THE LAST CARGO SHIP

"Set on board a cargo ship, the John Bede, its maverick Captain Lovelace (rough diamond drunk) is relieved of command after disgracing himself before a female company director. His replacement is the universally loathed Rupert de Vere Frogmore.
... I had great fun reading this... very funny... details of life on board... are engaging and vivid to the extent I found myself totally immersed in the fictional world... It's bawdy and full of life and very entertaining."

from an André Deutsch report. Since then the book has developed. It is bawdier and has got queerer. Captain Frogmore is now a complex man with an exotic past.

Paul Mann served in cargo ships, troopships, passenger ships, tankers, landing-ships-logistic and educational cruise ships during the sixties and the early seventies which were the last great days of the British Merchant Navy.

ALSO AVAILABLE FROM PARADISE NORTH

The Queer Commando
The Seaman's Mission
Nailing Frank
Stowaway

THE LAST CARGO SHIP

Paul Mann

Paradise North

Manchester and Brighton

The Last Cargo Ship is published in Great Britain in 2008 by Paradise North,
Manchester & Brighton

British Library Cataloguing in Publication Data.
A catalogue record of this book is available from the British Library.

ISBN: 978-0-9553543-4-2

Cover by *Wry Grimace*, Newhaven

some praise for Paul Mann

"Really quite something" CHRISTOPHER ISHERWOOD

".. a riot of acerbic wit and authentic characterisation." *ONEINSEVEN*

"...an overview of a world that has all but disappeared. Great fun." *THE SEAFARER*

"...situations exude the zeitgeist of shipboard life..." *NAUTICAL MAGAZINE*

"one of the greatest books about Royal Marines... just as true of the Royal Marines today..." A MARINE in IRAQ ~ *THE PINK PAPER*

"...heartfelt story..." SEBASTIAN BEAUMONT *GAY TIMES*

"...a great book." *OUTNORTHWEST*

"Poignant..." *BBC*

"...Humour, insight and tragedy, what more can you ask." *AMAZON*

"If Somerset Maugham had got gritty and worked on a ship today, he would have written something with this panache and gustiness..." DR JO STANLEY - *HELLO SAILOR*

"...a strong narrative voice." JONATHAN BURNHAM *CHATTO & WINDUS*

"...did enjoy *Nailing Frank*... seek it out..." *CHROMA*

"...Paul Mann's best book yet." *OUTNORTHWEST*

Nailing Frank – priser *ILGCN WORLD CULTURAL CONFERENCE* Vintersolstand Fest, Stockholm

STOWAWAY supported by MERSEYSIDE MARITIME MUSEUM

This book is not dedicated to that handful of cantankerous bastards who I was unfortunate enough to have sailed with. Such captains will have now hopefully passed on to the great storm-tossed ocean in the turbulent sky. They, in comparison, make the dyspeptic Captain Frogmore in my tale appear to be an absolute pussycat.

ONE

QABAHBAH

"IS FROGMORE board yet?" asked Captain Fred Lovelace, using his month old copy of the *Daily Mirror* to keep the flies away.

Alex shook his head and pointed to the foreman from ashore, a few yards off, who was draped over the ship's rail. "He wants to buy the cadet."

Captain Lovelace put down the *Daily Mirror* and studied the foreman. "*Buy* the cadet, purser?"

"He's offering the local funny-money – go for dollars."

The captain scratched his large belly beneath a singlet, clean that morning but now stained after an irritable confrontation with a stubborn bottle of HP sauce at lunch. "Cadet Smith's horrible. He's got bony arms. There's no flesh on the lad."

"Think *Billy Budd.*"

"Who the fuck's Billy Budd?"

Alex helped himself to crisps out of the glass dish on the white plastic table on the deck outside the captain's accommodation. "The cadet's blond."

Lovelace squinted speculatively at the foreman who had his back to a sun high over Qabahbah. The foreman straightened up and approached. He rested large brown hands with gnarled nails on the back of one of the four white plastic chairs which Captain Lovelace had ordered last call at London. These, and the table with its jaunty Martini umbrella, gave the captain's deck the appearance of a large private yacht, which the *John Bede,* as a working general cargo vessel, was not.

Lovelace's age alone should have given an indication of authority, but did not. The captain's crumpled shorts, his varicose veins, and his beer belly, which pushed unpleasantly at the stained singlet, together with his nondescript face, made the foreman look away, and his glance fell, with some sexual interest, on Alex who cut rather a dash in his starched white uniform shirt and shorts.

"No can do, Squire," said the captain.

The foreman's opaque blue eyes stared ahead. He was clearly bewildered by this old man, perhaps wondering who he was, or maybe he was unable to understand Lovelace's Yorkshire accent.

"You can't have the boy," interpreted Alex, then aware that the captain was watching keenly, added, "The boy with the nice buttocks."

For the first time Captain Lovelace showed surprise.

"How much you want?" asked the foreman whose left hand gripped the back of the chair. His right hand dropped and fingered his fly.

"Buttocks?" hissed Lovelace.

"He's a true blond. They're very thin on the ground out here," said Alex.

"You're blond."

"Cadet Smith has youth. And I am given to understand that the foreman is much taken with his legs. Me – long in the tooth, though I am not giving up. I may well be next if I read the signs right. One cannot but gain some satisfaction; even coming second on his shopping list for boys."

Lovelace took a Benson and Hedges from the box on the table. "Where the fuck's the fucking matches?"

The foreman's right hand came up from the front of his trousers. A rasping nail ran the head of a match. Lovelace regarded the sulphurous flame with suspicion as he inhaled.

"Evidently, Fred, blond hairs on youth's legs are the in-thing in Qabahbah," said Alex, milking the situation.

"I don't give a monkey's testicle what the fucking 'in-thing' is in Qabahbah, purser." Then contemplatively Lovelace smiled; his wicked humour triumphed. "What would head office say?" He scratched his belly, searching for an apposite way of phrasing his thoughts. "Would the foreman want the cadet for… er, temporary relief or something more long term?"

"Definitely long term. Penetration would be involved as well as sucking cock – that's the way I read it, but I may be wrong. Do let me check."

"No you don't!" Then fed up with the game. "Get rid of

him!"

"No can do," said Alex to the foreman whose eyes were sad with disappointment.

"No can do, Squire. Savvy?" said Lovelace in slow English.

The foreman, not understanding the captain, spoke to Alex, "Money? I have the money."

"He has a certain admirable doggedness, don't you think?" said Alex.

Re-emerging was Lovelace's humour which had, from time to time, got him in very deep water with head office. "You reckon we should consult the cadet?"

"Negotiate terms, you mean?"

"I collect the monies from the gang," the strong voice interrupted.

"Oh, he's passed the plate round – just like church. Oh, my Delilah!" Lovelace's rheumy eyes glistened. "Think on it, Alex, I can sell the cadet – who ain't great shakes anyway – then cable head office." He drank deeply from his beer daydreaming. "I'll inform them that Cadet Smith has been sold into male prostitution." He sat back in the shade provided by the Martini umbrella, enjoying the imagined reaction of head office.

Suddenly, Lovelace waved his arm dismissing the foreman at the same time shouting, *"Allez! Allez!"*

The man, understanding French, grasped Alex's hand sadly before shuffling down the companionway leading to number three hatch.

Captain Lovelace, scarcely the film star image of an old seadog, had binoculars trained on a launch heading out from the shore. His voice showed disgust for the first time, "Frogmore's armada. Go to the gangway and meet Captain Rupert de Vere Frogmore, purser."

"Not on."

"Tell the bugger, I'm pissed."

"Fred, please? I'm on my knees."

"He's hell. No normal human being joins a ship in this arsehole of a port," said Lovelace, with no romanticism for the East.

THE LAUNCH was out of Conrad with its fringed canvas awning and gleaming brasses. The native crew wore smart uniform blue shirts and shorts. A monocled Captain Rupert de Vere Frogmore stood imposing in the stern: gaunt-faced, skin unhealthy from too long in the tropics – everything but the fly whisk. He boarded the *John Bede,* followed by four porters carrying his baggage.

"Been away from the UK for some years now, sir?" said Alex, not extending his hand.

"Still in cargo ships?" said Captain Frogmore with mild satisfaction.

Alex smiled uncomfortably; being with Frogmore meant discomfort. He did not reply.

"Have you no ambition?"

"Ambition for a simple soul such as I, I consider dangerous and unwise, sir."

"You do yourself no favours with such glib replies. What you say, and the way you say it, tells me that you are putting authority in its place."

As the porters climbed the swinging aluminium gangway, the two officers waited in silence. They had sailed together in a passenger ship. Rumour had it that Captain Frogmore had been transferred because he considered passengers were animated cargo; and his authoritarian manner had upset most of the officers and crew. It was said that Alex, after a complaint being lodged about him being drunk, had been demoted and transferred to the *John Bede,* which suited him fine; for the work was not exacting and discipline did not exist, and the run was to Australia, which was much sought after. His punishment was in fact a reward.

The porters had stacked the luggage on deck and were silently waiting for a tip.

"Where's my stateroom, purser?"

"Pilot's cabin, for the time being. Spare cabin's being painted."

Frogmore spoke in the local tongue to the head porter then turned to Alex, "Do you still read?"

"Er, books? Yes."

"I have a copy of *Daisy Miller* you might care to borrow."

Alex said, "I thought you only went in for nautical stuff?"

"Goodness, if I did that I would be in danger of becoming an expert on the sea rather than a seaman and that would never do."

Alex said nothing, aware that Frogmore was often consulted on matters nautical.

"One would have thought, purser, that an officer with your experience would be in a vessel somewhat more prestigious than this. The *John Bede* has the reputation as a refuge for down and outs."

Alex visualised Frogmore in some Middle Eastern port, attended by servants, courted by royalty. He felt that Captain Frogmore would rather lose his luggage than lift a suitcase, such was his grandeur.

"Can you tip these men and put it on my account? Dollars preferably. Don't stint. Damned fine chaps, damned fine." He then spoke to the head porter before turning to Alex again. "What I say is only for your own good."

"I do so appreciate your advice, sir."

"You answer with irony and concealed aggression." He turned on his heels and disappeared into the accommodation.

Alone, Alex was very much aware that Frogmore had arrived. Frogmore had the gift for making his presence felt. Alex regarded him with disdain. He was an anachronism. The Empire clung to him, as the heat clung to the ship.

For the remainder of the afternoon he hung around on deck. The ancient open-steam-winches hammered, shook the vessel, and sometimes they screeched. When the last of the cargo was discharged, the hatches were closed up and the dunnage was heaped at the ship's side, along with some condemned saloon stores, ready to be thrown overboard when the ship was deep-sea.

As the telegraphs rang stand-by-below, Cadet Smith, so recently toast of the town, supervised the deck crew securing the gangway.

"The mate shut me in the office all bloody afternoon. Only allowed out when the gangs left," said Cadet Smith.

"The fair maiden coy in her chastity belt," said Alex.

"You what?"

Forward, the windlass noisily took up the anchor cable. And as the *John Bede* swung, a hot blanket of wind caught the starboard side. In a motorised barge immediately below were the last of the stevedores ready to return ashore. Cadet Smith examined them.

"Which one is the foreman?"

Tinkering with the barge's engine was a stately man, a hawk of the desert who had the features of royalty. "Him!" lied Alex in a consolatory way, to reassure the cadet that he had not been lusted after by an unsavoury man with an eye problem. Cadet Smith wasn't consoled. He picked up two rotten apples from a box on deck and threw them with a skill learnt on the cricket pitch of his fourth rate public school.

"Pervert!" shouted the cadet, who held an arrogant assumption that he was better than most, certainly better than foreigners.

The desert sheikh wiped the splattered apple from his forehead and screamed with some justification, *"Fucker!"*

How odd, pondered Alex, that I find these colourful men likeable in comparison to the pallid humourless cadet. Then he reprimanded himself for his loyalty must be to his shipmate, so he threw an apple at the desert sheikh, missed him by yards and caught a roguish stocky man in baggy trousers. The man drew a long curved dagger and made alarming upward thrusting gestures. Alex's talents were for the arts rather than the cricket pitch, so with his sense of theatre, he raised both clenched fists and orchestrated the packed barge into a chorus of chanting.

"British! British! British!" he shouted.

The throng in the barge caught his fever immediately. In unison they raised their fists.

"British bastards! British bastards! British bastards!"

Cadet Smith, with unfailing sporting accuracy, pelted the stevedores in the barge with rotten apples, and when the apples ran out he threw bad egg after bad egg. His aim was unerring. One egg broke on the desert sheikh's cheek.

"Stop that, idiot!" said Alex.

The barge, which had been drifting away from the ship, suddenly got underway, and as its engine fired both Alex and Cadet Smith panicked. Cadet Smith fled aft. Alex raced the edges of numbers two and one hatches heading for the bow where the first mate was at anchor stations.

"When are we sailing, Morgan?"

"What's that chanting?"

"Some stevedores with egg on their faces. I know the

feeling."

"He's on about it. Got his knickers in a twist." Morgan pointed to Captain Lovelace who was pacing the bridge wing.

The anchor cable crawl-clanked out of the clear water.

"Heat and sand and what else?" said Morgan looking at the small town.

The two officers hung over the side as the barge came into sight. The stevedores, several splattered with apple and bad eggs, were raising rhythmic brown fists chanting ceaselessly, "Fucking British! Fucking British! Fucking British!"

Captain Lovelace did not bother with the bridge telephone, he leant over the dodgers and screamed at the mate, "Get that anchor up or slip the fucking thing! They've got a line on board!"

Alex raced down the side of number one hatch. He freed the heaving line and dropped it back in the barge.

The main engine, at emergency double full astern, shook the *John Bede* violently. The anchor hung clear as the barge crossed the ship's bows. The ship ceased shaking when the telegraphs were put to stop, then full ahead. Below, the faces of the desert sheikh, the myopic foreman and the knife-carrying man showed hate.

As the ship gathered speed, the barge bumped along the starboard side. The stevedores, realising the *John Bede* was escaping, chanted climatically, "Fucking British!" with all fists held aloft in a final contemptuous thrust.

The *John Bede* turned a dignified stern as it steamed away from the port.

TWO

AT SEA TO UK

A FAST FALLING sun deepened the golden brown veneer of the bulkheads in the officers' dining saloon. The four deckhead fans turned lethargically. Captain Lovelace and Alex were seated at the large oval, top table drinking beer before dinner.

"Our passenger…" said Lovelace

"Captain Frogmore."

"Was thrown off a passenger ship and exiled to the East. Anyplace would do so long as it was at least two thousand miles from head office. First he was condemned to Aden, then sentenced to Rangoon, and in an attempt to get shot of the old bastard, darkest Africa – without quinine and Paludrine."

Alex knew this was hogwash. Frogmore had the reputation of being the shipping company's trouble-shooter. He was held in great esteem; some of the lesser directors ran scared of him.

He said, "What's he on here for?"

"Why ask me? Read his appointment letter."

"You've got it," said Alex. The captain had a drunken habit of heaving head office correspondence over the ship's side, screaming, "I know who wrote this crap. I hereby condemn it to the Big File."

"Frogmore tells me he's on passage to the UK for reappointment." Captain Lovelace turned to his steward and said, "Nuts please, Gomes."

His steward smiled with familiarity. He had sailed with the down-to-earth Lovelace on and off for ten years. He brought a dish of peanuts from the sideboard.

Alex said, "He's shore-based permanently, I heard?"

"Scarcely satisfying for a man seeking the sea. He'll be given one of the older cargo ships for one voyage before his retirement."

"You're not thinking what I'm thinking?"

"Fucking right. The vulture hovers. My throat will be torn out and my flesh will soon hang from his talons."

"What does Frogmore do for sex?" said Alex, angling for gossip.

"He and the Pope don't do it."

"He's not religious. On the passenger ship he told me that he thought Divine Service was a primitive ritual created by politicians. He never attended the church services at sea; the only captain, I've sailed with not to."

"He's above God. The man's a machine, walks with a ramrod up his arse. That voice of his sounds like General Montgomery addressing his men." Lovelace glanced at the bulkhead clock. "Thirty seconds to go. He'll arrive at five minutes after seven on the dot. Bets?"

Leather heels sounded as Frogmore crossed the dining saloon to join them at the top table. He waited for Gomes to draw his chair back and when seated, he acknowledged the captain. He looked at Alex, but said nothing. Alex interpreted this as a good evening, so smiled awkwardly.

The chief engineer arrived shortly afterwards. "Trip okay, Rupert?" It was difficult to make out what the chief said because he had been drinking, but Frogmore picked it up all right.

"Not straightforward at all, chief, I'm afraid. I was used. Head office had me set up an agency in Mena-al-Ahmadi. A cock up in Basra took two weeks to sort out. I flew from Dubai to Qabahbah. The plane was a bazaar." He carefully unfolded his starched linen napkin and positioned it on his knees, then studied the menu card through half-glasses, and said to Gomes, "Soup, boy." Then he turned his attention back to the chief engineer. "I find, that however wealthy these chaps are, they are still very much of the land. On the aeroplane I sat next to a goat."

Alex sniggered

Frogmore eased himself back to allow Gomes to position a bowl of mulligatawny soup. "You find that amusing, purser?"

"Did it have the window seat?"

"I last met you in Port Soukatha, *Rupert*," said Captain Lovelace emphasising the Rupert for ridiculous effect.

"Boujiba, Captain. I was seconded to Boujiba."

"Some arsehole of a place. So hot you could fry eggs on the deck."

The chief engineer chuckled.

"Was there anything on the BBC?" asked Frogmore, irritated by Lovelace's manner.

"I don't listen to the news, Rupert. They make most of it up, you know."

"Indeed. I'm more than curious about the violent verbal abuse the ship was subjected to in *Qabahbah*." Frogmore's pronunciation was guttural. He pushed the soup away which he had hardly touched, and said to Gomes, "Fish, boy."

"What trouble?" said Lovelace.

Frogmore tested his plate to make certain it had been warmed then, as he helped himself to a fillet of sole from the salver, said, "Had the same goings on in '67. I was in command of the *Eric Bede*." He snapped at Gomes, "Tartar sauce! Tartar sauce!" Then he continued, "Communists, you know. And they were in league with pirates. That shindig this afternoon brought it back vividly. Same set up. Hatches closed up, engine at standby. Labour being transported ashore. And the same frenetic chanting. This time they were more aggressive – showed open hostility."

"Not political, Rupert. Merely a domestic matter. The purser was trying to sell the cadet into male prostitution."

Captain Frogmore glanced up sharply, aware he was being ridiculed.

Lovelace could not let such a rich vein of humour drop, "The purser's the ship's tout." As Alex and the chief engineer snorted with laughter, he said, "Beer, Rupert?"

"Not for me," said Frogmore, rapping a spoonful of tartar sauce on the edge of his plate.

"Go on, have that beer?"

"I seldom drink after sundown – my ulcer restricts my socialising, I'm often thankful to say. When in command of the *Eric Bede* in the approaches to the Red Sea, pirates attempted to stop and board us. Might I suggest that you keep a keen watch. Station a *kalassi* in the crow's nest – just in case."

Frogmore's acute hearing caught Lovelace's muttered derisory aside to Alex, "Crow's nest?"

Examining the menu, he said, "Is this *Aus*tralian chicken,

purser?"

"Yes."

"Is it all right?"

Alex's defence of Australian chicken was shelved, saved by the captain's call light which was sited in the deckhead above the large top table. A light used only in emergencies: it now winked blue and bright.

"Captain, your call light!" Frogmore abandoned his half-glasses to firm a monocle in his eye.

Captain Lovelace leisurely wiped the condensation from the outside of his glass of lager. "I think I'll have the Australian chicken."

Frogmore was on his feet. "The bridge, Captain!"

As he sped out, Frogmore bumped into Francis coming out of the pantry. He knocked the tureen out of his hands. It spun and fell; potatoes and peas littered the linoleum. Frogmore's heels sounded urgently as he doubled up the stairs leading to the bridge.

Lovelace grinned as he announced to the dining saloon, "I told Jack on the bridge to test it."

The junior engineering officers and deck officers on the side tables laughed.

Lovelace said to his appreciative audience, "Frogmore was in the Gestapo. He was about to interrogate the fucking chicken."

"You ever met his wife, Fred?" asked the chief engineer.

"Buttercup, wasn't it? Something to do with cows."

"Priscilla. A tall lady and well built. Very much the senior British wife in Bombay."

"I remember the Amazonian dyke. All six-foot-two of her dominated those fuck awful *memsahibs'* cocktail parties. The British abroad – God help us. No wonder we lost the fucking Empire."

What is more frightening than a woman who lusts for position and power, is a man who has it and misuses it, thought Alex.

Frogmore didn't return to finish his meal. He stayed on the bridge to watch for pirates. Later, when Alex checked with the second mate; Jack confirmed Frogmore's story. Pirates had attempted to board the *Eric Bede*. With the use of high powered deck hoses, the pirates had been repelled. If

Captain Frogmore had not ordered that the hoses be put on standby, there was no doubting that the ship would have been taken.

FROGMORE was to mar the voyage to the UK. It seemed to be his talent to spoil pleasure.

The purser was summoned to the captain's dayroom where Lovelace was in a frenzy of alcoholic concern, tugging at a head office letter which lined the cat's litter tray.

"What you up to?"

Lovelace waved the suffered letter. "Read it."

Below the heading *BEDE STEAMSHIP COMPANY LIMITED* and the die-stamped crest, Alex managed to make out the name Captain Rupert de Vere Frogmore. "And?"

"He joins as a supernumerary it says. A supernumerary what? Can you make out the next word?"

"The cat has pissed on it, Fred."

"It says as a supernumerary captain, that's what it says."

"So? A supernumerary is a passenger."

"Supernumerary captain. That's what it says," shouted Lovelace. "And don't you dare say it."

"Say what?"

"I'm imagining things."

Alex took little notice. Lovelace hardly had a history of stability. A year ago in Tilbury docks he'd been carried off the ship after talking to the toast rack at breakfast. Initially, Alex and the chief engineer had dismissed the incident, thinking it due to too much alcohol the previous evening. However, at lunch the marine superintendent was discussing using Southampton as a container port when Lovelace had disappeared under the dining table. No one could persuade him to come out. Gomes, who steadfastly looked after his captain, brought him coffee and he sat drinking it under the table until the ambulance men arrived to carry him ashore.

Also Alex knew of two separate stays in discreet private nursing homes which treated patients suffering from alcoholic disorders.

EGYPT: clear dry air and marvellous light. The *John Bede*

anchored for six hours in the Bitter Lakes before sailing north through the Suez Canal – the desert on the starboard side; to port a ribbon of road.

The ship departed the Canal at Port Said as if in a hurry. The town's lights sped by. The ship's agent stepped adroitly from the foot of the gangway into a flagging launch, his musk perfume lingered. The launch, with the Bede Line's company's flag fluttering, fell quickly astern.

After several days of sun in the Mediterranean they sailed through the Strait of Gibraltar. The weather dampened and the Atlantic was cold and green. In the accommodation steam rattled the old fashioned radiators. Now, instead of wailing Eastern music, or a fading Voice of America broadcasting the news in slow-English, the BBC medium wave programmes came in strong at night.

As the ship was passing Trafalgar after lunch, Alex was busy in his office calculating the wages for arrival UK. The door curtain was pulled back by Lovelace who held a confidential finger to his lips. Carefully drawing the curtain closed behind him, he went though into the adjoining cabin, signalling that Alex was to follow. Together in the cabin the captain dramatically shut the door.

"Haven't you got a beer in this rabbit hutch?" He accepted a Foster's and said, with a touch of Mata Hari, "Frogmore's planning to take over the ship."

"Where'd that idea come from?"

"He's on the bridge a great deal."

"Thank God someone is."

"You've seen him. After we left Qabahbah, he stormed onto the bridge as if it was his right."

"Jesus Christ, Fred. Your call light was on. The call light means an emergency and you ignored it. Captain Frogmore acted with the decisiveness of a man used to command. You played the gallery and made a fool of yourself."

"You go too far, purser."

"No, you went too far, *sir.*"

"Your career at sea is scarcely unblemished, purser."

"Fred, now you're scoring points, getting at me for being constructive. Frogmore has pull in head office. Why not invite him in for a drink, be nice to the sour-faced sod."

"Would you?"

"It's not my head on the block."
"Help me."
"Frogmore mellows now and then – rarely but he does," said Alex, thinking that Captain Lovelace had committed suicide – careerwise.
"Frogmore kicked you off a passenger ship."
"Did he?"
"You were pissed and you were thrown off."
"Fred, that's malicious gossip."
"Why do you stay in this ship?"
"The ship's company's okay. You're okay. And there are the six to eight weeks drinking on the Australian coast. Face it, Frogmore wouldn't want this ship, it's on the Aussie run."
"He doesn't like any place. He detests today. He detests me. He detests white crew, Elvis and everybody – other than the county set who live in thatched cottages, read *Country Life* and have a daily in to poke the Aga. Point is, he's got family in Sydney and he's nuts about the *John Bede*."
"This ship? He could have any ship he wanted."
"Old values. Built during the war. Bofer mountings on deck. I caught him photographing that brass notice on the bridge. The one which says 'Dim lights when under attack'." Lovelace emptied his beer glass. "He'd get a first class ship's company."
"I said they were okay, not first class."
"He's phoned London office. Ask Sparks subtly what he said."

SUBTLETY AND SPARKS did not go together. Sparks was a man to call a spade a fucking spade.
But Sparks, to Alex's way of thinking, was the definitive seaman. But to others, Sparks was the antithesis of a seaman. He called the deck the floor, and the bulkheads were walls. But he had a woman in Valparaiso and Rio and Road Town. There was a bargirl, he couldn't be one hundred percent sure, though he was pretty certain, that he had married in Manila. Plus, he had spoken teasingly to Alex of a ménage à trois in Greenwich Village. He had had several doses. He often spun sailor's yarns, but Alex resisted the bait when he said,
"I got this bobby-dazzler – caught it in Bangkok. The

Vietnam Rose."

"I do not want to hear about Vietnam Rose."

"Super syphilis."

"Just as well we've stopped kissing."

"The quacks gave me malaria. My high temperature hit those little bastards on the head, I hope."

Sparks usually lolled about in jeans and T-shirt, or in a jumper with the sleeves rolled up, showing off his birds of paradise tattoos done by an adept Chinese man in Taiwan. This artwork was spoilt: beneath an exquisite swooping bird on his right arm, some hack had tattooed two cherubs holding up the word *Mum*.

The bulkheads of the radio room – radio shack was a more apt description – were papered with centrefolds. They darkened and closed in. Alex found so many female nudes overwhelming.

"Frogmore's telephone call to head office, Sparks?"

"What you after?"

"What'd he say?"

"That call was confidential and scrambled."

"What did he say?"

"I've taken the Marconi-atic oath."

"What did he say?"

Sparks retrieved a piece of chewed gum stuck onto the front of the main transmitter. Alex waited, aware that all radio operators were mad or eccentric; a madness caused by isolation and listening to Morse for eight hours a day.

The gum shifted. Sparks also shifted his bare feet along the desk. "Frogmore was on about rioting natives in Qabahbah."

"And?"

"Alex, what's the name of that company director? The one with the walk?"

"Debrence."

"Debrence don't like Frogmore much at all. But Frogmore wouldn't shut it. Stuff about a dangerous command. On about Lovelace never going on the bridge sober."

"What did Debrence say?"

"The company director with the walk, you mean?"

"Jesus!"

"The ducky director said, 'Quite'. In fact he said 'Quite'

quite a lot." Sparks took out his gum and plunged it into the sugar bowl.

"The old man thinks that Frogmore is trying to get command of this ship."

"I love Lovelace, man. Maybe one or two minor faults." Sparks grinned. The tattoos disguised a gentle easy-going young man. "But he fucked up bad with that call light. He can't show up La Frogmore in front of everyone and get away with it."

"You're being unusually perceptive, Sparks."

"Self-preservation, man."

"He mentioned the call light to head office?"

Sparks nodded. "And by the way he was talking, I reckon that La Frogmore might well have one-and-a-half feet in the door."

FOG IN THE CHANNEL. Windows heaved up tight, blankets on bunks. After the *John Bede* rounded Ushant, the BBC medium wave came in clear during the day. Cadet Smith set up the TV, which flickered unwatched in a corner of the smoke room. As the ship altered course, the picture went to snow.

Alex did a stocktake of the spirits and cigarettes in the bonded storerooms, then he chased up the crew's customs declaration form. He finished off the accounts and roughed out store requirements for the next voyage before turning in early to be ready for the ship docking the following day.

IT WAS TWO IN THE MORNING when the apologetic Indian *seacunny* woke him. Alex wrapped a towel about his waist and pulled on a sweater as he dragged himself up top.

"You seen the time?"

The captain's theme was unchanged. "I am about to be usurped by a martinet and you whine. Have a whisky."

Lovelace used his captaincy in a chummy way. His 'Come up for a drink' was a command. And whether the invited officer wanted to listen to his drunken ramblings or not, he had little choice. Alex often hid in the second engineer's cabin to avoid these summonses. And afterwards his steward would report that Lovelace had been on the prowl, shouting 'Where's that fucking purser?' Hiding became frequent, but a two-o'clock in the morning summons, he could not avoid. For if he did not report then the *seacunny* would get it in the neck.

The black cat, which the captain nursed, hung on with sharp claws. "Can you promise me something?" Lovelace was in familiar territory. The mournful quartet had tuned up.

Alex opened a side window before turning off the heat. He marched into the bedroom where he took a Paisley patterned dressing gown off its hook from behind the door. He strode back into the dayroom dropping it on Lovelace's lap.

"What you up to?"

Lovelace was in pyjama bottoms, his chest bare, his white larded breasts hung and a red line marked his waist where the pyjama cord had dug into the flab.

"This place stinks of cat's piss. And it's overheated. Put your dressing gown on. Cover yourself up." Alex was on his knees rummaging through the drinks cabinet, searching for the whisky. He pulled out part-bottles of Cherry brandy, sherry and Gordon's until he discovered a full bottle of Haigs.

As he sipped his whisky, he wondered how a man so physically repugnant could display himself to all and sundry. In uniform the captain might command some respect, but half-naked?

The Indian *seacunny* tapped softly on the outer door, then padded across to the large desk and placed a chit, sent down by the officer on the bridge, on it. On his way out, the *seacunny* salaamed his *burra sahib*. And Alex thought how wrong it was that a dedicated Indian quartermaster should give such respect to this wreck of a man.

"If I'm superseded, Alex, you must promise me one thing?"

Alex downed his scotch then refilled his glass.

"I want you to look after my chum," said Lovelace tearfully.

"You mean your stinking cat?"

"Felicity'll stay with you."

"That greedy bitch'll stay with anyone who feeds her."

Alex went to the desk and read the chit. "Shouldn't you be on the bridge?" The traffic in the English Channel was heavy, and at times alarming, but when Alex recognised the second mate's handwriting he relaxed.

"I can't have her quarantined."

"She pisses on important correspondence. She's got that going for her." Alex poured himself several more fingers of scotch.

"Promise me? I know you love her."

"Oh, Jesus Christ, give it a fucking break. I'll look after the bitch."

"Thank you, thank you."

It was a corny geriatric movie, except that Alex couldn't escape the cinema and was stuck listening to the hammy lead. He downed the scotch rediscovering his fondness for Haigs.

"The chief engineer would have her but he's retiring next trip."

"You could've asked Sparks. He won't be transferred to passenger ships, that's for sure."

"You won't either. I've been putting you were not suitable on your confidential report." Catching Alex's expression of alarm, he said, "Nothing bad – only that you weren't refined."

"Not refined coming from you is the ultimate condemnation," said Alex, hoping that head office would take little notice of what Lovelace said about anyone.

"Come, lad, you and I will sup usquebah. And when six bells sound, we'll toast the dawn and your forthcoming voyage to Oz."

Alex said, "You are kidding me, about saying I'm not refined?"

Lovelace roared with laughter.

THREE

LONDON

The Thames Estuary was as grey as the grey sky.

A Trinity House pilot was on the bridge. The VHF crackled. The *John Bede* steamed upriver; into the lock, to berth in the vast Royal Albert Dock late morning.

After the port health officer ordered the quarantine flag to be taken down, Alex put him in his cabin with a beer to wait for lunch while he dealt with the customs. The customs boarding officer was given VIP treatment because he controlled duty-free fags and booze. Francis, as acting storekeeper, brought along the immigration officer who was put with the port health officer in the cabin while Alex escorted the customs officer below to seal the bonded store.

The shipping master closed the vessel's articles of agreement in his office and drank a beer while Alex scoured the accommodation rounding up officers to sign off. When he returned, he found a lean-faced policeman drinking with the other officials in his cabin.

The ship's chandler arrived but didn't join the drinkers because he wanted an order for saloon stores. A role-reversal situation, Francis sarcastically put it, as he dumped the chandler in the saloon pantry with a cup of tea.

The dulcimer sounded. The cabin slowly emptied as the officials went to lunch. All twelve spare seats in the dining saloon were filled. The port officials knew and chatted with the marine and engineering superintendents and with several unexplained grey-suited men, who looked as though they sucked blood at night.

His cabin and office now empty, Alex decided to pay the Indian crew an advance against their wages. Advances were a pain in the neck, because the sums paid to Indian crew were limited by esoteric Indian currency regulations to a measly twenty-five percent of the crew's measly salary.

The *serangs* summoned the deck and engine room crew

and Alex's small office became a bazaar. There was dissent from Baboojan whose buffalo had been shot or taken by a tiger, Alex couldn't be sure which. Ghafoor's wife was heavy with child. And the pleas for money did not stop there...

BADSHA MEAH, the young fireman, was the negotiator. He ushered the crew out through the doorway where they waited on the narrow strip of deck, then he shut the heavy weather door to cut out their babble.

While Alex saw sex in everyone, and was often repelled by what he saw, Badsha Meah did not repel him one little bit. Badsha Meah outwardly treated Alex as a *sahib,* but they were equals. Badsha Meah had long ago sensed a vulnerability in Alex and with Indian doggedness, had pursued him. He would tap on his door at any old hour, and he would *salaam* outrageously when they ran across each other on deck. But Alex was not taken in. He had Badsha Meah organise the crew and liaise. For this service he paid him a much larger advance of wages than was allowed. All was compromise. Alex was paying lip service to red tape. The ship was at such times very much in the East.

Badsha Meah's brown thumb was firm and warm on the purser's forefinger, pinning it to the desk."Three hundred rupees, *sahib?*"

"Two hundred." The smell of diesel oil in the fireman's hair was a heady perfume, an aphrodisiac to the purser's frustrated nose.

The young fireman leant over him and ostensibly studied the advance sheet in the typewriter. His coarse boiler suit open to the waist, his soft sex nudging Alex's bare arm.

"Okay, three hundred, but piss off."

Badsha Meah held his sex against Alex's elbow and they both pressed for several seconds. Saliva ran into Alex's mouth. Then the twenty-year-old fireman called time on the tease and sat cross-legged on the carpet watching as the purser altered the list. When he finished typing, Alex said, "Wheel 'em in."

"Acha sahib. Me first *sahib"*

"Why not sign?"

The two were alone in the office; the young man had his bare brown chest inches from the purser's face, as he allowed him to roll his thumb on the ink pad and then let Alex press his thumb gently on all four copies of the advance sheet.

Having done his bit, a smiling Badsha Meah rubbed his inky thumb in his thick black hair before allowing the crew in, one by one.

ALEX PUT ON HIS REEFER JACKET when the superintendent of supply arrived with a man who he didn't know nor wanted to know. The other officials were drifting back from lunch and his cabin, which led off his office, was beginning to fill up again. A man of about sixty, wearing blue overalls, popped his head around the office door.

"Okay for a beer?" he said.

"Who are you?"

" 'Fridge engineer working on the German ship ahead."

"Go away," said Alex.

When a riveter started, the superintendent of supply left, trailed by the grey-suited man who definitely sucked blood. The riveting was heaven-sent, it came in deafening bursts, it drowned conversation. It caused the shoreside freeloaders to flee.

IT WAS SEVEN THAT EVENING when Alex dropped his heavy reefer jacket on the daybed. He lifted his arms, sniffed each armpit, then decided on a large medicinal brandy before taking a shower.

A fine featured young man, with broad shoulders and wearing brand new reefers that showed the white tabs of a cadet, tapped diffidently on the office door.

"Where do I find the captain, sir?"

"You hot, or is it me?"

"It's warm, sir."

"Call me Alex. You call the captain 'sir', if you can speak after the initial shock." He remembered his own bewilderment on boarding his first ship. Adept at the throwaway remark, which only he appreciated and therefore he alone found amusing, he said, "Allow me to show you the way. The exercise will do me good."

THE CAPTAIN'S dayroom intimidated with its field of deep

carpet. The subdued light from glass-shaded wall lamps pooled on the satinwood bulkheads. The captain was sprawled in an armchair; his unbuttoned reefer jacket was peppered with cigarette ash; a fag dangled char-like from his lips and the cat was asleep on his lap.

"Do not salute, cadet, I forbid it," he said, putting his glass on a drip mat on the coffee table. "Fancy a beer?"

"Not at the moment, thank you, sir."

"Don't you drink?"

"Now and again."

"You smoke?"

"Maybe one or two in the evening, sir."

Lovelace, puzzled by such virtue, said, "Any hobbies?"

"Soccer and rugby, sir. Mostly soccer."

"My eldest boy was accused of being a sissy for coming last in some running event at school. I told the headmaster that whether my son came last in the race or not was unimportant. Whether he was a sissy or not was immaterial. It appeared that my son's offence was that he had not taken the race seriously. It is a wise mind which scorns primitive competition." The captain paused, said, "Cadet, do you pull your wire?"

Cadet Jones concentrated on the large desk.

"Fred, for fuck's sake, you're making me squirm and I'm thirty-five. He's sixteen."

"Be quiet, purser. We're having an introductory chat. Aren't we 'er..."

"Jones," said Alex.

"I know the cadet's fucking name, purser, without you sticking your nose in." Captain Lovelace had had a full day entertaining the marine superintendent with ship's account booze. "I warn you, Jones, we almost sold your predecessor out East. Rum, bum and baccy, lad, eh? What?" His voice was that of the decadent seadog. He coughed and as the smoker's cough took hold, the cat rocked on his lap. "Are you the one percent, lad?"

"One percent, sir?" said Jones, scarlet with embarrassment.

"Fred, that's enough!" Alex pushed the cadet out the dayroom.

Lovelace shouted, "Don't you bully me."

In the alleyway, Alex said, "He'll know what bullying is in the morning. You fancy a natter, Cadet David Jones?"

They walked slowly down the stairway and then went out on deck.

"No, thank you very much. I think I'll sleep ashore. I don't live far."

The ship was berthed dead centre of the Royal Albert Dock. It was a mile and a half trek to either gate. Alex doubted whether the cadet could afford a taxi. "Have a beer first. Don't worry about me. I only bully captains. It's a I-hate-all-authority thing."

"What did he mean by the one percent?"

"Take no notice."

Alex indicated the armchair. The cadet perched on it with his cap on his knee. Alex took the cap when he gave him a glass of beer. "Tonight he was drunk as a skunk and pig ignorant." He kicked off his shoes. "My feet stink?"

"Nope."

"I'd take a shower but it interferes with my drinking time." He topped up the cadet's glass before sitting on the day-bed. "You're on the booze now. Captain Lovelace has that affect on people."

The new cadet, even though he was not blond – his hair was dark but leaning towards gold, and henna flashed when he moved his head – would go down a wow in Qabahbah.

"Relax," said Alex. "Take your coat off."

The cadet hung his reefer jacket on the back of a chair, then he rolled up the sleeves of his white shirt, showing muscled forearms. "Thanks for being nice to me." His voice was deep and slow, like the Thames. "The one percent?"

"Ninety-nine percent of men masturbate. One percent are liars." Alex flicked his lighter and the cadet inhaled. "He's supposed to be responsible for your well-being."

"Seems like it's you doing that."

Refusing a second beer, Cadet David Jones stood up. "Thank you very much for the drink. I best turn in."

The hesitancy in his voice made Alex say, "You off home?"

"It's not far."

If he went ashore to sleep, Alex doubted whether he'd return and he might get to regret that for the rest of his life. He tugged open the bottom bunk drawer and pulled out two snowy-white blankets. He took a wooden coat hanger from the wardrobe and hung the cadet's jacket on it. "Sleep on my daybed."

It was as though the cadet was taking orders: David Jones nodded and sat down to take off his shoes and socks. As he undressed, Alex switched off the lights and poured himself a drink. Soft illumination seeped in through the door curtain from the alleyway.

In his bunk he said, "I know what it's like. I went to boarding school."

"I'm sixteen."

"The bully makes you feel alone and miserable." He poured another sherry into a beer mug and sipped it. "If you wanna piss – the heads are forward. I use the sink. Dig in, make yourself at home."

"Thanks."

"Report to the mate tomorrow morning, 'bout six-thirty in working gear. I'll show you where – or Francis will."

"Francis?"

"My steward. I am bullied by him, but nicely. He'll get you tea."

"I would like to thank you for being so kind to me."

Alex stayed drinking sherry until he heard the cadet's breathing deepen and slow, as sleep overtook him.

ON DECK he tried not to look at the dockside because it was moving when he knew it was not.

Cadet Jones, muscular in blue denim trousers and working shirt, was pushing something into Alex's trouser pocket.

"I don't know what you are doing but those two dockers are thinking evil thoughts," said Alex.

Dishy David Jones dazzled. He exuded life, he was entrancing. Grinning, he removed his hand. "The mate told me to grease wires. Where'd I get the grease?"

"Forward store. See the *cassab.* He's clued up. Good English."

"You've saved my life." Cadet Jones rubbed the purser's arm affectionately.

One of the watching dockers gripped his genitals with cupped hands and shouted at the cadet, "How about it, darling?"

"No chance!" Cadet Jones said with a confidence that Alex had not heard before.

"Couple of quid do it?" shouted the docker.

"Fuck off and look in the mirror."

HEADING for the officers' accommodation, Alex wondered if his own reputation, as the ship's pimp, had followed him from the East to the Royal Albert Dock.

In the quiet engineers' alleyway, he took out the quarter bottle of scotch which the cadet had thrust into his pocket.

Rodney, immaculate in reefers, was locking his outside cabin door. Rodney was the refrigerating engineer, and unlike Cadet Jones, would never make it to be the toast of the Royal Albert Dock. He said, "You look shit."

Alex glanced about him to see if the coast was clear before drinking deeply from the bottle. He handed it to Rodney. "Finish it and hold my hand, I'm not at my peak today." The third tumbler of sherry last night had been the killer. "I'm suffering from gastric discomfort."

"You've been on the piss." Rodney drained the bottle.

"Peace is what I crave, not a voyage meeting."

"Load of shit," said Rodney, consoling Alex as he sometimes did. He opened the heavy glass door to the dining saloon, and gently pushed the purser in ahead of him.

Alex mumbled, "Good morning." to those already seated and he slumped in his seat at the large oval table. He shuddered as slings of cargo banged into the sides of number two hatch which was immediately forward of the saloon. Debrence, a company director, ignored a docker working on deck who swore long and loud. Debrence smiled at Alex, as if he were a friend, but he advocated the division between management and the workforce. Alex had difficulty with the concept of himself being management and, never in his wildest dreams, did he consider himself as a member of any workforce. He did so little work when the ship was at sea that he would often ask himself, 'How did I get this job?'

The saloon steward had been busy. There were set-out notepads and new pencils; the ashtrays had been polished and roses were arranged in a plain silver bowl. Opening the glass entrance doors to the dining saloon, Francis ushered in a Ms Oliver, who was someone of importance in management. She had the impressive title of Modernisation Co-ordinator in Chief.

Alex discretely swallowed two aspirins, while the first mate confessed, with hand-wringing sadness, of cargo pilferage. Then the chief engineer explained that the five days delay in Perth waiting for engine parts was just one of those things. And, when questioned as to why a domestic freezer chamber's temperature had soared – so that fruit had to be condemned and hurled over the side at the natives in Qabahbah – the chief engineer said, "Over to you, purser." Alex was tempted to explain that the temperatures hadn't been read because a junior engineer refused to visit the freezer chambers because of a ghost. He sipped water trying to shift an aspirin that clung to his tortured oesophagus. He coughed for several moments, then lit a cigarette. More composed, he said, "The thermometer in the veg room was broken. It read, consistently, thirty-six degrees."

Typical management latching onto small issues. It was only fruit and vegetables. Oh, he'd forgotten about the eggs. Four boxes with 360 eggs in each box.

"Refrigerating engineer?" said Ms Oliver.

Rodney, seated at the bottom of the large table, said, "The thermometer read thirty-six degrees day-in and day-out, and instead of being suspicious and taking note when the purser told me that the chamber was warm, I ignored him." Alex had in fact pleaded with Rodney who had told him that he should 'Read the fucking thermometer and stop being such a fucking old woman and let the engineers get on with their job'.

"The losses are relatively insignificant," said the superintendent of supply, rallying the troops and making an ostentatious note on his pad.

OUTSIDE IN THE ALLEYWAY, on their way to the smoke room for drinks before a curry lunch, Alex put his hand on the refrigerating engineer's arm. "I thought what you did in there – owning up – was singularly British, Rodney. You're a thoroughly decent chap."

"How could I watch you martyring yourself – you'd enjoy that far too much."

"Will you be joining the *burra sahibs* for drinkies?"

"Load of wankers," said Rodney, with a directness that revealed his Northern roots.

Rodney rude, or Rodney tetchy, or Rodney flamboyant was okay with Alex who said, "Stop bellyaching and keep me company."

"Your arrogance keeps you company."

"What's up, Rod?"

"Nothing."

"Tell me, you miserable shit."

"My ma's had a fall."

"Heart?" said Alex, looking him in the eye.

"Pissed." Rodney slipped away along the engineers' alleyway, as though on a mission of some urgency, leaving Alex to traipse up a flight of stairs to the smoke room and there to slowly sip a lager in an attempt to ease his hangover.

CAPTAIN LOVELACE was cornered by Ms Oliver who had the aloof manner of all the Bede Line directors. She had their remoteness. The remoteness of royalty: the benign smile, the proffering of the hand – and the devastating way of putting sea staff in their place. Alex sensed that one should wait for her to speak first but Lovelace, with his senses dulled by too many hairs of the dog, seemed unaware of her authority.

Ms Oliver offered drinks, handed round a dish of seen-better-days crisps which had travelled over fifty thousand miles and had experienced freezing temperatures and temperatures of over one hundred and forty degrees. She should have attended one of her own tedious courses on personnel management for she was taking charge in Captain Lovelace's ship.

"My thoughts on management are that if one can manage – say a bakery – then those management skills can be applied in other situations."

Lovelace said, "Are you saying that the manager of a bakery can command a ship?"

"What are your thoughts on my circular about container ships, Captain?"

Fred Lovelace regarded her blankly for she was no doubt referring to correspondence that he had condemned to the

Big File or which had lined Felicity's litter tray.
"Quite," he said.
"Sorry?" said Ms Oliver.
"I haven't fully digested it."
"Does the business of command fill your every minute?"
"I do little. The tricky bits come when the ship nears land and then a pilot boards and takes over," said Lovelace.
"Do you anticipate doing very little if you are appointed to a container ship?"
Luckily, Debrence asked Ms Oliver to join him at the bar.
Fred whispered to Alex, "Who the fuck is she?"
"Ms Oliver. She's joined the board."
"Did you see the bitch's face?"
"Mobile. She takes no prisoners."
"What does that fucking cow know about ships?"
Alex shrugged. "What does management know about anything – certainly very little about managing. It is the posing and posturing that they do so well."
"Fuck all. I tell you, they know fuck all." Lovelace downed his brandy, signalled a steward for another, and when fortified, glowered at Ms Oliver.
Ms Oliver was tackling a well travelled gherkin. The gherkin was a social accessory to be held and nibbled, in the same way as she delicately sipped her gin and tonic. She could leave an hour later, and most of her drink, together with most of her gherkin, would remain. When she talked to Debrence she put her head to one side, showing her face to Alex. Hers seemed a face that was never still, the muscles moved as if electronically.
"The bitch must have her vibrator in," said Fred with uncanny intuition, for it was rumoured that Ms Oliver did have a habit, admittedly in palmier days, of chasing chambermaids. It was fortunate that Lovelace did not know this for he could well have recalled the bartering for the cadet's doubtful charms in Qabahbah. And then he would have put the boot in, saying conversationally – glancing at Alex and at the company director – "As a heterosexual, I'm in a minority here."
When Ms Oliver summoned the captain, Alex went behind the bar so he could eavesdrop.
"The management wishes to discuss crew manning with

you, Captain," she said.

"What?" Lovelace signalled Francis by waving his empty glass.

"You will carry a Dr Trimmer on your forthcoming voyage. He's an expert in work study."

"What does he know about ships?"

"His expertise is work study."

"Sounds like some shoreside freeloader to me."

"Are you questioning the decision of management?" Ms Oliver's expression showed that the electrical device was running at an increased speed.

"A ship's doctor we don't need. A work study expert, who knows sod all about ships, we definitely don't need."

The electrical device seemed to have short-circuited for Ms Oliver's face showed great consternation. She drew back in alarm but the captain, with resolution, moved closer and fixed her in a corner near the bar. A frond from a potted palm, brought in especially for the voyage meeting, touched her cheek. She jumped.

"He knows bugger all about the sea. Admit it, woman!" shouted Lovelace.

Ms Oliver abandoned her barely touched drink. She dropped the nibbled gherkin in the ashtray. Brushing Lovelace aside, she surged out, heading for the privacy of the spare cabin opposite, which was used as a ladies' cloakroom. But escape Lovelace she could not. He clung like a burr. She turned right so did he. The door of the cabin was shut in his face. But Lovelace was not deterred. He shouted through it,

"There's fuck all wrong with this ship."

THE FOLLOWING morning Alex learnt of Lovelace's impending departure from his steward.

"The transfer letter came by special messenger. The captain's steward read it."

"Gomes doesn't read English."

"You should never underestimate a Goan." Francis irritatingly tidied the papers on the purser's desk.

"Well?" said Alex.

"Well what?"

"What was in the bloody letter?"

"Can I say, Captain Rupert de Vere Frogmore?"
"Can I say, fuck?"
"Yes indeed, sir."

IT WAS A SOBER LOVELACE who summoned Alex to his dayroom.
"You have my sympathy. To sail with Frogmore is to sail in the dark ages."
"I'm putting in for a transfer."
"Not a prayer. Frogmore is here to sort out the ship, and that includes you."
"It doesn't need sorting."
"I consider my command has been ahead of its time. One should be suspicious of institutions, one should two finger the establishment."
Alex nodded.
"Feed Felicity," said Lovelace, gripping his desk and with eyes brimming tears, he gazed fondly through the forward windows at the foredeck where a shoreside crane was discharging cargo out of number two hatch.

THE FASCIST REGIME started straightaway. The once over-heated dayroom was cold as the windows were opened to get rid of the smell of cat. The ship's carpenter inserted fitments in the desk drawers to take the Gestapo files; an accumulation of official mail, which spasmodically Lovelace had flung into the bottom of his wardrobe, was sifted through. As the bathroom was disinfected, Wagner played on the record deck and jackboots sounded in the alleyways.
Felicity, with the self-preservation of all cats, moved to Alex's cabin and settled in a corner of his daybed.
"May I ask, sir, where precisely you require me to site the excrement tray?" said Francis
"Stick it next to the cockroach trap."
On the office floor, between the outside bulkhead and the large green safe, stood a beer glass. In it a mound of cock-roaches moved about a piece of bread. They could not escape because the inside of the glass was slippery with butter.
"Will it be my duty to empty the excrement tray, sir?" persisted Francis.

"Stop calling me sir. Stop calling the litter tray the excrement tray."

"Am I to clean the cat's excrement tray, sir?"

"I'll do it."

"You'll be attending to it daily – as did Captain Lovelace."

"What am I to do, Francis?"

"Get rid of Captain Frogmore."

"Oh, sure."

"With Captain Lovelace you had little to do – now there can be purpose in your life – get rid of Frogmore."

"And how am I to do that?"

"You're forever telling me how clever you are. With your I.Q., I'm sure you'll find a way."

"With Frogmore around I have the feeling of always being in the wrong."

"We can't have you suffering from perpetual guilt, can we, sir?"

"You have to do that?"

"What, sir?"

"Jeeves, you ain't. Ditch the smart backchat and stop calling me sir every other word."

"I have to inform you, Alex, that I escorted the new doctor to the shipping office this morning to sign on, Alex."

"He's work study."

"So he told me, Alex. You might be interested to learn, Alex, that this voyage is to be Australia via Brazil, Alex."

"This news is from Dr Trimmer?"

"I cannot reveal my sources, Alex."

"You ever experienced torture? I'm thinking about squeezing your arrogant neck."

"Strictly entrez-nous my source is not MI6 but the Gomes-spy."

"Gomes-spy?"

"A mole maybe, but on the side of good."

"Francis!"

"Loading London, but first Amsterdam." Francis shifted his weight from foot to foot and said in a voice which made Alex look up, "Rather your cup of tea, one might surmise?"

FOUR

LONDON – SECOND CALL

ALEX enjoyed his time spent in a hotel bar in Amsterdam, a bar which catered for certain tastes; but he had not enjoyed the upstairs bit afterwards.

Despite loving the Continent, he masochistically relished the return of the ship to London on a cold damp day, an English winter's day, when it never really got light. He considered Britain to be a country to dislike, a country made alien by climate, by prejudice, by the establishment, by its class system. A country to escape. He should delight, thinking about sailing foreign again. But, he considered when abroad, Frogmore would represent the old values of the UK and implant them in the ship.

STANDING WELL BACK from the river was a row of terrace houses. He rang the bell of number twenty-three. Inside a smell of expensive perfume hung in a neat front room that was claustrophobic with a sixties three-piece suite and wallpaper on which were large cabbage roses.

"Should last you until you rejoin," said Alex, placing two packs of duty-free fags on the lace tablecloth, then he perched on the Rexene settee.

"Thank you very much." Cadet Jones put the cigarettes in the sideboard drawer. "Tea?"

"Pass."

A pink scar ran the cheek of the cadet's face, the other cheek was swollen. Before he had been a superbly built young man whose face was beautiful, but now the flaws had added a rugged glamour.

"What'd you get up to in Amsterdam, Cadet Jones?"

"Nothing."

"Define nothing," said Alex, lighting a cigarette.

Cadet Jones stared at the window but didn't speak.

Alex could hear the tick of the clock above the fireplace. "Okay, if I smoke in here?"

"Thing is, my mum's not too keen, not in this room."
Alex inhaled, tapped his ash in a plant pot. "Well?"
"Well what?" Dave handed him an ashtray.
"Tell me how you got injured in Amsterdam?"
"You know..."
"Trust me. I haven't told a soul of your shame."
"My shame?" said Jones alarmed.
"How you don't bash the bishop."
"For Christ's sake!"
"Is it that you can't wank, or you don't know how? I give lessons – no fee. In your case, I'll pay. You have a high drool factor. Shall I draw the curtains?"
Alex stared at the cadet, forcing him to speak.
"In Amsterdam I didn't do anything wrong. I went with a woman and paid her. And 'cos I refused to play with the bouncer's dick, he threw me through a window."
"I see."
"Mum said I didn't do nothing wrong."
"You *told* your mother?"
"Why not?"
Alex could never imagine his mother coping, if he mentioned he had had sex, never mind brothel sex. His mother's life was the Women's Institute, the vicar, and organising talks, usually with slides, given by doughty ladies who had all-in-wrestler's arms and travelled abroad a great deal with cameras and good intentions. It was all too much when Alex's imagination had his mother greeting him: "Darling, that dreadful scar!" And after he had explained how he had come by it; her saying, "Darling, wasn't that just *too* awful. I hope you won't find it too dull here in the country after shagging yourself fucking stupid on the Continent?" That mountain over, he had Mummy at the village fete, which she had organised for the last three years. "Oh, by the way," says Mummy, as she is judging the bramble jelly competition, and is torn between delicious Jar number seven and wonderfully tart Jar number nine, "darling Alex got his dreadful scar in a brothel in Amsterdam. The dear boy was only after a bit of cunt. They threw him through a window because he refused to play with the bouncer's cock. As I told the vicar, I've never heard the like." Alex shuddered and lit another cigarette.

"You've just lit one," said Cadet Jones.

"Do you have a small medicinal brandy. My nerves are quite shredded."

"The bouncer said to me, 'You Americans are all the same'."

"You're American?"

"He only thought me a Yank."

"Oh, my God, can this get worse? You won't know this, of course, but my mother's vicar had the most ghastly trouble with the Yanks during the War when they requisitioned the church hall to make doughnuts."

"Alex, will you come down to earth?"

"Sorry, I was in Little-Trumpington-in-the-Wold. Wold means barren land; it's rather appropriate."

Dave picked up and smoked Alex's abandoned cigarette. "Mum's not too happy about my scar. You know, me getting it at sea, and that."

"With your looks, why do you pay for sex?"

"No complications."

"That didn't work," said Alex. "After you were hospitalised in Amsterdam, two Dutch policeman boarded and told me that you had been in a fight ashore in a brothel."

"And?"

"The policemen told me to inform the captain."

"What did the captain say?"

"I didn't tell him but he'll find out because the agent's report will go to head office."

"I really appreciate that, thank you."

"Cadet David Jones, stop thanking me. I'm only after your body."

The large grey mongrel dog pulled herself upright and rested her muzzle on the cadet's knee.

"Mum'll be back soon. Doesn't like her in this room." He opened the door and called the dog out. "Anything I can do for you. I mean it. Anything at all."

"I'm but a simple sailor, Jonesy, my needs are those of the ordinary tar. Why couldn't you be in hospital?"

"Why?"

"Give the nurses a treat. They'd bed-bath you, soap your bits and I could bring you symbolic grapes and stroke your forehead."

"You can do that here," Dave said, his fine eyes beautifully lashed.

"Do what?"

"Stroke my forehead."

"I was gonna bring you something to read," said Alex, almost at a loss for words.

"Blokes in our road don't read books, only girls read."

"Very funny, cadet."

"The doctor said I'm gonna scar." Cadet Jones again glanced at the clock on the mantelpiece next to a cut-glass vase of silk flowers. "Mum'll be back soon."

"I'm being thrown out. Seems to be some kind of theme going on."

Jones blushed. "Don't talk stupid." then, "Please!"

"What?"

"Don't put your ash in there." He moved the plant away, then to cover his embarrassment, said, "She's a bit house-proud about this room."

"I'll see you back on board. And..."

"Yeah?"

"Keep it shut. Careless talk costs lives. The mate blabs."

"You wanna meet my mum?"

"This visiting-the-sick is cutting into my drinking time and I need to ditch my dog-end in the street."

"Is it okay if you and I go ashore when I get back on board? No one else, just you and me, I mean." Cadet Jones held onto Alex's hand, not shaking it, but holding on and squeezing it. "Me treat you, to thank you for being a good friend."

Alex didn't know what to say because his own family didn't go in for touching and holding other human beings.

At the end of the street, he waited at the bus stop near a shop which had boarded up windows. One of the boards had been ripped off and inside was litter and water on the floor and what looked like excrement.

Hoping for a taxi, Alex looked this way and that. He saw a woman putting her key into the lock of number twenty-three. Mrs Jones. Alex had imagined her in a headscarf and a wrap-around pinny, but Mrs Jones was done up to the nines; she must have been in makeup for three hours. A look which did not go with waxed fruit and floral wallpaper.

He shook his head. He had hoped for laughter while he visited, not an ill at ease young man, wanting to get shot of him, yet at the same time not wanting him to leave.

"I must be depravity. Maybe I act camp. I am the dirty magazine to be read with hand moving urgently under the bed sheets," he said out loud, to the astonishment of a young mother pushing twins in a pushchair.

ALEX stomped into his office. His strong fingers grasped tight hold of Francis' Indian white cotton shirt. "What am I to do? Tell me, for pity's sake! I am on my knees."

"I take it from your demeanour that you've been in converse with the captain?"

"Oh God, you're in pedantic mode. Where have you hidden my fags, serf?"

Francis handed him the pack off the desk. "You'll never manage to act the prima donna convincingly – you're too British."

"I'm not rising to your insults."

"You'd prefer to be Indian, sir?"

"I love your colour," said Alex, who thought Francis, not handsome, but very attractively dark; his eyebrows glistened and his thick black hair shone.

"And you'd wash yourself in a Calcutta drain?"

"That has some appeal if you did my nails."

"I..."

"I have just been up top to tell *La Grande Dame* Frogmore that Cadet Jones will rejoin and all he could say was, had I been ashore dressed like that?"

"In jeans, you mean?" said Francis.

"A navvy, he said. Why is it whenever I set foot in the captain's cabin, he gives me shit?"

"Because you're a bolshie sod and you dress like a fucking tramp."

"Francis, you go too far. But if you stopped, I would not like you. Captain Frogmore pointed out that when in uniform I must wear my cap – especially when reporting to The Command."

Francis laughed.

"I shall slit my throat."

"Wouldn't it be easier to wear a cap?"

"What's he on about? Wear a cap! It's six-o'fucking-clock in the evening, and it's Saturday."

"What's Saturday got to do with it?" asked his steward.

"My day off."

"You have every day off."

"I do my job," said Alex.

"Indeed, sir. As you have often sagely remarked, you have functioned quite brilliantly, when pissed, on all five continents."

"Beer, please, steward?"

Francis opened a can of Allsopps and expertly poured the contents into a smooth-sided glass before handing it to the smiling purser.

ON MONDAY THE PUSH WAS ON.

There was a race to load the vessel before the Trades Union negotiations broke down.

Francis came into the office waving a sheet of paper. "I've had the most stimulating conversation with the doctor about Descartes."

"Six thousand eggs are blocking the stores-flat. Forget Descartes."

"This note is from the doctor."

"I haven't seen him since he boarded. He's sick or something?"

"He's gone to the City."

Alex read the doctor's scrawl. "Three crew names. Enlighten me?"

"Abdul Samad is suicidal. You must arrange for him to fly home to Calcutta today."

"I'm not Christ."

"Indeed you are not, sir." Francis struck a match.

The purser took a long drag on his Rothmans. "The other two crew?"

"For the clinic dealing with sailors' diseases." Francis added primly, "The doctor said you had a great deal more experience of that sort of thing than he."

The purser leapt to his feet.

Francis jumped back but Alex only swung open the heavy safe door; took out five one pound notes which he gave to his steward. "Phone a taxi. Organise the two crew for the clinic. Take Abdul Samad to outpatients. Show them his identity book – merchant seamen get priority. Demand a psychiatrist. I'll give you a letter saying he's suicidal."

"What about the storing? I can get Badsha Meah to help."

"No way!"

"I am surprised. I would have thought that Badsha Meah's charms you are unable to resist." Francis rushed on, "Do not worry, I'll go ashore for you, sir, that should give you time to quaff an ale, or ten, in the officers' bar."

Alex had been goaded enough. He closed in on Francis. "I do not find it reassuring that a steward rams the fact that he's smarter than me down my throat."

"Me saying, you being unable to resist Badsha Meah's charms got right up your nose, didn't it?"

He pushed two pounds in Francis' shirt pocket. "For you."

"Why, sir, thank you, sir. Forgive me, sir, for forgetting myself and acting above my station, sir."

The telephone, which was a direct link to the captain's cabin, buzzed. Alex wondered if he dare risk it and go up top without a cap.

SEATED AT HIS DESK, CAPTAIN FROGMORE was in deep conversation with the marine superintendent.

"I could have demanded full leave after my extended tour out East but I put the Bede Line first. Though, I will admit that my appointment to this ship gave me the opportunity to get back to sea. It's ironic that I was forced to work ashore for years. The genuine seaman is but a foreigner ashore, divorced from the sea. The seaman's passion is to return, to hoist sail and watch the spume fly."

Captain Lancaster, the marine superintendent, relaxing on a sofa, was a onetime ship's master now permanently based ashore. He stifled a smile and avoided looking at Alex. Sinking further into the sofa, he said, "Lovelace's taking leave, I hear."

"He is a man seldom sober. His antics are those of a drunk at chucking-out time on a Saturday. Like many a drunk, he is loud. If he were efficient and loud, he might be forgiven."

"Rupert..." Captain Lancaster attempted to silence him but Frogmore was in full flight:

"He's an incompetent. He's a malicious man; a fact he

masks with his hail-fellow-well-met manner which is lapped up by toadying officers. The only good I can say of Lovelace is that he is seldom on the bridge." Frogmore became aware of Alex in the doorway. "Why are you eavesdropping?"

"I'm not."

"Haven't you the courtesy to knock?"

"He did knock," said Captain Lancaster.

"Where's your cap?"

"I'm storing."

"So? Wear it! Wear it! What do you want?"

"You ordered me to report to you, sir. And reporting, I am..." inspired by Francis he threw in an extra, "...sir."

ALEX returned to the real world where the engineers cleaned the filthy bilge tanks, where cargo was manhandled in the hatches, where a confusion of four months stores was jammed in the stores-flat, where an angry deliveryman waited for Alex while he had been delayed by the captain discussing the fish course on the next day's dinner menu.

As Francis was at the hospital, he spent four hours stacking cartons in the dry storeroom.

Badsha Meah appeared in the doorway.

"Oh God, it's Liability Badsha. Tell me you're not helping?" said Alex.

"Much to do, *sahib*. You wanted on telephone urgent."

In the cross-alleyway outside the dining saloon, attempting to get to the phone, Alex scrambled over a heap of bulging canvas bags containing dry-cleaned loose covers.

Abdul Samad was on the other end, at the hospital, and was shouting as only a man with experience of the telephone system in Calcutta could.

As a riveter started on a plate in the ship's hull, Badsha Meah accepted a delivery note from a driver.

"No!" Alex panicking, trying to get hold of the delivery note before Badsha Meah signed it, caught his shoe in the telephone cable and tumbled, cutting his hand on the chrome trim on a sand-filled box used to douse cigarette ends. Blood ran. Badsha Meah abandoned the deliveryman to wrap Alex's hand in a linen napkin.

Alex reversed charges to the shipping company's head

office, and during lulls in the riveting, he learnt that Francis had arrived with a psychiatric report from the hospital. Abdul Samad was booked to fly home to India. Alex turned to Badsha Meah.

"Pack Abdul's gear and list it. It'll be air-freighted out tomorrow. He flies home at six this evening..."

The captain arrived on the scene.

"Purser, am I hearing you aright? Are you authorising a crew repatriation without my approval?"

"He's suicidal and his wife is seriously ill."

"Who says so?"

Alex was silenced as the riveter came in strong. Badsha Meah clung to his bandaged hand as if they were dating.

Captain Frogmore shouted above the din, "Purser, I am waiting."

Alex pulled his hand away but Badsha Meah would not let go.

"The ship's doctor..."

"A man I've never sighted."

"Abdul Samad's story has been checked by the welfare officer in Calcutta. Two psychiatrists ashore have examined him. Head office has authorised his repatriation."

A deliveryman with boxes of bonded spirits guarded by a customs officer pushed forward to see if the captain, as unmistakable authority, could help.

"Do us a favour, me old darling, and put your moniker on this. I'm due in Tilbury an hour back."

Frogmore gave the deliveryman a withering glance. It was as though Frogmore were royalty and above it all, never getting his hands soiled, never touching bank notes, having others do menial tasks. He turned to Alex. "Under no circumstances will you authorise crew changes." Straight backed he climbed the broad stairs that led to his quarters.

The riveter stopped. Frogmore stopped too to raise a hand to summon Alex to follow him. His was the monarch's elegant hand, a hand that moved as if palsied from behind the limousine's reinforced glass. Adoring subjects gazed respectfully, and enthusiastically cheered and waved.

But times were changing. The deference of hoi poloi for authority was diminishing. The deliveryman was openly contemptuous: "You're what's wrong with this fucking country, Adolf. Too many fucking chiefs and not enough Indians."

Alex's anger showed clearly on his face. And the lowest of the low, the brown-faced crew member's attention, was not on supreme authority, but on the purser's injured hand.

For Frogmore, this was a rare occasion when he was not in control but he dealt with the open hostility as best he could by ignoring it. He made a dignified retreat, unhurriedly, to the sanctity of his spacious quarters – his Balmoral, in contrast to Alex's box-like cabin on the working deck. But Balmoral was even a greater distance from the bleak dormitories of the crew quarters, which suffered vibration from the propellor shaft, where Badsha Meah lived.

The incident had the cosiness of a conspiracy. Alex was elated with the conception of being mates with the deliveryman, in the brotherhood of the trades union. It gave him purpose.

At four o'clock he made time to type a letter which he took up to the captain and placed before him on his desk.

"It's to head office, sir, requesting an immediate transfer for personal reasons."

"Personal reasons being I told you to wear your cap."

"The absurdity of wearing a cap while storing is certainly an issue, but my main concern is your criticism of the way I dealt with Abdul Samad."

"I will concede that you handled the matter correctly but you have to keep the command informed." Frogmore pushed the letter aside.

"Will you countersign my letter, sir?"

"I am tempted to endorse it *highly recommended.* However, matters concerning discipline are to be resolved on board. You will not flap a letter to head office in my face every time you are told off. No, I will not countersign it."

"You have to countersign any letters to head office."

"If you insist, I shall endorse it that the short staffed saloon department requires a purser of your experience and it is my wish that you stay."

"You must hate me."

"It is not a question of like or dislike, purser. All in all, I have no criticism of your work. It is your manner which appals."

"I don't want to sail with you." As he trudged out of the dayroom Alex's stomach lurched.

Frogmore followed him into the alleyway. "You will leave my ship when I say so, not when you throw a tantrum."

"Jesus!"

"Act your age and do your job, purser. If you and I have open confrontation who do you think is going to win."

EVENING. Exhausted, Alex at last had time to relax. He lifted the cat out of his armchair and sat down. He opened a beer; rested his feet on the low table.

A tall man tapped at the doorway which led from the office into his cabin.

"Trimmer," said the man who settled uninvited on the daybed. "This looks good." He reached for a can of beer and the opener.

"Do allow me to get you a glass," said Alex, not moving.

"Had one fuck-awful day," said Dr Trimmer.

"On board has been uneventful. I spent most of the day finishing a rather complex jigsaw of the *Cutty Sark*. The rigging was an absolute bugger."

Dr Trimmer tilted the blue can and drank deeply.

"A glass is in the cabinet above the desk – if you feel the need."

"I've been having a bad time of things lately. My marriage is over – a decree absolute or some such nonsense. Your hand?"

"Francis redid the bandage after Badsha Meah embalmed it. Francis and Badsha Meah are bright new India."

"Abdul Samad? What about him?"

"Repatriated."

"And the other two?"

"One has N.S.U. The other has gonorrhoea of the back passage."

"Nothing to worry about."

"Hardly good news, I thought."

Dr Trimmer pushed back his long hair. "I spent half my day travelling." He paused while he helped himself to Alex's sandwiches. "What a peculiar place the Bede Line head office is." The doctor spoke with some difficulty. Alex noted he was no phantom but a tall man tending to overweight, definitely scruffy and discernibly drunk.

"Am I being work studied now?"

"Debrence insisted on lunching in the boardroom of dark wood and leather. Models of dated ships in glass cases. Gilt-framed portraits of bewhiskered men on panelled walls. An elderly waitress served the meal. Everything old, everything dated." The doctor swayed unsteadily on the daybed, more ash fell. "I don't care for ritual dining. I thought the merchant navy wasn't boardrooms but denim and lime juice."

"Lime juice is no more. The crew are issued with vitamin C tablets which are more convenient to resell in India."

"Can I have another of your excellent beers?"

"Finish my sandwiches. They're my evening meal."

The doctor's second beer foamed. He sucked the spillage from the outside of the can.

"You didn't drink out of a can at lunch, did you?" said Alex.

"Let's drink to Thomas Thomas."

"Who is Thomas Thomas?"

"Was, my dear chap. Was. His remains for burial at sea. In an off-white plastic urn with a label on its screw-top lid. A Welshman called Lewis gave this very tacky urn to me. The Welshman wasn't a bundle of laughs."

"The company's chairman is named Lewis and is Welsh. He doesn't do jokes."

"The lunch was mostly liquid. Caught the tube back. Got off at Poplar. Is it Poplar? Bought four Guinness in a supermarket to keep me going 'till the pubs opened." He crammed the last of Alex's sandwiches in his mouth.

"Where are the remains of Thomas Thomas?"

"I had him in the supermarket because he fitted in rather snugly with the Guinness in the carrier bag."

"Where's the casket, Doc?"

"I must've left the old darling someplace."

Alex poured himself a sedative brandy. "You've lost the remains of a friend of the company's chairman? Where?"

"A pub – of that I'm pretty sure."

"A pub? Which pub, for God's sake?"

"My dear chap, you sound like Lady Bracknell."

"Lady Bracknell?" said Alex.

"She did not use expletives. However the situation is not dissimilar. Miss Prism lost a baby..."

"Miss Prism was not pissed nor dealing with the Welsh dragon."

"She..."

"Nor were you on the fucking Brighton line."

"District line. The station is immaterial. I had Thomas Thomas, not in a handbag but in a plastic carrier bag – its logo I am unsure of."

"You said a pub?" persisted Alex.

"What?"

"You said you ditched the remains in a pub?"

"Francis said I'd like you. I'm not so sure."

"It's certainly not my hospitality that's lacking – it must be my manners. You'll have to instruct me."

"Irony is a tool used by those who have something to hide."

"You are hiding the name of the pub. I will ask again. Where the fuck is this fucking pub?"

"How should I know? I say, my dear chap, I'm about all in. Can't we leave this until the morning?"

"The pub? The pub? The pub?"

"A pub. Near the dock gates. You must know it. The formidable landlady has large forearms and bottle-blonde hair." Dr Trimmer shut his eyes and slumped in a drunken stupor on the daybed.

FIVE

THE ADMIRAL BENBOW

ALEX hauled the doctor to his feet then thrust his hands under his arms and dragged him the length of the cream-painted alleyway, empty and quiet except for the hissing from an overhead lagged pipe carrying steam. The doctor's heels bumped as Alex pulled him into a cabin which had a small metal plate above the door which read *Ship's Surgeon.*

After dumping the doctor in the armchair, Alex hurried back to his own cabin. He knocked back a large scotch before pulling on a green Jaegar sweater to cover his uniform shirt. He went back into the alleyway but this time, headed forward. He sped past door after locked door. Hearing the sound of the television in the officers' smoke room, he doubled up the stairs but found the smoke room empty.

He ran down the stairs and raced the engineers' alleyway on the starboard side looking for someone to help him. All doors were shut and locked. He remembered that the chief engineer had led an expedition ashore to 'an intimate club' he knew where 'the women had the price chalked on the soles of their shoes'. Alex doubled back to the foyer where he phoned a taxi before climbing the companionway to the cadet's cabin at the after end of number three hatch.

Cadet Jones had rejoined. A cobweb of stitches gave a curious glamour to his face.

"Can't offer you a beer, Alex, I'm stony."

"Don't suppose you know a pub near a dock gate which has a blonde landlady built like an all-in wrestler?"

"*The Admiral Benbow.*"

"Sure?"

"Vera's big. Nice breasts."

"Take me there and don't spare the horses."

"I'm on duty and in working gear. And I'm broke."

"Do you have a problem going ashore with me? Am I an embarrassment to you?"

"I'm not allowed ashore."
Alex peered out the window. "Cut the crap. Taxi's here."

A SMELL OF STALE BEER hit them when they entered. A padlocked bike, with a broad worn saddle and rusting spokes, rested against a wall in the narrow entrance hall which led into the barroom where two polished spittoons stood on bare scrubbed floorboards.

In the pub Cadet Jones was assured and at home. His manner gave a lie to his age. Alex, in his Jaegar sweater and tailored uniform trousers, was way too elegant for the joint. At first he kept his mouth shut and let the cadet make the running.

He marvelled how the cadet smiled and charmed the formidable landlady, and charmed the not bad-looking middle-aged man seated on a bar stool. Cadet David Jones was mannerly, but in here his accent coarsened and his attitude changed. He was one of the family and proud that Alex was part of it too. He casually put his arm about the purser's shoulders to introduce him. "This here's Alex. He's okay. Looks after me and that."

Alex bought the landlady and the man at the bar a drink before sitting at a table near the fireplace.

Cadet Jones followed him with the spotlight trailing. The audience of two were beaming their applause and Alex seemed to be included, which was pleasant. Dave winked and put the drinks on the table then handed Alex his change.

"Thank you so much for the beer."

"Thank me again and I'll scream."

"That's Mark." Dave indicated the man at the bar, then nodding at the two shots of whisky, said, "Bought me a scotch. You okay to drink it when he's not looking?"

"You seem to be well in with the landlady?"

"She does Mum's and my hair."

"You come in here with your mother?" said Alex, keeping all surprise out of his voice.

"Her, me and Mark on Saturdays. Mark runs a stall."

"So does my mother," said Alex, thinking of the W.I.

"Mark sells shellfish. Your mum handle that?"

"Maybe. I won't devalue her by saying she couldn't."

Though Alex did have to stretch his imagination to see his mother shovelling pints of cockles and whelks.

"And take a load of mouth off the customers?"

"Does he sell live eels? I don't think the mater could cope with live eels."

"The stallholders come down the boozer afterwards – on Saturdays, see?"

Alex had a vision of his own mother going down the boozer and putting on a brave face when attempting to sing *Down at the Old Bull and Bush.* She would not yield to the temptation of a port-and-lemon but instead plump for her customary amontillado. Or perhaps she might join the natives and partake in a nice cup of rosey-lee. Or perhaps not. She seldom touched Indian, for it was a 'tad' acidic. Perhaps they'd have a Ceylon blend somewhere. She'd recently enjoyed a milky Ceylon at the Braithwaites.

Dave said, "My mum sings."

Alex immediately had the two mothers doing a duet. Though what, he could not imagine.

"What kind of music?" he said.

"The Stones mostly," said Dave.

Alex's mother and Mick Jagger had very little in common, but if the mater could shovel cockles and whelks, then the sky was her oyster, as it were.

"Lawks-a-mussy!" said Alex. It was an ejaculation, he thought, from the East End, but Cadet Jones looked at him quizzically.

In reality, his mother would have thought Mrs Jones' makeup a touch overdone; though she would have never said so. There might be a glance, but never an "Oh dear."

Dragging his thoughts back to the reason why he came ashore, he said, "Did you ask about the urn?"

"It's behind the bar. Vera thought it was curry powder left by them Malays they had in." As Jones leant forward on his seat, the scabbard of his deck knife caught the chair.

"Do you have to wear a dagger ashore? This is really too much."

"Only when ashore with you. I thought you'd go for the macho touch."

"I do hope, Cadet Jones," said Alex, with assumed pomposity, "that you are not of that breed of young men who bare their chests and belch and sniff their armpits in male display. It's only necessity that brings me ashore with a dissipated youth with a dagger between his teeth."

"I falls in love with you when you talks like that, me old mate. You does it for me every time." Jones leaned back, his chair scraped the glossy brown wall.

"Mate – china plate. I'm really very good at this. I'll ask the mater where she gets her barnet cut."

"You can have my body any way you want it, and in public too, just so long as you drop the rhyming slang."

He was entranced by David Jones but he forced himself to examine the shoddy urn. It was made of plastic which had yellowed. Cheap or old stock, or perhaps it had been reused; not what one would expect of one of the chairman's friends. There was a label fixed in its screw-top. The inscription was in longhand and clearly written was *Thomas Thomas*.

"Let's celebrate the urn's arrival," he said, ordering another round.

"Great wake this," said Jones, looking at the casket which sat on the table between them. Alex saw not Jones' working boots but Texan soft tooled leather cowboy boots with noisy spurs. "If this Thomas Thomas was a sailor he'd want his wake to be in a seamen's pub." Jones sipped his beer and pushed the whisky chasers towards Alex. "Maybe he's a weekend sailor. You know, in those poncy caps – like they wear down the yacht club. Not like us."

"I'm not like you. You've been arrested in a foreign port."

"Jack says you've been inside."

"Not bleeding likely. But I do admit to having had cabbage stalk soup for breakfast in a Belfast jail, but that was due to the natives. So broad a dialect, I was misunderstood, not like here where I slip easily into the patois." Alex said, "Cor blimey, me old china, you must be fucking famished. I'll get you a bite."

"Vera does a pea soup with fatty bacon and fried bread, don't half set you up of a cold night."

"One can imagine it warming the very cockles of a stallholder's heart." Alex's stomach baulked at the idea of food, though he might manage one poached egg on a round of brown bread – no butter – if pushed. At Vera's prompting, he ordered one soup and four slices of fried bread with fried eggs for the cadet.

As he waited for Vera to prepare the food, Alex talked, as he loved talking, with Mark, who had footballer's legs; his muscles pushed at the too-tight worsted slacks. Mark wore the most striking of tweed jackets; a dusky mauve affair with thin red stripes crisscrossing through it.

"Harris?" said Alex.

"Back of a lorry, mate," said Mark.

"Would you Adam and Eve it. Knocked off, rather than spun off in some remote Hebridian croft, one imagines, but it suits you."

Mark exploded with laughter.

"No, being serious. It's certainly garish and would do nothing for me at all, but with your dark colouring it works a treat. And I simply love the pattern. One could not get its like in the high street – one would hope." Alex found himself trying the jacket on, with Dave Jones watching. "I don't have your shoulders." A heavy weight, from whatever was in a side pocket of the jacket, had him whispering, "Do you pack a gun?"

"Small change for the stall."

Alex bought Mark a large scotch before returning to Cadet David Jones, who relished his soup, fried bread and eggs. "Very tasty. Vera's done the eggs how I like – all burnt and curly," he said. All four eggs, thought Alex as he toyed with a bag of crisps.

"Oh dear, closing time already, just as I was getting into the mood," said Alex.

"THEY LOVED YOU," said Dave happily, as they walked in the damp night air, heading towards the docks, not noticing the chill breeze.

He put his arm in Alex's. "Mark said that you was what I needed – the toff. Pull myself up in the world."

"That makes me sound a snob."

"You ain't no snob but you didn't go to no secondary modern, that's for sure."

It was then Alex realised that Dave had been showing him off; that he was proud of him. And that was a new experience. "I liked Mark, a lot. No side to him," he said, remembering the warmth of the jacket as he had tried it on.

"Play your cards right."

"Does he take it up the Khyber?"

"Vera reckons. You could be in there with a chance, mate." Dave took his arm away and found a hanky. He offered it to Alex. "Dry your face."

Alex had not noticed how the rain had dampened him. Returning the hanky, he said, "Oh shit, no!"

"What's up?"

"I'm groaning. Him!" He pointed to a badly parked Mini.

"The driver who is throwing up?"

"Rusty. When he's on watch in the engine room – pray."

Jones helped Alex drag the drunken third engineer out of the driver's seat and haul him into the back of the car.

"Dave, take the urn out the carrier. Use it as a sick bag in case Rusty spews." Alex fumbled in the driver's seat; swore as he banged his bandaged hand. "I've only ever driven the mater to the shops in the Rolls when Smithers was out of his fucking skull on cheap wine."

"Your parents have a Roller?"

"You got some idea I live in a castle?"

"Your accent goes with castles."

"No castle – a small house, no car. My ma lives in the country in a house which will never feature in *Country Life*. She drives a Morris Minor which I borrowed without asking and we talk through lawyers now." Alex managed to get the car going and drove towards the dock gates.

"You want I should drive?" said David Jones.

"Am I that bad?"

"Fine, fine."

The rain, coming down heavily now, showed in the light from a lamp which hung above the dock entrance. The lamp swung in the wind, lengthening and shortening the policeman's shadow as he slowly approached the car.

Alex swivelled in his seat. "Dave, open your fly. He's got a funny walk."

The policeman put his head through the car window and drew back sharply at the smell of vomit. Then, he spent an age examining the singing Rusty. Slowly his flashlight moved to pinpoint Alex's bloody bandaged hand. The flashlight moved again to illuminate Cadet Jones' scarred face. The beam then shone on his deck knife.

"What's this then? Drugs?" he said, lifting up the casket.

"The ashes of Thomas Thomas. To be scattered at sea," said Alex.

The policeman carried the casket into his brightly lit hut where he unscrewed the lid and tipped some of the contents on a copy of the *Evening Standard.*

Alex's imagination had the Bede Line's chairman opening his *Financial Times* and reading that three of Captain Frogmore's ship's company had been arrested. *Two officers had recently sustained knife wounds and the third was puking. The trio were in possession of the alleged remains of his lifelong friend Thomas Thomas. The remains were with the drugs squad for forensic examination. It was reported that this drunken band had taken Thomas Thomas for a carouse in The Admiral Benbow – a tavern frequented by low sailors and stallholders.*

The lean-faced policeman's next words brought him sharply back to reality. "You're off the Bede Line ship." He held out the casket. Alex took it apprehensively. "You'd better watch it in future, purser. You're lucky I'm off duty in ten minutes and the wife's expecting." He stood back and waved the car through.

Alex drove with excessive care on the deserted road inside the dock.

"How'd he know you?" asked Cadet Jones.

"God, you're good looking."

"Where'd you meet the cop?"

He shrugged. "Dozens of officials on the ear-hole pass through my cabin." He parked the Mini behind the shed at the berth ahead of the *John Bede* in case it had been stolen.

Jones swung Rusty over his shoulder with little effort. "Fireman's lift," he said, strolling along the dockside.

On board Cadet Jones' offloaded the third engineer; rolling him gently onto his bunk. Later, he sat relaxed in Alex's cabin.

"This Rusty? He's...?"

"...shallow and not trustworthy and a friend of mine."

"No, seriously?"

"Seriously. You know what. I drink with Rusty daily at sea, but know less about his background than I do yours. He lives in a house on the Thames, I'm pretty sure. I get the impression that his parents discovered early on that he was the black sheep and sent him to sea. Whisky?"

The cadet shook his head. "Good evening we had."

"Did you not notice that I was almost arrested for being drunk in charge?"

"Now I am back on board, I speak proper English."

"I've noticed."

"You're an amazing man, getting things fixed and stuff."

Alex on reflection, was not pleased with his run ashore. He had saved Dr Trimmer's neck, but then he had assumed that the doctor would be on Frogmore's side.

He got that wrong.

GREY LIGHT told him it was morning.

All senses were heightened after the poison alcohol had been absorbed into his body.

Alex noted that Francis was reproving as he handed him a fizzing Alka Seltza. The smell of frying bacon coming from the galley registered unpleasantly with his nose and this drew his attention to his stomach, which had not only suffered an affront of beer with chasers in the pub, but, several enormous scotches on board, when he and Cadet Jones had discussed life. Alex's stomach and his intestinal tract were signalling rebellion.

He gingerly made his way on deck and stood ready to rush to the shoreside lavatories. The ship's heads being out of bounds because they discharged directly into the non-tidal Royal Albert Dock.

Rusty, short and cute wearing John Lennon spectacles, and cuddly in a white boiler suit and fisherman's knit jumper, was returning from ashore. He handed Alex the large lavatory key.

"Stinks of Jeyes."

"You look like a Home Counties pygmy. See the German ship in the next berth? The Mini is parked behind the shed."

"I think I'm engaged."

"Not the old biddy with high principles and black suspenders?"

"It's making me ill – physically. I threw up just now. It's the worry of it all." Rusty's face screwed up in confessional guilt.

"I'm so sorry."

"Tina is black suspenders and she's not old. The one I'm engaged to is Barbara. You know how these things go."

"No, I do not know how they go. I've been pissed often. I've swung from chandeliers. I've woken up in the embrace of a Russian ballet dancer – sans cod piece – that was a disappointment. I've opened my eyes to filed teeth and tribal scars. And, on one memorable occasion I awoke in the tight embrace of a female all-in wrestler with notable body odour. But I can say I've never become engaged. Engaged is convention. Engaged is to be avoided at all costs. And what's disgusting about you, is that you've become engaged and you're not sure about it. That's like committing suicide and waking up and wondering if you're dead."

Alex's sermon was interrupted. The forbidden was happening. An onboard lavatory was flushing. A discharge from the ship's side was shooting out sewerage onto the dockside. Human waste splattered around four dockers manhandling a large crate marked SYDNEY. A fragile sheet of toilet tissue clung to the crate. The four dockers stopped working.

"Fucking ship'll be fined fucking thousands!" One docker shouted up at Alex.

It wasn't that event that triggered Alex's bowels but the sight of the approaching lean-faced policeman of last night, who was walking purposefully along the wharf. Alex's senses signalled alarm. Involuntary actions were taking place. His digestive tract screamed that it could take no more. Gripping the lavatory key he clattered down the aluminium gangway. It was a race. He bumped into a young docker and winked. "Not me. I'm off for a pony and trap." They both laughed. Alex two-fingered the four dockers as he skirted the crate; then he waved gayly at the policeman as if he were an old friend. The timer was ticking. His bowel went into spasm. The large key was in the large lock. Door open. Door shut. Fly ripped open, pants down and he had made it. He gratefully slumped forward on the wet wooden seat, in the dank, Jeyes-smelling, white tiled cubicle.

He stayed in the 'officers only' lavatory for fifteen minutes, hopeful that the policeman would have moved on.

There was no sight of him when he returned onboard.

Unfortunately, he could not avoid Frogmore standing at the top of the gangway. The captain was running ten minutes late for breakfast and that meant a crisis. In the shelter of the entrance to the midships' accommodation lounged Dr Trimmer. Alex guessed that it was the doctor who had illegally flushed the onboard lavatory.

Alex eased himself between Frogmore and the ship's rail. River mist, which clung to the captain's jacket, rubbed wetly on his bare arms as he slid by.

Frogmore stopped berating the doctor and said casually to Alex, "You're improperly dressed."

"I've been to the lavatory."

"Therefore you have been ashore."

"Have I to wear a cap to defecate?" Alex thought that the captain with his medal ribbons on his chest and gold rings on his arms and oak leaves on his cap's peak, looked ready for the stage. Perhaps he was comparable to a Peruvian admiral. He wondered if, given the choice, Frogmore, as the epitome of the British sea captain, would prefer to be compared to an efficient German rather than a flamboyant Latin.

"I will see you later, purser. My cabin after rounds."

Alex hurried to his office where he pushed five packs of Rothmans in a brown paper-bag. Minutes later he was doubling down the aluminium gangway. He strolled up to the small band of dockers and pushed a note surreptitiously in the foreman's hand. He smiled at the dashing dark-haired young man and casually left the brown paper bag containing cigarettes near him on the crate. He stayed talking with the dockers for ten minutes. The fine was avoided.

SEATED IN HIS OFFICE, Alex wondered at Frogmore's love of England for he was seldom there. Thinking about it, he now wondered if Frogmore was hooked on England at all. What he could be certain was that the captain did revere old standards. There was his obsession about officers being properly dressed at all times. Though, to wear a cap to have a shit, Alex thought, went beyond all boundaries. Did the Queen wear her crown on the throne?

Hanging in the open doorway was the young docker he had chatted to on the dockside.

"I'll have a short, if you've got one," he said.

Alex brought a bottle of export-strength vodka from his cabin and poured a ship-sized peg into a glass which had the Bede Line crest on it.

"Nice smooth glass, for this bit of rough," said the docker.

"You ain't no rough."

"You not having one, Alex?"

"Tomato juice for me. We've got the Voyage Inspection any second." Alex was curious. "You look Mediterranean?"

"Name's Gypsy." He downed the vodka in one. "That hit the spot."

"How come you know my name?"

"Asked the cadet on the gangway, didn't I? Knows him, don't I? Said you were okay. Didn't know if you were up for it, though." He rubbed his chin, which was black with stubble; his forehead creased in thought. Alex poured him another shot.

"You got dangerous cargo, mate."

"I have?"

"Radioactive –in number three. It's lead protected. We got paid extra."

"I see."

"Don't tell the others 'bout the booze," said Gypsy, with an air of a conspirator.

"Can I ask how old you are?"

"Old enough for a quick fifty, mate. Pity you ain't up for it." The sexy hand held out the empty glass. Gypsy's dark eyes were on Alex as he poured a hefty peg. "Last one, otherwise I'll get so pissed I'll fall down a hatch."

"I wouldn't want that."

Gypsy looked at the slave clock fixed to the bulkhead. He drained his glass before putting it carefully on the desk. "Work fucks us up. I am due Vic Docks in about two hours – there for a week." Gypsy stepped back into the alleyway, bumping into Frogmore. Not intimidated by the brass, he said, "Sorry about that, mate. See you, Alex."

Alex was left feeling he'd missed out, had somehow fucked up.

It was normally Frogmore's presidential style to summon the purser up top, so Alex was surprised to see him in his office.

"What's that you're drinking, purser?"
"Tomato juice, sir."
Frogmore glanced at the bottle of vodka on the desk. "For your nerves, one supposes?"
"Some of the Catholic clergy take beer for breakfast," said Alex, hoping for a change in Frogmore's mood.
"I do not see you as a man of the cloth. You do not have that false sanctity, nor that pious put-on plummy pulpit voice. However, we have but ten minutes before we meet the director at the gangway for the Voyage Inspection." He added, as if he were a BBC newsreader announcing that the country was at war, "Have you a thing about the church?"
"I do indeed, sir. I'm as uncomfortable with religion as I am with unjust authority."
"You are certainly comfortable with your position in my ship. You saunter about with a cigarette in one hand and a peacock feather in the other." He pushed the bottle of vodka out of Alex's reach. "However, your dealing with the dock labour was exemplary. You put that work study doctor's nose out of joint. Showed him how things are done. That was one of the four dockers I bumped into just now. A striking young man. You get on?"
"They're people." Alex shrugged, feeling intense shame at Frogmore mentioning Gypsy, as if he had been caught doing something wrong.
"You have the common touch. Like me – you communicate well with the man in the street."
Alex glanced up at his captain, unsure if he was joking. He felt that the ice between them may have cracked some. Frogmore's attention turned to the activity on the dockside. Alex joined him at the office window.
"Oh dear, the traffic must be inexcusably light. I see the company car arriving."
"It's large enough to have gone astray from a cortege."
"Gangway, purser."
Alex looked about for his cap. "You want me to report to you later?"
"No."
"I am not in the doghouse?"
"I grant you absolution."
"Do I have to salute the director?"

"He would note it and would like it. I don't bother. But then you are not me, nor do you have my authority, even though at times you assume it," said Frogmore in revolutionary mood.

THE CAPTAIN, the first mate, the chief engineer, the purser and the doctor stood at the head of the gangway to greet Debrence. Immediately he boarded they began a tour of the ship.

Several dockers stopped working to watch this odd band carrying out the Voyage Inspection prior to sailing deep-sea. Debrence moved elegantly, the captain strode, the chief engineer walked with whisky-purpose and the first mate's gait was steadied by gin. The doctor took notes and Alex tagged on, lagged behind, as if hoping to get lost. He was bored by it. And after the Inspection there'd be drinks before a lunch of the usual chicken curry and gammon steak.

Debrence waved a hand at him. "Come along! Can't you keep up with us old 'uns?"

This odd British procession, headed by a man in a Savile Row suit, followed by officers in reefers, wove its way along the main deck, avoiding the dockers, avoiding slings of swinging cargo. It was the importance of Debrence that not one of the many dockers – the gangs had been doubled up to get the ship loaded to sail on time – made a comment when Debrence gaily fluttered fingers at a trailing Alex, who was avoiding looking down the open hatches into the vertigo holds.

Aft, the inspection party stood importantly in the crew galley while the *bhandary* cooked chapattis on a coke-fired stove. Then the steering gear was examined. The Asian crew lavatories were but briefly looked at. Frogmore had had his fill of lavatories that day.

On their return trek, standing amongst a group of dockers, was Gypsy. He made no sign of recognition, nor did Alex acknowledge him. Gypsy might think him a snob, but Alex was too shy to be openly friendly with him – a much younger man not of his own class. It was the sex thing that stopped him saying hello, not snobbery. Gypsy watched as the inspection party made its way back along the main deck, heading for the midship storerooms where Francis and the pantryman had spent much of the night stowing and tidying the dry stores.

But half-drunk, Gypsy no longer lurked, he took a step towards Alex as the Inspection party stepped over the weather sill to disappear into the accommodation.

"How's it going, Gypsy?" said Cadet Jones, slightly out of breath. "I saw you from the poop. You're still here?"

"Give him this," said Gypsy, angrily thrusting a quarter bottle of scotch into Dave's hand.

As they watched him roll his way towards the gangway, David Jones said, "It's from number three – broached cargo. The dockers dropped a sling on purpose and now there's a stack of it." The cadet was watching Gypsy's back. "He's a funny bugger. The moods on him. Maybe 'cos he was in care. His brother's doing time in the Scrubs."

"How old is he? Sixteen?" said Alex.

" 'Bout that. He'll be sixteen or seventeen anyway. Kirsty at number ten fancied it like mad and asked him to come down Top Rank with her one Saturday – she'd pay. He told her to go fuck herself. I'll stick the booze in the fuse box outside your cabin."

ALEX turned in at nine that evening. His cabin cosy in the low light from two shaded lamps. The tape recorder was playing softly; Felicity was on the daybed, and outside the docks were night quiet. The director had long gone. All the labour was ashore and all ship's company had signed on and were on board.

It was one in the morning when a *seacunny* woke him for departure.

The last minute mail he handed to the shipping company's driver. Two men ashore manhandled the ship's lines and after casting off, the *John Bede* was manoeuvred by tugs into the lock where it waited for the water in the lock to level with the Thames. Alex completed two forms. He guessed at the fuel remains on board, and then he forged the master's signature. He rolled the forms around the large lavatory key and secured the package in a huge bulldog clip which was made fast to a long pole held by a man in a peaked cap who stood far below on the side of the lock. Ritual. This departure ceremony of the man in the blue trench coat and official cap, who carried a pole in order to retrieve two bureaucratic forms and the officers' lavatory key, was quietly British.

The ship sailed downriver. Tilbury slid astern. On the port side was a flat stretch of marshy mud and clustered oil storage tanks; to starboard an ugly power station and a shingle shore strewn with plastic detritus. Further out a red lightship was dulled by an English dawn. But for Alex, the true moment of departure had been in the lock where the ancient ceremony of the landing of the officers' lavatory key had taken place.

SIX

THE ATLANTIC

THE *JOHN BEDE* had shaken off the land. Unwanted dunnage and saloon garbage were thrown overboard, the decks washed down and seagulls held station above a white wake.

"He's confined to bed," said Dr Trimmer, who perched on Alex's office desk, getting in the way.

"Who?"

"The unfunny man up top who wears starched pyjamas and is lying to attention reading Joseph Conrad."

"Didn't Conrad know Henry James?"

"I was summoned. His stomach. Ulcer playing up – he says."

"Is it?"

"He shows stress which has possibly aggravated the ulcer." The doctor lit one of Alex's Rothmans and dropped the spent match on the square of carpet. "Such a dreadful man. His attitude to life is a manifestation of self-loathing. Certainly caused during early childhood. Manifestly sexual."

"Has he latent cravings?" Alex moved his legs away from the doctor's falling cigarette ash.

"You've hit the nail on the head. Almost all physical illnesses have a sexual cause."

Influenza? thought Alex. He stood up to hook back the varnished heavy weather door. A weak sun streamed into the oblong white-painted office. "So you think his stomach upset is psychosomatic, Doc. A sexual problem?"

"I like the way you're thinking. He's divorced. There's been no partner – man or woman – for years." Doc drew heavily on his cigarette. "I told him he needed regular sex."

"You're kidding?"

"I suggested – and here the conversation got somewhat heated – various causes which might be at the root of his gastric upset."

"I'm agog," said Alex.

"Latent homosexuality, curries and suppressed masturbation and an inability to communicate. He takes aspirin too, and that disgusting pipe he smokes can't help."

"I was right to be agog. Next time you go a-calling, tell me. I'll eavesdrop with both ears."

Dr Trimmer puffed neurotically before aggressively extinguishing his part-smoked cigarette. He immediately lit another. "I tried to reassure him, pointing out that excessive patriotism is linked to mother love."

"Mother love?" said Alex.

"It's well known. Oedipus. I suggested that he and I have long talks. I assured him of my total confidence."

"Like the way you're blabbing now?"

"He has a very short fuse – sexual deprivation, of course. He became unnecessarily heated. Particularly when I asked if he had had a live-in nanny. Came out with drivel that doctors are only any good if they can *see* what's wrong with a patient: a broken leg – that type of thing. Any difficult diagnoses they put down to nerves or sexual problems."

"That's the shrewdest remark the old bastard's ever made."

"He didn't care for the cut of my jib."

"Doc, use the ashtray."

"Oh, I do so apologise. I'll sweep it up."

"Francis'll do it. He thinks you're adorable."

"My dear chap, it is simply not okay. I shall clean it up." He grasped Alex's arm. "I thank you for pointing out a very slovenly habit."

BOREDOM HANGS ABOUT SOME PEOPLE. Certainly not Dr Trimmer who read a great deal, regretting there were not more hours in the day, nor Captain Frogmore whose running the ship – which already ran itself – had Alex typing many lists. Morgan, the first mate, got bored. Morgan was a dull man in his late thirties who looked fifty. He doted on his wife. Her photograph – she posed with their thin-faced children in their nice garden – stood on his desk. Morgan drank. His drinking was clandestine until ten hundred hours. After ten he carried a peg glass of gin, pink with Angostura bitters.

Alex never got bored. Alex read and talked and drank.

At twenty after midnight Rusty, just off watch from the engine room – but already showered and towelled dry except for his hair – sat in Alex's cabin with six cans of beer at his feet.

"I saw the doctor naked," he said.

"When."

"Minutes ago. I was writing up my log in the engineers' mess room. You can see the pantry from there. Doc was raiding the fridge – naked."

"You speak to him?"

"You're kidding?"

"That's your hang-up."

"Not speaking to a naked man at midnight is not a hang-up."

"You'd speak to me if I was naked?"

"Sure."

"The doctor didn't do anything for you sexually – that it?"

Rusty was used to Alex winding him up. "You would've spoken to him?"

"Sure as hell I wouldn't have played Peeping Tom in the mess room."

Rusty drained the large can of Foster's, shook it to make certain that no lager remained then crumpled it and spun it noisily into the gash can. "I was not peeping. I was writing up my log. Doc was pissed. Lurching. Naked. Ramming food into his fat face."

"You hid watching all that?"

Rusty stayed calm. "Usually at midnight there is no one around. I maybe bump into Jack coming off the bridge and we gab some. Maybe Felicity comes into the mess room on the cadge for food. It's really, really nice."

"I do so understand," said Alex.

"Rodney was on about seeing him naked."

"Rodney sure as hell wouldn't have complained if Cadet Jones had been naked," said Alex. "Your cap I borrowed? Can I keep it?"

"Is the doctor one of your lot?"

Alex lit a cigarette, poured a Foster's into a smooth-sided glass. "Am I missing something?"

"It's fact that you queers flaunt it."

Alex said, "You're not lending me your cap because I am

queer? You a bigot or something?"

"Keep the cap." Rusty opened another beer, pulled his feet up and lay back on the daybed. "This captain getting up your nostrils?"

"And how. Tomorrow there's a caffeine session."

"A what?"

"Dr Trimmer's idea. Personnel relations crap. A daily meeting at zero-eight-zero-zero for heads of department. Resolve problems socially over coffee. I'm thinking about presenting myself as queer."

"You won't have to work at that."

"Where the fuck do I learn how to mince properly?" said Alex.

"My trouble is too many girlfriends."

"Fiancée?"

"Scary. Should I try sex with men?" said Rusty.

"I don't think they do courses."

"Teach me? You could suck me off after I've had six beers."

"Did I mention that the doc told the captain that his ulcer was due to tension. And what he needed was a good shag?"

Rusty caught his breath and coughed up a dribble of beer.

"I think my role at the caffeine sessions will be rather *Tatlerish.* A society reporter, with camera, recording snippets of news in an artistic pose. You know the kind of thing: *Mr Chumley-Bottom-Smythe enjoys a cigarette with Philomena Willomena Potts-Handlebar on the stairs.* I am striving to achieve an openness, an honesty. I will be like Mozart, dazzling, inspiring and bathed in genius."

"Tomorrow you'll be tongue-tied, hungover and wondering if you're gonna throw up." Rusty opened a can.

"It's my nerves. They're quite shredded."

"You're starting to enjoy this old man, aren't you?"

"You've got that very wrong," said Alex.

"Four more beers to go," said Rusty.

"Fat chance."

SEVEN

THE ATLANTIC

NEXT MORNING Alex climbed the two flights to the captain's accommodation without *Tatler* zeal. He was without cap too. That had been retrieved after Rusty mentioned it again, and Alex had told him he could keep his pig-shitting cap. On their fifth large export strength Foster's – a lager of truce – they jumped on such a symbol of conformity. A final beer had been poured ritualistically into it and Rusty, loath to see beer go to waste, drank it.

The outside door in the captain's dayroom was hooked back; clean sea air blew in. The chief engineer hadn't shown. Alex sat next to Morgan on the settee. A cup of pale tea was handed to him as though it were a treat. Alex left the tea untouched on the low table. He ignored the proffered inlaid mother of pearl cigarette box and lit one of his own.

Doc entered the dayroom without knocking. It seemed from his appearance that he missed his wife. His long hair untidy; his creased white shirt had pulled out from the waistband of his army surplus shorts; one sock was inside out, and his shoes were stout brogues suitable for tramping grouse moors.

"You wanted me, Captain?"

"You're a qualified doctor?"

"Certainly."

"And you specialise in work study too?"

"Quite."

"You are a talented man."

Alex detected more than a whiff of disapproval in Frogmore's remark.

"I was considered a minor genius early on in my career."

Frogmore said, "Can I mention Cadet Jones?"

"Why?" said Doc.

"What precisely is the cadet suffering from?"

"Why?"

"I asked – that is why." No expression showed on a face handsome twenty years ago.

Doc would have to ditch his Hippocratic oath for Captain Frogmore had him on the carpet. Morgan had blabbed for sure, thought Alex.

"Cadet Jones has gonorrhoea," said Frogmore.

"It's P.U.O. – a pyrexia of unknown origin."

Oppressive silence. Alex made a mental note to consult the dictionary later. Pyrexia seemed to hint at fire. He wrote *fogo* – the Portuguese for fire, according to Francis – in his notebook.

The captain tapped his bony knee where the starched shorts stood away from his white legs. "Doctor, he is sixteen. He is a cadet under my protection. He has gonorrhoea."

"You are talking rubbish, sir."

"Do not be insolent!"

Morgan had blabbed for sure. Morgan, who had kindled the *fogo*, toyed nervously with a box of matches.

"Gonorrhoea is easily identifiable by a discharge from the penis. He has no discharge. Gonorrhoea exists only in your imagination," said the doctor with insulting tolerance.

Morgan spilt the matches on the Formica tabletop.

"It's the ship's surgeon's statutory duty to inform me of sickness amongst the crew – not to play silly beggars."

A frenetic burst on the dulcimer told Alex that Francis was in the alleyway below. The dulcimer meant escape from the dayroom. Alex's eagerness to leave attracted the captain's attention.

"Purser, do I have to remind you daily to wear a cap?" said Frogmore, firing a parting shot.

LATE THAT MORNING THOMAS THOMAS was to be committed to the deep. His ashes were to be scattered from the main deck aft.

Alex knew that Frogmore was a man keen on uniform, and keen on ceremony too. On one occasion he had made a two hundred mile journey to London to watch the Trooping of the Colour. Alex would have made a two hundred mile journey to avoid it. He had expected all officers and crew to muster on the main deck, and for the ensign to fly at half-mast and the ship to be motionless on a glassy sea – but there was none of that. The captain was dressed in dated, and seldom worn nowadays, number tens; the high Mao-style collar showed white across his bearded throat. His cap he carried under his arm in respect for the departed. The cadet, exuding life, held the remains. Alex gripped a battered, dried-out cap which stank of beer.

At the starboard rail stood Francis, smart in white starched jacket with braided red epaulettes, and alongside him was the old saloon *topass,* Budhia, who was not a Christian.

The saloon galley was located at the after end of the midships accommodation block on the main deck, so earlier Alex had warned the chief cook about the need for silence. The chief cook took it into his head to attend the burial service and wore a never-seen-before chef's hat. In deference, he stood out of the way, close to the accommodation alongside the second cook. The second cook wore no head covering at all, but had a great deal going for him in the way of looks.

Frogmore said, "The cooks are both Christians and more qualified than I to read the service." Out of his respect for others' faith, it almost seemed that Frogmore was prepared to delegate the ceremony, and even his position, to these two lowly men, if they had been capable of MC-ing the proceedings. He beckoned the two Goans to join him, which they did; but when he summoned Francis and Budhia, Alex intervened, saying that he thought that they would prefer to stay where they were.

Alex stood between dishy Cadet Jones and the sexy Goanese second cook, who smelt of pastry and who had no hang-ups about touching others, for he clasped Alex's hand in a sympathetic grip; only letting go to put his own hands together in prayer, showing Alex the way he thought the burial ceremony should go. The company of these two young men, during the disposal of the ashes of Thomas Thomas, was affording Alex some very pleasurable companionship.

Before the captain started reading, he said, "Are you a Christian, cadet?"

"No, sir."

Frogmore glanced at his first mate, then at Alex and turned his back on them, as if knowing it would be a waste of time to ask. He talked fluently with the chief and second cook in Hindi. The second cook reached out and took the plastic casket from the cadet and held it tight to his admirable chest. Frogmore spoke again and the second cook nodded and walked aft. He stood a solitary figure at the ship's rail. His full attention was now on the casket as he carefully unscrewed the lid. This young Goan, with a square-face and high, well-defined cheek-bones, had skin which was as black as a Tamil's. His white teeth shone; perspiration beaded his smooth forehead. Alone at the rail with head down, his raven curls catching the sunlight, he kicked off his shoes. His thick, broad bare feet moved and his toes wriggled on the warm iron deck.

A smell of curry came from the crew galley aft. The Muslim *bhandary* had stopped cooking, and he too came out on deck with a dishcloth in his hand. The *bhandary's* solemn expression kicked Frogmore into gear. Alex had no idea what language he was speaking, but the *bhandary* nodded twice.

As a shoal of flying fish broke the surface of an oiled sea, the captain started his reading of the burial service and when he paused and nodded, the second cook allowed the ashes to trickle from the urn. The draught of air, caused by the movement of the *John Bede* steaming at fifteen knots, caught the fine ash, held it, then let it go to float down, to be committed to the deep. The same draught moved Cadet Jones' thick hair and dried the perspiration on the handsome forehead of the second cook.

The second cook extended his arm, black and hairless, and dropped the empty casket. It bobbed on the flat metallic sea then was caught in the wake. The funeral party watched it floating, watched it being pushed away from the ship by the wake as it rocked rapidly astern. When it sank, the second cook put his hands together in a *Namaste* of farewell and respect for the dead.

The *Namaste* gave an exotic final touch, Alex thought, to the Christian burial, garnishing it with a flavour of the Hindu religion: it was the act of a devout man symbolising contact with the Divine.

The chief cook, before crossing himself, pulled off his chef's hat for the first time to show thinning grey hair.

Nodding at the two Goanese cooks, both barefoot and clad in ragbag clothes, Frogmore said to Cadet David Jones,

"Take note."

When the black second cook came and stood alongside the cadet, who had a peaches and cream complexion and a muscular frame that filled and firmed his starched white uniform shirt and shorts, Alex could not take his eyes off the two. The chief cook and Captain Frogmore were looking at them. The two elderly men gave, what Melville described as *the tribute of the stare*. What fascinated Alex was that the two young men were unaware of the power that their rare beauty commanded.

The chief cook threw all caution to the winds and embraced him, holding him tight as a fellow Christian, which Alex was not. And as Alex's cock jerked from being in such intimate contact with another man, he thought that if it had been the second cook who was embracing him, his cock could well have bruised that young man's thigh.

AFTERWARDS, HE ASKED CADET DAVID JONES to join him for a drink. Dave was about to say something, perhaps that he didn't drink during the day, but he nodded and, when in the smoke room, ordered a bitter lemon from Francis.

"Mum has it with her gin," he said, sitting down at the card table. "First time I've tasted it."

Francis carried the mood that existed on deck into the comfortable room. The burial had affected them all: Alex disinterestedly sipped his beer and Dave Jones toyed with his drink.

"You don't act the only son – but you are an only son. I'm not, but act as if I am," said Alex.

"You have a brother?"

"An ornithologist. My mother told me on the telephone that he's saving eggs in Scotland. Some bird or other, near extinct. We're not alike."

Dave nodded.

Going down for lunch, Alex held open the dining saloon door for the cadet who gently kissed him on his cheek and said, "If I was at home, I would've kissed you on the mouth."

Alex was aware that those in the dining saloon could hear but let the cadet talk:

"I kiss my mum. I kiss Terry. Terry I've known since I was a nipper. Both on the mouth. And my grandpa and uncle too."

"How about Mark in the pub?"

"Not in a thousand years! He'd read something into it that ain't there."

"Beware the Khyber Pass."

They both laughed on their way in. Alex sat at the top table, and Cadet David Jones at the junior officers' table, next to the third mate, Brewer who said loudly,

"You two make a lovely couple, David darling." Brewer, large, angular and plain, and never the most sensitive of souls, added, "You dance together?"

Sparks, sitting opposite, said, "You snigger like some kid behind the bike shed, rubbing himself and thinking things dirty when they're not."

The captain, the chief engineer, the mate, two fifth engineers, the third engineer and the refrigerating engineer, all heard, all looked up.

Dave, breaking a crusty roll, smiled warmly at Fernandes, thanking him for the bowl of minestrone soup. He then asked Sparks about the longevity of fish. Sparks was an enthusiast. He rose to the bait, as it were, and spoke animatedly.

Brewer looked foolish. He had isolated himself. He sat, not saying a word, and was ignored. His innuendo had not gathered the applause that he had hoped.

But to Alex, it was Sparks who was a revelation. This was a new Sparks: Sparks, the conservationist. Sparks talked of voyages in trawlers and onetime he had sailed in a whaling ship which he had loathed and he had been logged for arguing with the skipper. Normally his voice would not be heard by those seated at the other tables, but he raised it slightly, as if he was at a lectern. "...the obscenity when seabirds were caught in the trawls..." "...the blood and blubber and the stench of death..." All in the dining saloon were enthralled and inclined their heads to listen.

But his spellbinding lecture was abruptly stopped. The doctor arrived, twenty minutes late, seemingly the worse for wear.

"One must consider the crew. I would have thought that would be a prerequisite for anyone who preaches work study," said Frogmore, shattering Alex's mood. "I assume that you know the quotation about politeness and punctuality?"

"Too right," drawled Doc, in a put on Australian accent.

A giggle was heard from the junior engineers' table.

The captain was unperturbed for he had other things on his mind. "I'm not the man to read the Bible and preside over the ritual of the burial service. However, it is the ship's master's job."

Job? Alex should have been fascinated by Frogmore airing his unconventional views on religious matters, but he wondered why he was talking in such a way when he had presided over what was a dignified and memorable ceremony. "I thought it very moving," he said, in what he hoped was a noticeable rebuke.

But attention was on the doctor, who was using his fork as a shovel. His face was held close to his plate and his head and arm movements were synchronised as he shovelled food into his mouth. This was not a sudden greed; the tablecloth had been so splattered at earlier meals that a clean napkin daily covered his place-setting.

"The disposal of a body is comparable to it being junked," said Dr Trimmer, his mouth full.

"The dead body should be disposed of with dignity. I merely question whether it was suitable that I – a man who disdains the church – should do it," said Frogmore sharply.

"I'd already junked Thomas Thomas in *The Admiral Benbow*."

"What are you on about? Your diction, which is not clear even on a good day with the wind behind you, is muffled by food."

"I mislaid the casket on my way back to the ship from head office."

Alex glanced at Cadet Jones.

"Mislaid?" said the captain.

Dr Trimmer broke a crusty roll, crumbs fell. His elbow caught some cutlery on the linen tablecloth and a soup spoon rang on the linoleum. "I loathe the City. And the tube was hell. I was in need of sedation after experiencing a frenzy of people rushing hither and thither to no avail. I placed Thomas Thomas in with them."

"In with what? If you'd stopped eating – it might help."

"I bought carry-outs from Tesco's."

"Tesco's?"

"A supermarket."

"I am not a high court judge. I am aware that Tesco's is a supermarket. I will put my question to you directly, *What are carry-outs?*"

"Not a judge but the prosecuting counsel," said Doc.

"I say again, *What are carry-outs?*"

"Mine were Guinness in rather a jaunty carrier. It had a toucan on it."

The chief engineer looked up. Rodney, sitting at the engineers' table, had something in his throat.

"First off, I left the wretched carrier on the tube and had to rush back and rescue it from a youth with a shaven head and a forceful vocabulary."

"You mention an hostelry? *The Admiral Benbow*?" Frogmore's fish was untouched.

"Before the pub, I drank in the park. I talked about Rasputin to a charming man who was drinking cooking sherry on a wooden bench donated by a worthy citizen – the bench, not the sherry. The sherry would have stripped its varnish. His dog was not charming: a Doberman, or some such terrifying breed, but thoughtfully on a length of rope, stout enough to hold a ship alongside; it did not interfere with my companion and I as we shared the carry-outs." The doctor spoke to Francis in a voice only mildly muffled by food, "Might I have the cold meats and salad?" His audience of officers and stewards had to wait while he heaped his plate and subsequently made a fuss retrieving a slice of tomato from the cloth. "I decided to reflect on life and death in *The Admiral Benbow* inn."

"You left the remains of a personal friend of the chairman of the Bede Line in a public house?" said Frogmore.

"Lady Bracknell again," said Doc to Alex, in a loud aside.

"Lady Bracknell?" said Frogmore.

"Oscar Wilde. *The Importance of Being Ernest.*"

"I am familiar with the play. At this moment the only line which comes to mind is 'Australia! I'd sooner die!' However, the subject we are addressing now is the remains of Thomas Thomas and *The Admiral Benbow* inn. When precisely, Doctor, did you retrieve 'the remains' from the taproom of this four ale bar?" All officers stopped eating. Alex could have sworn that the captain was being ironic but his expression was fierce.

"The following day. I visited *The Admiral Benbow* – a smoke-filled tavern where tobacco-juice stained a worn plank-floor, and sailors slumped drunkenly in chairs, and a landlady – a full-bodied woman with arms of formidable size – who had yellow hair from a bottle and a metal hook for a hand."

Alex pushed a fist into his mouth. This was too much.

Doc continued, "She had rescued Thomas Thomas from her dustbin. And this is the point of my story. One must ponder on the symbolism of the dustbin. The junking of the remains. Do you see the connection, Captain?"

Alex was laughing uncontrollably, as the doctor said to him, "In the taproom, purser."

The lunch, which might well have been sedate, was not. It was not a wake, not a celebration of a man's life, it was theatre. And however outraged Frogmore appeared to be, there was an element of self-satisfaction in his performance. He was to show all in the dining saloon that the doctor had met his match.

A strong captain dictates the atmosphere in any vessel: In a moment the mood in the saloon changed from humour to foreboding. Frogmore's face held malevolence and contempt. He stared fixedly at the doctor with distaste. But then addressed Alex, "That conflicts with the policeman's tale."

"Sir? What policeman?"

"You recall the policeman who came on board when Dr Trimmer used the heads illegally in the London docks?"

"Yes, I do."

"It appears that the policeman was on duty at the dock gate when you returned from ashore, purser. His story of your return did not reflect well on the ship, nor on the occupants of the car which you drove. But his story must be believed. The policeman is not a liar." He glared at the doctor. "But you are a liar, sir. Now hold your tongue." He turned his attention to his plate, tasted his fish, then snapped at his steward, "Take this away, boy. It's stone cold."

"DAVID JONES, how's your clap?" Alex sat down in the

cadet's armchair without being asked.

"Mum wasn't too pleased about my face being cut. When she hears I've got this dose, she'll go mental."

"You do not tell your mother. In your letters home you tell her the weather is nice and the captain is a decent chap and the purser takes a fatherly interest in your well being – and is firmly suppressing his longing to fondle your genitalia. No mention is to be made that if he were to go down there, he might catch something really rather nasty."

"I tell her everything."

"Pass on this one. You want I should telephone your mater and say you're okay?"

"From the ship? You? No way," said Jones.

"That does sound very much like a no. I am good with people. I've attended courses."

"Your accent, Alex. It's public school."

"I wish it were public urinal. All I was going to do is reassure her, tell her you're fit and happy – in an avuncular voice."

Cadet Jones, unsure whether Alex was pulling his leg or not, blushed. "No phone. We use next door's." And as if wanting to change the subject, said, "They had a lot of queers at your boarding school?"

"If only. Mind you, I expect that I missed out stinking somewhere along the line. Always slow on the uptake. At school we were taught the essential things: like which knife and fork to use. How to act when presented to royalty, but stuff like fucking we had to find out for ourselves." Alex regarded Dave as having a natural poise which contrasted to his own elegance which was a mask which he had to learn. "I'm really quite good at this paternal stuff, don't you agree? I should concentrate on my journalism, now I have *Tatler* connections. If I had a sex change I could be an Agony Aunt. Any problems – you know where I am."

The cadet stared at him, saying nothing.

"Days are okay, but if you visit nights do wear protection."

"Alex, can I say something?"

"I'm apprehensive."

"You're sounding camp."

"Excellent. I thought that no one had noticed. Does it bother you?"

"Nope. Wear a bra and that's okay by me, any day – or night – of the week."

ALEX used to be very much at home on the bridge. In the Lovelace era he had learnt to steer and take sights. 'Only ship in the company where the purser can stand a watch,' Lovelace had boasted.

That afternoon Alex crept onto the bridge feeling the interloper. He judged that after lunch would be the most likely time when Frogmore would be taking a siesta. He was wrong.

"What are you doing on my bridge?"

"I need the ship's position for this morning's burial – the Official Log Book entry." Alex longed to cut and run, but instead he copied the ship's position from the Rough Bridge Log Book which lay open on the chartroom table. Irritated at being watched by the captain, he handed him the typed draft Official Log Book entry, certain that it would annoy him. Even Lovelace would not have approved it, for Alex was cutting new ground with his reference to an Indian member of crew taking part in the burial service in the European Log Book.

Frogmore put on half-glasses and slowly read it. Alex had typed that the service had been conducted by Captain Frogmore and that the remains of Thomas Thomas had been committed to the deep by the devout Christian, Joaquim Lobo, second cook. The entry was to be signed by the captain and the mate – as was usual.

"Have the second cook sign it," said Frogmore.

"He doesn't write, sir," said Alex, surprised.

"Then have him thumbprint. Send copies to the chairman."

"Thumbprinted copies, sir?"

"Of course."

It seemed to Alex that Joaquim Lobo, second cook, would briefly make it into the big time. If only he had a photograph of him to attach to the log entry – that would have made his, if not the chairman's, day.

HE ESCAPED to the radio room and the comfort of Sparks.

"That mean man's been on about my teeth."

"I love your teeth – they remind me of a burnt-out fence."

"I did have two sets. First set I lost calling for Hughie in Lourenco Marques. Second set I left by the bed in a cat-house in Houston."

"Has he mentioned your tattoos?"

"You can say he sort of brought them into the conversation."

Now in shorts, Sparks' amazing serpent showed. It started at his neck then slithered green and mauve out of sight down his back, circled his waist then plunged at his navel to run the length of his pecker. Most ship's company knew this for Sparks, with scant encouragement, happily exposed himself after a couple of beers.

"You show him your willie?"

"You know something? First watch out from UK and I had on my woolly hat and the green Bombay tartan shirt, you admire." Sparks imitated Frogmore, " 'This is not a trawler, radio operator.' Je-sus, to fuck, I know it ain't. I been on a trawler. I hated fucking trawlers. I hated the fucking skipper too. Urine George, who drank gallons of beer and pissed in the cod liver oil tank."

"Right." Sparks was prone to go on at length about his eventful seagoing career, so Alex didn't question him about the cod liver oil but made a note to tell his mother to stop buying it from the chemists.

"How'd you get along with the fucker, Alex? I'd say he don't take over-well to your laid-back attitude."

"I grovel. Kiss his ring. Conform – as you have. I'm a very subservient person, you know."

"Man, I fucking know."

"Now I have to pose at these daily caffeine sessions – at eight in the morning. Him and his orange pekoe or Brazilian blend. Afterwards you can see me screaming, with knuckles white, gripping the rail, my glazed eyes fixed on the beckoning sea."

A red light on the bank of knobs and dials came on. Sparks swore, for the red light meant work. When he threw a switch the muted Morse came in loud. He scribbled on a message pad. It wasn't until Alex reached the foot of the stairs that he remembered his reason for popping in to see Sparks was to check if he would be going to the captain's drinks party that evening. Alex laughed out loud at such a preposterous idea.

He'd ask Rodney. Rodney would be the ideal guest. Rodney was into shallow conversation, preening and posing, and was adept at circulating – which was what cocktail parties were all about.

But Rodney was not overjoyed. Indeed, after Alex had settled uninvited on his daybed and asked him if he would be coming, he said, "No fucking way."

"Do not be beastly to me, Rodders old horse. Without you there, there'll be no one I can talk to."

"Talk to Francis – he's brighter than me."

"Not permitted."

"This captain a bigot or something?"

"It's a question of status. One does not drink with the servants except at Christmas when the eggnog is handed round."

"You should be more than enough for anyone. With me there they'd be overdosing."

Alex was serious for a moment, "You manage to get North, see your mum before we sailed?"

"A neighbour's looking after her." Rodney glared at Alex as though he had said something wrong. Alex rubbed the engineer's cheek with affection.

"Fuck off." Rodney looked at his shoes.

Alex switched the conversation back to the drinks-do that evening. "Cocktail parties I loathe, but I can amuse. I consider myself a cabaret performer rather than packing 'em in at the Palladium."

"Not your style to drum up business. What you up to?" Rodney turned the page of his *Time* magazine but he wasn't reading.

"I want to support the doctor."

"No fucking way."

"Nothing I can do to persuade you?"

"A suck would do it."

"If only I had the time," said Alex, getting up.

EIGHT

THE ATLANTIC

THE SMOKE ROOM'S décor leant heavily towards Odeon but the overall effect was spoilt by a philistine superintendent of supply who had covered the original jazz age linoleum with a fitted carpet.

"Never thought the old fart would agree to this drinks do. Not after the brouhaha at lunch." Dr Trimmer kept his voice low so Frogmore and the chief engineer on the port side of the smoke room couldn't hear. "This type of get-together is good in a work study context."

"No one will turn up," said Alex.

"Then he'll know he's not liked."

"But he knows he's not liked. He doesn't care that he's not liked. He likes being not liked, so what's the bloody point of this party?"

Dr Trimmer scooped up peanuts in greedy handfuls from the glass bowl on a card table. "I've never met anyone so determinedly unpleasant." His voice was held low in dramatic conspiracy. "Keep it under your hat but young David here has the clap."

Cadet David Jones's muscular frame was all the time in the corner of Alex's eye. Clap or no clap, Dave's appearance registered purity. "You're unsullied," he said, handing him a brimming glass of beer from the bar counter.

"Can't. I'm on antibiotics."

"Don't drink and Frogmore will be certain you have it."

"The way you take the cadet so firmly under your wing is telling of your sexuality," said Doc, silencing Alex's reply with a held up hand and causing Cadet Jones to turn pink. "Once his gonorrhoea clears, you two must get together. Heavens forbid that I play the psychiatrist, as well as cupid but the way you hold back from sex with him, might suggest coitophobia."

"If you mean frigid – say frigid," said Alex. "I like the cadet. I like Rusty. I like Larry. I like Rodney – but about liking you, I'm not sure. And to put you straight on the holding back from sex, Doc, I had a fuck in Amsterdam."

"Putting me straight, eh? Holding back, eh? Amsterdam eh? I admit to having had sex with men. The love was there all right but I never got used to who dominated who and I suffered severe problems when I enjoyed being passive. Being brought up in Australia, my urge to be seen as macho had me denying my longing to be screwed – a result of being bottle-fed, most certainly. Denied the breast in infancy, you see."

Cadet Jones stood in awkward silence.

"Gonorrhoea is an illness to be treated like influenza," said Dr Trimmer, slurring his words.

"Have you been at the wine gums, recalling your nights of frustrated passion with the dominant men of your dreams?" said Alex.

The doctor said ear-splitting loud, "This is a super party. I must admit that I had imagined a Frogmorian soiree would be singing sea shanties around the binnacle, nursing a toddy of black rum. Yo! Ho! Ho!" Having fully caught the captain's attention, he said, "What have we here?"

He knew darned well what he had here. It was a Frogmore souvenir: a framed tie which hung on the bulkhead to the left of the bar counter. Indeed, there was a spread of Frogmorian memorabilia: plaques of six ships, a dated photograph of a cricket eleven in Port Elizabeth, and a photograph taken outside the *Taj Mahal* in Bombay, which showed Frogmore shaking hands with the Bede Line's last chairman. Alex thought the collection charmingly dated.

He moved away but could not escape the doctor who pushed the framed tie under his nose. He saw that the Indian craftsman had trapped a fly beneath the glass. A patch of tropical damp had discoloured the inscription: *Presented to Captain Frogmore from The Bungo Polo Club.*

Doc said loudly, "Memories of India flood the mind. The club. Native bearers. The Maidan. *Chota pegs* on the verandah." Dr Trimmer then faced Frogmore. "And baize notice boards."

"You are intoxicated," said Captain Frogmore.

"Garden parties and double-chinned *memsahibs* playing bowls. A ripple of applause from the chaps as Boddington scores a six. The National Anthem. Chinless wonders educated at elitist schools – clap. Jolly good sorts. Damned fine."

Dr Trimmer seemed to leap from eccentric sobriety to wild drunkenness in one stride. He teetered. He lurched. He waved the framed tie as if it were a trophy. He shouted, "It will be a shrine."

Frogmore, straight-backed, stood his ground. He grasped hold of the framed tie and wrenched it out of the doctor's grasp, then he adroitly side-stepped as the doctor lunged in his drunken approach.

Dr Trimmer collided with the door jamb, shouting, "Obsolete traditions. The Club and Kipling are a legacy of the British in India which history will view with contempt."

His passage out of the smoke room was marked by small pools of vomit, that was until he lost all bodily control at the top of the stairs. As he was waving his hands about trying to locate the banister rail, he showered the steps.

Why is it always carrot? thought Alex, as Francis rushed out to return with a floor mop and bucket.

The captain calmly repositioned the framed tie on its bracket and said to the chief engineer. "The doctor has left the task of cleaning up his filth to a Goanese steward who is worth ten of him."

Alex whispered, "That seems to have broken the ice."

"That doctor makes me sweat," whispered Dave Jones.

The two were drawn into the conversation by the chief engineer who put his arm about Alex's shoulders, saying, "The doctor's marriage has finished recently. I expect he's under the weather."

The captain said, "I wonder he qualified at all. One can only imagine the medical examination board were inept or quite mad, or perhaps they had a bizarre sense of humour, letting such a man loose on the world. One must assume that when elevating a student to be a qualified doctor, they must take into account the character of the applicant. Perhaps they do not. But it is the way of the world. Deck officers, once they obtain their Master's Certificate, are not only qualified to take command of large deep-sea vessels, but also to take charge of crew and passengers. Many have scant ability in either direction. Many have little charm and some are unable to get on with their fellow man. Is that not so, purser?" Frogmore's eyes held Alex's.

"In my ten years at sea, I've never sailed with a flawed ship's captain, sir. They have all been quite exemplary and I am humbly grateful for my luck."

"Your tongue is much in your cheek. But the diplomatic way you put me in my place, is acknowledged. This is not the occasion for confrontation – a fact that might be pointed out to the errant Dr Trimmer. Purser, tell me the worst captain you have sailed under, and do not include me, or I will have you keel-hauled."

"There is one captain who, when I pointed out that he had signed his name in the wrong place on a document of some consequence, told me to shut my stupid mouth and not to argue with The Command."

"Goodness, how uncomfortable for you. You have my sympathy, for he sounds very much the dictator," said Frogmore, with apparent seriousness, but those about him laughed. "While it would be indiscreet to ask his name, perhaps a physical description might point me in the right direction?"

"His visage reminded me greatly of Edith Sitwell?"

"Ah, a distinctive physiognomy indeed. I know our man. All were grateful when he retired to a bungalow, where, on his front lawn there flew a flag on a tall white pole. This flag he raised at sunrise and lowered at sunset. And when the mayoral car passed by, fluttering its standard bravely, he dipped and doffed his hat. It was rumoured that he penned a letter to H.R.H. upon learning that the Queen was to open a hospital in the nearby town. He asked the monarch to make a detour along Acacia Avenue – or wherever."

Alex said, "What flag was it?"

"The Union Jack – which said a great deal about him: his misplaced patriotism, and his sense of self-importance."

"Ships dip at sea," said the chief engineer.

"That is something else – an acknowledgement; the courtesy of saying good morning when one meets a fellow hiker on remote moorland."

"Is he dead?" said the chief.

"He died of apoplexy quite recently. There was a piece about him in the Bede Line magazine – last May, I think.

Whoever wrote it, kept it gratefully short."

The chief engineer said, "I know who you're on about. It's old..."

"No names. One should not speak ill of the dead, though with him it is very hard – nay impossible – not to. At my age I am often at funerals – sometimes people I like, which is upsetting. But it is the going to the funeral of people I dislike – and that is more frequent – that gives me particular joy. But even when they are in the grave – or in the oven, these days – some stupid act that they have committed will not go away, it becomes embedded in the mind and embellished in the telling. It is a sad requiem to be a joke at a cocktail party – but at least he is remembered when many of the other fools are not."

There was something final about the way the captain glanced at the clock, listened to the dulcimer being played in the alleyway, that told them the party was over.

He made a brief speech in the doorway on his way out: "Cocktail parties are inevitably silly. The only good one can say of the doctors appearance, and dramatic disappearance – for which we can be grateful – was that he livened it up no end. Indeed, he made an unmemorable occasion into a memorable one." Before turning on his heels, he studied Cadet Jones with a monocled gaze, then headed for the dining saloon without another word.

"You see the way he looked at me?" said the cadet. "What've I done?"

"Nothing. You laughed in the right places and you were getting nicely happy and not seeming to be drunk. Frogmore can understand that. Officers and gentlemen do that."

"I only had two halves of beer."

"Then have more. My cabin after dinner. You can get back on your medication tomorrow. I need medication now – sanity tablets – and you'll do nicely, someone sensible to talk to."

"If only, but I've got to write up my journal."

"Forget it. I'll clear it with the mate."

Cadet Jones had no friends on board other than Alex who he treated with open affection. "I was gonna leave the sea in London but it cost Mum a bomb for my uniforms and stuff."

"You talked to the mate about this?"

"No."

"Don't. Trust few, and I would steer well clear of the doctor after tonight. If your clap doesn't clear up, I'll fix you up with a shoreside clinic. You can tell Rodney anything, but give him half a chance and he'll rip open your fly."

"I can cope with that. I can't cope with the captain getting at me. Getting at me when I don't do nothing wrong."

"Right."

"Can I trust Rusty?"

"I'm just about to have hysterics."

AFTER DINNER, the cadet shyly ran his knuckles down the outside of the purser's jalousie door. He perched on an upright chair.

Alex pushed him into the armchair and put a glass of beer in his hand. "Tell me about it."

"I got ticked off again. He said I'd lied."

Dave's hands were trembling. Alex lit him a cigarette and poured him a small scotch.

"He glared at me and I was crapping myself but I kept to the lie."

"Why couldn't he talk to you about it. He's turned sex into something dirty."

"I've never shat myself before."

"You want to stay the night on the daybed?"

"Yes, please."

"And no hanky panky. I don't go for redheads."

"Am I a redhead?"

"Gold, auburn, chestnut, your hair changes colour, to tell the truth. And very sexy it is too."

Dave said, "Can you cut my hair for me?"

"I do Rusty's. Have you *seen* it?"

"Save me paying the *cassab.* I'll give you a tip – whatever you fancy," said the handsome young man.

HE DID NOT HEAR CADET DAVID JONES LEAVE.

Alex became aware of the remorseless tap-tap-tap on his bunk-board. This was the signal to get up. Francis' irony, for today his role was the servile soft-footed Goan servant.

"*Chota hazri*, *purser sahib.* It's sunny today." Francis

positioned the plastic tray, with its serviceable white crockery emblazoned with the shipping company's emblem, on the ledge besides the bunk.

Alex watched him pick up a pack of Rothmans, then hook a brown finger in a green pot ashtray and position them on the tray.

"A whore's breakfast, *sahib*."

Alex ignored him.

"Tea and a cigarette – a whore's breakfast."

"You're killing a feeble joke with repetition. Piss off."

"You will be familiar with the quotation, *sahib*, that all prostitutes and madmen smoke?"

"Jesus, why can't I have a normal fucking steward."

"Could you confirm it's Dostoevsky?"

"Francis, my second thought on waking is that there is less than one hour to the hell of the caffeine session. My first thought is that my smart-assed steward will be trying to get one over on me."

"Is your tea all right?"

"It's barely drinkable which suits my mood."

Francis surveyed the cans which Cadet David Jones and Alex had ritualistically bent with one hand during their previous night's thrash and had chucked dead-eye easy into the metal gash can. Francis' role as the soft-footed Goan was shelved, he became the long suffering wife. He filled a cardboard box with noisy spent cans. He groaned as he wiped sticky rings off the Formica top of the coffee table.

Alex sat up in his bunk, and resting his head on the cool iron bulkhead, he watched his steward go into the office to clean Felicity's tidy tray, with an air of martyrdom. The tidy tray became a noisy reprimand as he shook a bag of Fuller's earth.

Alex escaped to the washrooms.

Still damp after his shower, he sat naked on the lavatory. Felicity too had escaped Francis' ruthless duster. She slunk under the bottom of the lavatory door and rubbed against his legs.

"Felicity, we are both perversely in the doghouse," he said.

The tropical heat had dried him by the time he wrapped a towel about his waist and flip-flopped back to his cabin.

"Would you be looking for these, sir?" Francis held up two white uniform stockings. "I discovered one behind a cushion and the other in the filing cabinet under 'Asian Crew Allotments'. By the way, the underpants you are putting on are inside out." He paused, "Not that anyone will notice, one presumes, though, of course, one never knows, it might be your lucky day – after a lucky night, perhaps?" He produced the cigarettes which Dave Jones had left. "Your acolyte's? I shall deliver them to him personally, unless you want the pleasure of that communion, sir?" Francis left the cabin to reappear in seconds. "You're late."

In ten minutes Alex, in uniform whites, was in the alleyway. The bulkhead on his right was warm despite its thick insulation – behind it was the engine room. The cool bulkhead on his left led him to the pantry with its red-tiled floor and hot presses and stainless steel working-surfaces and refrigerators.

Francis was waiting with a glass of chilled tomato juice.

"Aren't we behind schedule?" He handed him the hard-backed menu book. "I've changed the whiting at lunch – not much left." He followed Alex out of the pantry into the foyer, grand with its polished light green linoleum and its wood staircase that flared splendidly.

"If you handed me the menu book without comment, it would help. I want the calming inner peace of Eastern religions not your gaudy Catholicism. I do not need that 'behind schedule' crap either. And I don't care if it's sunny today or not." He gave his steward the empty glass. "Fuck it, I'm late."

"Tell the captain you've been checking the potato locker – to cable an order to Panama?"

"DO THEY HAVE POTATOES in Cristobal, purser?"

"Sure." Potatoes were not foremost in his mind when he recalled Panama. Alex's vivid recollection was being excited by a soft damp mouth.

"How do you know?"

"We picked up potatoes in Cristobal last year."

"Ah," said Frogmore, as if winning his point, "but last year isn't now. I shall cable and ask."

"You have to be kidding?"

"Why should I – as you colloquially put it – be kidding?"

"Because they have potatoes in Panama, sir." Alex in the moment of tension downed the tepid milkless tea that he had intended to boycott.

"The matter of potatoes is hypothetical. You'll have to store fully in Brazil – just in case." He turned to Morgan. "I shall proceed to New Zealand by way of The Horn."

Morgan's homely round face registered discomfort as if he had experienced an unanticipated and extremely loose bowel movement.

Frogmore pulled the stem of his pipe away from the bowl and poked about with a wire pipe cleaner. Brown dottle marked a paper serviette. "I shall head south after Brazil and thence sail to New Zealand via the Cape of Storms."

Alex heard a thousand drowned mariners cheering.

Morgan was aghast. "The Horn? The wrong way?"

"Against the prevailing winds – if that's what you mean by the wrong way."

"Captain Bligh couldn't make it," said Alex.

"I am not Captain Bligh, though you might think so. Nor is my ship under sail, though whether or not its crew is mutinous, I make no comment." Frogmore's smile was without humour. He wiped his pipe stem, ditched the stained serviette in the wastepaper bin beneath his desk. "I'll have the second mate plot a course. I shall make a great circle from The Horn to New Zealand."

"Go south? A great circle goes south!" said Morgan.

"I shall save my Panama Canal dues."

"The Horn is the grave of many fine ships and men," said Morgan nervously.

This was a comment of some importance coming from a man who slept and ate on the fence. Morgan coughed as a sixty-a-day, two-bottle-of-gin-a-day man in severe shock can. He was so shaken that he forgot to help himself to the Rothmans in the cigarette box on the coffee table, and lit one of his own.

"The waters are charted. The wrecks are marked. And there at the foot of the Americas the albatross soar."

"Sailors' souls," said Alex.

"I have misjudged you. You do have saltwater running in your veins, purser." He stood and peered through the forward facing window at an empty glittering sea. "A great circle, indeed. I could sight ice. I've seen a wall of ice, you know – a solid wall, as high as Beachy Head. It stretched for miles." He filled the cleaned pipe with tobacco and lit it.

"Head office go along with it?" said Alex.

"Why shouldn't they?"

To hell with breakfast, Alex thought, after the insanity of being interrogated about potatoes in Panama when the ship wasn't going there. And, to hell with being forced to listen to Dr Trimmer's facetious comments on any goddamn thing just so long as it got up Frogmore's nose.

As the captain and Morgan headed for the saloon, Alex climbed the inside stairway to the bridge.

The wheel was on automatic. The doors to the bridge wings were slid open and the ship's movement pushed cooling air up and over the dodgers. Here was a tranquil zone with Jack on watch. Jack, who had never bothered sitting his Masters Certificate, knew more about ships than anyone in the shipping company except Frogmore.

"How'd you get on with this old man, Jack?"

"Good seaman. Not frightened of land like some skippers. He passes ships so close they think he's playing chicken. Stays sober. He knows how much cargo we've got and where it's for and how it's stowed." He handed his seven-by-fifty binoculars to Alex and pointed. "Whale."

The sea ahead, seen through the bridge windows, shimmered. Alex searched for the waterspout.

"You missed the whale." Jack lit a rolled cigarette. The slim tube burnt unevenly.

"Frogmore's on and on about me not wearing a cap."

"I don't wear a cap. Never says anything to me."

"And he bullies Cadet Jones – that's not right."

"He told me he was doing it for the cadet's own good."

"You buy that?"

"Maybe not," said Jack.

"You know he's taking the ship round The Horn?"

"Drakes Passage then a great circle to New Zealand."

"Is that sane?"

"I'll check it out. You didn't see the whale?"

"Was there a whale, Jack?"

"You don't believe me, do you? You only see what you

want to see. Quotation for you."

"Oh, please no – dear God, not one of your quotations. Do not do this to me."

"Even if a snake is not poisonous, it should pretend to be venomous. Tell the cadet that."

ALEX headed for the radio room.

Sad bits of sticky tape were left on the bulkheads; the paint was white in squares, nicotine-brown edges silhouetted where the pin-ups had once been before being removed under the Frogmore regime.

"It's to be repainted. Duck egg blue was vetoed for Bede Line white. Is there no romance left?" Sparks yawned. "You wanna see a confidential Marconigram?"

"God, I'm gonna have to beg."

"The Horn – got head office's reply ten minutes ago."

"What'd it say?"

"FROGMORE YOU ARE A WANKER" Sparks pulled down a box file marked CONFIDENTIAL and with the stub of a nicotined forefinger – the tattooed L had been cut off in Mombasa so the remaining three fingers read OVE – he jabbed at the file copy of the cable. Alex read PROCEED AS PER LETTER OF INSTRUCTIONS VIA PANAMA CANAL STOP CONFIRM REPEAT CONFIRM

Sparks said, "You know why he smokes a pipe?"

"You'll tell me."

"Same like his monocle. Same like his cap fetish. Same like his stupid beard. All these nautical fuckers smoke pipes, wear caps and dream of top gallants and futtock shrouds. You hear about my teeth?"

"Sparks, I am loaded down with quotations – can I cope with your bloody teeth?"

"The new teeth. I have been ordered to get new teeth."

"Is chippy making them? Varnished mahogany would be a conversation piece. They could double as castanets on a dull voyage."

"I'm getting them made ashore."

"With Brazilian teeth you could crack nuts."

"Alex, for fucks sake."

"The false teeth, Sparks?"

"The captain was most reasonable. Melbourne teeth.

Down Under porcelain will do."

THE THIRD MATE flopped his large body in Alex's spare office chair.

"The mate was drunk, " said Brewer.

"What's new," said Alex, thinking Brewer an odd forename for the abstemious third mate.

"He was pissed on watch."

"Much shipping about?"

"Can I send money home from Panama?"

"You want I should telex head office and increase your allotment?"

"Frogmore does the mate's watch."

"You're kidding me?"

"Hours of darkness, he's on the bridge. Cut the air with a knife."

"Is Frogmore on the bridge with you, or when Jack's on watch?"

"Not unless we near land or something hairy crops up. Even then he's pretty much laid-back. He lets me get on with it." Brewer bent forward, rested his cheek on the Formica desktop. "Check out that lump on my neck."

Alex pulled down Brewer's shirt collar and seeing his broad hairless back, said, "Can't you get a tattoo or something?"

"Look at the lousy lump and stop viewing me as sex."

Alex examined a lump, the size of a plum, on the back of the third mate's neck. He pressed it gently and clear liquid shot out. He went into his cabin and returned with cotton wool and Dettol and wiped it. "A cyst. See if the doc can cut it out."

Brewer sat upright, his small intense blue eyes in a homely face drew and held. "You are just so fucking kidding. I'd rather you do it."

"You want I fix you up with the quack in New Zealand?"

"What's a cyst?"

"A sac containing fluid. I could hit it with the family Bible."

"I'll go for the shoreside quack." He stood but hung around, his doeskin shoe tapping the linoleum.

"What?"

"Alex, have a word with Frogmore about the way he goes

on at the cadet?"

"For fuck's sake. The cadet is deck department. See Jack."

"You know Jack."

"I'm not happy about this."

"You're the one with balls."

"Queer balls."

"Dave Jones never stops going on about you, and your balls come into it, I would think, by the way his tongue hangs out. All the more reason."

"You see sex in everyone."

"You don't?" Brewer raised his eyebrows questioningly.

"The cadet looks on me as a dad."

"The cadet wants you for a fuck. I'm married and looking at him, I get one hell of a stalk," said the third mate.

"You want I should use the Bible on your fat skull?"

"You gonna up my allotment to Karen?"

"I expect it'll be for decorating the guest room when you take Cadet Jones home."

Brewer smiled, reached down and touched the pack of Pall Mall on the desk. "My taste. I see sex in you."

"Fuck off, third."

"Increase my allotment to Karen by twenty pounds a month and see the old man?"

"Fuck off, third."

"Does that mean yes and yes, darling?" said Brewer laughing as he left the office.

Alex felt bewildered and unsophisticated.

NINE

THE ATLANTIC

THE POTATO LOCKER was sited on the poop deck above the Indian crew's accommodation where the propeller vibrated the red-painted steel deck. Blasts of coke fumes came hot and choking from the crew galley's narrow flue. Alex daydreamed of going ashore in Brazil in the Lovelace tradition of getting drunk. His daydreaming made him late for rounds.

On rounds the captain strode with Morgan at heel. Alex dawdled, caught up when Frogmore halted to run a finger along a shelf – seeking dust.

Pomposity incites ridicule, he thought, but said, "Pity The Horn is out, sir."

"Overruled by some clerk in head office. A clerk who thinks that Milton Keynes is in Thailand."

In the smoke room Francis, in 'humble servant' role, knuckled his forehead.

The captain ran a diligent dust-seeking finger on each of the eight window ledges.

When he opened the bar refrigerator, he said, "Why isn't this cooling properly, purser?"

"Because we're listing. If the ship lists, the refrigerator shuts itself off."

"What are you on about?"

Alex added, "It's *Aust*ralian."

"Do your job. Have it fixed in Panama."

Alex smarted at the unfair rebuke, and the fact that the captain failed to remember that the ship carried a refrigerating engineer. But he put it down to Horn deprivation.

Francis was everywhere. With adept timing, he managed to dash ahead of the inspection party to sit in the office typing menus. He bowed his head as the entourage arrived which was Francis' way of sitting-to-attention. As Frogmore's dust-seeking finger ran the top of the box files, Felicity leapt off the desk and knocked over the cockroach glass. Legions of cockroaches bolted for freedom. They mounted the assault course of Axminster. They clung to the hairs on Alex's arms as he righted the glass. Felicity, defensive because her territory was again being invaded by that man, arched her back and spat in frightful comment.

Frogmore left the office without a word.

Francis, loving the theatre of rounds, looking at the emancipated cockroaches, wrung his hands and said to Alex, "My goodness, *sahib,* what to do?"

As Alex hurried along the alleyway to catch up with the captain, he heard Francis caressing and consoling the cat, possibly explaining in Portuguese about the strange antics of Europeans. Frogmore, denied The Horn, glowered, stalked, examined. Worn baize linings in the cutlery drawers in the saloon were totally unacceptable. In Larry's cabin he pointed to the black ceiling. "Get this deckhead white."

"I'll check with the chief engineer," said Morgan.

"White! White! White!"

The coke-fired cooking range was drawing for lunch making the galley stifling hot. On a workbench a block of frozen fish lay defrosting.

"What fish is that, purser?"

"Fish fish," said Alex, not knowing what fish Francis had substituted for the whiting.

"You don't know and you are in charge of catering."

Alex counted to ten.

"Note this, purser, I will not have crew typing in the officers' accommodation."

"He's acting storekeeper."

"Then he can work in the storekeeper's cabin aft."

The doctor's cabin Frogmore could not bypass. Opened files were scattered about, stoppered pots of liquid stood on his desk. Sheets of foolscap were stuck on the bulkheads. One sheet read ERGONOMICS, another MONOMANIA. Dumped on the carpet was a pile of short-hand notepads.

Frogmore, taking in the once neat cabin now turned squalid, glared at the doctor sprawled in his armchair. "It reflects your personality. Your steward is deserving of much *baksheesh.*" Without waiting for a reply he rounded on Morgan. "Rounds are finished."

Morgan scurried away, but something held the captain,

who was looking his purser in the eye, so much so that Alex was unnerved. It wasn't a look of malevolence but one of sadness.

"I shall be in the cuddy."

When he left, Dr Trimmer said, "Cuddy? Ridiculous. He only uses the word because he knows we are unaware of its meaning."

"Nautical, possibly the officers' mess. He may have used it incorrectly. I'll mention it to him, if ever he experiences a good mood."

"I had a stimulating talk about metempsychosis and karma with the deck *cassab*. Events that happen cannot be altered or avoided – such is fate."

Alex escaped to his office where he stared miserably out the doorway, beyond the narrow alleyway of open deck which separated the office from the ship's rail. The trade winds were blowing; small waves were breaking white.

Francis hissed at him. He followed his steward out on deck. They skirted numbers four and five hatches and entered the crew accommodation aft. Underfoot the linoleum was dark green.

Two decks down was the small hot office, which doubled as Francis cabin. Short chintz curtains hung limp either side of the open port; its brass fittings gleaming. A rush of sea sounded on the ship's hull. There were no ornaments, no photographs. Francis' bunk was militarily neat. The sole tubular chair was at the small desk.

"Best not use the office for a bit."

"The chief cook told me." Francis kicked off his *chappals* and walked barefoot to his bunk. He sat on it and opened the menu book.

Alex concentrated on the white-flecked sea and sat next to him. "I'm queer," he said, holding Francis' hand.

"You've put lamb chops on again. I'll change it to Irish stew."

"Irish stew – never."

"I'll call it ragout."

"It's still Irish stew." He placed the Indian's thin fingers on his fly and leant back against the steel bulkhead, his eyes half-closed. The tropic sun flickered, colouring the cabin.

"Is mutton biriani okay?"

"Brilliant."

Francis' hand, which rested gently on Alex's fly, squeezed his approval and squeezed his approval several times. He took his hand away to correct the entry in pencil as Alex pumped into his underpants.

When he finished writing, Francis reversed roles and became the tolerant boss, coping with an underling. "The sun is over the yardarm. Open the bar for me. I'll be up when I've finished." He glanced at his *Favre Leuba* watch, which he had bought to resell in India, then he crossed barefoot to his desk. "And..."

"Yeah?"

"You can leave your underpants in the *dhobi-bag.*"

Reflections of the sun on the sea were playing on the deckhead as Alex fled.

Guilt. Shame. The blood pounded in his ears. He hurried to his own accommodation to get changed. Before going up to the bar, he hurled his underpants over the side.

HE sat, as he usually did at sea before lunch, with Rusty in the smoke room. On the card table between them were two Australian bitters. There was a dictionary too. The officers played their word game. The Oxford Concise dictionary was their sometimes referee.

"What's a cuddy?" said Alex.

"What?"

"Captain Frogmore said this morning that he would be in the cuddy. Nautical. Know your ships, third engineer."

Rusty looked it up. "Closet. The thing you are mincing out of. What's a tosspot?"

Francis arrived and collected the bar keys off the table.

"A tosspot is a piss-artist. What's a limey?"

Rusty's golden eyes shone behind his spectacles. "A British sailor 'cos they had an issue of lime juice."

"Wrong. To lime means to hang out. The British sailor would hang out with prostitutes, hence limeys."

Rusty, leafing through the dictionary, said, "That is so much shit, Alex. How does micturition strike you?"

"It's masturbation." Alex turned for support to Francis, who was behind the open bar.

"With great respect, sir, I wouldn't have thought it that. To toss off a tosspot could be a pleasant experience while micturition is not pleasant; it is a morbid desire to pass water." Francis was staring Alex straight in the eyes.

Rusty sped across the carpet to the bar and reached over the counter and brought out the dictionary which Francis had concealed on a lower shelf.

Francis held his head in mock shame, then lied, "Sorry, sir, Alex told me to cheat."

Their game wasn't about winners and losers. If it had been, Francis would have won hands down. And, for a fleeting moment in the familiar comfortable room, with the trade winds pulling at an out-of-date magazine on a side table, life was fun again. Life was as it had been when Lovelace was in command.

Alex was happy, he was back in his steward's good books.

ONLY ONE *TATLER* caffeine session before Brazil.

Alex was early for a change. The dayroom was deserted. The monocle lay on the broad desktop demanding to be tried on. It fitted well. It sparkled as he straightened his back and goose-stepped his way about the carpet. He longed for an audience, longed for Rusty's applause. He snapped to Gestapo-attention to admire himself in the scrolled mirror behind the drinks cabinet, then he raised his right arm in a Nazi salute.

A sound. He turned. Through the borrowed eyeglass he saw a hazy Frogmore. Neither spoke. Alex removed the monocle and placed it carefully on the desk.

"It's quite strongly sighted, sir."

"Did you imagine it to be plain glass? Had you supposed I wore it as an affectation? As a prop? Am I out of *HMS Pinafore?*"

The idea had Alex covering his face. "No, sir."

"Do you think I have leanings towards the Third Reich?"

"Of course not."

"You obviously find my glass humorous?"

Alex stared at his shoes. He would sometimes sneak a glance at the monocle when Frogmore wore it, and would stifle a smile. It was as funny as a waxed moustache or a painted on beauty spot. "Yes, sir, I do."

"At least you are man enough not to deny it. Do sit down. I want a word with you alone."

Alex perched, ill at ease, on the long settee.

"I mention your antics in the Thomas Thomas affair. I know that you collected the urn. The policeman spoke of you driving a car with other rabble from this ship, rabble who showed the scars of war – he told me in the most graphic way. However, my main reason for sweeping the incident under the carpet was that the cadet is being kept under review by head office. But, my guess is that you retrieved the urn from the hostelry where the irresponsible Antipodean lost it."

Alex stiffened with apprehension when Frogmore shouted. "I will not tolerate you thinking me the Hun! I sunk two U-boats in the North Atlantic while you were at school. And I will not have you colluding with the enemy on board my ship. Do you understand?"

"No, sir. I mean, yes, sir."

"That ridiculous man ridicules me."

"Sir."

"Pour the tea."

Alex poured two cups then sat down again.

"I expect he was a hippy – that unhygienic bunch who sat crossed-legged and sang of San Francisco; a city which has more in common with Sodom than Nirvana."

"I am mentally a hippy, sir."

"Do you understand your position in my ship?"

"How'd you mean?"

The captain's face was impassive. "You're a senior officer. I must have you acting as one, not as a childish prankster."

Alex belched nervously.

Frogmore wrote *purser* on the lined foolscap pad he kept on his desk. "Do you want some bicarbonate of soda?"

"No, thank you, sir."

They sat not speaking but it was not an uncomfortable silence. Indeed, Alex suspected that Frogmore might have been teasing him.

The dulcimer sounded in the alleyway for breakfast.

"Dashed uncomfortable – indigestion. Brought on by stress or by guilt, although the doctor says it's caused by sexual deprivation. I claim mine is stress, you can admit to guilt."

RODNEY said to Alex, "You don't think they look like breasts?"

"What?" Alex was thrown by the question.

"My pecs."

"Your whats?"

Rodney touched his muscular chest.

"Anything but."

"You've got good legs." Rodney said in such a way that Alex snapped back,

"I can't help them."

"He hasn't got much between his." Rodney leant on the rail and gazed at Cadet David Jones painting the winch on the foredeck below.

"How'd you know?"

Rodney sniffed. It was as though his special branch of homosexuality picked up on such things. "How'd he get a body like that?"

"He's just got it."

"I detect a fan. Go for it."

"He's not queer."

"*It takes one to know one* – is a phrase that does not apply to you. Oh God, the arse on it. And he fancies you rotten, dear."

"Do not call me 'dear'."

The rolled up sleeves of the cadet's blue work shirt were tight on his muscular arms, his shirt buttons were mostly undone and showed a broad chest and a firm stomach. Alex thought he should be on film, in a commercial perhaps, as the most handsome young man around.

Rodney made a loud sucking noise with his mouth which was clearly sexual.

Cadet Jones picked up the signal and grinned. This grin of friendship was then interpreted by Rodney, "You'll definitely be all right there."

Annoyed with Rodney's put-on camp, and his assumed esoteric knowledge, Alex doubled down the companion-way to the foredeck.

"You okay, Dave?"

"Rodney's gone?"

"He was being stupid."
"Why's that?"
"Said you fancied me."
"Play your cards right," said the young man.
"But you're straight?"
"Why should I want a woman when you're around?"
Alex turned and headed up the companionway. He hesitated at the top of the steps to look back. The cadet stared. Alex stood there, was held there for seconds, then he hurried aft because his irrepressible erection was pushing at his shorts, giving comment to the encounter.
Rodney was hovering in the engineers' alleyway, eager for chit-chat and gossip. He prodded the purser's erection "He would have helped you with that."
"It's not only Dave. I'm so frustrated even your ugly mug would get me hard."
"Let me do something about it, otherwise you'll go through life with a perpetual limp."

HE was to return up top after breakfast.
"You wanted to see me, sir?"
No reply. A black mood of sullen, sulking silence hung in the bright dayroom. Alex longed to cut and run. Frogmore kept him standing for several minutes. Finally: "You will accompany me." The captain handed him a Marconigram. "The doctor and I have been instructed to attend a shippers' party in Brazil hosted by Mendes. The doctor cannot be seen as a representative of the Bede Line."
"But if he's invited...?"
"The man can't hold his drink. You will come instead."
"Who is Mendes, sir?"
"An important shipper. Incurably Latin. Smarmy – some call it charm."
"I've arranged to go ashore in Brazil."
"This is ship's official business."
"Not quite the evening I had in mind," said Alex.
"I can be quite a riot when I let my hair down. I crack jokes and play the ukulele."
"What's wrong with Mendes?"
"Not out of the top drawer."
"Not British, sir?"

"I'm aware that you're being facetious, but even you are cognisant of the fact that many British are flawed."

"I'm perpetually ashamed to be one of the tribe."

"If Mendes were British he would be a member of parliament. Indeed, a cabinet minister, such is his integrity."

"But I can't let my hair down?" said Alex.

"Certainly not. And no Nazi salutes nor goose-stepping either – though one never knows in Brazil. Try it and you might get recruited."

Alex went below to his cabin with the improbable image in his mind of Frogmore playing a ukulele to an obese South American wearing a S.S. uniform – and underneath the uniform, it seemed, he might have on fishnet tights.

He decided to return to the captain's quarters, and did so with an enthusiasm that he rarely felt.

"What're we supposed to wear at this shippers' do?"

"Very little going on past form. It's not a question I dare put to Mendes for he might suggest a frock. Slacks and white shirt and a tie would not go amiss. Everything about Mendes is showy. The lavatory paper is embossed by some Italian fashion house. I cannot think how they had the ill judgement to put their logo on it."

Perhaps, Alex thought, the evening ashore might not be all dull.

TEN

BRAZIL

"MY DEAREST, ALEX!" Mendes gushed, and was shaking hands with him for a third time. His grip was dry and warm and his hand pleasantly lingered as they walked together towards the long low building. "I have sent Rupert back to the ship in a car."

"Am I being chucked out too?" asked Alex, delighted to see the back of Frogmore and charmed by this swarthy man with intense black eyes.

"I would be heartbroken if you left me. Rupert was suffering from a migraine, brought on from meeting me – and ghosts from his past, no doubt."

Alex nodded.

"He spoke of you in a manner which made me curious."

"Saying what?"

"He talked of you as though you were the prodigal son."

"The prodigal son was forgiven?"

"Rupert is incapable of showing if he likes people, but he has passion." Mendes whispered, "Perhaps Rupert is closer to you in some directions, than you imagine." He pressured Alex's hand in his own. Alex squeezed back, it seemed the polite thing to do. "Your accent is attractive. You're English?"

"I loathe being English. I was brought up in a school where to admit liking poetry was to declare oneself into high heels and a blouse."

"I adore poetry. You can borrow my court shoes. But then I am Brazilian and am quite unacceptable. I am so dark that it is said my grandmother slept with a slave."

"What cargoes do you ship?" said Alex.

"Canned goods. Coffee. Ore too – that is major. Sometimes nuts – Brazils seem appropriate."

They both giggled like schoolboys.

"This property seems to stretch for miles. Please do not tell me this is the front garden?"

"Those men who wish to impress, seldom do, and those

who do impress, do not give a fig what others think of them. Rupert impresses, but not with wealth, but with his authoritarian manner." He squeezed Alex's hand again and Alex found himself responding eagerly. The man was warm and smelt of cigars. "Rupert is very wary of me."

"Why?"

"Because he thinks I will blab."

"Think of me not as your guest, Mr Mendes, but as an interrogator. I have you hard up against a wall. My knee is in your groin. My arm pressures tight across your throat. And as you choke, the light is harsh in your eyes. Now, the question you have to answer is *Why does Rupert develop a migraine to get away from you?*"

"You will not charm all details out of me, I'm afraid. But you have detected that I'm a weak man, my dear Alex. I might submit to all your punishments with some glee, if you call me Maria."

"Tell me more, Maria. I've packed my whip."

"Rupert's ambition is the sea. He seldom relaxes, but there were times when... Perhaps he has never forgiven me for giving him the opportunity to enjoy himself. He can be the live spark, you know. And his horsemanship drew the admiration of the gauchos." Mendes rested his hand on Alex's shoulder to guide him over the worn flags. Above their heads lanterns hung in trees; on each side of the broad path urns cascaded garish blooms. Mendes stopped to introduce him to three smartly dressed men who went out of their way to be pleasant. Alex sensed he was being courted. There was a mission in the air, a frisson of an unexplained delight. The three men's talk was camp and bawdy and laced with innuendo. They acted rather in a childish way, or perhaps as some businessmen act when on the loose – having left their wives at home.

Alex, avoiding an invitation to a late supper, changed the conversation, and asked one man what cargos he shipped.

"Ore," said the man.

"Alas, an unattractive cargo and low freight. I should know," said Maria Mendes but added, getting the conversation back on track, "But we have an attractive cargo in Alexio."

Alex thought it rather a rum do as he listened to another

man – fighting middle-age – let drop an invitation that Alex might accompany him later to his town house for a nightcap.

Mendes saved him and they walked away. "When you get back on board you must inform Rupert that I told you about the time he got utterly smashed."

"You're being deliciously indiscreet, Maria, but Captain Frogmore governs his appetites. He neither gets drunk nor lets his hair down."

"In his younger days, he was invited to a banquet at a Chinese trade delegation in Hong Kong. The Chinese consider themselves the superior race – they are as arrogant as the British. Their *yam sing* is a barbaric custom that they impose on us Westerners to get us stupidly drunk while they look disdainfully on. At the shout of *Yam sing!* one's drink must be downed in one. I knew the form so was on tonic water. Rupert was on gin and he got so sick he couldn't make it to the bathroom. You must remind him how he threw up on the tablecloth at the banquet."

"I must?"

"The table was oblong and long and laid out with place settings. There were floral centre pieces. Frogmore vomited. The waiters had to cut the tablecloth in order to remove the soiled section then replace it and relay the places. It was a prestigious do. An orchestra."

"A forty piece orchestra?"

"That many? I never counted."

Alex said, "How can I believe anything you say?"

"Tell Frogmore and watch his reaction."

"You are a wicked man."

"We make a formidable couple."

Alex, side-stepped over an irregular flag as Maria guided him on a narrowing path that led to a black wrought iron gate.

He said to a young man standing by the gate, "Shut it behind us and keep people out." He led Alex into a large courtyard with a central splashing fountain. At the perimeter of the courtyard was a colonnade, and in a niche, in half-darkness, Alex and Maria settled on a black chesterfield. The man who stayed at the gate, as if on guard, glared at them.

Maria said, "Spying on us and jealous is Rodrigo Fernandes. Surly and not overly bright, but he's handsome enough – though not from a good family."

"Given his looks, his family background might be unimportant."

The Brazilian said, "Look not at Rodrigo but at the sky. There is a storm brewing." He took Alex's hand and placed it on his hard cock. And that act gave, to Alex, a whole new meaning to a 'shippers' do'. He closed his eyes, leant back and felt warm dry fingers touching his face. Opening his eyes he saw, in the light of suspended paraffin lamps, the shadowy figure of Rodrigo Fernandes standing on the other side of the gate, facing them.

"We've got but five minutes before I have to get back and make a tiresome speech," said Maria coaxing Alex's head down as he unzipped his fly and in moments Maria's mouth was kissing the back of Alex's head which moved as urgently, but not as frantically as did the hand of the watching Rodrigo Fernandes peering through the wrought iron gate.

FLATTERING AS THE ATTENTION was that Maria Mendes lavished on him and, as exciting as the sharply erotic interlude had been, Alex knew that here was not what he really wanted. He wanted the company of rougher joints.

It was an hour later and he had joined the other guests. He had his eyes closed and was smiling at Mendes' talk, shutting out a swimming pool coloured turquoise from submerged lights, shutting out the statuesque palms and the long building which had a lofty foyer with low hanging brass lamps – maybe fifty of them – and walls lined with dark oil paintings. There were several black leather chesterfields and occasional tables dotted about. Opening his eyes, he spotted side arms on the security guards who mingled with the guests.

Rodrigo Fernandes, who had energetically masturbated on the wrong side of the wrought iron gate, had snake hips and wore Cuban heels; his slicked back hair was the colour of jet. But most striking were his muscular forearms coated with black hair. His dark eyes surveyed Alex and Mendes and, catching their attention, he raised a bottle of champagne high in the air and let it drop on the flags. Chunks of glass were everywhere. With an arrogant expression, and his back straight, he watched as waiters and waitresses picked up pieces of glass.

"Accident," said Rodrigo Fernandes.

"Go to bed, Fernandes." Maria's use of his surname was an open reprimand.

One waiter, who was dangerously young, made eyes at Alex as he helped him pick up chunks of glass. It was the same youth who had followed him earlier. It now dawned on Alex that the waiters and waitresses were on offer along with the trays of canapés and the champagne. Maria nodded his approval at the waiter, who reacted as though he had been slipped a twenty dollar bill. He stood up and approached Alex shyly, and kissed him softly on the ear.

"He speaks little English, but no matter. Stay the night and he will cut your English mustard."

At lofty gates, operated by a burly man, Maria pressed a gilt-edged card into Alex's hand. "Such a pity – had your ship been in over the weekend, you would have stayed with me. Weekends I have guests over. Houseguests of our persuasion. Sophisticated men, not a boy in sight – although that could be arranged. But I prefer good conversation to double beds. But, alas, my dearest Alexio, I fly to Mexico tomorrow on tedious business." He smiled at the youthful waiter who had tagged along. "With Salvadore. Do come?"

The boy, Salvadore, gripped Alex's hand as if anchoring him. Alex said, "If only. I have some typing to do."

Mendes caught his irony and smiled, insisting that he take a limousine back to the ship. Alex would have none of it. He wanted the freedom of choice. He did not want to be ferried in a chauffeur-driven car nor fly in a private plane with a boy on offer, especially a boy who had not started to shave.

But Mendes held him back, held his arm. "You seek the truth?"

"Don't we all?"

"Keep on the road for half a mile. When you see the railway lines, follow them and you will come to a solitary building, an adobe cantina where men drink and play cards. There you will find what you seek: the real men of this great country. If you chance upon Ignacio, tell him Maria sends him, as always, his devotion.

ONLY WHEN HE WAS OUT OF SIGHT, did Alex shout and sing and run on the rough road, kicking stones.

The storm that had been threatening all evening broke. It was a deluge. He slipped; slithered into a broad ditch that ran the edge of the unmade up road. Landing badly, he grazed his forehead on a rock. Scrambling up the side of the ditch, he regained the road and ran as lightning lit the sky. The storm tore at the trees, the rain drenched him, it flooded the road. He danced drunkenly in ankle deep water. He waded. He sang and jumped in the air; again falling – this time bruising his hand. He teased himself that he could bleed to death alone in a South American storm drain.

The neon lights of the small town were lost in the downpour but he located the rail track easily enough. He walked the shiny lines with his arms outstretched and his palms held up to the cleansing rain. Foot followed foot. He went faster, then slipped again and lay face down in mud, marvelling at the evening.

But his evening was anything but ended. He lifted his head and as the rain stopped, he saw in front of him, at the top of the rise, what he was looking for. Light spilled out of the adobe bar.

"You speak English?" he asked a man whose brimmed hat, stained dark with sweat, rested on the scarred bar counter. Next to the hat was an unlabelled bottle of spirit.

Not speaking, the man filled a small glass from the bottle and gave it to him.

"I'm Alex."

"I am The Man from the Pampa."

"The Man from the Pampa?" Alex was in awe of such an introduction. He tossed back the shot of liquor. "What do you do?"

"I drink," the man said, refilling Alex's glass.

"I fall down storm drains."

"Your forehead has blood on it. You also are covered in mud." He used a laundered white handkerchief and wiped Alex's forehead and showed him the blood.

"It's ruined your hanky."

"No matter."

"Your English is beautiful?"

"I was taught by an Englishman years ago. And later by Maria."

"Maria Mendes. You are...?"

"Everyone knows him."

"The gun at your hip?"

"I am a gaucho."

"You should have your portrait painted." The man's body was muscular and young, yet his face was creased. He'd be around thirty but it was hard to tell with his superb facial bone structure and dark skin. Alex went to order drinks but the man's broad hand firmed down on his.

"We have a bottle to finish."

They settled on high stools. The motor of a large Kelvinator rattled. There was no music in the bar. Alex could hear soft conversation from the men who drank at the tables; one group played cards.

"You are a little drunk perhaps, Englishman?"

"I've been to a party where the waiters and waitresses were on offer and the wine came from France."

"I was invited."

"You are Ignacio? Maria sends his love."

"You perhaps wonder how a humble gaucho knows such an important man? I tell you. He picked me out of the gutter when I was a beggar. You are an important man also?"

"Far from it."

"If you like the simpler things, then this bar is more your home, I think."

"Is this Tequila or Nirvana?" Alex looked over the rim of his glass. He could smell horse on the man.

The rain came again with force on the roof, spilling noisily out of the gutters, cocooning the small group in the bar. In drunken confession, Alex talked animatedly of the ship and the gaucho showed a keen interest. He questioned him about the captain's manner and attitude. He became angry when Alex told him how Frogmore bullied the cadet.

The man's thick hair was flat and black, combed straight back with no parting. He wore bleached Levis and a spotless white T-shirt; a poncho hung on a stool.

"You're Indian?"

"In Brazil the races are mixed."

"Come back on board and listen to Joan Baez?"

"I'd like that." The Man from the Pampa added,"Over there – my uncle." He acknowledged an old man drinking with others at a table.

Alex felt the evening marvellously surreal. It was as though he was watching a scene being shot for a film when the cracking of thunder stopped conversation. He didn't flinch when, without warning, a man wearing a policeman's uniform burst into the bar. Water dripped off the black peak of his cap; his leather holster flapped open, a long-barrelled pistol was in his hand.

"Move away! Over there!" hissed Ignacio.

Alex remained next to his new friend.

Dark eyes held Alex's. "Move!"

Alex took his drink to the far end of the bar.

Ignacio's uncle stared at a tabletop marked by cigarette burns as the policeman spoke to him. The old man shook his head. The policeman's hand slammed hard on the old man's head and he fell face down onto the table. His grey-white hair showed a patch of blood.

Ignacio spun off his stool to stand between the policeman and the crumpled old man.

A bolt of lightning held the bar in a tableau of white light.

The Man from the Pampa pushed the official. The policeman's peaked cap spun. His pistol and baton dropped to the hard dirt floor. Alex was on his feet and inspired by watching mediocre films during long sea voyages, he shouted at the official.

"Guardia fascista! Bastardo!"

He saw now that three policemen covered the front. The squall stopped. But more shocking the Kelvinator stopped too.

All in the bar was silent and still.

ELEVEN

BRAZIL

RUSTY, as the duty engineer, had to keep ship. Late the following evening he settled on Alex's daybed.

"You remember that girl I was with in the club?"

"I didn't go ashore with you, Rusty."

"Filmy dress and too much makeup?"

"You're pissed. I wasn't ashore with you. I was yak, yak, yakking at the shippers' do."

"She asked me to wash it first."

Alex yawned, pretending to be bored.

"I ended up in the *favelas*. A narrow bed and a wood-burning stove. Outside came the sound of breaking glass. A Frenchman screamed. There was a crucifix above the bed."

"A convent?"

"Afterwards a man came in and took my wallet."

"Not a convent. You put up some resistance?"

"I never fight."

"You can't be a coward to admit such an act of cowardice."

"That makes me brave?"

"Without question. You are a man I honour deeply. If, as an old seadog, I might give you a tip?" Alex had been drinking all evening. Rusty had been drinking all day.

"Tip?" said Rusty suspiciously.

"I suggest that you keep your money in your sock when going ashore."

"Very convenient if you pop into Woolworth's."

"You were not popping into Woolworth's. You were in a knocking shop. This is not Tilbury."

"She was fourteen. The guy who took my wallet drove me back in his car – a '67 Cadillac, very nice indeed."

"You do have a history of instability, don't you?"

"How come you got that cut on your forehead?"

Alex dramatised events as he told of his arrest in the bar, making it sound as though he was roughed up by the police, then he said, "I was flung into jail with the scum of Brazil.

Lowlife colourful only in their vile language. They applauded as farts ripped the fetid air in the cell."

"How'd you get out of prison?" asked Rusty impressed.

"Money – in my sock. My friend bribed the guard."

"Your friend?"

"The Man from the Pampa."

"Oh, please, give me a fucking break. The Man from the Pampa?"

"One does not use names," said Alex, glancing about his cabin. "And his uncle was incarcerated after being pistol-whipped."

"Such shit."

"You wanna hear my story, or not?"

"Too right. It sounds blissfully squalid."

He needs entertaining, thought Alex. Rusty comes in here because I'm good company. I am the song and dance man.

"The stench in the cell was such that I am unable to speak of it." In reality the senior police officer had released him after only an hour. There was no charge or fine. The officer said courteously that he hoped that Alex would accept the fact that The Man from the Pampa was a political animal and his uncle was without papers and wanted for sedition. Alex was driven back to the ship by a charming elderly man with grey-black hair who came on board for coffee. A man who had positioned a blanket over Alex as he started to doze drunkenly in his armchair. A man who had left his card.

Alex looked about the cabin again. "I have a direct contact in the police ashore." He showed Rusty the pasteboard card.

"This criminal you picked up in a bar – what was he like?"

"*Mi amigo* had a stubble chin, breath of garlic, gun at his hip and hypnotic deep eyes. His powerful macho body was hidden under a rain-soaked poncho until he took it off to reveal muscles beneath a stretch of white linen and faded denim. His hands were leather. The smell of horse was on him. He talked of miscegenation, of rights, of getting back at Frogmore."

"You're saying that some old fellow was pistol-whipped in this *cantina* and macho man, who was sweating like some hot whore in his rain-soaked poncho and stank of horse, was arrested and you went to his support? You supporting anyone in a time of danger, I find very difficult to believe.

And you ended up with him in jail where you and he discussed Captain Rupert de Vere Frogmore?"

"It is the gaucho code, *Gringo.*"

"It's the gaucho crap."

"In the cell, the rough stone hewn wall behind this intimidating figure – all man and dressed to kill – was pock-marked with bullet holes. It was not the Savoy."

Rusty was drawn in but Alex had conned him so often.

Alex said, "I went to bandage his bleeding wrist but The Man from the Pampa, whose leather skin was dripping blood, said, 'Desist! Play the innocent and they will think you an official from Oxfam.' And later, as we parted, my friend clasped me as tight as a brother and said that Frogmore should be served the calling card of retribution."

Rusty blinked. "So this unhygienic Pampas Queen, who despite having Portuguese or Spanish as his native tongue, uses words like miscegenation – which you only know from our dictionary game – and he grasped you? You being a not unattractive blond, and you did say the light was poor. He was seeking your roll?"

"My roll?"

"Not the one in your sock." Rusty was taken with Alex's tale but would not allow his appreciation to show. "You turned down beautiful paid-for waitresses for some rough jail bird in a bar? Sounds to me like you've found your promised land."

"What're you saying, Rusty?"

"I'm asking you what exactly you did with The Man from the Pampa?"

"We gelled, bonded as machismo men in adversity do."

"Did you bond in doubling spurts?" said Rusty, his eyes gleaming through spectacles.

"Do not judge others by your own crass needs."

"When you had sex...?"

"How dare you, you foul-mouthed beast."

"Do you fancy me?"

"Haven't we tediously been here before?"

"I am the Casanova of the Bede Line. Women queue for me. Bathe me. Kiss every part of my beautiful body."

"A body which is going to seed. You're losing your cuteness." Alex spun a spent Foster's can into the half-full gash bin.

"You do want to do it with me, don't you?"

"Are you serious?"

"Maybe we could try it, just so long as you don't have a too powerful suck. I had rather too much of that last night." Rusty, cute and cuddly, sat forward on the daybed, his knees widened. He was wearing nothing under the towel that was wrapped around his waist.

He's adding me to his trophy list, thought Alex, keeping his eyes away from what was on display. "Is this your subtle approach?"

"You don't go for subtle." Rusty closed his legs and primly tugged his towel over his knees.

Alex poured his beer into a glass. "Did you sign for these?"

"Don't be stupid. How can I? I put them on your tab."

"Why?"

"I'm cutting down. The chief engineer said the captain had complained that my wine account was in orbit."

"And what about my wine account?"

"For fuck's sake, don't be so selfish – think of others for a change. You'll be seeing this Pampas Queen again?" As he used the opener, the can foamed and beer spilled down its blue sides. Rusty lapped the spillage with a flicking sensuous tongue.

"I may prison visit." Alex examining the third engineer's appealing face, said, "I've a plan. You're going to help. Consider it payment for drinking on my wine account."

Rusty didn't say anything as he watched Alex walk into his adjoining office and take an egg carton off the top of the large green safe. Bringing it back into the cabin, he held it under the third engineer's nose.

"Oh, Jesus! What the fuck?" said Rusty, gagging at the stench.

"Two sausages smeared with cat shit."

"I suggested you suck me not sniff cat's shit. You queers get off on that?"

Still standing, Alex said with pomposity, "Follow me, third engineer."

Rusty could refuse him nothing after such entertainment. He trotted obediently after him into the alleyway.

They walked drunkenly past the deck officers' showers then climbed the companionway that led out onto the deck at number three hatch. Then up another companionway and in two minutes Alex was unlocking the captain's outside weather door with a passkey.

Inside the large, cool dayroom, he made his way towards the desk but froze on the acreage of carpet as a groan of uneasy sleep sounded from the bedroom.

Alcohol did not stop the silhouetted Rusty shaking with excitement as he hovered in the doorway, ready to cut and run but he was held watching the purser cross the carpet on the sides of his feet, making no sound. Alex gave a low laugh as he tipped the contents of the carton onto the captain's desktop. He used the stem of Frogmore's second best pipe to free one sausage which had stuck. He turned imperiously to speak to Rusty, but he had fled.

NEXT MORNING, well before the smell of frying bacon came from the galley, Alex made his way to the captain's suite.

The circulating air from the air-conditioning unit stank of cat's mess.

"Sir, you wanted the *topass*? He's loading stores."

"Where is your cap, purser?"

"Can't wear it. Bruised forehead – bad cut."

"How?"

"An altercation ashore."

"Mendes is many things but not a violent man."

"No, sir. I was in manly contact with a ditch when walking back to the ship."

"I do not see how you could fight a ditch. Did Mendes not furnish you with transportation?"

"I turned him down, sir, preferring to soak up the atmosphere of the country. I ended up in the caboose."

"The caboose? The ship's galley? Are you concussed?"

"I did a short spell in choky."

"Let us stop this now, purser. You're making less sense than usual." Frogmore pointed to the sausages on his desktop. "Your cat."

"No, sir."

"I will speak slowly as obviously the wound on your

forehead has further impaired your already diminished intelligence. *Your* cat has defecated on *my* desk."

"No cat would shit on glass. Their instinct, on home territory, is to cover their mess. These turds are much too large. Human, I would say."

Frogmore stepped back a good pace when Alex eased up the end of one sausage with his ballpoint pen and sniffed, holding his nose close to it.

"Have you expertise in faecal identification, purser?" said Frogmore grim-faced.

Gomes, eavesdropping in the hallway, hurried in and peered at the sausages.

"Oh, my goodness, not Felicity's, *burra sahib.* Much too big."

Alex picked up a circular showing the Bede Line's logo and headed: HEAVY LIFTS – AUSTRALIA and scooped up the sausages and put them in a paper bag which Gomes held open.

"For God's sake, wash your hands," said the captain.

Alex called out above the noise of the running water in the bathroom, "Can I use the towel, sir?"

"Drop it on the deck when you've finished."

The captain stopped him before he went below.

"A word, if I might. Last evening, was your reason for refusing a car because of Mendes… 'er, touching you?"

"Touching, sir?" said Alex wide-eyed.

"You are being deliberately obtuse. Did Mendes touch you in an unnecessary way?"

"Certainly not, sir. A colleague of his did invite me for a drink in his town house. 'Back to my home for something long and hot' was his exact phrase. I must say I was rather taken aback."

"Indeed one might hope, or one might not hope, that you were taken aback," said Frogmore. "A black man, immaculately dressed?"

"Very dapper."

"That wound on your forehead wasn't…?"

"Nothing to do with him, sir. Do you know him?"

"A confused gender role – Dr Trimmer would spout. He is a chap to be watched very closely indeed. And what I have to impart to you now, must be kept within the confines of this dayroom." He glared at his steward who moved out into the alleyway, shutting the outside door after him. "The black man told me that I had nice eyes."

Alex giggled so uncontrollably that he started to choke, so much so that Frogmore called his steward urgently to pour the purser a glass of chilled water and to bang him heartily on the back.

THOSE OFFICERS DRAWING MONEY to go ashore that day admired Alex's scar as if it were a campaign medal.

Larry, despite his preference for Oriental women, decided that local women would have to do. Rusty pushed his spectacles nervously up his nose as he forsook the onboard excitement of nocturnal commando raids for something more to his taste.

The telephone that linked Alex to the captain buzzed. "I had Mendes' secretary on the phone, purser. I am to convey to you that he was quite taken with you. Said you are a credit to the shipping line and he was writing to the directors to tell them so. Mendes is a charismatic diplomat. But one must watch one's back pocket – not that the wallet will be picked – the opposite. It will be stuffed full with dollars of corruption."

"Sir," said Alex.

"Anything you wish to discuss with me – you have my ear." The phone went dead – that was Frogmore's way.

Alex was cheered because the evening with Mendes had been pleasant and the memory of it had lingered and left him with a comfortable feeling. Such companionable encounters were so rare, that it was an event of note; but to repeat the encounter might perhaps spoil their association, but Alex would grab at that chance. Mendes, the man of the world, had understood Alex's needs and appreciated his lack of guile – "It is that in you which appeals to me most," he had said at that moment of intense climax, when Alex was quite unable to speak.

Nearing lunch hour, he was at his desk when the *seacunny*, deferential in the doorway, informed him that a *peon* was wanting to see him. The *peon* was standing behind the *seacunny*, and he wasn't deferential at all. It was Rodrigo Fernandes from the shippers' do: the broad-shouldered, smouldering young man who had stood guard at the gate to the courtyard. The same young man who had later deliberately smashed a champagne bottle in a fit of pique. Today he had on the blue uniform shirt of a messenger. His uncovered forearms were rivetingly black with hair. Black hair showed, in an attention seeking way, at the open neck of his shirt.

"Sign here!" His brown forefinger smoothed a line in the receipt book he held. The nail was manicured, the half moon defined.

Alex looked at the large well-wrapped parcel but did not take it. It would be a present from Mendes. "I can't accept it."

The man's eyes were hidden behind intimidating black glasses. He tapped his pistol.

"Dear God, do I get shot if I refuse?"

"No, you are my friend," Rodrigo Fernandes said, with an immediate and devastating smile which almost took the intimidation out of his earlier sullenness.

"I feel we have something common," said Alex, thinking of Maria Mendes.

"You could be coming back with me in the car, if you wish, but I tell you that Maria is in Mexico."

Alex scrawled his name on the receipt.

"I'm told to unpack it in front of you." Rodrigo Fernandes bent over the large package and began peeling off layer after layer of brown paper; it was as though it were a striptease. Revealed was a flat box, some two feet square, made out of ply. He indicated the paperknife on the desk which Alex gave him. He positioned its point under the large blob of sealing wax and flicked it off. Inside the box was an oil painting, of some distinction, in a substantial gilt frame.

Rodrigo Fernandes was dark-skinned and as exotic as Alex could have wished, and he hinted of danger with the holster at his hip. He had one final task to do. He picked up the gallery's invoice that lay open on top of the painting and after folding it slowly – slowly enough for Alex to see how much the painting cost – he slotted it in his shirt pocket.

He was in no hurry to leave – he lingered as though wanting to confide in Alex. "This! This!" He angrily tugged at the material of his smart starched shirt and his matching blue cotton trousers. "He makes me wear this to humble me." His face was a child denied sweets in the shop. Alex had to console him, to stop him screaming and crying real tears and banging his angry heels on the floor.

"Rodrigo, in rags you would look stylish and handsome. Old clothes, any old thing you can wear. Seeing you now I am standing erect."

"Thank you, thank you," said Rodrigo, checking out Alex's crotch with a steady look.

"Do you have to wear those glasses?" The glasses were disconcertingly black, his eyes hidden.

Rodrigo's left hand opened all the buttons on his shirt. Revealed were black nipples and hairs that were smooth and everywhere, symmetrically they headed down beneath the broad leather belt which was perched on slim hips. His right hand took off the seemingly opaque dark glasses. His eyes were lustrous.

"The hair is on my back too." The Brazilian shut the outside office door that led onto the deck, then he bolted the inner door. He took off his shirt. "You can touch my back, Englishman."

Alex ran his hot palms over the superb back, following the direction of the hair, tucking his hands into the broad leather belt.

"What do you think?" said Rodrigo.

"You're magnificent. And you know you're magnificent."

Rodrigo nodded and put his shirt back on before unlocking the door. The sunglasses were back on too, as was the scowl. "What you think of my English, Alexio?"

"What is wonderful is your lack of an accent. Your voice is very manly."

The child had had his sweets and the beaming smile was back on. He thought that if Rodrigo now volunteered to remove his trousers to show the hairs on his legs, he would be on his knees as a supplicant; his mouth was already salivating lubricant.

After Rodrigo left his office, Alex felt as though he had had sex. Rodrigo had titillated, like a stripper, but more brilliantly than the common or garden stripper, for he had left his own goods covered while the other veils fell. And he was heavily endowed, unless what Alex saw outlined in Rodrigo's pants was a very large courgette. Rodrigo had delivered a memorable performance and Alex had applauded. His applause was concealed: a damp patch of notable size, sticky in his underpants. He thought that he should rush down the gangway to tell him about it, knowing that Rodrigo would be very pleased, but then again he might arrogantly have expected it and he would not deign to come back on board to look.

The smell of the Brazilian, his perfumed soap, or perhaps it was the scent he used, lingered. Alex rushed to the window to watch him disembark. He expected autograph hunters thrusting books. Flashlights popping. But there was only a face that was gloriously sullen, exotic and arrogant. His mood was conveyed in his scowl as he stared up at Alex, who was thinking, *My God, that Latin dreamboat must think of me as the competition.*

The Cadillac purred along the jetty, went out of sight. And he was alone and life was dull until he studied the painting with an expert eye. It seemed that the shippers' do had provided him with a reward far beyond any gift that he had received in his life. Alex, who always hated the bother and embarrassment of giving and receiving presents, now had accepted the most munificent gift.

He replaced the painting of a mulatto boy in its box. He positioned the box on top of the folded blankets which were stored in the long and deep bottom drawer under his bunk.

AT THE END OF THE WORKING DAY he was still elated about the gift and desperate to show it to somebody – somebody who he could trust and whose judgement he respected.

In his cabin Cadet Jones was washing his face with ship's issue buttermilk soap. He lathered his neck too, and his cleansing was as meticulous as any surgeon. Not once did he glance at himself in the mirror above the sink.

"Your dose cleared up?" said Alex cheerfully.

"Ages ago."

"Why aren't you ashore?"

"It's okay."

"Has God been getting at you?"

"I'm okay," said Jones, studying his feet.

"Come ashore with me?"

"I don't want to drink." David Jones reached for the towel.

"My intent is missionary work, not alcohol, nor sex. I wish only for your kind Christian arm to lean on. I shall visit the local jail and deliver largesse. Afterwards we can get a burger – paid for by the Bede Line." Alex would foot the bill, but would not tell the cadet. "I'll put you under entertainment allowances. You can dance or sing or do something truly wild."

"You're good to me."

"I'm hot for you – now you are certified clean. And I go for fifteen-year-olds," said Alex.

"Almost seventeen."

"In which case it'll be food, not sex."

Cadet Jones beamed. It was the right moment for Alex to show him what was in the box.

"Where'd you get it?"

"From a man at a shippers' party. A shippers' party, I've never seen the like."

"Tell me?"

Alex told him everything, and finished by saying, "Thinking about it, have I become a highly paid call boy? Extraordinary. I'm not good at sex."

"Sex is easy. It's the people you do it with that are the problem." Dave held the painting away so he could examine it, then he held it close to his cabin's central light, finally he propped it up on his bunk. "The boy's almost ugly, but he's got something. He's got a lot of something. I'd photograph him."

"Gets you randy?"

"This boy's parted lips are sensual but it's the animal he has in him – wild and dangerous."

"He's a boy who is sexually mature and it's on offer– that's what it's about," said Alex. "You ready?"

"I'll have to shower first."

"Forget the shower. Showered or not, you suit me any old day of the week."

Dave Jones beamed.

"Come down to my cabin when you're changed."

TWELVE

BRAZIL

AS A GOOD SEAMAN, DAVE was neat and tidy.

He carefully folded the sheets of brown paper that littered Alex's office desk. His tidying revealed a long white envelope.

"Open it," said Alex.

Dave extracted a single sheet of paper which he handed to the purser, who read aloud, "*My dearest Alexio, This is a favourite portrait of mine. I was going to hang it in the long hall but there it would be dwarfed and lost. It has an earthy quality which I think you will like. The painting is suited to a small room. The intimacy of your cabin – and when, on a lonely night at sea, you look at it and your thoughts are of self-stimulation. It is then that you will remember me, be with me. That is the legacy and selfishness of my gift – Maria.*"

Alex understood now that Maria Mendes had been giving the arrogant and mouth-wateringly sensual Rodrigo Fernandes, a sharp message. The young man must've been a favourite who had grown too big for his boots, so Maria Mendes rubbed his nose in it to cut him down to size. Alex had gained an expensive artefact and Mendes had gained control over the young man. Alex felt himself deliciously used, but he consoled himself that he came at a high price. He fingered the painting. "You can have it, Dave."

"No." The cadet was alarmed.

"It'll only be left in my bottom drawer."

"You're kidding?"

"Did you see the chauffeur?"

Dave shuddered. "Arrogant."

"Fuego."

"What?"

"He was hot."

"You know those flamenco dancers who toss their heads and give that 'look at me, I am so wonderful' stare. He was one of them."

"He was one of them, all right," said Alex.
"You'd photograph well. Can I?"
"You're kidding?"
"Your skull's a good shape."
"Definitely kidding." Alex blurted out, "I thought the chauffeur the most beautiful creature."
"You're looking at him with your cock."
Alex took the cadet's hand and gently kissed his palm which smelt of buttermilk soap.
"Alex?"
"Yeah?"
"Rodrigo was part of the package."
"How'd you mean?"
"He came along with the painting. He would think you were playing hard to get. He'll be as used to putting it about, as you are not."
Alex said nothing, recalling the courtyard.
"I reckon this Mendes is some big shot and big shots demand control – control over the chauffeur," said Dave.
"And Rodrigo was on offer."
"He's anybody's and gagging for it. You're better off having a wank."
Alex said, "You're worth a Velázquez or two."
"You reckon we could get egg, chips and beans ashore someplace?"

CADET DAVID JONES leant across the table in the small bright restaurant near the docks.
"Shutters," said Alex, emptying the remains of the fourth bottle of *Vinho Verde* into Dave's glass.
"Your parents' house has shutters? Are they millionaires?"
"No, Jones. I'm not talking about my mother's house but about my home."
"You're home is at sea."
"I'm at home with seamen – comfortable with the likes of you."
"Shutters? Do you mean the jalousies that you pull up to cover the windows when you pull off?"
"I do those lines, cadet."
"Call me Dave, please?"
"How can I call you Dave, when with you it has sexual

connotations and I am frightened, Dave."

"You can't be frightened of me. You call your steward by his first name."

"Francis is cleverer than I, but then you are too." Alex fiddled with his cutlery. "My house is near the beach."

"It overlooks the sea?"

"Well, sort of, but not in a grand way. It's one of a terrace on the coast – barren land in front because nothing will grow on it. The shingle gets thrown up from the beach in the winter gales and it pounds the house – so there are shutters to protect the windows, that's all. No one wants to buy it because of the shingle."

"I wank."

"Oh, goodness me, Jones, you're going to be a problem, I can tell. You promised me faithfully that we wouldn't drink and now we're drinking. I certainly am not going to discuss nasty sex. Sex between men is very beastly indeed. How many times a day?"

"About the shutters?"

"You want shutters up to iron tank behind, don't you, you dirty little iron tanker?"

"You're doing it again," said Dave Jones.

"But I'm so awfully good at rhyming slang. I'm rather good at languages too."

"You speak Portuguese?"

"Fluently. Francis taught me – in case of spies." Alex then ordered two coffees with two large tequila chasers then said to the waiter in appalling Portuguese, "Your house has shutters?"

The waiter, wrinkling his broad nose, said in English, "Of course, and a garden with the flowers."

"That's really nice. That music? What's that music?"

"You don't know James Brown?"

"He screams," said Cadet Jones.

"Sorry," said Alex, "but who is it that screams?"

The waiter said, "James Brown is soul, man. Every person into human dignity likes James Brown."

The waiter, who was black and no longer young, left to get their order. David Jones leant further across the crumpled tablecloth. "Ask him if James Brown's house has shutters." He added, "Doesn't proper tequila have a worm in it? Ask him."

"Worms, shutters, James Brown and a Brazilian waiter's garden – it's too much."

"Best times ashore are with you." Dave reached to grasp Alex's hand, gripping it tightly on the top of the tablecloth.

The waiter positioned their drinks, saying huskily, "I'll change the music – Julie London."

"I need to get you back on board, Cadet David Jones, for several strong coffees. You were right, you do need that shower – and very cold indeed."

HUNG OVER, but up and about, at eight the next morning Alex joined Gomes. The two eavesdropped outside the captain's dayroom.

"Not one of the crew." They heard Morgan say.

"Must be an officer. Only officers have passkeys." The captain's voice. "It is not uncommon for thieves to leave their calling card in this unseemly manner."

"Nothing stolen?"

"Correct."

"The purser not joining us?" asked Morgan.

"Are you suggesting it could be him?"

"The doctor's a strange beast."

"Ah, the doctor," said Frogmore, with dawning comprehension.

Alex pushed aside the curtain and sank into the low settee. Bleary-eyed he watched tea poured into a cup of the fine blue china that was reserved for captains and chief engineers.

Veins stood on the back of Frogmore's hand as he handed him the cup. "Purser, I have a telex from Panama to confirm they will be able to supply potatoes."

"Francis."

"Who is Francis?"

"My steward, the acting storekeeper."

"You call your steward by his Christian name?"

"I've told Francis that he may use my office again, sir, if you have no objection."

Frogmore stared ahead, focussing on nothing. A hand waved in front of his eyes would not register.

Morgan drew heavily on his cigarette, the ash lengthened

and trembled.

Frogmore said, "Why have you countermanded my orders?"

"Mendes mentioned in some detail – that he knew you in Hong Kong, sir."

"What are you on about?"

"A reception? Given by Chinese shippers?"

"What?"

Alex borrowed a leaf out of the doctor's book. He was rehearsed. "A banquet, sir. Tables glittering with cut glass and polished silver. Red roses quivering in studied floral arrays that were eventually disarrayed, according to Maria Mendes. Dinner jackets on the men; the bejewelled ladies splendid in long frocks. He mentioned a forty piece orchestra."

"By God, Mendes imagination is as flamboyant as is his lifestyle. He was, as you are, deliberately going over the top, but that's to be expected. It was a restaurant dinner for men – and all men of character – except for Mendes." Frogmore examined his pipe before speaking to Morgan. "Chief, would you excuse us?"

When the chief mate had left the dayroom, the captain spoke again, "He was not discreet on other matters?"

"I'm afraid not, sir."

"How much not discreet?"

"I promise you that I will not repeat gossip, sir."

"Many men have skeletons in their closets. But as you are a man of integrity, purser, when you discover such a skeleton, then you will let it be." Frogmore was far more rattled than Alex had expected. His face was the most intense red. His hands shook perceptibly. He grasped his left elbow and groaned. "To whom of this have you spoken?"

"I said, sir, no one."

"Do I have your solemn promise that not a word will be mentioned to a soul?"

Alex thought that Frogmore's reaction was totally over the top, it was as if Mendes had told him he was a thief or a murderer. "I've said so."

"You and I have had our differences but I am happy to accept your word." He opened a small gauze pad. "Could you fix this about my elbow?" As Alex wound a bandage to hold the heat pad in place, Frogmore said, "Sometimes I want to shout out, the pain can be intense."

"There are codeine in the dispensary."

"That means the doctor."

"I've got duplicate keys."

Frogmore grimaced. "A splinter of steel during the War. I'm unsure how much steel is left in."

"The muscles in that arm are wasted."

"How observant of you to notice, purser."

Alex hurried below and brought back a small bottle of codeine.

"Give them here." The captain shook out two tablets and swallowed them with tea, then he discussed the works of Conrad at some length. Alex was impressed by his knowledge.

When rising for breakfast, Alex said, "Is it okay then, sir?"

"What? What?"

"Can the storekeeper use my office?"

"Oh, that. Yes, of course," he said, then he added mysteriously, "Sometimes it's a relief to get something off one's chest, however indirectly; even when such a revelation is forced upon one. And I admit that it came as a shock. But I trust your discretion, but I warn you that you will gain no quarter from your knowledge."

Alex understood clearly that there was a dark secret in the captain's past and it had nothing to do with Frogmore being ill at a meal given by Chinese shippers.

THIRTEEN

AT SEA TO PANAMA

AS THE *JOHN BEDE* altered course leaving the harbour, a shaft of late afternoon sun streaming through the open office doorway, shifted.

Dr Trimmer, perched on the long, fitted desk lit one of Alex's cigarettes.

"Sparks tells me that I was invited to this Mendes' shindig?"

"Not your cup of tea."

"Frogmore sidelined me. He cannot be allowed to get away with this abuse of power."

Alex pointed out the doorway. "Look at the tropical vegetation, at the scenic port and the architecture of the old town. See how picture postcard it is. But when you get ashore and regard the exquisite buildings, with their iron balconies, and you visit the grand Catholic churches, you note the rust and decay."

"I shall report Frogmore."

"He's convinced that you shat on his desk."

"Persecution complex. Quite common in cases of deluded grandeur. Brilliant move – you planting those turds."

Sober, Alex thought the act embarrassingly childish.

"Terribly telling with its penile and anal symbolism."

"Morgan fed the rumour that it was you – what with you being naked at night."

"Thank you so much, you've given me an idea for a topic of conversation at dinner."

Alex shifted his legs out of the warm shaft of sunlight which had steadied now the ship had set course for Panama.

"My reason for being on board is to advise on modernisation. Modernisation means getting rid of men such as Frogmore."

"Will you succeed? He has friends in high places."

"You planting the sausages can be seen as an opening

shot in the war of attrition. We must be relentless. Is that slice of toast going spare?" When Doc spoke again his mouth was full. "I shall get rid of him – of that have no doubt."

"GLAD TO SEE the back of South America," said the captain at dinner. "Last time I was there a third mate, taking his vessel's departure draught, was shot in the head."

Dr Trimmer laughed.

"Surely, you can't find that funny?"

"I thought you were joking." Doc's long hair had been combed and his clothes were unusually neat. Tonight he would not discuss Radclyffe Hall – a confused chief engineer had asked if Radclyffe Hall belonged to the National Trust – and Freud was to be shelved, but only temporarily. Freud was so much in vogue that Alex saw symbolism everywhere. The meal table was littered with phalluses: the salt and pepper pots, and Alex had given up cornflakes since his using the sugar shaker to sweeten his cereal was now deemed masturbatory.

Removing a pineapple slice from his gammon steak, Dr Trimmer said, "I shall stop walking about the ship naked."

The captain stared at him.

"I do hope I'm not being greedy." The doctor's plate was so heaped that a potato was about to roll on the cloth. "My coarse Australian way." Doc's voice thickened as he crammed gammon steak into his mouth. "I was once a vegetarian. I'm still a naturist." He said to the captain, "When the children were small we bathed together."

Frogmore made no comment.

"We rented an apartment in the South of France – part of a nudist enclave. There was a supermarket where the checkout girl served one at eye-to-crotch level. I thought the naturism rather overdone. One night we drank gin and tonics at a cocktail party – all naked. It was a chilly evening. The studied naturalness of the naturists seemed unnatural and all of us would have looked better clothed." Dr Trimmer leant across the battlefield of crumbs and stains that marked his place setting. "I expect you agree with Michelangelo that the reproductive organs are ugly?"

Frogmore remained silent.

"I'm for freedom of choice. There is no reason why stewards can't serve meals without clothes in this hot weather."

Francis caught Alex's attention and mouthed what Alex could have sworn was 'Fuck off'.

"Something to put in your report, no doubt," said the captain.

Excluding Joaquim Lobo, the second cook, and Cadet Jones, who were both on a pedestal, whether clothed or unclothed, Alex thought that no one in the sixty-odd ship's company could get away with being naked. Francis was far too skinny, Larry used to have it but had lost a great deal of it, and Brewer, although young, had little going for him.

The doctor continued unabashed, "We all feel liberated when unclothed. It would certainly make the queers amongst us stand up, would it not, Alex?"

Alex looked over the chrysanthemums – lasting brilliantly – to see Frogmore contemplatively putting a grape in his mouth and openly studying the doctor. Perhaps he was visualising the doctor naked, defecating on his desk.

Dr Trimmer went far too far, as he always did. He called on Freud. "I have a deep interest in problems of a sexual nature." He leered at Frogmore. "We all know about Napoleon."

The captain cast his eyes down and concentrated on his meal.

"Oedipus. Excessive patriotism. And all which that entails," said Doc darkly.

The captain glanced up and glared; a glare which said, 'Shut up.' The two men peered over their half-glasses like duellists.

The doctor was unfazed. "Future generations will sweep aside such pettiness. Uniforms worn by certain classes in our class-structured society will go."

"What classes wear uniforms?" demanded Frogmore.

"Clerks in grey. The county set in checks and green wellingtons – that sort of thing. When in France a Dutch couple invited us to dinner. My wife was nude, as were the hosts, of course. I wore a cocktail dress – the New Look – but no knickers, in deference to naturism."

The fourth engineer, Keith, overweight and not cuddly-overweight either, snorted with laughter. Alex thought that the snorted applause could be the straw that would break the camel's back. He was spot on.

"Now listen to this, Trimmer. I will not tolerate your asinine talk."

"Sir, my apologies if I have upset you."

"Upset me? You have already done that in spades."

"I have?"

"It was you," said Frogmore.

The doctor's face showed puzzlement.

"You shat on my desk. And, by God, sir, you will not get away with that."

ALEX would have liked to have the memory of Mendes fading nicely; hidden like the exquisite painting snug between snowy-white Bede Line blankets. A reminder, perhaps, to surface when the cold weather came.

But for Captain Frogmore the spectre of Mendes clung. He had been made vulnerable. Their re-meeting had affected him deeply.

The breakfast table, Alex considered, was the place for eating not talk.

Frogmore was not of the same mind. "Of course, he's religious."

"Who, sir?" said Alex politely, glancing about the dining saloon, almost empty – a drama in the engine room had claimed all the engineers. The only officers breakfasting were Cadet Jones and Brewer, the third mate.

"Your chum, purser."

Alex instinctively knew who he was on about. The Hong Kong banquet and the unexplained happening, which Frogmore had alluded to, had certainly hit home. "Is believing in God a bad thing?"

"You attend church?"

"Only against my will. The frenzy of crossing oneself gets up my nose."

"Can I ask if you were Catholic?"

"Lapsed, lapsed and lapsed. My mother deserted Catholicism when she heard that the retired admiral and Lady something-or-other in the village were amongst the congregation of the Church of England."

Frogmore seldom laughed, but he did so and heartily. Both Brewer and David Jones regarded him with mild astonishment.

"Purser, it's naïve to consider that all the congregation believe in God when many clerics do not. For the top church jobs, only administrative skills are required. Many church high-ups are like our world leaders: they have no morals and their sole objective is to stay in power. The Christian religions are all political. They take sides during wars. They are greedy too – they demand money for saying a few words at funerals and so on. The major religions have their own administrative bodies which rule and decree – but they are not democracies. They opt for the benign dictator who waves at crowds and tells people what to believe."

"Mendes did not strike me as a religious man," said Alex, who was drawn to Frogmore when in rebellious mood.

"He loves that ceremonial malarkey. Satisfies his longing to dress up. I had the misfortune to stay with him one dragged-out and, dare I say, fagged-out, weekend. If ten course dinners weren't enough, they were followed by tedious chit-chat over brandy, and the chit-chat went on into the early hours. And, as a final punishment, I was expected to attend church, as part of the social weekend. A fleet of limousines took us there and..." Frogmore broke off to chuckle "...there were outriders. Two men on motorcycles. American machines with too much horsepower and much too much chrome."

"A presidential cavalcade."

"What sticks in my memory was there was a mendicant on the steps of the church. A youth of some distinction and bearing, I might add; but humbled in poverty. Mendes gave him a hundred dollar bill. The boy fainted with shock." Frogmore watched Alex closely. "He had a servant drive the boy to his property where he was employed."

"And did Mendes leave a hundred dollars in the offertory box?"

"How well you cotton on, purser. How well you cotton on."

"You participated in the service?"

"Ritual has its place. Without the Lord and the royal family, we would be denied much excuse for dressing up. And that would be a pity for those who wear ermine and those of us who delight in waving our patriotic flags on sticks."

The idea of Captain Rupert de Vere Frogmore waving a union jack, bought from a street vendor, stretched Alex's imagination. He said, "Church wasn't on the menu at the shippers' do, that's for sure. He's, without doubt, utterly charming."

"But his charm is put on, you know. With me my charm comes naturally." He looked directly at Brewer on the deck officers' table. "Why are you smirking, third?"

Brewer wisely did not field a riposte.

Frogmore then ignored him and talked directly to Alex. "At least during the rigmarole of the church service, Mendes got on his knees in a gesture to acknowledge a higher Being."

Alex recalled that he too had sunk to his knees, with probably more enthusiasm, in that ill-lit alcove in the courtyard, and on offer then was something impressive and it had been washed and perfumed with the aphrodisiac of wealth, just in case a supplicant happened along, as it were.

Half-turning in his seat, Alex saw that Brewer, seated at the junior officers' table, was leaning back in his chair, openly listening to Frogmore, who said,

"Did I mention that Mendes sent one of his staff on board."

"Who?" Alex was much concerned, for Mendes did have a track record of spilling the beans.

"A man of little consequence. A driver? A messenger?"

"A dark-skinned man in a light blue uniform?"

"Dark indeed and he did wear some such garb in a gabardine material – American inspired, no doubt. Name tag on the pocket – that sort of thing: Have a nice day, Miguel – it could've read, but in his case, the wearer would not be caring about my day, nor anyone else's, come to that. He was a surly brute."

"And?" prompted Alex, with more than a passing interest. "What did he want?" He had an improbable vision of Rodrigo frantically ripping off his shirt. Alex's imagination had Frogmore naked, with his hands passionately smoothing the swathe of black hair on Rodrigo's memorable chest. A nautical finger was flicking a black nipple when

Frogmore said,

"He brought me flowers. An exchange of flowers in India can be the coming together of two souls, but I did not think that Mendes had that in mind. I gave them to my boy immediately. Flowers are not a gift one man gives to another man, me thinks."

And giving them to a male steward is all right, thought Alex, but said, "You'd been ill. Flowers are usual."

"Quite," said Frogmore, dismissing the idea. "You are in Mendes good books, purser, but I can tell you this: get on the wrong side of the man and he can be ruthless."

"I'm sure you're right there, sir," said Alex, but he was at that moment remembering Rodrigo's chest, and he was chastising himself for not understanding that it was an advertisement for the goods below. And below the large courgette was demanding urgent attention. And Alex was now kicking himself very hard, for not having attended to that. But on reflection, he did not understand how anyone so utterly desirable could be interested in the likes of him. Last night Alex had stimulated himself with the courgette in mind and the knowledge of the mulatto, not too far distant, in fact supine in the bottom drawer, resting on a soft white blanket. And, by God, that did the trick – very speedily indeed. The two images were linked to Maria Mendes, who he could never forget. But he was cruelly aware that, in a month or so, Rodrigo would not remember him at all, and perhaps all he would be for Mendes was a notch on his bedpost.

Had it been the aphrodisiac of Mendes' wealth, or a hunger for Alexio, that had made Rodrigo's cock gorge so eagerly?

"Purser!" said Frogmore, breaking into his reverie.

"Sir?"

"Are you with us? Your boy has asked you three times if you want tea or coffee."

As Alex turned to give Francis his order, he caught Cadet Jones smiling at him from the deck officers' table. Alex beamed back. Brewer caught Alex's eye and made kissing movements with pursed lips.

"Third, why are you doing that extraordinary thing with your mouth? It looks most unseemly," said Frogmore.

"Nerves, sir. A twitch, sir," said Brewer.

"In that case you'd best lie down in a darkened cabin. I would not advocate seeing the doctor, for seemingly he is unwell. It is unlike that trencherman to miss a meal. I do hope that his indisposition is not serious, for his presence is greatly missed. A prolonged illness one wonders? Third, after breakfast, could you pop in and see him and check on his health and let me know? One could hardly bare the rest of the voyage to *Aus*tralia worrying – if the doctor is to be confined to his bed."

All in the saloon, other than the captain, openly smiled. Alex dismissed visions of dark South American men, far too young, and returned to comfort: the comfort of the familiar world.

"Sir, you get the revised E.T.A. all right?" asked Brewer.

"Why didn't the second mate do it?"

"He did. I brought it down to your dayroom so you could revise your arrival cable soonest."

"I do wish you'd stop trying to impress me, third, for you fail quite miserably."

Brewer winked openly at Alex; that wink was telling Alex that Brewer knew darned well that he had impressed Frogmore. Frogmore noticed it too, but made no comment until he was on his way out, then he paused to speak to Brewer, "I expect that the extra money will come in handy, when you're promoted to second mate."

"I'm not due for promotion, sir."

"Do you not want promotion? Do let me know if that is the case, then I will put something quite frightful on your confidential report."

All, including Cadet Jones, laughed and Alex felt a liking for Frogmore, but that was not to last.

FOURTEEN

PANAMA

THE SHIPS ARRIVAL AT PANAMA was joyless. The cadet had hoisted the Panamanian flag unaware that the Canal Zone was United States territory.

"Take that thing down," the American pilot said.

Captain Frogmore turned to David Jones. "You are reliable. You prove your ineptitude every day. One would ask you to buck up, but are you worth that effort, one wonders."

Cadet David Jones looked miserably at Alex who was in the chartroom gathering information from the Rough Bridge Log Book for arrival forms. When the cadet was out of earshot, looking in the locker where the various country's ensigns were stored, the mate said to Alex. "I told that bloody bastard of a captain we'd hoisted the wrong flag and he said, 'Good. It'll get up our American cousins' noses'. He wouldn't allow the cadet to change it."

"Have it out with him, Morgan. Stand up for the cadet."

"Can't, can I. He's got me over a bloody barrel."

Alex had to get off the ship, to get away from its claustrophobia and the captain's varying moods.

OUTSIDE THE BAR were ornate wrought iron columns that held up a balcony which shaded wrought iron tables, and wrought iron chairs on which sat business folk and shoppers. Alex left the steamy warmth of the outdoors and pushed his way through swing doors into a familiar bar. It was air-conditioned and the artificial light made the bar seem strangely night in contrast to the harsh daylight.

His heart wasn't in the postcard he was writing. He shredded it and started a fresh card.

"Who's the lucky girl?" asked the woman behind the bar, sweeping the torn pieces of card into an ashtray.

"A man who wears a wide-brimmed hat, knocks back raw spirit in one throw, and whose even teeth grip a perpetual cheroot."

"That's your third. Where's mine?" she said, pointing to his beer.

"Get yourself one. I'll have a vodka and orange."

"That's a woman's drink."

"Make it a double. I'm into sex orientation therapy." He watched her fix the drink then took the long glass and drank it straight down.

"Another?"

"Sure. Hold the ice and ease back on the orange but I want a fresh swizzle stick and three cherries. Your face is very familiar."

"I was sucking your cock last November."

"Is there a shop here that sells potatoes?"

"Potatoes?"

"King Edward's would be a plus," said Alex.

"Give me five dollars."

"For three drinks?" He put a five dollar bill on the counter.

The woman pushed the note between her breasts and whispered confidentially, "You can make money with that man."

Alex glanced in the mirror behind the bar and saw the reflection of a middle-aged, podgy man nursing a beer.

"If you go to the bathroom and wait, he'll follow," she said, her face close to his.

"Is the lavatory wrought iron?"

"Stay in there long enough and he will display himself."

"Explain."

She shrugged. "He has only a little thing. You'd call the shots. Suck him – twenty dollars. That's a lot, a lot of money."

"I don't need the cash."

"You need the sex – it's not the wrought iron that pulls you out back."

Alex placed two more dollars to cover his drinks on the bar counter and stood. "I'll give Biggles a miss."

"Biggles?"

"The little prick." Looking at his reflection in the mirror, he said, "Even in a bad light I ain't got much to offer. Am I worth twenty dollars, you reckon?"

The woman studied him. "Maybe he's into tat."

"These are my best jeans."

"Settle for ten. I'll be your pimp. I charge fifty percent up front." As Alex turned to leave, she said, "Where you go to, Joe?"

"To sit in a bar where the tin tables are buckled and the chairs are rickety and there the flies are thick and stick on a hanging yellow tape where they slowly die. A sour smell comes from the lavatory and the bartender has a killer-glance."

"Give me twenty bucks."

"Don't think that you can demand money from me, you bolshie woman. I'm a customer not a rent boy."

"Boy? Go check the mirror. I'll put on the cleaning lights and lend you my makeup."

"You're worth twenty." He gave her two dollars.

"See you next time your ship is in port, sailor." She smiled farewell as he pushed his way through the swing doors to leave the artificial cool of the bar. Outside he skirted the wrought iron chairs and the wrought iron tables. From the street came the smell of melting macadam and petrol fumes.

He strolled to the agents to pick up the Panama Canal Certificate and the Ship's Register, then he hailed a taxi to take him back on board.

HEADING FOR THE CAPTAIN'S QUARTERS, he lingered in the cross-alleyway listening to Spark's music which was abruptly silenced.

Alex heard the captain's voice coming from Spark's cabin. "I will not have that racket inches from my ear."

"You want I shouldn't play my music, sir?" Sparks voice.

No reply.

Alex knew that Frogmore's inches were several yards and his ears were protected to a great extent by a thick steel bulkhead, but it was fact that Spark's speakers were laced with tweeters and woofers.

"What do you want, purser?" said Frogmore, coming out into the alleyway to find him smirking.

"To report that the ship's papers and crew are on board."

"Have you returned to the *John B* the only seaman sober?"

"As always, sir."

"Have you not been wallowing in the groggeries of the

port?"

Frogmore's manner made most officers uncomfortable. But Alex had become fascinated by a man so unusual, a man, who outwardly, was incapable of passion – other than dull anger. Yet his reference to the *John B* had to be from the song and the captain was assuming that Alex knew it.

Sparks hung in the doorway of his cabin.

"Would you not agree, purser, that the radio operator – whose tattooed body offends all good taste – affronts with that noise?"

"I'm not into Hendrix, but fair dos, taste is the age gap."

"I do not expect the young to listen to Bach but I'm a fair man." He turned to Sparks. "You may play your music." The captain rounded on Alex. "Where's your cap?"

"I'm excused cap, if you recall."

"That's as maybe, but you are required to carry it under your left arm when reporting to the command."

"Could I mention Cadet Jones?"

"Why?"

"First trip away from home – and that. He studies evenings. He's not some layabout sporting earrings and getting drunk."

"What's brought this on?"

"He should be treated as a human being, not bullied."

"By God, purser, I have never heard the like. You're ticking me off."

Sparks was wide-eyed; his mouth hung open, showing an absence of teeth that made Alex smile.

"Are you finding this an entertainment, purser?"

"I'm like the Chinese, sir, I smile when I'm nervous."

"You're glib-tongued and exceed your brief."

Sparks tried to cut and run, edging his way to freedom between the back of his captain and the white painted bulkhead.

The captain shouted at him, "Stay where you are!"

It was as though Frogmore had looked in the mirror and seen himself, or rather, had heard himself. He stepped to the side and waved the radio operator through.

"I'll have the cadet round this evening for a coffee, sir?" said Alex.

Frogmore stared at him but said nothing.

"Is that all right, sir?"
"Why should it not be all right. I have no objection to him socialising. He is an apprentice training to be an officer. Sign for six beers – put them on my account."

"GOD TREATED YOU TO BEERS. We're transiting the Panama Canal – one of the world's greatest engineering achievements – I'm to tell you." Alex opened the office outside door and they watched a crocodile slither from the bank into the water. "Over five thousand people died building it."
The three large beers apiece did not lead to Alex's usual whiskies in generous measures. Instead, Dave made coffee in the pantry. He detoured to his cabin on his way back to collect a pack of photographs: photographs of rocky foreshores, barges and silhouetted dock cranes. The notable one was of an old man wearing a jacket suitable for the ragbag.
"His expression – so well caught," said Alex. The man's face was sagging, as though he were wasting away. It was the look in his eyes – a look of almost envy, of longing. "He wants your youth."
"He gave me a roll-up. He was on sailing barges. I went back to show it to him – never found him."
As Alex studied the other photographs, Dave said, "You get away with murder 'cos you're posh."
"What's brought this on, cadet?"
"Your dad is what?"
"Was. Something in the City."
"You don't want to talk about him?"
"Towards the end, he couldn't go out – not unless my mother drove him, and then he had to be steadied by whisky. My mother is the mistress of the dignified silence. Her stiff upper lip comes reinforced. She's perpetually ferrying meals on wheels, or picking up the elderly then rushing back to cook something 'decent' for me. Grilling the special steak because I'm home. I'd rather make do with beans on toast in front of the fire and a natter. She never understood Dad's weaknesses. His trouble she swept under the carpet. My liking for men was brushed there too. Alcoholism happened in other families and homosexuality

was a no-no. I talk too much."

Dave Jones nodded, urging him to continue.

"There was a church worker, a Mr Smith, who never smoked nor did he visit the pub nor did he follow sport *like other men*." Alex inhaled deeply then stubbed out his cigarette.

"You should talk about it."

"I'm thirty-five."

"So?"

"Your mother kisses you, you said."

"Sure."

"Embracing is reserved for the cinema screen. Mother hugs the dogs, she doesn't care for the dogs, she loves them. She cares for the family and is obligated to look after them."

"Your ma would be strong like you."

"It got so my dad relied on her more and more. Dad could understand how I was flawed, because he was damaged goods. My mother wears those waxed hats with a brim – the kind the royal family sport when they massacre defenceless birds for fun. But she would never shoot anything – perhaps an intruder who broke into her house to damage her family, who are already irreparably damaged."

Dave flicked a cigarette. Alex caught it and over the hiss of a lighter, the cadet said, "Mum don't know who my dad was." He inhaled, holding the smoke in his lungs.

"He was a handsome brute."

"You queer, Alex?"

"You straight, Dave?"

"I thought so but when my hand rubs my dick, it's you I think about." The cadet, now relaxed, closed his eyes and leant back on the daybed. Alex carefully replaced the photographs in their brown envelope.

Before turning in, he left the desk light burning so he could keep an eye on the youth who stirred.

"You okay?" said Alex.

"You want me to go?"

Alex propped himself up in his bunk. "Mr Smith."

"The man in your ma's church."

"...got caught with a choirboy. In the woods – real Sunday newspaper stuff. Four years, he got. Arthur at the pub said the boy was up for it."

"You iron tank?"

"I'm a stiff hanky man."

"That's something we can do for each other," said Dave.

"My mother said in her letter that she had to wash both the dogs after they rolled in something."

"You want I should piss off?"

"Francis'll wake you at six." Alex moved to his desk where he sloshed sherry into a beer mug. "Want one?"

"Why don't we do it, Alex?"

"I like black men."

"Question: Do you fancy me?"

"I plead the Fifth." Alex climbed into his bed, putting the bunk light on. He positioned the sherry bottle and glass on the ledge where Francis rested his morning tea-tray.

"Can I ask you a question?" said Dave.

"What?"

"I'm scared to ask," said Dave.

"Ask it."

"Does your mother have a shooting stick?"

"She does take the weight off her plates of meat when she exercises the dogs. Mater uses her shooting stick to rest her arse when shopping in Boots."

"We're okay together, Alex."

"Shut up, I'm drinking."

"Do you have a lilac smoking jacket?"

Through the mists of alcohol and in the poor light, he could make out the tears of laughter on the cadet's cheeks. Some tears stayed and clustered on the ridge of his scar.

Dave's subsiding giggles turned to soft snores. His tear-streaked face looked content. Alex topped up his glass for the third time and watched the younger man. He envied his naturalness, the way he recognised that Alex liked him. He sipped his sherry which was strong enough to relax him, but not strong enough to make him so drunk he'd do something stupid.

As he was dropping off, he leant over the bunk-board and carefully positioned his glass, with about an inch of sherry left in it, on the broad ledge.

Dave was awake and moving towards the door. His hand went up to draw back the door curtain.

"Where you off to, Shitface?"

"Piss."

"Use the sink."

Large, but never lumbering, and wearing only tight underpants, Dave crossed to the sink and hung out.

Over the sound of water running from the tap, Dave Jones said, "What's sherry like?" He let go the tap, stopping the flow of freshwater, and took the glass from the ledge and downed the warm sherry. Afterwards he sat cross-legged on the daybed. "Mum's letter said I should come ashore and see about getting a job in a building society."

"Try art school. I did."

"Alex..."

"We talk some more in the morning."

FIFTEEN

THE PACIFIC

Next stop – New Zealand.

The Pacific should have been bright and sunny but it was sullen and overcast.

At breakfast there was ice in the butter dishes, and large brown bottles containing salt tablets stood on each of the tables in the dining saloon. Alex wondered whether Frogmore would remark on him missing the *Tatler* caffeine session – but the captain's mind was on other things.

"You won't have heard about Guthrie, chief?"

"Doc Guthrie, you mean? Not for years."

"Dead." Frogmore added with mild satisfaction, "Several years younger than I."

"How'd you hear?"

"A Marconigram from Devaney-Smythe in personnel."

"Heart? Guthrie carried way too much weight."

"He died with his boots on."

"Sorry?" said the chief, puzzled why Frogmore was beating about the bush.

"He was attacked by lion."

"A lion?"

"Guthrie was walking back to the ship from a club in East Africa. By all accounts the club had gone to pot – run by an *Aust*ralian."

The captain seemed oblivious that the silence in the dining saloon wobbled, was about to explode into laughter.

"Whereabouts in East Africa?" said the chief.

"Laku – one of those little used ports built for the Groundnut Scheme."

"Guthrie on safari? Hunting animals? I can't see that happening," said the chief.

"I said he was at the club. Mauled on the road returning to his ship. One cannot blame the lion." He examined his bowl of cornflakes for weevils. "Fine chap – one of the few good doctors at sea." Before Dr Trimmer could field a riposte, the captain said, "Poor Guthrie – a loss. For a few weeks he was my ship's surgeon in the *Resourceful Bede*."

The chief said, "You sailed with British crew? That's a turn up for the books."

"I've sailed with Chinese, Malays, Indian, Pakistani, Philippino and African crews. But British crew only the once. I informed head office that it was to be Indian crew for me if possible. They demonstrate order."

"Why not British crew?" asked Dr Trimmer, who was wearing a battered and faded, black baseball cap.

"Multitudinous reasons."

"Sex?" said the doctor, pushing his luck.

Frogmore fixed him with his eyeglass, as if aware of his attempt to ridicule him. "For a change, you have hit it on the button. I have some understanding of carnality, but self-control must be exercised, must it not, purser?"

"I couldn't agree more," said Alex.

Dr Trimmer said, "You're a patriot. How can you object to British crew? And what has sex got to do with it?" He absently shook sugar onto his grapefruit. The fallout reached Alex's knee.

"You brought sex into it. I was only confirming your assumption."

"Please tell?"

"One of those boring yarns you so much despise from us old seadogs, I'm afraid."

"I'm all ears."

"My ship was crossing the North Atlantic and dashed cold it was too. I was on my bridge when I observed in number one lifeboat a British rating rattling on top of a passenger. In clear view of the three deck officers taking the noon position. They concentrated not on their midday sights, but on the sexual activity in lifeboat number one. They were hysterical with laughter. And who can blame them. The act itself is ridiculous. The act in public can only be erotic or disgusting or hilarious. That is what one has to put up with with British crew. Indian crew don't do it, you see." He drew in breath sharply in recollection. "By golly, that female passenger was not in her prime."

"Old?" asked the chief.

"My second mate described her as 'yesterday's meat'."

The captain poured diluted tinned milk on his cornflakes.
"The rating?"
"Wore an earring in the left ear."
"Did you have him sacked?" asked the doctor.
"Goodness no. The earring, you see."
"Because he was a seaman who had rounded the Horn?" said Alex.
"Quite so. I logged him two days' pay and put his lapse down to sexual heat – or perhaps she paid him, for he did cut something of a manly figure – Horn or no Horn."
Alex chuckled and looked away but his eye caught Dr Trimmer's baseball cap which he also found funny.
The captain said, "It was a round the world cruise. Not places I care for: New York, Florida, the Caribbean then, as if that wasn't enough..." He paused deliberately, as if waiting for the doctor to speak.
Doc said, "Australia?"
"Got it in one."
"You must've gone down a wow on passenger ships," remarked Doc, scanning the sideboard for the blackberry jam.
Frogmore gave him a sideways glance. "Your headgear does not go down a wow in my ship. The Bede Line handbook dictates that headgear at table is only to be worn by Sikhs or those of the Jewish faith. As you are neither, I suggest that you follow the company's guidelines."

"WHERE THE HELL ARE WE GOING?" said Rusty, bumping into Alex's back and pushing him against the iron bulkhead in the port side alleyway.
"Keep it down."
"Who is going to hear us at two in the morning?"
In the foyer, outside the dining saloon, Felicity the cat brushed against Alex's bare legs as she ran on ahead. His torch lit her eyes at the foot of the steps that led down to the stores-flat.
"Ernest saw the ghost there," said Rusty, annoyed at being parted from his after watch beers. "He refuses to check the freezer temperatures."
"Ernest is the reason why we condemned the odd ton or two of fruit last voyage and the reason why Rodney got in

the shit. I think I was in the shit too, but as I am so often in it, it is hard to recall if I was."

Alex's powerful torch lit broad iron steps that led down to the saloon storerooms. "The ghost is the *topass* who broke his neck when he plunged to his death two and a half years ago."

At the bottom of the steps, near the waterline, was the stores-flat. Steel doors guarded the beer locker and the dry storeroom and the bonded store which housed the ship's spirits and cigarettes. To their left was a door with a spin-to-open wheel – like a bank vault – which led to the domestic freezer chambers. Further along the alleyway was an insulated door to the engine room which Alex heaved open. There was the immediate noise of the huge pistons, a blast of heat and a smell of oil. He let the door close automatically.

"What you after?"

"The AC converter for the air-conditioning units in the old man's and chief's cabins."

Rusty took the torch and shone it on a small motor high on a shelf in the alleyway.

Alex stood on a crate of engine spares and reaching up, pulled a long lever to OFF. The whirring of the converter stopped. The dying motor disturbed Felicity. She brushed against Rusty's bare legs.

Rusty shrieked. He dropped the torch as he tripped over the crate of spares and fell face down on the deck. Felicity, with a cat's curiosity, returned to swish her tail against his arm.

Rusty doubled up the steel companionway. When at the top, he called down. "Alex?"

There was a long silence. Alex, faking hysteria, shouted, "Please, please help!" But Rusty, wisely, Alex thought, stayed at the top of the steps to grab his shoulders when he finally made it to the safety of the officers' accommodation.

Alex had not finished his nocturnal tasks. He led Rusty to the chief engineer's suite on the starboard side of the dining saloon. As they entered the bedroom the chief stirred but Haigs held him under. Alex opened all three windows and humid salt air blew in.

The cat was on his daybed when they returned to his

cabin.

"As a Socialist I've never approved of air-conditioning for the *burra sahibs* while we sweat," said Alex.

"You're a Socialist now?"

"Of course, I'm a working man."

"Queer and a Socialist. Both are recent conversions?"

"I have emerged from my closet bedecked in red flags and waving my tool and sickle."

"The chief knew you were going to switch the converter off, didn't he?"

"I've underestimated you, Rusty."

"What're you up to?"

"I thought you liked japes."

"Japes?"

"At that constipated engineering college you attended, they taught you – *sweet Jesus, hear us, for those in peril on the sea* – to be a leader of men. Well, to be a leader, one must play sport and partake in japes."

"What?" Rusty stuck his greedy mouth to an opened beer can.

"A midnight feast in the dorm – that's a jape."

"You are so full of it. First off, you say you turned off the air-conditioning because you're a queer Socialist and now it's a jape. How about you planting Felicity's shit in the old man's cabin. Jape?"

Alex was silent.

Felicity stopped grooming her tail, her eyes widened. She miaowed.

"The spirit world is trying to get in touch with us through the cat," said Alex."

Rusty eyed Felicity suspiciously then sucked hard at his can like a child sucking greedily at its mother's nipple.

SIXTEEN

THE PACIFIC

THE CAPTAIN'S dayroom was sticky, damp and reeked of stale tobacco. As the restarted air-conditioning unit laboured to cool it, coffee was served on deck. The air was sapping and the ocean flat; flaccid seaweed hung below the water's surface.

"I telephoned the O.O.W. in the engine room..." said Frogmore. The officer on watch was Ernest. "...who refused to attend to the converter because..." here the captain guffawed "...a ghost haunts the stores-flat."

The plastic table wobbled as Alex leant on it dreaming of the Lovelace days.

"I then telephoned the chief engineer."

"At four in the morning?" said Morgan.

"The chief said that the unit does turn itself off."

"It will if the DC input surges," said Morgan.

"It was turned off deliberately. And I know who."

Alex looked up questioningly.

"The doctor."

"Does the doctor know where the converter is? Does he know that the converter converts DC to AC and that it runs your air-conditioning unit?" said Alex.

Frogmore spoke down to him, as he spoke down to everyone, including the shipping company's directors. "Do you happen to be the doctor's crony, purser?"

"No."

"But you play his brief. Get him now."

"I'm not going to be bullied by you, sir."

A gathering of perspiration on Morgan's forehead pooled and ran down his nose. It dropped onto his shorts. He mopped his face with a Bombay sweat-towel. "Alex, ask Gomes to give the doctor the captain's *salaams*, please?"

Anything for a quiet life, thought Alex, as he sought out the captain's steward.

When he returned and sat down, the captain said, "Purser,

I would mention for your own good, that your attitude does not go unnoticed."

Alex did not have a chance to reply for Dr Trimmer arrived. On his feet were overlarge sandals, worn without socks; his shirt was a drab green colour and made out of an unsuitable synthetic material which was stained black with perspiration under the arms.

"I hear your cooling system has broken down. What a shame," Doc said, making a note in a shorthand pad.

Gomes was hovering in the background and he and Alex shared a look when Dr Trimmer settled in a chair.

"*Char, doctor sahib?*" said Gomes, seizing the moment.

The doctor, who had been summoned for a ticking off, was being served tea.

"It would appear, Doctor, that you consider yourself in Bohemia."

"Bohemia?"

"Your hair."

"Ah."

"It is a question of order."

"I'm almost fifty."

"It is my misfortune that you came to sea at any age and it is the Bede Line's misfortune to have you advising them."

"I see."

"If it comes down to the nitty-gritty, you are signed on this vessel's articles of agreement with the ship's master."

"As a passenger."

"You are a member of my ship's company – two years foreign-going sea service."

"I don't dig that."

"You are digging your own grave. I recommend that you steer a careful course." He added darkly, "I have the power of the law behind me." Frogmore turned to Alex. "Correct?"

"Guess so."

"You guess, purser?"

"To be fair a supernumerary is a signed-on passenger."

"Signed-on. Read the conditions of service. *No whistling on the poop deck. Attend divine service when required.*"

"Anachronistic."

"It is your legal contract with me. The ship's articles state that you be neatly attired in the company's uniform."

"I see."

"Your hair – I can fine you two days' pay."

This was absurd for a supernumerary was signed-on at a notional sixpence a month. It was not for the first time that Alex wondered if the captain confronted the doctor for mental stimulation. He could see no other purpose. A smart telling off in private – followed by a cable to London office would have sorted Trimmer out fast. Frogmore had that pull.

The doctor stood. "Your cholera injection. I'll pop up?"

Frogmore ignored him.

When the doctor was out of earshot, Frogmore said, "Did you know that the redoubtable Conrad was given a *Declined to Report* during his sea service. An endorsement that nowadays would finish any officer." He watched Trimmer lazily stroll the deck then he made a lengthy note and turned the pad upside down so Alex could not read it.

ALEX loved the dining saloon which was not the usual run of the mill British cargo ship design. The designer had a thing about the twenties. Chrome handles decorated the built-in walnut sideboard beneath an oblong clock. Nowadays the splendid walnut tables were shrouded in felt and Irish linen, which was just as well taking into account the doctor's eating habits. Alex had complimented the décor by obtaining four large potted palms from a grateful ship's chandler in a foreign port. The frosted glass wall lamps and the polished art deco linoleum in yellow and brown made the gilt-framed portrait of Her Majesty seem out of place.

Francis, a Goanese steward not a flapper – to the regret of only some of the ship's officers – held Scott Fitzgerald in some regard. He and Alex had had many a sharp exchange about beaded purses and cloche hats and, in heated moments, *The Black Bottom*. But despite the high jinks of the twenties, the dining saloon had never witnessed the like of Dr Trimmer.

The pale wood jalousie blinds were lowered and two large standing fans turned at slow speed.

The captain studied the menu then turned to Gomes. "Kedgeree, boy."

There was grease paint in the air when Dr Trimmer said, "Kedgeree on the sideboard, peacocks on the lawn, will there be crumpets for tea?"

The chief engineer interrupted diplomatically, "Did you hear about the match, Rupert?"

"Abandoned because of hooligans."

"Sport is war without weapons," said Alex, his hangover making the conversation surreal.

"Rubbish," said Frogmore.

"The purser is quoting Orwell," said Dr Trimmer.

"Orwell was a Communist." A blue-veined hand shot out, seized the pot of chrysanthemums and repositioned the plant, putting Alex in the wings and leaving the doctor centre stage. "Orwell fought in Spain for the Communists."

"*Animal Farm? Nineteen Eighty Four?* George Orwell loathed the Communists, my dear Captain."

"Do not address me as 'my dear Captain'."

Remembering the missiles of decaying fruit hurled at the natives in Qabahbah, Alex said, "Sport is an unfailing source of ill will. It is the strong in continuous triumph over the weak."

Frogmore stood and peered at him. "You certainly didn't get that cut on your forehead playing soccer, did you?"

"No, sir. I slipped whilst doing *The Black Bottom*."

A sensation of mirth started at the engineers' table behind Alex. It travelled, as if in stereo, to the junior mates' table where Sparks and Cadet Jones were eating. It bubbled over to the top table. It hit the chief engineer whose good-natured smile became a steady grin. Even Morgan managed a sixty-a-day splutter. The master mariner was silent but smiling, seated in his carver chair beneath the portrait of H.R.H. It was a comment on his authority that when he chuckled, only then did Rodney break up completely.

THE WEATHER FRESHENED as the ship caught the trades. Most afternoons Alex sunbathed aft of the old-fashioned tall smoke stack on the sundeck.

The second engineer's sweat-soaked boiler suit clung to his once fine physique; his body was now heading to flab; his good blond hair had been hacked by the *cassab* and it showed some grey. He appeared to be nearing forty but was twenty-nine. He stood with his back to fast white clouds and an emerald sea.

"I've gotta check this out with you."

"You look very much the Western movie star, Larry, to my hero worshipping eyes."

Used to Alex's nonsense, he said, "I'm cleaning out the ventilation system's ducting on the captain's deck." The second engineer squatted Indian fashion. "What's in that package that Francis gave me?"

"Offal and rotting fish."

"And you want me to place it in the blower system in the captain's bathroom?"

"Is that a problem?" Alex shaded his eyes.

"You don't mind me bringing it up?" Larry appeared laid-back but was, in fact, a keen engineer and he could not help but observe the trail of black smoke from the funnel, which should have been a clear vapour that distorted the blue sky. He said, "Rodney'll be doing his nails."

"Another favour?"

"I'm preparing to jump over the side."

"Can you sit in your wardrobe at eleven o'clock tomorrow morning for rounds?"

"I'm glad you didn't get Francis to pass that on," said Larry. "Rig of the day?"

"Do you have a Stetson?"

"Are you out of your mind?"

Alex sighed. "Naked? It's very much in vogue."

"Rodney, what are you up to?" said Larry, horrified as clouds of black smoke poured out the funnel.

As he headed for the bridge to use their phone to contact the engine room, Alex said, "You used to be co-operative."

"Six crates of beer might do it."

"Dream on," said Alex.

THE STENCH OF ROTTING FISH filled the dayroom. Morgan was taking out the Gestapo filing drawers in the large desk. Frogmore was on his hands and knees, smelling the carpet near the outer door.

"Something sure stinks in here," said Alex, as he bounced in. "You want I sniff out the bathroom?"

"You stay put, purser." Frogmore hugged the skirting then ran a slow, low exploratory nose over the walnut veneered drinks cabinet. His nose reached the ventilation grill. "By Jove, it's strong here."

Dr Trimmer burst into the dayroom holding a kidney-shaped enamel bowl in which lay a hypodermic syringe. He winked at Alex as the syringe entered the captain's upper arm. The syringe emptied, the arm was wiped with cotton wool. Doc left.

Frogmore sat at his desk.

"Well, that's your cholera over and done with," said Morgan.

"If it was cholera."

"Sorry?"

"Could be anything. The man's an expert in subterfuge." Frogmore rubbed his upper arm and glanced about. "He spent twenty minutes in here yesterday advocating breathing exercises. Suggested – as if I were a fakir – the seated position to restrict the blood supply to the genitals to suppress sexual urges. Can that remark be made by a sane man?" He said sharply to Alex, "The smell's gone."

"It ain't."

"Do you smell it, chief?"

"I'll have chippy check your drains."

Frogmore grasped his stomach. "Blasted ulcer."

"You sure it's not the injection, sir?"

"He's not man enough, purser. Overt murder is not his style. Mark my words, he's the coward who stabs one in the back."

YESTERDAY WAS MIDSHIPS ROUNDS, which was on Saturday, so today was Sunday. But not so – for Frogmore had crossed the International Date Line – the ship had in fact crossed it on Thursday – but Frogmore leapt from Saturday to Monday, therefore Sunday was Monday and Frogmore could save head office paying the ship's company an extra days pay for a Sunday at Sea.

Alex ignored such paucity and credited all ship's company, except Frogmore, with an additional days pay, then he went to the smoke room to spend two hours drinking, instead of the weekly one hour, before the customary Sunday chicken curry lunch.

Condensation ran the outside of Rusty's glass of lager.

Alex broke his mood. "Everything all right, is it?"
"What are you on about?"
"You put five pounds on my wine account."
"What?"
"You signed for and drank six million beers and put them on my wine account."
"You can farm them off onto ship's account."
"That's known as theft, Rusty."
"I'll pay you cash."
"Oh, sure, like last time." Alex tapped his foot on the thick carpet. "Can I mention the lovely Eleanor?"
The third engineer shifted uncomfortably in his chair. "Sparks blabbed and that bastard's taken the Marconi-atic oath."
"I did happen to be casually chatting with Sparks – *Tatler-wise* – over a glass of *lime pani* this morning – and, in passing, he did mention that Shrew Eleanor phoned you from Sydney, darling. Darling? How suburban. Sparks said he had a tattooed hard-on listening to you. We both did wonder how anyone so stunted and hirsute could pull a bird like Shrew."
"Do not call her Shrew."
"Shrew! Shrew!" screeched Alex.
"She might fly from Sydney to New Zealand," said Rusty, turning brick red.
"By plane?"
"Do not go there." Rusty narrowed his golden eyes.
"Is the broomstick in for a service?"
"She likes you."
"Oh, fuck off."
"Fond of you."
"Fond of me, darling?"
"You've got this very irritating habit of repeating things."
"She despises everyone on board except darling Rodney, because Rodney's sensitive and cares deeply about the important things in life, like clothes and makeup." Alex pulled the Band-Aid off his forehead and examined the fading bruise in the mirror at the back of the bar shelves. "Ditch her. Seriously." But Alex knew that Rusty wouldn't ditch her. Rusty's perception was clouded. He was the celibate sailor contemplating the certainty of good old sex.

SEVENTEEN

NEW ZEALAND

NO STREAMERS, NO BUNTING, only one port health official and one customs officer.

And Eleanor, who waited on the dockside, as the *John Bede* went alongside.

"I would have thought that Rusty could have snatched a couple of minutes to meet me after the journey I've had," she said, marching into Alex's cabin interrupting him reading his mother's letter.

"Lovely to see you, Eleanor."

"Where is he?"

"Engine room. You must be exhausted. You want to rest in his cabin?"

"Am I in your way?"

With the stupidity of sarcasm, Alex said, "It's so wonderful to have female company for a change."

She eyed him for a full minute. "You should try a different hairdresser. Those highlights do not suit you."

"The *cassab* does my hair. His tools are hand clippers and a cut throat razor – which I might borrow." He had an improbable vision of the sixty-year-old *cassab* mincing about, doing his ends.

She examined the armchair before sitting. "Yesterday I saw Deborah."

"Debs okay? I'll ring her when we dock in Sydney."

"She's in Melbourne at the moment."

"Right."

"You still chain smoke."

"Down to a hundred a day."

"And you've put on weight."

"Same weight."

"I can't understand what Deborah sees in you. She's years younger and intelligent and pretty. Trouble is she's a sucker for lost causes." Eleanor tidied the already tidy tea-tray. "Glorious hair. With her money you'd think she'd go to a decent hairdresser."

"Was your flight draughty, Eleanor?"

"The woman in the window seat went to the lavatory ten times." Eleanor fanned the air with her magazine to remind Alex he was smoking.

Perhaps, he thought, it was the confidence of her looks that made her such a bitch. Larry said she must be ace in bed because out of it she was poison.

As if reading his thoughts, she said, "Is that second engineer on board?"

"Larry?"

"Slime that lives under a stone."

"Not Larry."

"He needs professional help."

"Why?"

"Japan for starters." Her grip tightened on her magazine and her full lips tightened too. "I practically stopped eating in the engineers' mess room because of him." She wasn't supposed to eat in the mess room. Larry usually ate there to avoid the dining saloon which meant changing into uniform. "He told me that all Western women are without sex appeal."

"That's..."

"...not normal." Eleanor pushed her magazine into her large leather bag. She pushed Felicity away who crept up to gain her warmth. "He never comes out of that weird cabin except at night. He's a slug."

"Larry's my friend."

"I wouldn't boast about it."

"He doesn't have a vanity thing about sunbathing."

"He blinks in sunlight and he goes on and on about Japan."

"Never." With anyone else Alex would have agreed that Larry had a Japan fetish.

"He's certainly not going to meet a decent girl if he repeatedly says how feminine Oriental women are." Eleanor pouted. Felicity had backed off and stood watching her. "He told me..." Eleanor hesitated for bitchy effect, "...that European women look like men. That's queer."

"I'm queer."

"Oh, do shut up, Alex."

"Have you seen my boa?"
"Larry was friends with that shuddery Pugsy who stank and masturbated continuously."
Pugsy had left the ship in London. Alex said, "We all iron tank."
"What?"
"Iron-tank – wank."
"Just *how* long have you been at sea?"
"About forty-five iron-tanks."
"You don't have to say that everyone wanks, like you don't have to say everyone shits."
"Got you there, Eleanor. This captain does neither."
They both laughed.
Eleanor again straightened the teaspoon in the saucer. "I hadn't intended to bring this up, because I know you two are close, but when I first met Larry... Well, Rusty was drinking in his cabin." She breathed in deeply, but her magnificent bosom did nothing for Alex. "Those brothel curtains tight shut and that decadent black ceiling... Everything but mirrors over the bed. And that garish lantern from a Chinese restaurant." Eleanor lifted her cup, it remained poised. "I'd been there minutes when there was a drama in the engine room. Larry sent Rusty to sort it out, of course." She sipped her tea, then took another sip to check out the taste of chlorine and tinned milk. The cup went firmly back in the saucer. "Larry sat with his boiler suit gaping so I could see his front." Eleanor was at her malicious best. "I made small talk and asked him if he was married. That disgusting slug with his front bare to the elastic of his underpants, and showing a great deal of pubic hair, said, 'I'm married to Hand'."
"You must've been outraged," said Alex.
No one seeing Eleanor with her bouncing hair, her stage makeup, her long nails, and clothes which hugged her eye-riveting figure, could believe her narrow minded. Alex thought her strident. He wanted to drape muslin over her, gag her, then stand her many yards downwind.
He lit a cigarette.
"You're chain smoking."
"You covered that in Tirade One."
"Rodney's the only sensitive human being on this boat."

"Ship. In this ship – not on this boat. I thought you spoke fair dinkum English, me old cock Antipodean sparrow."

"Rodney knows how to treat a woman."

Alex picked up his mother's letter, which was the usual two sheets of blue vellum. The vicar's new wife fitted in. He immediately saw her as a woman of thirty dressing like a woman of fifty. He said, "She'll wear stout walking shoes."

Eleanor glanced at him. He smiled at his letter which sent a signal to Eleanor, who appreciated the importance of mail to a seafarer.

Alex was unusually grateful to his mother until he read that Mr Smith, who had been incarcerated because of the choirboy in the woods, had died unexpectedly. His mother thought it was for the best. Prayers were said, of course. Mr Smith was given four lines while the retired admiral's fruit bushes warranted half a page.

"You crying? Bad news?" said Eleanor.

"Something in my eye."

"Alex, is there something I can do?"

The telephone buzzed.

"Hadn't you better answer it?" she said.

He put the letter down. "The captain. He'll want to see me. I'd much rather be here with you." He picked up the phone. After he replaced it, he said to Eleanor, "He uses the telephone as though it has just been invented."

"I heard. Poor you."

"If I'm not back in ten minutes come up and rescue me. Bring your right hook and have your tongue on standby."

ELEANOR had left by the time he returned.

Eager to get off the ship, he strolled ashore to post the ship's mail, relishing the warm New Zealand weather, feeling good until he returned on board to be met by the *seacunny,* on gangway duty, who told him he was wanted up top.

"Why was I not informed you were going ashore, purser?"

"I went ashore to post mail."

"Give the mail to the agent. That's what he's paid for," said the captain. "I understand from my first mate that an engineer has a female guest on board. Why wasn't I told?"

"Engineers' guests come under the chief engineer – you

know that."

Frogmore was taken back by the sharpness of the purser's tone. "It would have been courteous of you to inform me."

"You're telling me to be courteous?"

"What?"

"You're shouting again." Alex's was outwardly calm. "I'm going ashore tomorrow – all day. I've planned on Rotarua. If you don't want me to go, just say so but please don't shout at me when I get back. And you are still shouting at the sixteen-year-old cadet."

Frogmore slumped in his seat breathing through his mouth.

"By God, you do my digestion no good, purser. Get me the bicarbonate of soda. Bathroom cabinet – top shelf."

Expensive unstoppered cologne did not mask the sulphurous stench in the warm tiled bathroom. Returning through the bedroom, Alex noted the slippers at attention, the silk dressing gown neat on the broad bed. The sole decoration was a framed dated photograph of a young merchant navy officer wearing a third mate's braid.

He placed the packet of bicarbonate of soda, together with a glass and spoon and a Thermos of iced water, on the desk. Frogmore mixed and swallowed his medicine.

"It's not your place to talk to your captain about a deck cadet."

"No one else will, sir."

"No one else has your spunk."

"Is it all right if I go to Rotarua tomorrow?"

"You are a young man, purser."

"I'm thirty-five."

"Clear it with the first mate and take the cadet with you, if you so wish." The captain sat with his lips tight, showing his discomfort. "For the young, pleasure is the main purpose of their lives. Pleasure is happiness but happiness is ephemeral." He added without rancour, "Is that all? Nothing else I can do for you?"

"No, sir."

"Do go away."

Alex was reluctant to leave, sensing that Frogmore wanted human contact. But when below, he was annoyed at himself for feeling sorry for the man. He'd admit it to no one, but he was shaking from the encounter; his heart was pounding fiercely.

BACK FROM ROTARUA that evening Cadet Jones was cheery and talkative as he changed into working clothes for a spell on cargo watch. Alex lounged in the armchair, watching. He handed him his shirt. "Cover yourself up. You drive the troops wild."

"What troops?"

"I'll get my jack boots."

"You get mail from your ma?"

"The two dogs are continuously muddy and Mr Smith died."

"The man who went to jail."

"When I was having trouble at school I pissed in the font while Mr Smith was watching. On my way out he asked me if I wanted to talk. I told him to tell my mother what I had done. And I talked to him about how I was bullied and he saw the vicar who made my parents take me out of boarding school."

"Let's have sex. Mr Smith would approve."

Alex said, "We are talked about – and that's when we do nothing. To do something would fuck up your career and mine. Frogmore is an unpredictable man and, as an indentured apprentice, you are under his protection. Two men in bed is not on the curriculum."

"Alex, there is no hurdle. You've already pissed in the font," said Dave Jones.

ALEX listened to Larry groan, watched his powerful back lift as he gripped the sides of the porcelain wash-hand basin to vomit in agony. Eleven years at sea, and the stopover at a bar on the drive back from Rotarua, had taken its toll.

Alex eased him to the side, held down the taps sluicing the sink clean.

"Leave it out."

"My job. I've a steward who intimidates me, tells me – like Oscar Wilde – he never travels without Balzac. And a captain who tells me I'm a moron." Alex shook cleanser into the basin and scoured it with a cloth.

"Give it here!"
"Think of me as wanting to do it because I like you."

"THAT WAS A SORT OF HEAVY THING TO SAY," said Larry, as they made their way to the smoke room.
"Eleanor tells me you flashed at her?"
"She walked in on me. I was bollock naked."
"Not the way she tells it."
"True. She didn't knock."
"Tell me?" said Alex.
"She wanted to stay."
"You got rid of her?"
"Sure."
"And she was offering it?"
"She stares at it. All the time she stares at it. Finally she says, 'I'm looking for Rusty'."
"You didn't touch her?"
"I did nothing. It signalled."
Eleanor was in the smoke room wearing a cream linen dress. Long white nails on suntanned fingers tapped the framed tie.
"Someone likes sport," she said.
"Our captain. Convention. Decent standards. Likes ties on men, and women to be kept in their place," said Alex.
What you drinking?" Larry sipped the beer Francis served him. He relaxed as the anaesthetic took hold.
"Nothing, if you're buying," said Eleanor.
"You're such a lovely bitch."
"Vodka okay?" said Alex.
"With tonic, darling." She glared at Francis. "He won't let me sign. I have to pay cash."
"I'll fix it."
"You've got manners unlike some," said Eleanor.
"Why aren't you with Rusty?"
"Larry put him on duty."
"It's his watch," said Larry.
Eleanor's comment was ditched when a monocled Frogmore entered the smoke room wearing what he had decided was suitable for an English gentleman abroad in the colonies. He seemed to be dressed by the same bespoke tailor that Alex's mother patronised. His trousers

were cavalry twill; his jacket was country check, his knitted tie was a sedate beige and matched his Viyella shirt. Alex thought that his brogues developed the bespoke tailor theme nicely.

"Good evening," said Eleanor.

Frogmore considered her thick hair, her sensational figure accentuated by a broad belt, her heavy makeup suitable for women who wait under street lamps. He did not reply. He crossed to the glass cabinet which housed the Seafarers' Library.

Eleanor glared after him but Frogmore was immersed in the stuff of life. He was reading hardback books of endeavour, of top gallants and futtock shrouds.

"Can't you speak? Who do you think you are?" said Eleanor, piercing the brief silence.

Frogmore held his pipe in his hand. His face expressionless. "This is my ship," he said. "Now you have my reason for being on board, may I be permitted to learn yours?"

"I am the third engineer's fiancée."

Larry mouthed, "Fiancée?"

Then the captain put the boot in. "One should have hoped in a civilised society that it would not be necessary to remind guests about manners. Are you an *Aust*ralian?"

A winch vibrated savagely at number three hatch.

But Frogmore's attention was drawn back to more important matters. His eyes widened, the monocle dropped. He took his gold rimmed half-glasses out of a leather case and positioned them on his nose. He had spotted a book that had taken his fancy. He pounced on *Windjammers of the Horn*. Absorbed, he was reefing sails, watching green seas cascade over the ship's side. Delighted at his find, he returned his reading glasses to their case; reinserted the monocle and with *Windjammers of the Horn* tucked firmly under his arm, he marched to the door. He gave Eleanor a parting shot. "Company policy allows officers' guests to stay in my ship. But, it should be remembered that the ultimate authority is mine."

A Frogmorian staged exit, but Alex was still thinking about the captain's choice of clothes. Very similar taste to the retired admiral who his mother had mentioned in her letter.

He said, "And he wears a Glengarry. Isn't that just too much?"

"You've been at sea too long," said Eleanor, marching out of the smoke room. Her anger sounded as she stomped her way to the lavatory in the cabin opposite.

"She handled that badly. He won," said Alex.

"Rather him than her," said Larry.

"Oh, no, sir," said Francis, "that isn't the game at all. The game is the captain against the rest of the ship's company."

Eleanor returned and perched on an upright chair. When she spoke her voice was laden with innuendo. "There is something queer about him."

"About Alex?" said Larry.

"The psychopath."

"Did you hear that fake human being say *his* ship?"

"Ex-R.N. captains go that way." Then Alex imitated Frogmore, " '*I* shall be sailing in two days. *My* draught will be twenty-six feet. *I* shall be taking on two hundred tons of water.' *My* men. *My* ship. It's R.N. *unchi*."

"Unchi?"

"The Japanese for shit," said Larry.

Eleanor heard the engine room door open and close. She stood, said, "Being at sea makes you act like fools."

After she left, Francis dropped the bar keys on the card table. "Is it okay if I use your office to read my book?"

Alex nodded but Francis did not leave. He said to Larry, "May I hazard an objective observation, sir?"

"You don't usually ask before you stick your nose in."

"Maybe Eleanor's aggression is a manifestation of sexual want. And, if I may say so, sir, you do have an obvious masculinity. Subconsciously, she wants to rip off her clothes and sacrifice herself to you – you being the dominant male."

"Larry, ask her why she was fascinated by your knob," said Alex.

"That would be bad manners."

"You call her a bitch to her face and mean it – that's bad manners."

"Perhaps, it might be worth considering her wrath, Alex? It could be used against Captain Frogmore," said Francis.

"I thought you were going to read your book?"

"You must know from your earlier readings of Eastern philosophies – I'm talking of the time before your downward path to alcoholism and homosexuality – genuine or not, one hardly dares to go too deeply into that – that retribution might be her. As you are aware, sir, retribution comes in surprising ways."

"Says Catholic you. The Pope's into karma nowadays?"

"Your own efforts at getting rid of the captain are scarcely valiant or determined. You have pussy-footed about like a timid old maid. I can say that the fiery young woman certainly has…"

"Do not say spunk."

"Why, sir! No, sir! Why, bless your heart, sir, we servants knows our place, sir."

"Okay, you can say spunk, Francis."

"I was thinking of balls."

It was idiosyncratic of the ship, that neither Larry nor Alex remarked on Francis' outburst – quite unsuitable for a steward, particularly a Goanese steward, for the Goans were renowned for their gentle and reserved and courteous manner.

But Francis was allowed licence. The three were at that moment together and Francis was then very much one of them.

EIGHTEEN

THE TASMAN SEA

TWO days later Captain Frogmore sailed – together with the *John Bede* – for the port of Tamana Prospect in South Australia.

Straightaway the ship ran into heavy seas. Alex's Angle-poise lamp became alive and moved like a praying mantis. He gave up trying to type and jammed the heavy machine alongside the green-painted safe on the linoleum. That night he hardly slept. His muscles tensed as he rolled between bulkhead and bunk-board.

During the *Tatler* caffeine session he sat cowed on the settee. Looking through the forward windows of the captain's dayroom, he could judge when the ship would shudder before slipping into a trough, and when it would rise to dip again. Earlier, on the bridge, with an albatross keeping station to port, Alex had looked through one of the spinning panes of glass in the bridge windows that gave a clear view of the flung-up white water and the heavy seas running the foredeck. He had enjoyed being there with the sliding doors to the bridge wings closed. But in the captain's dayroom he was depressed by the force of the ship's movement.

"Hope the weather's fine in Aussie," said Morgan glumly. Morgan longed for rain in the UK because rain stopped cargo and delayed sailing, and that gave him more time with his family. Abroad he prayed for fine weather to speed up the ship's cargo handling.

Suddenly the *John Bede* broke routine. Alex saw the horizon and fast clouds in a blue sky before the ship slid down a wall of water. Then up again. Breaking wave tops flung spray in bright light.

"The third engineer had the gall to request that his doxy travel in my ship to *Aus*tralia," said the captain.

Alex was annoyed with Rusty for he had put himself in such an obvious no-win situation.

"She would have paid passage money. The company wouldn't object," he said, irritated at the captain misusing his power.

"Are you not cognisant with company policy on the carrying of doxies?" said Frogmore.

"She's not a whore, for Christ's sake," said Alex, bravely hitting out as the *John Bede* shuddered. The patterned carpet dipped. He clung to his seat as he rose with the settee. He hung for a moment, to drop suddenly as if to land on a rubber deck. The forward windows streamed water, blurring the sky. The racket he could barely tolerate. Below in the accommodation, doors banged violently. A chock and wire on deck made a terrific din, the books on the shelves in the cabinet on the after bulkhead, slid; the glass doors chattered.

Larry burst into the dayroom without knocking. His white boiler suit was stained with oil, his face creased with worry.

"Too much speed, captain. The prop is out the water."

"The ship will take it."

"Too much speed. The governor is cutting in."

"Safety device – no problem."

Larry hung in the doorway. "You sailed under canvas?"

"Yes, indeed," said Frogmore.

"It shows." Larry was gone.

Alex was on his way out too. He handed his cup to the steward, then addressed the captain, "I'm going on deck to get some air."

Leaving, he heard Frogmore say, "The purser is suffering from *mal de lager*, do you think?"

Alex's queasiness excused him breakfast. At nine his phone buzzed. "Report to my quarters."

Felicity, upset by the violent movement of the ship, had headed for her old home, maybe hopeful that after a stay in port Captain Lovelace had returned. The cat stood her ground with back arched, spitting at Frogmore. Alex swept her up in his arms and her claws hooked into the coarse linen of his uniform shirt.

"Purser, the book is going round. Boat stations at ten hundred hours. And keep that animal secure."

"Her problem is that she is unable to comprehend rank."

"She might be reading my mind," said Frogmore.

DURING Boat Stations the weather made it impossible to swing out the boats. The ship's company stood pointlessly on deck for forty minutes. Afterwards Alex visited the radio shack.

Sparks lolled in his chair. "Before Frogmore we'd all get together and jaw some and tell tall stories, but now since Doc and him have arrived, the ship's gone to pot."

"Yeah."

"Doc was up here taking notes. Jesus, I sit here for a two hour stint, four times a day, listening to Morse Code. I don't do nothing. My job is to be here doing nothing. And Doc takes notes. That pisses me off."

Alex, worrying about the captain making dark hints about the cat, nodded miserably.

Sparks said, "You hear Eleanor is joining the ship in Tamana Prospect? It's the fucking back of beyond. And we're in port less than twenty-four hours."

Alex peered through windows encrusted with salt. "She'll have one hellavua headwind. What's the broomstick flying time to Tamana Prospect?"

NINETEEN

TAMANA PROSPECT

THE *JOHN BEDE* was the first ship to dock in Tamana Prospect in two years, the pilot informed Alex.

"I double as port health and customs and immigration. I have been issued with three different caps."

"Not much to do here – other than wear caps, I suppose?" Alex looked out the window at a bleak mud-covered foreshore.

"A donkey farted last Tuesday and we had a party," said the pilot, accepting a Foster's. "That skipper'll get you Poms a bad name. He bad-mouthed the cadet then he was gonna have a go at me. Thought better of it." He placed a small pile of arrival forms on the office desk. "Got Hitler to sign 'em. Started to read the small print. I told him I hadn't time to hang about – having three other jobs and that." He pointed at Felicity. "That cat shouldn't be loose."

"She won't go ashore."

"Too bad if she does. The captain's signed an indemnity form."

"Will he be jailed if Felicity escapes?"

"Ditch the mog and I'll have a word with the judge."

"I'm on the scrounge. A lift into town?" said Alex.

"Town? Are you in therapy? What we have ashore is a handful of buildings of despair and disrepair. We hold pray meetings at *Joe's Bar. Joe's* doubles as the post office." The pilot became confidential, "I promised a lift to an engineer. Ham-sized arms and sort of..."

"...spends a lot of time in the gym?" said Alex stifling any further comment.

THE PILOT dropped Alex and Rodney at the end of the long wooden jetty near the dismal muddy foreshore. The two walked the couple of hundred yards to the low-lying settlement which included a wooden hall and a shuttered building which Alex guessed to be a shop.

"What's that?" Rodney prodded Alex in his ribs.
"What you on about?"
"That blue thing you're wearing?"
"It's called a shirt."
"I could have lent you something half-decent."
Alex said, "You've no taste. If it's expensive, you wear it. My mother looks classy in old Wellingtons and a mac."
"You've inherited it, you bastard."
They were passing half a dozen clapboard bungalows with corrugated iron roofs and rain butts in the yard. One front garden had an edge of white paving decorated with blue painted scallop shells and brightly coloured gnomes.
Joe's Bar suited the dreary landscape, suited the dirt road where tumbleweed should have rolled. The two seamen hesitated on the unpainted verandah, then pushed past a stack of blackened lobster pots to enter a L-shaped room, its walls bare other than a tacked-up notice which told of a house sale three months back.
Alex knew it wasn't high summer because the customers weren't wearing their broad-brimmed bush hats with dangling corks.
"If you wanna piss – hang out in the road. The sit-down is Martha's – one door down," drawled Joe behind the bar.
The six male customers, all in working-shorts and showing tree-trunk legs, openly stared at the two seafarers.
Joe accepted the ship's mail, which Alex handed to him for posting, saying "fuck" because the mail needed stamps for exotic Britain, India and Japan. He stacked it on the top shelf behind a notice: *SUICIDES NOT PERMITTED*, said, "Jane will let the agent know how much."
"It's pointless to ask for a Pils, I suppose," said Rodney in a loud aside.
"Ask, for fuck's sake," said Alex, exposing an earthy side now he was Down Under, but definitely not out, Down Under.
Rodney's nose lifted as a mutt came off the dirt road to cock his leg on the lobster pots outside the door. A discarded black plastic bag slapped against the verandah's bleached rail in the hot breeze. "You notice how Australians finish each sentence as though someone has stuck a finger up their arse? Men's fashion here is a hairy chest and shorts

and the fashion accessory is a tinny."

"Dare I say you might be a little overdressed." It wasn't only bravado that had Rodney ashore, glittering and waving, and strutting his stuff for his *cause.* Rodney was vain and wanted to look good.

"I'll bet you any money that you bought your shirt for five rupees from a *box wallah* in Bombay," said Rodney.

"Two bob in Singapore. I got a couple of hankies thrown in."

"You are you, and I am me."

"Trust me, Rodney, you ain't you at all. You've been through makeup so many times, you don't know who the real you is."

"Am I to dress like a tramp because we've docked in Hicksville?" Rodney's Italian slacks were way too tight.

"You're lipsticked and rouged like a popinjay."

"For your information, Mistress Alex, I am not wearing makeup."

A laid-back, yellow-haired customer wearing an open-necked white shirt, which was not embroidered silk nor imported from Italy, surveyed the seafarers speculatively. The yellow-haired man scratched red fuzz on his broad chest and drained his schooner before saying, "Seems we got ourselves a loud-mouthed pommy woofter."

Alex was intrigued because woofter was the Cockney rhyming slang for poofter but this was not a good time to discuss it, he thought, keeping an eye on the exit.

Rodney stood his ground and said loud enough for all to hear, "One expects the customers in this backwater of all backwaters to trail their knuckles on the ground."

Alex's eyes misted. His head spun. He gripped the bar apprehensively for the man with yellow hair was not slightly built by any means. He wondered if he could faint, he was certain that he could not outrun anyone.

Joe had a publican's tact. "Keep it level, boys. Okay?"

Another man held his hand up, held the audience of five men back – all of whom had very large torsos that grew intimidatingly out of their large tree-trunk legs.

"Cool it, Scott," he said.

The man Scott, who had called Rodney a woofter, said, "You gonna let the Pommy fag get away with saying us are gorillas, Aidan?"

Rodney's crack about prehensile knuckles had hit home. The sensitivity of the natives showed. Alex felt the room spin again and in the panic of the moment he found himself gripping Aidan's hand.

"Alex."

Aidan nodded at Rodney. "Maybe The Mouth should finish his beer on the verandah."

"Rodney, piss off," said Alex.

Rodney stayed were he was.

"Mate, what don't you understand, the *piss* or the *off?*" said Aidan softly.

Rodney moved sullenly to the verandah to stare moodily at the bleak shoreline. Alex trailed after him.

"Where you going?" said Aidan.

"The ship."

"Stay. You think we are ignorant Aussie gorillas?"

"Rodney's my friend."

"He's just wiped your nose in it. I've been watching him playing the cunt since he came in."

"Rod's an acquired taste – like some exotic food. At first it tastes so foul you think you've been poisoned but then you get use to it and start to like it."

"He wanted an audience while he pushed your nose in it. We're the audience – I don't think so. Our bar. And no one in here wants to listen to his shit."

Alex didn't get chance to answer. The sound of an approaching vehicle had all drinkers in the bar out on the verandah. On the shore road was a small open-back vehicle that threw up clouds of dust.

Things were happening in Tamana Prospect. The vehicle cornered at a dead tree, and with a turn of speed raced up the narrow strip of road. Eleanor braked on the dirt sidewalk. Rodney ran to open her side door and peck-kissed her on alternative cheeks in a theatrical way.

One can only vomit, thought Alex.

But Eleanor was not seduced by Rodney's tender reunion. Her language caught the atmosphere of the place nicely. "What a dump. One fucking murderous journey. Flew from Sydney to Melbourne then I bussed partway. I hired the Ute for the last stretch."

The land, had she bothered to look on her journey, would have been littered with the bleached skulls of cattle; there would have been miles of arid earth, maybe some burnt trees, thought Alex. He said, "Bet you could murder a coldie, doll?"

Eleanor ignored him. She hugged Rodney again. She held onto Rodney's hand. She drank from Rodney's glass and the two of them talked close up, like lovers do. Theirs was a love unsullied by sex. Their relationship had everything but the orgasm. They were as close as some women can be. They were loyal, dependant, gossipy, and able to expose their feelings to the other.

Entertained by the activity, all customers in Joe's were still on the verandah. They took in not only muscular Rodney's styled hair and his pants which appeared to house a codpiece borrowed from Sadler's Wells, but the centrefold Eleanor. Glamour had arrived in Tamana Prospect.

"We've had models here before," said Aidan to Alex.

"Were they woofters?"

"All male models are after your tackle, mate. The lot we had got themselves photographed up outside the mine entrance. Posed alongside the junked machinery. Came out in one of the fashion magazines. The wife bought several thousand copies." Aidan sucked his beer. "Reason being, they asked me to pose with them."

"I can't see you in silk pants."

"Jeans," said Aidan. "I got paid good money for it. Got chatted up too – by both sexes. It was all good, clean, dirty fun."

"A career change?"

"It was suggested, but they wanted me erect."

"What you do here other than being a freelance macho model who is into intimidating simple sailors?"

"Manager at the mine – chief engineer."

"But you're a *child?*"

"Twenty-five with a degree – that piece of paper did it." He added, "*He's* performing again."

"His life is a performance. Few know who the real Rodney is."

The Ute's engine fired. Eleanor waved farewell to her audience as she and Rodney bumped along the road, heading for the jetty and the ship. Alex felt gratefully abandoned and relaxed for the first time since coming ashore.

Through binoculars, borrowed from Joe, he focused on the ship. He could see that Eleanor's arrival was not garlanded. He picked out the figure of authority on the patio deck. Eleanor waved to the figure. But Frogmore's face was as uninviting as the drab shoreline. He turned on his heels and marched into his dayroom. Perhaps the captain was unable to comprehend why this truculent woman, now draping herself over the small, hairy and bespectacled third engineer, should make such an uncomfortable journey for a twenty-four hour stopover in port.

Alex's attention was distracted when Aidan said, "I got cans at my place. Have a look at the magazine?"

"I gotta get back on board for lunch."

"Eat at my place. The wife's in Perth."

"You do cheese butties?"

"Port Salut or store cheddar."

"Cheddar but cut off the mould," said Alex.

"Stop for dinner, if you like. Crash out if you get too pissed."

Alex, not one for socialising usually, was grateful for the company of this pleasant Australian. Stopping ashore would mean a break from Frogmore, and from Eleanor who would no doubt make the the trek overland to rejoin the *John Bede* when the ship docked in Melbourne.

TWENTY

MELBOURNE

MELBOURNE was the *John Bede*'s main storing port. Eleanor arrived on board with the crew mutton.

Alex was supervising the storing, leaning on the ship's rail with a can of beer in his hand.

"He's after you," said Cadet Jones, resting his arm on the purser's shoulder.

"God is?"

"I'm to tell you to report to Him after you've finished storing," said Dave. "I've just had a Frogmore experience."

"I'm agog." Alex stopped watching the trail of crew carrying the frozen carcasses on board.

"You see me and him on the dockside?"

"And?"

"We were talking about ship construction."

"You should have called me – I'm sure I could've livened up the conversation no end."

Dave Jones was in working jeans cut off above the knee that showed his footballers' legs, suntanned and glinting golden hairs. "You listening?"

"You've no idea how I hang onto your every word." Alex drank beer from the blue can.

"The captain said, 'Lovely bottom'."

He stopped drinking. "He said that you have a lovely bottom?"

"The ship. He was talking about the ship. You are always thinking about sex."

But Alex wondered if the captain had made the remark with Dave's bottom in mind: maybe in jest or even admiringly, for the old bugger missed little. And Jones was a pedigree. A stallion that was superbly graceful when moving, and stylish when still. He wasn't a centrefold like Eleanor – a page to wank over – Dave Jones was a work of art. Alex thought that he should point this out. "You're very, very beautiful, Cadet David Jones."

Dave gave an impatient shake of his head, and concentrating on the distant music coming from the accommodation, said, "Roger Miller. You want to come up and listen to me play guitar?"

"You're bound to be intolerably accomplished. Anyway my lord and master is taking me ashore."

"For lunch?"

"Doubt that."

WHEN FINALLY Alex made it up top, the captain was in a playful mood.

"Do you now have the time to come ashore with me, purser? You seem to be a man who is perpetually busy. My steward informed me that you were rushing to get changed and you would be up to see me when you could – which was after you attended to some quite major disaster in the galley. Is all resolved now?"

Alex waited, not speaking, in the doorway of the dayroom.

"Are you booted and spurred, purser?"

Alex nodded.

"Too exhausted to speak. You can rest in the taxi. Melbourne is a city which is attractive – in parts – so you can gaze at the view and recover your customary *joie de vivre* and cheer me up."

When in the taxi, the captain was silent. Alex, ill at ease, looked out the window.

Frogmore added to his discomfort when he lit his smelly pipe. "This doesn't offend you?" he said puffing away.

The taxi driver, shielded behind a thick reinforced plastic screen, fully lowered his window, giving Frogmore his opinion. Frogmore sat back smiling, as though he had scored a point.

THE SHIP'S AGENTS offices were high-rise and had whoosh-elevators and fitted cord carpets. A poised receptionist examined long red nails, repositioned a vase of flowers once, repositioned long legs twice, while she listened to Captain Rupert de Vere Frogmore informing her that he had to Note Protest for insurance purposes as he had suffered adverse weather conditions which might have damaged his cargo.

Today his manner was urbane and teasing, tomorrow rudeness and irritability could be on the cards. He was a man of moods caused by sexual deprivation according to the doctor – who might accord the same reason to his own bizarre behaviour, thought Alex. But Alex never understood whether sexual deprivation meant abstinence from masturbation. He had no doubts whatsoever that Frogmore was an exception to the ninety-nine percent rule. He would never do it. The doctor freely admitted that he did, but that was to be expected.

"Purser, you seem to be miles away."

"Daydreaming – escaping, I suppose."

"Escaping? As my witness when I Note Protest, I doubt whether I can allow that. One supposes, it will not matter that you are only a purser. I shall grant you honorary deck department status – no doubt that will make your day," said Frogmore when outdoors in the busy street. Alex suppressed a smile as Frogmore pulled out a pocket watch and said, "The court offices are closed at lunchtime. We have one hour and seventeen minutes to kill. You are more *au fait* with *Aust*ralia than I, what do you suggest?"

"How about a drink?" said Alex, suffering from last night's thrash. He indicated a bar sign.

Frogmore studied the advertising red neon which glowed faintly in the strong daylight.

"You know this place?"

"It comes recommended but from a dubious source."

"Then we must live dangerously. Just so long as it is not one of these *Aust*ralian beer-dispense urinals that serve frozen beer in chilled glasses."

"An intimate atmosphere, I'm told."

"Ah, then they would serve beverages other than frozen lager, one presumes. I understand that by law it must be served at thirty-four degrees. Extraordinary. American influence, no doubt, though Canadian beer, while not so numbingly cold, is served with salt. One restrained any comment in deference to the country."

"You don't like Canada?"

"Goodness, you pose the question as if I dislike any place which is not Britain. How bigoted you must think I am."

Alex was in a mild panic for Rodney had recommended

the bar. But it was too late, they were already committed to obey the neon light that brightened to flash an arrow of intense red pointing to a swinging entrance door at the foot of the broad concrete steps.

The joint was quality-carpeted, the music was good and not overly loud. The place hummed with three hundred men squeezed into a barroom licensed to take one hundred and fifty. Alex carried the drinks back from the bar, pushing his way through the crowd.

Standing alongside a reproduction statue of David, Frogmore inserted his monocle. His high forehead sloped back, the whites of his deep, dark eyes were tinged with yellow, his nose was prominent, as were his ears which suited his austere bearded face. He commanded attention ashore as he did on board. A nerve moved in his left cheek. Alex wondered if he might be amused.

"Sir?"

"Not 'sir' in this place."

"You've been here before?" asked Alex stupidly.

"Indeed not. It has an artificiality I would have remembered."

Alex thought the bar a transient place, a place to say hello and move on if the response was not what it should be. Ill at ease, he said, "Artificiality?"

"Everyone is so bright. The place has the appeal of a brittle cocktail party that has gone on too long. But again a man of your sensitivity might say that any cocktail party has gone on too long."

One bald headed man, who had very little going for him, found a patch of carpet on which to dance. He seesawed his arms energetically. Alex turned away, embarrassed at such a poor dancer making a spectacle of himself.

Near to them stood a man whose eyebrows were severely plucked, his neck scrawny; he was delicate as if a slight breeze might knock him over. He smiled and lifted a frail hand in a gesture of friendliness which Frogmore acknowledged with a bow.

"Can I squeeze through?" The man with the plucked eyebrows was brushing by, brushing Alex; his light blue eyes flashed humour, they lingered. The man moved slowly on.

Alex shook his head at a proffered cigar. Frogmore

inhaled. The smoke aromatic.

A man approached wearing shorts. He had hair on his back and shoulders and chest. He was ten years too old, ten pounds too heavy for the clinging sleeveless vest. His friendliness showed when he said in a small voice, "Love the eyeglass."

Frogmore took the intrusion in his stride. "I have been told it is an adjunct – part of my costume as a ship's master. Everything but the parrot, one wag said. The wag was a man I respected a great deal. A ship's surgeon, and a good one too, I might add. Name of Guthrie. Guthrie was eaten by a lion. Quite recently. In Africa."

The man glanced nervously at Alex before scurrying away.

Alex smiled at him, but was unashamed that he was in the company of a person of such haughty distinction.

Frogmore said, "It is a credit to Guthrie's idiosyncratic humour, that I'm certain he would applaud my telling that tale in order to get rid of that man – that is, if you wanted me to get rid of him? Have I been crass? How very rude of me. He was only being pleasant. Shall I run after him and call him back?"

Frogmore had obviously enjoyed the encounter. His relentless examination of the room continued. He took in the crowded long bar with its hammered copper counter and its array of rude, stuck-up postcards with silly joke captions.

An Aborigine, tubby but handsome with a square jaw, who was sleepily smoking a cigarette, signalled Alex with a wink. Alex blushed and turned away.

"Shall we try some other place?" he said.

"My shout, I think."

The clock hands stayed rock still.

Frogmore displayed no outrage, no prim concern; in fact his cheeks had gained some colour and his jaundiced eyes had softened. He handed a note to Alex. "Whilst I do not want to play the captain when ashore, I cannot face that crowd at my age. Would you?" He paused, looking at the all-male customers, "Make a safe passage."

They finished their second drink without any event until a customer overstepped the mark. A crude man, topping middle-age, groped a bright yellow plastic banana taken from a bowl of dusty fruit, and held it aloft.

"I can take that," he shouted.

Frogmore fixed him with a monocled eye. The man trotted the room, parting men, sucking and fondling the banana. He should have crumpled as Frogmore gave him a *You are something I've got stuck to the sole of my shoe* stare but he beamed. Frogmore did not.

"Suck that," said the man brandishing the bright yellow plastic banana at the captain.

Frogmore turned his back on him and said, "Time to Note Protest, me thinks."

He sailed ahead. Alex, the bobbing dinghy, followed in the wake of this splendid yacht cutting passage through choppy water.

Free of the bar, when on the steps leading up to the street, they paused.

"You might recall, purser, an Aboriginal man on my right?"

"No, sir."

"Looked younger than he was. One can tell by the neck, you know. Passably good features, though chubby. He wore a diamond ring which he used to signal to you?"

"Sir?"

"Surely you remember him? He winked. His companion was a man I would guess to be at least five years my elder, and who had no doubt seen better days."

"I think I might know who you mean."

"I feel sure you do. I mention it in some detail for the Aboriginal man's comment might be of some interest, as it was about you. He said to his companion that he fancied the blond."

They recommenced their climb to the street. Again Frogmore paused before gaining the pavement.

"Should I have mentioned it earlier, purser? Would you care to pop back to exchange cards? There is ample time. I will happily wait."

ALEX had arranged to meet Dr Trimmer in a tiled bar where office workers drank. It was a modern hose-down joint, a puke on the floor joint where the floor tiles carried right on through to the lavatory. The stainless steel drip trays under the bar taps held violet dye. The refrigerated wall cabinets held chilled glasses for sadists. Beer guns were positioned ready to couple up to shoot near frozen beer into laid-out glasses when the five o'clock Swill Hour started. The Swill Hour was conveyor belt drinking.

Doc's clothes were so dishevelled and his hair so unkempt and long that he might have been in danger of being thrown out of the place. But his educated voice and his put on charm kept him there.

"Fine hostelry you have," he said to the barman.

"The office workers knock off at five, come in here and knock it back until six. At six o'clock I kick 'em out and celebrate the end of my working day with a shit."

Alex followed Doc, who moved to a counter that ran the length of the back of the barroom; no stools, however the counter was something to lean on, rest one's glass on.

"This is a Frogmorian urinal bar," said Alex.

"There is something exciting, almost illicit about drinking in here, like this, when outside is hot and bright and any sensible person would be on the beach. But we are waiting for the Swill Hour to force down as many beers as we can. I find it a charming custom. Must be a legacy of the British rule." Doc downed his schooner of beer.

"Are you lyrical or pissed?"

"Have you seen or heard me when I am not lyrical or inebriated? You look shattered. This will set you up." He poured Alex a schooner of beer from a large glass jug.

"I have arrived jaded from a gin palace of romping boys; a flagrant place for male pickups," said Alex, striving to get back to his old self.

"I am trying to decode what you said. My understanding is that you went to a gay bar."

"Ten out of ten."

"Was it crowded?"

"Crotch to crotch."

"Let's go visit?"

"Nope."

"Not friendly?"

"I was touched up once and given the eye."

"That fits my definition of friendly."

"I had Frogmore with me."

Dr Trimmer's interest was intense. "Frogmore's coming out of the closet? A closet he may be in but to come out of it, is not his style."

"His closet is crammed with marine paraphernalia."

"How'd he react?"

"He didn't cotton on," said Alex. "I took him there to shock him but he was blissfully unaware."

"Curious man. Sexless? Doubt it. His problem is sex. Oedipus – a classic Napoleonic case. He has notably large feet."

He glanced at Dr Trimmer to see if he was serious.

"The foot is a phallus. Freud makes that crystal clear," explained the doctor.

"Why do you get up Frogmore's nose so much?"

"It's my dislike of unfair authority. The Aussie in me."

"You sure are a sensitive man. That's what I love about you."

"Thank you, thank you," said Doc, his plain face transformed as he smiled his gratitude. He tugged at his baseball cap, suitable for someone half his age, and said without humour, "Did you discuss anal sex with Frogmore?"

"Are you nuts?"

"If you wish to indulge in anal intercourse then, by jingo, that's your right," said Dr Trimmer loudly, but gratefully not loud enough to catch the attention of four clerks, who although clad in clerical grey, were macho Australian. He peered over half-glasses, changed the conversation. "Was that letter I saw on your desk from South America? You can talk to me about it."

"I do not want to be analysed, nor labelled. I want a quiet drink and I want to rest. I need all my energy for tomorrow. We are taking out the lifeboat."

WEARING A WHITE BOILER SUIT and plimsolls, Alex shut his hungover eyes as he clambered down the Jacob's ladder that clung tight to the ship's iron side. He opened them as he neared the waterline to stumble into the lifeboat.

Ten of the ship's company, who were training for their Lifeboat Efficiency Certificate, were taking the lifeboat out under sail. It was a practical boat handling exercise in preparation for the examination the following day.

Underway the lifeboat manoeuvred clumsily. Alex perched on a thwart.

"You look like hell," said Rodney.

"Nerves. I've suffered a great deal of unnecessary worry and stress because of you."

"You're hungover."

"I went to that queers' joint you said was a must. I fear that my career at sea may be soon ended."

"You took Frogmore as your date."

"You know?" said Alex.

"Nigel."

"Decode?"

"The barman. He said you minced in there with an old fart older than death who wore a monocle."

"How'd Nigel know it was me?"

"A blond with good hair and poise, he said. Nigel has no taste and limited descriptive powers."

"Did Nigel mention my eyes?"

"You underestimate Frogmore if you think that a gay bar is gonna throw him."

"You reckon Frogmore is queer?"

"Alex, do grow up. No one can know, no one can tell. There are hundreds of thousands of men of his generation who play at being straight. For them to admit being queer would be death to their career, to their social standing, to their peace of mind."

"The doctor thinks..."

"The doctor thinks shit. He is shit. He looks shit. He talks shit. He makes shit remarks – and you applaud."

"You two-faced sod. You laugh as much as anyone," said Alex.

"All that posing and that camp, is so false."

"Oh, pardon me, Rodney-Wodney, I'm having hysterics. You've been putting on an act for so long it's stuck. You're naturally unnatural which, of course, might make you natural. But strictly *entrez nous* I suspect you are a not very queer queer, Rodney dear."

"You are so droll. All queens are."

Alex yawned.

"Work study – fuck off. That doctor never uses two words

when he can use ten."

"Very ponderous of him."

"Him and Frogmore are not of this world. They have their own stage on which they perform and spar. And we're their audience. You know what it's about?"

"You'll tell me, darling," said Alex.

"It's about power and control – forget work study."

"The doctor acts like a madman not a power freak. Frogmore could have stopped it – full stop. Kicked him off the ship. He had the grounds, but he keeps him on. This is where I consult the oracle and ask you, Rodney, my sweetness, Why does he keep the doctor on?"

" 'Cos Frogmore's gotta win. You don't stop a soccer match halfway through."

"We're agreeing. Isn't this nice? Sailing on a sunny day with a following wind and talking to a chum. Did you bring the hamper? I have my Panama. I rather fancy a Beaujolais with my banana. I shall *trail* my hand in the water and close my eyes while you wind up the wind-up gramophone and we can listen to lovely music."

Neither Rodney's nor Alex's attention was on the course the lifeboat was steering. Alex got to his feet to get his cigarettes out of his boiler suit pocket, and lost his balance. He stumbled into Badsha Meah who fell on Francis. Francis was steering. The combined weight of Alex, Francis and Badsha Meah rammed the tiller to starboard.

"Gybe!" shouted Jack.

The large ungainly sail touched Alex's hair as it slammed across. The lumbering lifeboat, now out of the lee of the *John Bede,* came alive. Jack hauled on the main sheet, gave an order to Francis. Ahead was the high white side of a passenger vessel. Francis put the helm down. The lifeboat went about but scraped along the passenger ship, taking off paint. Badsha Meah fended off. The lifeboat set off at a cracking pace passing under the *John Bede*'s stern well out of sight of the bridge and Frogmore's smouldering gaze.

Two hours later, the lifeboat was in its davits and Alex, with salt stiffening his boiler suit, sat in the mate's office eavesdropping as the captain riled in Morgan's cabin next door.

"They boarded like trippers!"

From a four ale bar, thought Alex.

"How could anyone but an incompetent ram *Canberra?* And that mad doctor taking notes and wearing that disgusting American baseball cap with his hair sticking out. I asked him why he had been in the boat. He said it was a test. Test? What bloody test? *Isn't life one great test, dear boy?* he said. *Dear boy!* What is this great shipping company coming to, employing such a devalued man?"

Dr Trimmer had a reason for being in the lifeboat. He had asked Alex to convince those sitting their Certificates that they should deliberately fail. Their failure would reflect adversely on Frogmore's captaincy. Head office would not be pleased.

Through the part-open door Alex watched Old Jack tap on the mate's jalousie door.

"Who was that incompetent at the helm, second?" said Frogmore.

Alex plunged a deck knife into the wooden beading edging the large blackboard which showed the stowage of cargo in all five hatches.

Jack's voice was low, Frogmore's wasn't. "The *purser's* steward. I might've guessed."

"They will do not too bad at all," said Jack, dragging the conversation back to the ten men sitting their Certificates. "Alex won't let me down, skipper."

Alex rolled off the desk and left the mate's office, heading aft. In the port side alleyway he was stopped by Badsha Meah cuddling the cat.

"Felicity, *sahib,* covered in oils. I cleaned her furs in case she is licking herself." Badsha Meah's arms were patchy with solvent, his smile was broad and he showed black gums; his teeth were stained a reddish-brown; his lips were purple-black, the whites of his eyes were flecked with brown. Everything about him was dark and exotic.

"You passing your lifeboat certificate tomorrow?"

"Francis – he already teach me, *sahib.*" Badsha Meah pressed Felicity into Alex's arms so that both the fireman and the purser held her warm body.

"Dump her in the alleyway. I'm on my way to the engineers' accommodation."

"Give me your cabin key. I lock her in and leave the key

in fuse box."

They both held the cat now and they both held the mortise key too. Alex surrendered the cat and the key, but Badsha Meah stayed close to him, pressingly close. Their hands touched. It was as if the fireman was wanting sex. Alex's excitement had grown and pushed its way out of the top of his underpants and showed at the V of his unbuttoned boiler suit. Badsha Meah looked at his cock as he gently rubbed Alex's hand. And Alex wanted so much to bend forward and rest his head on the fireman's shoulder. As he lowered his head, Badsha Meah stepped back.

"I see to cat," Badsha Meah said, then he walked slowly away, cuddling Felicity.

RODNEY'S cabin was spotless. Alex imagined Rodney perpetually cleaning. He visualised him wearing a knotted red-dotted headscarf, a wrap-around pinny and yellow Marigold gloves. Even the force of the air from Rodney's punkah louvres was stronger and fresher than in other cabins; his lights were brighter, the chintz covers chintzier.

"I'm binning *Carmen,*" said Alex, switching off the tape recorder.

Rodney was on the carpet doing press ups. He did not stop.

"If I go into any cabin in this ship, I'm offered a beer." Alex helped himself to a can of Foster's from under the wash-hand basin. "These are warm." He poured the beer into a smooth-sided glass; watching the foaming head.

"You all right for cigarettes?"

Alex lit up.

"Watch that beer on the carpet and use the pot ashtray – not the cut glass one," said Rodney, counting his press ups under his breath.

"You got to do that?"

"What?"

"Press ups while I'm talking to you, you ignorant shit." Alex reached up and flicked ash in the glass ashtray.

"I said: Use the pot one!"

"I said: Stop the press ups!"

"I keep my body in shape," said Rodney.

"You're *giving* your body shape."

Rod strove for beauty, but his body was manufactured. He could be an entrant in the Mister Muscles competition held in his local Northern town, but he would never make the finals. And his face had not much going for it either.

Rodney stopped, dumped the pot ashtray besides Alex then sat upright in his armchair. "You knock back beer after beer, you do no exercise and you don't put on weight. Is excessive masturbation your secret?"

"I've really fucked it, Rod."

Struck by the purser's tone, the engineer didn't speak until Alex had explained about what happened with Badsha Meah.

"Did you know he's married?"

"No."

"He's bought his wife not one frock but four. They're his size."

Alex had an improbable vision of the earthy fireman, with hands and arms shining with solvent, posing in a frock. A frock to spin in so that the skirt lifted as he twirled and showed his knickers and thin brown legs. Badsha Meah was losing some of his appeal.

Rod cheered him, "Forget him and Francis. In comparison, you and I are normal. At least we're almost honest."

"You bullshit beautifully." Alex stared at the engineer thinking him sexless; but if Rod made a move then, he would let him do it. Not out of manners but because he liked him and wouldn't want to hurt his feelings. "I always thought that the upper class and the working class were more laid-back about homosexuality. I mean it's us middle class that are hung up."

"The working class? Brutally honest – *The boy's a bit of Jessie* – that kind of thing."

"With my mother it's never discussed. Occasionally she refers to so-and-so who 'plays the violin' or who 'has long hair'. And there are 'those two unmarried men who breed spaniels and run kennels'." Alex buried his face in his hands. "I haven't the guts to defend them."

"Why don't you come right out of your closet?"

"I could hang prints of Diaghilev on my bulkhead, leave Firbank on my desk, and scour shops for green carnations and enjoy being queer like I enjoy being different." Alex squatted on his heels not wanting to mark the loose covers with his dirty boiler suit. "Tonight Francis is giving instruction on the lifeboat. You're coming."

"I'm eating ashore."

"Cancel it."

"He's flying down from Sydney."

"Sex can wait, this can't. Ask Ernest to come."

"Ernest is a peasant."

"You're on watch with that peasant – twice a day."

"Irritating hair."

"Rodney!"

"Ernest is *so* boring. Last trip he talked endlessly about engines. This trip Ernest is in love. He writes twice a day to his wee biddy lassie in East Kilbride or some ghastly Scottish backwater..."

"You've stuck your hand up his towel, haven't you?"

"Ernest's on about The Wedding." Rodney shuddered, helping himself to one of Alex's Pall Mall. "I'm pleading with him to talk about engines, but all I get is The Invitations and Auntie Morag's coming by sporran from Lerwick. And Uncle Jimmy – that's Uncle Jimmy on his side who lives near Glen Fartoch and tosses cabers – is rushing down laden with groats to pay for The Wedding Feast."

"I wonder, with my *Tatler* connections, whether I should attend his wedding?" said Alex.

"You want to wear a kilt – any old excuse to get into a frock." Rodney helped himself to a can of Foster's from under the sink then selected a glass from the cabinet above his desk which he polished and held up to the light.

"I haven't the legs for a kilt."

"Have you seen her photograph?"

"Whose?"

"Ernest's wee lassie."

"She's sorta..."

"One of the McBlands. Horse teeth and noticeable thighs under a not flattering green tartan."

"Rod!"

"I'm a bitch." Rodney rocked himself in the armchair, one knee hooked over the other.

"He's got a terrific accent."

"The accent's fine but what he says gets so very much on

my tits. If it wasn't for that body I wouldn't tolerate him for a minute." Rodney added, "I'll organise Sparks, if you want."

"No one organises Sparks."

"The divine Francis will. My dear Alex, I am *terrified* to walk into your office when you two are together. Francis dotes on you."

"If only."

"He's so very queer. He was on about hyacinths?"

"Hyacinth lives on. Nero and Narcissus are always with us."

"Jesus."

"Ditch your vulgar magazines and borrow Francis' university course – he and I bone up together."

"I am sure you do. Tonight is?"

"Cleats and reefs and boxing the compass."

"Afterwards we can drink black rum and sniff rope ends," said Rodney.

"Don't you have to rush ashore to meet your Sydney fuck?"

"Not until nine, dear – and who knows, the flight might be late and he can wait. I must put you and the ship first, darling Alex. Can I say something?"

"No, no and fucking no."

Rodney stood up and his hand slid inside Alex's boiler suit smoothing its way downwards. It stopped to gently squeeze his genitals. "Badsha Meah's a fool – you do it for me, any day of the week." He took his hand away and sat down. "You're feeling guilty because you've been made to feel your sexuality's wrong."

"Am I supposed to be proud?"

"Oh, fuck that shit. How can you be proud of something that makes you so uncomfortable?"

"You'd be just about bearable if you didn't play at being the Rodney of all Rodneys." Alex added, "I'll see Ernest."

"Oh, that will make you stand proud," said Rodney, running the tip of his tongue suggestively over his lips.

"See? That's what I mean."

ERNEST was as trustworthy as his name and he had the loyalty of the Scots. He loved to visit Alex. "I came for aspirin, please? he had said, being too shy to ask Doc. That had been the fourth time in a week. Worried about the wedding, Alex guessed. Ernest didn't drink much so was often excluded. That evening he sat in Alex's cabin as they all waited for Francis to finish working in the dining saloon.

Rodney talked about Ernest as though he was not there. "I've given up on Ernest. He's in his perpetual shell. Comes out of it only for you. He tells me you listen to him." Rodney sighed. "Inferring that all I do is talk."

"But, you have so much to tell us," said Alex.

"I do wish I was aggressive then we could wrestle. I'd like that." Rodney patted Ernest bare knee.

Ernest let the hand be, saying to Alex, "He's jealous of you – you having manners and looks. And he fancies you rotten."

"You're both silly children," said Rodney, taking his hand sharply away as the other two laughed.

Francis organised the evening, taking charge and testing the ship's company sitting the examination. He gave a warning. "And no drinking tonight."

"Now you can understand what I have to put up with," said Alex, after Francis left his cabin.

"You two should get married," said Rodney, "and you'd be the groom."

NEXT DAY Alex had expected a smile from Frogmore but unfortunately Ernest had tried to get out of the ordeal of taking the boat out, by inventing a dental appointment ashore during the lunch break. And to steady his nerves, he'd asked Rodney along. They had visited a bar.

Frogmore drew in a sharp breath. "The fifth engineer told the examiner that he had to go to Melbourne because of chronic toothache. So proceedings were delayed awaiting his return. I did not think it wise to mention to the examiner that I had espied the fifth engineer, together with the refrigerating engineer, knocking back ales in a bar ashore."

"The fifth doesn't drink."

"He does."

"It would be his nerves."

It dawned on Alex that the captain must have been in that bar too. A Bohemian bar because Rodney had told him of the incident. Ernest had been panicking, so beer seemed sensible medication. Rodney had said, "We sped our way back to the ship, as soon as I got Ernest pissed."

"Two beers?"

"His nervousness led to a heady third."

"It did the trick," had said Alex.

"Ernest told me that he didn't want to let you down. Why you instil such devotion, I do not know," Rodney had said.

THAT EVENING before dinner, Cadet Jones ran his knuckles lightly down the outside of Alex's jalousie door.

"Am I okay to sit down?"

"Why so formal?"

"With you it's like visiting the theatre."

"The front stalls." He pushed the cadet into the armchair and put a can of beer in his hand. "I do character parts – seldom revealing who I am. I am an enigma."

"Am I an enigma?"

"You are my ultimate wet dream."

"There you go again."

"But you want me to talk dirty, don't you?"

Cadet Jones reached across and stroked Alex's bare arm, then drew back sharply as though he had gone too far.

"You're so up for it."

"You ever do it with Larry?"

"Once. We held a seminar afterwards. Rodney was in the chair."

"I went for a meal with Debs."

"Debs? My Debs?"

"She came on board looking for you but you were ashore and, well, you know."

"Tell me about the *you know?*"

"She's good fun and sexy."

"Did you have sex?"

"She's loyal to you."

"So you did make a pass at her. Anyone with taste would."

"We have you in common." Dave downed his beer. "We walked the river bank and the water was muddy."

"And?"

"I cuddled her. She pushed me away."

Alex handed him a fresh can and opener. "Go on."

Dave placed the can on the table. "She said to me, 'Love

keeps one loyal and faithful'."

"Even when it's not reciprocated?"

"Isn't it?" Dave looked him in the eyes.

Alex turned away as though something had dawned on him. Then he turned back again and ran a forefinger over the young man's cheek, tracing the ridge of the scar. His finger, with the lightness of a feather, moved to Dave's lips...

The jalousie door banged open. Larry burst in carrying six beers.

Dave stood. "I've got to study. The captain wants my log-book at seven in the morning." He handed Alex his unopened beer. In the doorway he said, "Am I okay with you?"

"You always are. I'm seeing Debs tomorrow."

THE FOLLOWING afternoon he was daydreaming, leaning on the ship's rail.

"A pity that the disastrous dress rehearsal made for a successful first night," said Dr Trimmer.

"Ten sat and ten got their certificates."

Doc waited for a group of wharfies, manhandling a sling of cargo, to stop shouting before he spoke again, "You've enhanced Frogmore's reputation." The two men moved out of the sun into the accommodation, away from the noise on deck.

Doc followed Alex into the engineers' mess room, saying, "You will have enjoyed the drama of taking the boat out, the theatre: your hand on the tiller, taking command, playing at sailors. Your kind go in for that show business drama stuff."

"Your kind go in for bitchy remarks."

"I understand that your old girlfriend is coming on board to see you?"

Alex opened the refrigerator door. Behind a propped-up wine card, on which was written *LARRY,* were six beers. He took a can, wrote on the card *FIVE – ALEX*

"You should have failed your lifeboat examination. To want to achieve is an uncomfortable part of the human condition." Doc added, "Come ashore and avoid your girlfriend?"

"I don't want to avoid her. I like her a lot."

TWENTY-ONE

MELBOURNE

WHILST ELEANOR'S appearance hinted at an easy lay, Deborah's did not. Where Eleanor jangled ornaments of chunky agate, Deborah wore no decoration. Her naturalness, her lack of concern about her appearance appealed to Alex, her longing for him did not. He sensed that Debs' goal was the same as Eleanor's – marriage. Church and alarm bells rang. Alex considered marriage an unnatural state advocated by priests and perpetuated by jingoistic politicians who, in public, preached family values while in private enjoyed fellatio from the au pair or houseboy.

"So good to see you again," she said as they embraced. Her hair was lightened by the sun and her skin was berry-brown, her dark eyebrows and lashes attractive.

"How's things?" said Alex, thinking how nice she was and how hard it was to overcome his instinct to kiss her passionately. "Sorry about not answering your letter."

"I wept for a month."

"All my women do." He sighed.

"Eleanor said you were tensed up."

"Who wouldn't be with her around. You've lost weight – suits you."

"Why is that cat behaving oddly?"

"It's female."

"Alex, that's not like you. Come and stay with us for a few days?"

"Us?"

"Ulana and me at the flat. And we do not behave oddly. There'll be no fuss, no cooking – well, only simple food."

Claustrophobia came over him in waves. He went through into the office and hooked open the outside door, breathing in the fresh air. He came back into the cabin. "You're perpetually social. Little dinner parties – but don't worry because the dress is casual – and suppers, informal suppers. And people popping in and having something to eat – a plate on their knees. You cater for more folks than a railway buffet. It's not me. I don't do people."

"You remember Norman?"

"He asked you to marry him, you said in your letter. Go for it, he drives something which does several hundred miles an hour and cost the price of a decent town house in Chelsea." Alex seeing her expression, said, "Tell me?"

"I was invited to his house, I thought, for a party. No party – just me. A beautiful meal and gorgeous flowers."

"Oh, poor Norman. I mean he's okay."

"I was given a ring which..."

"Debs, were you thinking about marriage?"

"I'm twenty-six and he's so caring."

"I can't say anything, can I? Didn't you say he lived in a castle? Has it a moat?"

She said, "One of those houses where you can smell the wealth. Tapestries on the walls in the reception room and a housekeeper. I'm not used to housekeepers."

"You'd hate it?"

"I gave him the ring back. So embarrassing."

"Being with you, I just long to be straight."

She changed the subject. "My dog loves you."

"Labradors love everyone. They have no taste. And you have no sense of decency – you are bringing out the heavy weapons. I love your dog." Alex slid the serviette along the coffee table so it touched her hand.

"I'm not crying."

"I am." The large black cat jumped on Alex's knees. "It's the warmth she likes – hates me."

"That young man who showed me your cabin is devastating."

"Dave," said Alex.

"He said that I was to make sure you're all right." She blushed and lowered her head. "Tuesday, I came on board to see you, but you'd gone ashore. Dave and I went for a snack. We went Dutch."

"He told me."

"Why not bring him to stay. The settee opens into a bed. I did have a picnic in mind – that's all. It's only Ulana and Martin. You'd like him. He reads."

"Cookery books?"

"He doesn't talk about surfing too much nor beat his chest," she said. "His chest is worth beating though. Not into bullshit."

Alex said, "Does Ulana know?"

"Martin lives in the lower flat. He's a neighbour not her boyfriend." Then she said, "He can be so very funny and warm. You'd really love him. His humour is a lot like yours."

"That's the clincher. I'll pack a frock."

"That kind of humour."

Debs wasn't a lets-get-down-to-it girl. Instead of torrid sex, she was promising him poached salmon or salmon mousse with friendly friends. And there would be other friends who would pop in with bottles of wine. And there would be ritual dining and labelling friend's friends, and he would be seen as belonging to Debs or – but something had changed. There was Martin on the menu. And Alex was to bring along Dave who would share his bed.

"You stayed at the flat before," she said.

"That was you and me and the odd trainload of people popping in. I did dig your décor."

"The driftwood furniture."

"And that very comfortable floor I passed out on. I didn't realise the flat was yours. Thought it was a holiday-rent or something." The apartment had knocked-up painted wooden furniture and there was a large noisy fridge which had seen better days and when it cut out all were grateful for the silence. The comfortable fold-down bed settee was in the living room. The windows were coated with salt flung up by the sea on stormy days. What Alex had loved was a table lamp covered in seashells. When Debs had caught him looking at it, she had said, "It's the very devil to dust, so I don't." The LPs had no storage place, they were heaped – with or without sleeves – on the floor. The casualness of the place would have sent Francis into a frenzy of tidying.

"That crazy swim we had at six in the morning," she said.

"I bodysurfed, which had you in stitches. I lost all dignity and my costume. And got covered in sand."

"You were covered in goose pimples, not sand."

"And when we got back, I put on your dressing gown – I am into quilted pink satin."

"You were frozen," she said. "The scrambled eggs?"

"Okay, so I can cook eggs."

"It was all kind of nice, you know."

"Yeah." He lifted the napkin off the dish of sandwiches on the coffee table. "Chance it, the pantryman made them."

Felicity, sphinx-like, watched Debs.

"That cat's weird."

"Eleanor slagged off our captain to his face."

"She's got prickly after her operation."

"She had an extra tongue put in?"

"It's a women's thing."

"Hormones affects rationality. Fucks up men too. Having genitals, I mean. That's what fucks me up."

"No weekend this time, I sense."

"This ship is my home. And I've got agoraphobia and..."

"Alex!"

"Debs, come clean and admit you'd spend all your time cooking broccoli with a lime and strawberry sauce, and generally organising this and that, and trying to get me to see a psychiatrist because I'm demophobic."

Felicity jumped off his lap and rubbed against his leg. He reached down to pet her but she moved to centre carpet.

"Eleanor told me that your cat hated women." Felicity's round blue eyes challenged Debs to say something. "Has the cat been coaching you?"

"I don't hate women. Debs, I think the world of you but I hate the idea of a thoroughly normal married life. I don't fit in – but when I find I do, I kind of like it – you know? We never fall out. Trouble is I like you so much, but take it any further and it would be a big mistake. Eleanor is wrong, it's not that you're too good for me – well maybe you are – but it's that I'm queer."

"I admit I cooked fancies this afternoon."

"What?"

She picked up her handbag. "Small iced cakes – a selection."

"Who says 'fancies', for God's sake? This is some Freudian allusion to sexual orientation, isn't it?"

"Call me, okay?"

"Okay."

"What does that mean?"

"That means, I will call you. What's the rush? Why can't

you stop and talk?"

"I'd love to but I have to go."

"Oh God, you're cooking a meal! You were going to invite me to dinner?"

She tried to keep a straight face.

"How many people, *woman?*"

"Ulana and Martin and Rowena and her dad – he was at sea before he went into the church."

They linked arms as they walked the length of the alleyway. The gangway swung as they made their way down it, heading for her car. He kissed her on the mouth.

Feeling sad, feeling for her and wanting her, he watched her drive off between the sheds.

On deck, in the light from high up fluorescent lamps fixed to the underside of the warehouse eaves, he glanced at the stevedores working cargo, then, as if making up his mind, he sped back into the accommodation.

He ran the engineers' alleyway and scorched his knuckles on the second's jalousie door as he banged his way in. Seated, with a can in his hand, he told Larry of the evening with Debs. Then Alex shyly handed him the thin letter from The Man from the Pampa saying, "I like her best but I want his company and his respect. It's not even the sex with him. I'm weird."

"If you were normal you wouldn't be talking to me."

"You fancy sex, Larry?"

"Not when I'm drinking."

"You're always drinking. At least you could be gracious enough to plead a headache. What shall I do, for fuck's sake?"

"Have another beer."

Alex took a second can out of the mush of melting ice in the cool box that stood under the wash-hand basin.

"Then there's this party tomorrow."

"It'll be okay – no bullshit. Spark's organising it. Nice girls, so he tells me." Larry grinned. "You're coming – if only to watch the show."

"The Fucking Show," said Alex gloomily.

THE CARD TABLES in the officers' smoke room, together with the leather chairs, had been repositioned around the edge of the room. Sparks had replaced most of the light bulbs with his screwing-bulbs which gave a dull red light. It made Alex think of war films: films of submerged submarines where the lighting was a dimmed-red and a perspiring crew waited for their bearded captain, gripping the periscope, to shout *Fire One!*

Behind the bar Francis, standing in front of a cut glass mirror, said, "Man and church have laid down guidelines for human behaviour, but on occasions, when humans are free of such constraints, the humans will revert to the animal."

"You are the poor man's sage," said Alex.

"You don't like me?"

"I adore you and you adore me. But we are constrained by convention."

"You constrained? God help me when you're not," said Francis.

"If a majority of people do something, then it's okay. Like sport at school is okay, so those that despise it are outsiders and wimps. Like sex: heterosexual sex is okay but homosexual sex is condemned and illegal and punished by a judge who had at one time ogled his fag's buttocks when he bent down to make him toast in front of the fire."

"It's legal in England."

"Not in Scotland. One wonders if one's bedroom were on the English-Scottish border...?"

"It would depend if the genitals were in Scotland or England."

Alex said, "Practise *soixante-neuf* and...?"

From their vantage point they both studied the behaviour of the officers and their female guests. The females herded. Now and then, the herd would open and two females or more – never singly – would make a break for the lavatory to talk about the males who were drinking heavily.

Alex had earlier approached a woman who was over-tall and he had talked about how the ship was nicely old; chit-chat to put her at ease. "It's old all right," she had said in such a way as to dismiss him, make him feel that he should be ashamed of the ship he loved.

Francis pointed to Sparks carrying a tray of drinks to the herd.

"The tattooed male – as if displaying feathers – approaches tentatively but not too tentatively for he is the stronger of the species."

"He's out to get them pissed."

"Soon there will be a ritualistic dance. The Smooch."

Rusty interrupted, wanting a beer.

"Where's Shrew?" asked Alex.

"Ashore. Stopping the night. Having dinner with Debs."

"I'll be the entrée."

"Eleanor says..."

"Eleanor's gonna marry you."

"It's sex." Rusty shrugged.

"That too. A great deal of sex, I would say, what with her broomsticking it from port to port with her knickers in her handbag and her mouth in overdrive."

"You're frustrated, Alex."

"I masturbate contentedly – that's having it away with myself which is better than having it away with Eleanor – any day of the wank."

Sparks had rigged up a lamp which flashed long and slow every few seconds. It held the occupants in the smoke room; it froze them momentarily in a surreal tableau like the light from a distress flare.

The herd broke. A woman in a blue Can Can frock danced independently and in the tradition of the Can Can, high-kicked. Like the original dancers in the *Moulin Rouge*, she wore no knickers. Francis looked away.

Rusty, gripping his Foster's, had joined the dancers.

Larry had forsaken Hand and was seeking the real thing. His feet were planted, his body was fixed to a woman whose face was macabre in the strange light.

The Smooch. A chance to touch. The exhausted high-kicking Can Can dancer, with wisps of hair damp on her face, clung to Rusty for support. Rusty supported her very well as they staggered out of the smoke room.

Alex said to Francis, "I'm turning in."

Cadet Jones was hanging around in the alleyway waiting for the girl he had been dancing with, to freshen up in the spare cabin.

"Dave, have you got a photograph of yourself I can borrow? In bed I'll hold it in the other hand."

IT HAD BEEN an alcohol free evening. The four large Foster's he had drank, Alex considered being on the wagon. He awoke strangely hungry. His first cigarette tasted of tobacco. He sang as he showered. He cleared a backlog of work in the office, then wrote a letter to Ignacio in Brazil before ambling to the pantry.

D'Silva reported that Eleanor had returned on board with the milk to discover Rusty asleep clutching a sling back shoe.

"Whose shoe?"

"One of the ugly sisters," said Francis.

"Please tell me she is still on board?"

"Unfortunately not, sir."

Their conversation was interrupted by Eleanor's raised voice coming from the engineers' accommodation: "I go ashore for ten minutes and you are fucking a whore!"

Alex was distracted by Gomes smoothing his way down the flared staircase. Gomes' smile informed him that he was being summoned up top. Alex stuck out his tongue.

"Captain sahib's salaams," said Gomes.

"Piss off, you oleaginous smoothie. And to save you asking smarmy Francis, it means greasy."

"Oh, *sahib,* I am gravely upset." Gomes added, "Much to-do up top. You'll much enjoy the drama there also, I feel sure, *purser-sahib.*"

Frogmore was pacing the cross-alleyway. He ushered Alex into the smoke room. All the windows had been opened, but the smell of stale tobacco and last night's booze clung to the room. Someone had thrown a drink at the veneered bulkhead; it had left a sticky mark. On the carpet near the bar stood a cardboard box brimming with empties and rubbish. It was topped by a sling back shoe. Budhia was cleaning an islet of vomit off the carpet.

Alex switched off the tape recorder. The movement disturbed the chief engineer who, slumped in an armchair, opened his eyes then shut them again.

"Did the chief engineer give his permission for this row-de-dow?" demanded Frogmore.

"We assumed it was okay." Permission for parties had never been sought under the Lovelace regime.

"You gave permission?"

"Parties are usual in Aussie, sir. Vague invitations. Guests on board for cheese dip and light refreshment."

"Light refreshment, purser? I'm not talking about decent gels dropping in for lemon tea and cucumber sandwiches. You gave permission for this shindig?"

"Suppose."

"You suppose?"

"By default – yes."

"All you had to do was inform me. I would have agreed but would have kept a weather eye on the proceedings."

Alex did not reply.

"Who were they?"

"The guests I understand were ladies who had visited ships before. They knew their way around."

"By God, they knew their way around all right." Frogmore guffawed.

Alex pushed his luck. "I did show one lady where to leave her shawl."

"You are as always droll, purser."

"Another gave a demonstration of the Can Can."

"I suppose that the harridan in a blue dress I espied in the engineers' alleyway was Matilda – not waltzing but Can Canning madly? I did tentatively proffer her assistance for she was falling about a great deal. She declined – not graciously, I might add." Frogmore paused. "She shouted 'Fucking move it, mate. I'm gonna throw up'." The captain took a pull at his pipe. "Scarcely, me thinks, a maid with trembling bosom. Too much cheese dip, perhaps. She came from the third engineer's cabin. God help him, for such is his taste in women. His wine account is sky high, but I allow him leeway for if I were engaged to that *Aust*ralian female, I would be forever drunk."

"Did you see the party?" asked Alex intrigued.

"I looked into the smoke room on my way to bed. There were doxies plying their trade. Some jigged to discordant music."

A clean breeze blew in through the forward windows.

"There's little damage done, sir."

Frogmore indicated the vomit.

Alex seized a newspaper from a side table and said, "Move over, Budhia."

"That's not your job, purser."
Budhia firmly took the newspaper out of Alex's hand.
Frogmore's mood changed. "Where is it?"
"Sorry?"
"The tie, for God's sake. It's been stolen."
Where the framed tie had once hung was a sheet of paper which Frogmore plucked from the bulkhead and handed to Alex. In a flamboyant but firm hand was written:
YOU HAVE BEN WARNED – BARSTARD FFROGMORE. YOU IS TYRRANT
At the centre of the piece of paper was a blob of black ink.
"Oh my God, it's The Black Spot," said Alex, unable to suppress waves of laughter.
The morning sun reflected off the captain's monocle. "By Jove! *Treasure Island!* Was it not a sea captain who lodged in *The Admiral Benbow* inn?"
"Dunno about that, sir."
"You are versed in the literature of the sea. Do you not remember *Treasure Island?* The sea captain with a pigtail and cut face?" Frogmore's voice betrayed a delight that Alex had not heard before. "The sea captain weakened by a stroke, weakened by fear, weakened by a cruel cutlass, lies dying in *The Admiral Benbow* inn, dying of apoplexy. The sea captain was given The Black Spot." A spray of defiant spittle reached Alex. "By God, purser, I am no hulk beached on a lee shore." He seemed to have gained an inner strength as he paced the smoke room with a spring in his step. He re-examined The Black Spot and said triumphantly, "If this is not proof then I do not know what is."
"Proof?"
"Proof that The Black Spot was served on me by our Antipodean buccaneer."
"The doctor?"
"I saw *Treasure Island* resting on top of a pile of books that littered his daybed. I thought at the time that it was not a book he would read."
"But tyrant has been spelt with two 'R's. Bastard has got two 'R's." Alex thought it not tactful to point out the multitudinous 'F's in Frogmore.
The captain pondered. "I will concede it may not be the doctor's hand – but there may well be others in his gang."

"Gang? Come off it."

"By jingo, purser, you'd best watch your step, otherwise you might discover what it feels like to stand on the dockside without a berth, with your sea chest by your side, as you watch your ship sail."

"You'd kick me off?"

Frogmore thought carefully. "There is justification. Your record?"

"What record? Jailed for nothing in a South American country?"

"I'm talking about your attitude to me."

"It mirrors your attitude to me, sir."

"There you have it. From your own mouth. Guard your tongue."

"All I have done wrong is put my foot in it, sir."

"Do you wish to be removed from this ship?"

"No."

"I thought you did?"

"Not booted off, I don't."

"Now you have a clear impression of what it feels like when others are trying to oust you." Frogmore added, "The doctor wants shot of me. Also, I suspect you would delight at my departure."

The chief engineer snored then groaned. His arm dropped and hung limply over the side of his chair.

Budhia gave the carpet a final rub. The captain folded The Black Spot carefully, as if to preserve it as evidence, then he slotted it into the back pocket of his uniform shorts. He nodded brusquely as he left.

LATER THAT MORNING Francis perched impudently on the office desk.

"The captain visited the chief engineer's dayroom."

"Poor chief."

"D'Silva called me in to help change the chief's bedroom curtains and we happened to overhear…"

"You were eavesdropping."

"The captain said that the chief was setting a bad example."

"And?" Alex gripped Francis' thin thigh.

"Then the captain cross-examined the chief engineer

about something called The Black Spot?"

"Ah-ha!"

"What is The Black Spot?"

"Yo! Ho! Ho!"

"Alex, what is it?"

"You expect this intellectually stunted degenerate to know? What'd you say to me being resolutely queer?"

"You've been a vegetarian, a Buddhist, now you're an homosexual. Perhaps you could try being a black after you've tried being gay, you might masochistically prefer it. It reaps all kinds of bigotry. Overt and covert."

"You expect me to grovel?"

"One fad of yours that has stuck, is alcohol. You could become an alcoholic. Perhaps you are already."

"Do you think I should wear makeup and put on a mincing gait?"

"You're halfway there – you've got the talk."

"I'm attracted to men, but putting willies at random in every possible orifice is..."

"Wise up, Alex. You're thirty-five. Go have a fuck and take a shower afterwards. Keep yapping about it and you'll be wanking until your spunk runs out."

"Jesus, Francis," said Alex, truly shocked.

Rusty, in alcoholic confusion slunk into the office.

"What you two up to?" he said.

Because of the officer-steward barrier it was necessary that Alex's and Francis' mutual liking could not be shown, though it shone like a lighthouse beacon. Rusty saw it then. Even the shy Ernest had told Alex that Francis would cry if the two were split up.

Francis hurried out carrying a pair of doeskin shoes in need of Blanco.

"We're sailing ahead of schedule," said Alex.

"Have I done something wrong?" said Rusty with an alcoholic's remorse.

"You want I make a list?"

"Please tell me?"

"The captain talked to me about Eleanor and..."

"Eleanor didn't come back until this morning."

"And she found you naked and comatose in your bunk reeking of cheap perfume. And clutching a shoe belonging to Matilda Empress."

"The captain heard?"

"A cheap plastic shoe big enough for a fucking elephant."

"God, am I in the shit."

"Interesting the shoe – Oedipus afoot. Obvious sexual and pantomime connotations."

"Did you see *her?*" asked Rusty, in horrified recollection.

"Matilda in the blue dress? I was woken at midnight by her raucous voice."

"Oh, fuck."

"She didn't make it to the bog. Frogmore and I were inspecting her vomit on the smoke room carpet this morning. Have you noticed how people who throw up have always been eating carrots?"

"You have a thing about carrots."

"And, *en passant,* she accosted Frogmore in the alleyway when he returned on board last evening. Her earthy language he noted. You're a marked man."

"Not him too! I've enough on my plate with Eleanor on at me all the time."

"She has reason."

"It's her... It's her female stuff is the problem."

"She must be perpetually menstruating."

Rusty, sitting on Alex's desk, took one of his cigarettes. He tentatively inhaled then coughed violently. When he stopped coughing, he inhaled again.

"Is Eleanor familiar with *Treasure Island?*" said Alex.

"What?"

Alex lowered his voice, "Perhaps you'd best keep a keen ear to the deck when Eleanor is around. The Black Spot has been served on this ship's master – nailed to the bulkhead in the smoke room. The captain is taking it very seriously indeed. He suggested a conspiracy of *Aust*ralians. And, between you and me, his thinking is that Matilda or Eleanor may well be Blind Pew."

"You're so mad, Alex."

"Me, mad? You, mad? The captain mad? Dr Trimmer? Eleanor? It's a matter of the perspective of the other lunatics in the asylum called Earth. Can I have one of my cigarettes you've just pocketed?"

"You're in a good mood, Alex?"

"The old man is getting human."
He was to regret saying that.

"YOU WANTED to see me, sir?"
Frogmore gave five pages of handwritten foolscap to Alex. "The Voyage Report to be typed. You can mail it from Sydney." Bicarbonate of soda clouded the glass of water which he downed without a shudder. "Your cat was on deck this morning."
"She won't go ashore."
"How do you know?"
"Feline agoraphobia. I know the feeling."
"I've told you to keep her locked up. You promised me repeatedly that the animal would be secure."
"She will not go ashore, sir."
"Have it destroyed in Sydney."
"What?"
"Charge the vet's fee to the ship."
"Destroy Felicity? I can't do that."
"That is what I have just told you to do, purser," said Frogmore pleasantly.

TWENTY-TWO

SYDNEY

THE WORLD'S largest natural harbour was cluttered with brash yachts and several were hindering the passage of the *John Bede*.

The telegraphs rang stop. A cloud of rust rose as the cable ran out. At anchor, the ship swung and was buzzed by launches, looked at by passengers on ferries. Frogmore, instead of fuming at the delay, took the opportunity to hold a summit meeting.

The summit was on his deck. The senior officers sat on imitation wrought iron chairs around an imitation wrought iron table. The gay Martini umbrella of Lovelace days had been stowed away.

Frogmore studied the spectacular waterfront he hadn't seen in many a year. "The United States," he said in terrible condemnation.

The pilot, uneasy at being at anchor in a busy waterway, paced the starboard side as he waited for the officer on watch to tell him that contact had been made from the shore on the VHF authorising him to move ship. He declined Frogmore's invitation to partake in Kenyan coffee or *Lapsang Suchong.*

"Pilot, you are blessed with one of the most outstanding natural harbours in the world and you desecrate it with that." Frogmore indicated the part-completed Opera House. "There has been trouble over it – as one might expect."

The pilot, perhaps feeling he held some responsibility for the waterfront's architecture, headed back to the bridge.

"The British designed the Sydney Harbour Bridge which I've always considered impressive."

Frogmore's talk bored Alex. He concentrated on being photographed for *Tatler*. He posed, holding his cigarette so that the smoke drifted away from his face and positioning himself so the camera's lens could record the dazzle of sun on blue water and the coloured spinnakers of the yachts, as well as the distinguished company. He adjusted his Polaroid's that set off his fashionable beachwear.

"Are you with us, purser?"

"In body and soul."

"Is the cat locked up?"

"She's okay."

"I'm not asking whether the animal is okay. I'm asking if it is secure."

"Snug as a bug in a rug."

Frogmore said, "Your cat was not as snug as a bug in a rug when it was stalking number three hatch this morning."

"We were at sea."

Frogmore glanced about, not at the impudent ferries nor at the pleasure yachts unforgivably enjoying themselves, but for a possible eavesdropper. "And now you tell me that I've signed a form, pledging one thousand dollars if the animal disappears. Have her destroyed – after the party."

"Party?" said the chief engineer.

"What kind of party?" said Alex.

The captain smiled the smile of a skull. "Certainly nothing like the Melbourne junket."

"No women?" said Alex, thinking the party would be a shippers' do.

"Women."

"You mean a party for officers – with women?" persisted Alex, shocked by the momentous news.

"You object to women?" said Frogmore, with an ironic stare.

"No, sir."

"Would it help if you took notes, purser?"

"Notes?"

"Will you ever stop repeating what I say."

"I think I might be able to retain the information without the aid of notes," said Alex, lapsing into Frogmorese and that was easy – easy to be pedantic, to be rude. His tanned brow creased as he recalled how it used to be seated at this same table: with Lovelace with his cat asleep safe on his lap.

"We don't want a load of shag-bags at this party," said the chief, winking at Alex.

Morgan coughed.

"I have nieces ashore. One is studying modern history

and will be interested in the art deco features in the accommodation. The younger girl suggested dinner – bringing a few friends." He addressed the chief engineer directly. "One doesn't imagine that they will be shag-bags."

The chief engineer beamed. Morgan reddened.

"I will not have Saturnalia in my ship."

Bitch Sydney had firmly lowered the hem of her skirt.

"When's this knees-up?" said the chief engineer.

"Tomorrow. Perhaps you or the purser would inform the third engineer's woman that I wish to see her." He added, "With her track record one can assume that she will board as soon as the gangway is lowered."

ON THEIR WAY up top, Eleanor said, "If I'd known I'd have worn my dress with the shaped bodice."

Alex groaned. He had already waited fifteen minutes while she freshened her makeup.

"Miss...?" said Frogmore, trying to soften his voice.

"Eleanor, Captain. Alex has told me about your nieces. How lovely. Are they Australian?"

"Yes."

"What are their names?" said Eleanor with false enthusiasm.

Alex hoped for Gertrude and Heliotrope and was only partially disappointed when Frogmore said, "Charlotte and Emily."

"How lovely. I adore old fashioned names."

"With their friends, they will number ten. Tomorrow evening."

"And how can I help, sir?" said Eleanor, with barely disguised delight. Her use of 'sir' was so false that the usually impassive Gomes caught Alex's eye.

"It needs a woman's touch. Perhaps you could organise suitable music? The radio operator will lend his tape machine, I feel sure. And short-eats, perhaps? I thought a fruit cup?"

Full-painted lips slid on Vaselined teeth. "I'd love to." Alex turned away when she said, "Can we girls use the spare cabin as a powder room?"

IN THE SPARE CABIN opposite the smoke room Eleanor

took charge with masculine authority.

"Emily and Charlotte? He *read* their names off a slip of paper."

"Right."

"I can see those two Bronte girls in muslin and broad-brimmed straw hats. I expect they will wear fucking lavender gloves."

"Eleanor, you are the mistress of the extreme."

"What's for dinner tomorrow?"

"I don't know. I only make up the menus."

She smiled the smile of a winner. "Serve Australian wine. The captain pays." She added in the manner of a military strategist, "You'll never get rid of Frogmore. Not the way you pussyfoot about."

"My dear, sweet Eleanor, your aggression emasculates me."

"If that martinet ordered you to break wind you'd fart continuously."

"Am I tyrannised by Frogmore with multitudinous F's?"

Eleanor wasn't in the mood for riddles. "There are no ethics in combat – winning is what it's all about. And I'll want six bottles of vodka and eight of red wine – any old plonk will do."

"Sounds like your big push, darling." But Alex was puzzled. For Frogmore to invite her to organise the party was so out of character. Alex always did the bar and Sparks supplied the music at such events. Unless the captain had some hidden agenda? Perhaps he was into confrontation not cooperation.

AFTER ALEX escaped Eleanor's planning – or plotting, he suspected – he settled at his desk in the long narrow office.

The cadet came in to draw money.

Dave folded the Australian dollars and slotted them into his wallet. Alex swung closed the heavy green safe door, pushed down the handle and locked it.

"Thank you," said Dave.

"Okay."

"I mean thank you for being kind to me."

"You okay for midday tomorrow?"

"No problem."

"It's Rodney's friend's car. He's into animal rights and is outraged that Felicity is to be shot at dawn. Rodney will be busy – plucking his eyebrows – so if you're up for it?"

"I'm always up for it. You turn me on."

"Felicity's won't turn you on. Put her in a pillowcase in the boot and cover her with my dirty dhobi. Doubt if the man on the gate will look there."

"Okay."

"You don't hate Frogmore, do you?"

"I don't hate anyone."

"You've cause to," said Alex, about to lose stomach for the job he had to do the next day.

HE ARRIVED outwardly confidant on the bridge carrying a sheaf of papers.

"Later." Captain Frogmore was watching the discharge of cargo at number two.

"A signature, please? I've a customs officer waiting."

"He can wait."

"No, he cannot, sir. The cat has disappeared and he's due on another ship and he's getting shirty."

Silence from the captain.

"No problem. He's letting the ship off with a caution. No fine. He's in a hurry."

Frogmore's face showed his fury but all he said was, "By, God, purser, you give me no satisfaction in proving you wrong. Come!" He strode into the chartroom.

Alex followed with the forms, praying that his hand wouldn't shake too much and that Cadet Jones had made it safely out the gate with Felicity.

RUSTY and Larry and Sparks were knocking back the beers when Alex arrived in the smoke room.

"The old man's not coming?" said Larry.

"He's not a party person."

Sparks, even with tattoos covered, and sporting flashing new teeth, lacked certain social skills. "Is there to be no fucking at this fucking party?"

"What's that?" Larry pointed to a large glass bowl of pink liquid in which fruit and ice floated.

"When Eleanor stirred it, she muttered the Lord's Prayer

backwards," said Rusty, lowering his voice as he could hear footsteps on the stairs.

Alex, watching them arrive, thought how visitors from ashore intrude in cargo ships. They changed the very feel of the vessel. He suspected that Frogmore might feel the same.

There was no herding for this was a chat and circulate do. The chief engineer greeted the guests. The doctor was charming as he handed round drinks. Cadet Jones tempted with his smile and a tray of short-eats.

A woman, approaching Alex in his dugout behind the bar, said, "You shouldn't drink beer. Fruit punch is muchbetter for you."

"I wouldn't take bets."

The woman turned to Larry. "Tell me, what do you think of Australia?"

"It's big."

"You must have an opinion of Sydney?"

"Don't get to see much of it – only the bars."

"A bar is a bar is a bar."

Larry said, "In the Far East you go into a bar and it's quiet and there's a girl who comes to your table and sits and talks and she has all the time in the world. That's not just a bar."

"You pay these women?"

"That's how they get a living."

"They sell themselves to men?"

"Hey, ease up," said Alex.

"I'm for women's rights. This is my aggressive mode."

"I'll watch out."

"I don't bite – only in bed." She smiled. "You two are close?"

Larry said, "Close."

"I've nothing against homosexuality."

"We're not shagging only dating."

"You have no physical feelings for him?"

"Sure," said Larry. "He's pleasant to look at. But I don't see that as me being queer."

"And if he was fat and sixty?"

"You've just turned me queer." Larry poured her a beer. "Better for you than that punch – trust me."

"You spit in the punch?"

Larry laughed. "Worse."

Alex said, "You're Charlotte?"

"That's me."

"I thought you'd be serious with aggressive hair and not very good teeth."

"That's almost a compliment."

"You look good, but you're a Frogmore, for Christ's sake."

"Rupert's cuddly."

"I'm about to laugh derisively."

"I've gotta go up and see Uncle Rupert. You two coming?"

"I'd rather pull out my finger nails."

"I'll tell him."

"He'll identify me immediately."

"See you in a bit," said Larry, heading for the door.

Charlotte lingered in the smoke room talking to Alex. "What do you do on here?"

"Wasn't it dear Oscar who said it is an aristocratic art to do absolutely nothing?"

"You must do something other than quote Wilde and say rude things about my uncle?"

"I lounge about in a quilted dressing gown which is slightly frayed at the cuffs. And I smoke a great deal. I drink during waking hours – that is an occupation in itself. But coping with hangovers is my genius."

"I'll tell Rupert about you pulling out your nails." She headed up top to the captain's accommodation.

Alone and brooding, it dawned on Alex that the objective of this party would be no different to the objective of the party in Melbourne. The men were now dancing with the women. Drinks which were earlier sipped were being knocked back. A couple of fruit punches inside them and the event had changed from social to sexual. The veneer that hid the mating instincts had been stripped away. Cadet Jones was dancing with a slim young woman with raven hair.

"You okay?" asked Francis, curious at Alex's miserable expression.

"No."

"Grit you teeth and think of Australian surfers. Back in ten minutes."

The music became strident. The brakes were off. The dancers had ruthless intent. No one would flag, their purpose was clear. Heterosexuality reigned.

Francis returned and dumped a rattling box of mineral waters on the bar counter. Seeing the purser's expression, he said, "Go away."

Alex bolted. He was headed East – down the broad staircase to skid at the bottom on sisal paper which protected the linoleum in the engineers' alleyway when the ship was in port.

Larry had a beer ready for him. Johnny Cash was on his tape recorder. Johnny Cash was played a great deal in *Skysail Jack's* in Singapore. The two reminisced and talked about the East and places and people they knew. Two hours later they were brought back to Australia by Rusty bumping his way along the alleyway, seeking sanctuary from the hurly-burly of the smoke room.

Alex resented his arrival for Rusty was linked to the intruders from ashore.

"You off the leash?" said Larry.

"I'm in the heads." As Rusty slid drunkenly down the jalousie door, he dropped the empty mug he carried which bounced on the Oriental carpet. He reached under the wash-hand basin and lifted the lid of the cool box. Rooting around in the slush of ice, he grasped a can of Foster's.

"Rusty!" Eleanor's voice carried clear from outside the dining saloon.

The leash tightened. Rusty sat up as he heard her footsteps. Eleanor appeared in the doorway.

"Don't bother coming in," said Larry, his deep voice held no menace.

"It's Rodney," said Eleanor, sitting on the daybed beneath the gaudy Chinese lantern with silk red tassels. "Deeply upsetting news. Rodney's been with a woman."

"A pig flew by the porthole," said Larry.

"My reaction exactly. Enjoyed it too, he said."

Alex wondered whether, when Rodney's fashionable clothes had been dumped and the slap had been washed away in the shower, what remained was a Lancashire lad going out with a girl on a Saturday night.

"I hope you're not staying?" said Larry.

"I was so disappointed," said Eleanor.

"You're a bit jealous, darling? Because Rodney loves you?"

said Rusty.

"You don't mind, do you, darling?" she said, a frown on her handsome face.

"Darling Rodney will be as guilty as hell in the morning, darling, darling," said Alex.

"I worry Rodney might be turning straight," she said.

"He was ashore this afternoon for a facial and pedicure," said Larry.

"Are you changing your sexual orientation, Alex?" said Eleanor.

"Ten minutes with you is enough to turn any man queer," he said.

"Tell me?"

"My penis – my problem."

"Your problem is debating whether you should wear high heels and paint your nails black this voyage."

"That is so outrageous, Eleanor."

"That's what Rusty told me."

"What else did Rusty tell you, darling?"

"He doesn't have to say anything. I know. You and I go back a long way, darling Alex. You role play all the time. You've been a vegetarian. That health-freak kick lasted all of ten minutes. Then it was Buddhism one voyage, Yoga the next."

"That lipstick you're wearing is too orange for you, Eleanor."

"Clever, but you won't stop me telling it as it is."

Alex sighed, put his hands up to cover his ears, but he could still hear her.

"This voyage you are The Queer with the gay gaucho boyfriend who reeks of horse – who no one has seen. One notes that the 'imagined' boyfriend has to be very butch. He lassoed you. And you lay belly up – or bottom up – begging for it."

"Can't you kill the bitch, Larry?"

After Eleanor went on at length about Alex's sexual adventures with women last voyage. Alex said, "You're the camp follower, taking notes to store in your ammunition pouch."

"And there was Mary," she said, laughing with derision.

"Shut it. Tell her Larry."

" 'Tell her, Larry'," mimicked Eleanor.

"Two Marys. Hail Mary twice – how about that for gluttony?" Eleanor was unabashed.

"Mary and I practise Yoga, you silly witch."

"Oh right. That gorgeous figure – I was green with envy. And the second Hail Mary in Brisbane?"

"My mother's cousin removed several hundred times. She's fifty."

"Bullshit. Nearer thirty than fifty and was she hot. Question?"

"No," said Alex.

"Do you love Debs? Where you off to?" she said.

"I'm going to throw myself down a hatch."

The cabin was no longer the East, it was strident and anyplace. In the cross-alleyway he bumped into Cadet Jones. They walked together to the warm pantry.

"Where's the girl? She looked nice."

"She's good fun. Brewer's nattering to her."

"Come join us – Larry's?"

"I'm on deck at six."

"For someone so young you sound dull."

"The faithful often are seen as dull," said Dave, putting his cards on the table; putting his hands about Alex and holding him and kissing him softly on the mouth. He let go. "You gonna report me?"

"Come to Larry's with me?"

"You and I are good together."

"I am not for you. I like black men."

Dave moved quietly over the red-tiled deck; opened the door at the after end of the pantry and was gone.

Alex's hands shook slightly as he carried a tray of sandwiches back to Larry's cabin where he sat on the carpet, and rested his head on Eleanor's knees. She stroked his hair gently. "It's not dyed."

Rusty, so drunk that he was almost falling off his seat, said, "All those women he goes with proves he's queer."

"Pardon, darling?" said Eleanor.

"Surrounding himself with women, darling. All queers do that."

"That makes him queer, darling?"

Rusty snickered.

Eleanor said, "Alex has something – not so much looks but that something which women go for."

Alex was thinking about Debs, wondering if he was too drunk to telephone her.

Eleanor said, "He's a... What's a male nymphomaniac called?"

"Francis would know."

"Francis would know! That's another thing."

"What, *my sweetest*? You're turning me irrevocably to the comfort of my hand or any man's hand."

"That very unhealthy relationship you have with your slime-ball steward."

Alex sighed.

"He's so yuk. All that hair held down with sump oil."

"Coconut oil."

"Jeeves and Wooster. He – the smooth creepy servant and you the upper-crust chinless wonder." Her hand stroked Alex's cheek.

"Larry, why do you allow this dreadful creature in your cabin? She's so bitchy, she must be a man in drag."

"She's all woman, trust me," said Larry, moving to the daybed and sitting next to her.

Rusty's head was nodding in sleep. "Believe it, Alex's queer. He's tried to suck me off – twice. Bribes me with beers."

"Oh, be quiet, darling. Larry, my darling, I'll have my beer in a small glass."

"Don't give the witch a drop," said Alex.

Eleanor opened the small glass-fronted mahogany cupboard fixed to the bulkhead above the desk and took out a peg glass. "We have our little disagreements but he can be mature and understanding, can't you, Larry, my darling? I ask and you always obey."

"You are an evil witch but you are just so unbelievably gorgeous," said Larry, pouring her a beer.

The once giggling Rusty was asleep. Larry and Eleanor were kissing – tongues and frantic hand stuff.

Alex stood up.

Eleanor said, "If you're leaving, we can't do this." Larry's hand was under her skirt.

Alex stormed out, furious and jealous. His anger was

directed at the second engineer. It was as though Larry had betrayed him. He climbed the steps to the cadet's cabin, seeking reassurance, wanting to talk. Cadet Jones was deep asleep and did not stir when Alex pulled the blanket up to cover his broad shoulders. He sat in the armchair watching him for half an hour before going to his own cabin.

FRANCIS manner was brisk, his smile smug.

"News from France, sir."

Alex opened his eyes wondering if he could make the wash-hand basin before spewing.

"I've discovered Emily's movements," said Francis.

"Have we docked in Brest?"

"Emily!"

"*Emile.* Is it by Genet?"

"The captain's niece."

"Which port is this?"

"Sydney."

"Can I have a gin – no *tonique* and hold the lemon. I'm feeling a trifle *querelle* this morning."

Francis placed a large bowl besides the bunk, and said, "Emily was with Badsha Meah in the crew's galley."

"I expect they were enjoying a fried herring and *chapatti* breakfast. I'll note it for the *Tatler.* Did you take photographs? Was the herring *au beurre?* Did they pose *au naturelle?*"

"She was somewhat under the weather. Badsha Meah gave her tea then took her home in a taxi."

Francis, disappointed at Alex's lack of reaction, dumped a cold pot ashtray on his bare stomach.

"What happened to Charlotte?"

Francis, the imitation Jeeves, was now holding camp court: "You're referring to the elder of the two sisters, sir? The lady from Lesbos who disappointed your cruel expectations. I do recall, you had earlier said, rather bitchily, I thought, that she would be robustly built with layered chins and a severe haircut – reminiscent of Gertrude Stein on a butch hair day."

"You have to talk like that?"

"I've had a very good teacher, *cher* Alex."

"You're the worst *garçonette* out of Bombay. Stop looking,

you pervert." He sat up in his bunk and pulled the crested bedcover up to preserve his modesty.

"I have seen it before and it's not worth a second glance," said Francis, his dark eyes smiling, his chin smoky.

"Charlotte?"

Francis moved to the cabinet above the drop-down desk and took out a bottle of Gordon's and a peg glass. "She told the captain..."

"Gomes eavesdropping?" Alex sipped the neat gin; shuddered then downed it in one.

"She told the captain that she sat up all night worrying, waiting for her sister."

"I'll have ice with the next one, unless you're trying to kill me." Francis picked up the ice bucket and looked for the tongs. Alex said, "Play sexy, use your fingers. I feel like taking risks. You can rub my back with a melting cube."

"You are still drunk but I'm sober. Sober or drunk you are not a temptation."

"Charlotte?"

"She did tell the captain that Emily had been fed drugs."

"Charlotte's on board?" Alex took the bottle from his steward and poured gin over the ice in his glass.

"Went ashore in a taxi."

"I can't believe you made that remark about my penis." He swung out of bed; padded naked into his office where he picked up the phone to the captain. Francis followed, with his head averted, to primly drop a bath towel on Alex's lap as he spoke into the Bakelite mouthpiece.

"Sir, you worried about your niece Emily?"

"Do you know where the girl is?"

"One of the crew took her home in a taxi."

"Give him a pound and reimburse him the taxi fare. Put it on my account." The phone went dead.

Alex gritted his teeth at the captain's rudeness. He lifted the towel. "Something is happening. Rub my inside leg and get a tape measure."

"I'll get you two Band Aids, a large one for your mouth and a small one to hold it down."

"Be nice to me, Francis, and get me another gin – a smallish tot this time with much ice."

TWENTY-THREE

SYDNEY

FROGMORE said, "My nieces, purser?"
"Sir?"
"I'm old fashioned but not so old fashioned as to imagine that the young women sat around all evening sipping lemonade and nibbling game chips – but I had no concept that drugs would be taken."
"Me neither."
"Charlotte, the elder of the girls was most forthright on the telephone. Insistent that Emily had been fed drugs."
"Eleanor, you reckon?"
"Why not the doctor?"
"I've smelt ether outside his cabin. Does one take ether for kicks?"
"No idea."
"Me neither. I'm sorry."
"Sorry about what?"
"About Emily, sir."
Alex was fascinated as he watched Frogmore write in a leather pocket book. *Crojick – the lowest yard on the mizzen mast of a fully rigged ship.*
The captain said, "Do make yourself comfortable." He then sent his steward to summon the doctor who arrived looking dishevelled – that was usual; and sober – that was not.
"Doctor, when are you leaving my ship?"
"Is your stomach playing up again?"
"Please answer my question." Frogmore suddenly caught sight of Rusty's onetime battered cap which Alex sometimes carried about as a gesture to conformity. "Purser, what has happened to your cap?"
Dr Trimmer took a cigarette from the box and lit it with the table-lighter. "I can get someone to run a few tests on you."
"I was talking to the purser."
Dr Trimmer plonked himself in the captain's desk chair,

picked up an ashtray and placed it on his knee. "The hat, of course, is symbolic of the male and female genitals."

"Oh, do shut up."

"Freud." Dr Trimmer blew a smoke ring.

"You're leaving this vessel in Brisbane, are you not?"

"Right."

"I shall not be sorry. You have undermined authority. You have ridiculed the command. You have corrupted the gullible. You have tried to replace order with anarchy. You've shat on my desk."

Alex felt the need of a stiff brandy.

"You shouldn't be ashamed of mental illness."

"You have not practised medicine for some time, I would surmise?"

"Right."

"You gave up a philanthropic vocation for commerce?"

"My doctorate is in engineering."

This almost had Frogmore at a loss for words. He widened his eyes, spoke with great care. "Let me get this right. You have no medical degree?"

"I did nursing for a while. Get it?"

"Indeed, I have got it."

"I doubt if anyone likes you. You are a tyrant..."

"Tyrant with two 'R's, Mr Trimmer?" said the captain with relish. "Neither you nor any of your drug-crazed band will beat me."

Alex experienced unease. Maybe the captain's self-imposed isolation had affected his judgement. Or he wondered if Frogmore might be putting on a mood which hinted of a persecution complex. He wondered how much was the real Frogmore and how much was for show, for effect.

Trimmer stubbed out his cigarette, placed the ashtray on the desk, then stood. In the doorway he said, "Write to the board of directors. Repeat your accusations. Do you think the shipping company would believe that I put The Black Spot on you? That I defecated on your desk?"

After he left the captain said to Alex, "You were incarcerated in Brazil."

"You're not reporting that to head office?"

Frogmore said, "The so called doctor has already done so,

that was why I brought it up. Head office contacted me. I had Mendes telephone them and sing your praises."

"Oh."

"Stop your tomfoolery, lad. That malicious Trimmer acts with deliberate intent. I'm always on the side of my ship and my ship's company and on the side of what is fair and right."

"You had me chucked off passenger ships."

"Not so. It was a head office assistant manager."

"Tyler travelled that cruise?"

"Quite. You and I left with two other officers. Tyler's misjudgement. He's gone now and we remain."

Alex saluted Frogmore. The fact that he had saluted sent a shiver of embarrassment down his spine. He was immensely relieved that no one other than Frogmore had witnessed it.

TWENTY-FOUR

DRUNK AND OUT IN SYDNEY

ALEX enjoyed nothing better than a run ashore with his shipmates. As Cadet Jones was studying and Larry was sorting out a major problem in the engine room, he sought out Rusty. The defrocked Doctor Trimmer tagged along.

The *Gitchie Goomie Bar* had none of the informality of *Joe's* in Tamana Prospect although there was a flavour of the Melbourne gay bar. Some customers posed but most just looked. It was a sit-and-look joint. A place maybe to pick up sheilas or mates. Heterosexual sex hung in the air, and same-sex hung there too, but not predominately so. Sex was not Alex's intent. He was a seafarer getting drunk.

"Are you all right?" asked Trimmer.

"Define all right in a Freudian context?"

"You seem rather relaxed."

"Pissed, Doc. We are but simple sailors ashore."

"I've never seen you so far gone."

"I'm celebrating."

"Celebrating?"

"The demise of the virago."

"I can't follow you?"

"I've discovered Rusty has a backbone."

"Really?" said Trimmer, examining the wilting Rusty who was drunker than Alex.

Rusty lifted his heavy head, his speech slurred, "Did you know they've taken Felicity?" Then he nodded wisely at his beer as if in communication with it.

"Is this about Eleanor?" said Trimmer.

Alex said, "Eleanor is killing the sacrificial calf. There will be blood on the carpet tonight."

"Isn't that a novel by Gertrude Stein?"

"Gertrude Stein is much in vogue in Australia. An Aussie bar is an Aussie bar is an Aussie bar. She said when pissed out of her intellectual skull in Gay Sydnee."

"She wrote gibberish according to Evelyn Waugh," said

Trimmer.

"I don't want Gertrude," said Rusty.

"Eleanor would make a dashed fine wife," said Alex. "A powerful right hook and she's a spiffing cook into the bargain."

"Marriage is an outdated institution," said Trimmer.

Rusty choked as the leash of wedlock tightened.

Alex leant towards Trimmer. "Without backbone Rusty could well be doomed. He visited Shrew Eleanor's parents. They liked him."

"They did?" said Trimmer, looking at the swaying Rusty. "Can you describe them?"

"Doc doesn't want to meet the mother, does he, Rusty?"

Rusty pushed his head in his hands and groaned and sobbed. Tears ran through his fingers.

Alex said, "Bowls of flowers on polished tables and polished silver on polished tables, and take-your-shoes-off when you come through the front door before you tread on the polished floor. And tablemats. The tablemats were very worrying."

"You've been inside the house, Alex, or is it your febrile imagination?" said Trimmer.

"Would I have made up tablemats?"

"Indeed not."

"And a floppy clock – the Salvadore Dali' one – to show how intellectual they are."

"Deeply significant," said Doc.

"Freud again."

"Do not scoff. Floppy clock, slurred as you slurred it, sounded like floppy cock. A subconscious pleading by you, to inform us of your erectile dysfunction."

"When I lit a Pall Mall, I had several ashtrays thrust at me. 'Could you smoke on the verandah, dear'?"

"She's scary," groaned Rusty.

"Daughters grow to be like their mothers," said Trimmer.

Rusty rounded on Alex. "That garbage you came out with. How you adored the curtains."

"Pelmets! She had pelmets!"

"You were being sarcastic?"

"Eleanor's mother got it."

"God, you're so beautiful, Alex."

"Why do pretentious folk drink gin and tonic in a drawing room lit with so many chandeliers that it looks like a shop window."

"What exactly happened?" said Trimmer.

"I kept the parents company, chatting about pelmets, while Rusty and Eleanor dined outdoors on this special night. Rusty and the lovely Eleanor drove to the beach where they ate prawns and drank champagne. An evening in paradise: pounding surf breaking on the tropical shore, and palm trees that soared. Freudian, do you think, Doc?"

"Without one shadow of a doubt. The tree trunk is the erect penis, and the coconuts are the gonads and the coconut milk is the spermatozoa. And one must not overlook the palm fronds – and their obvious similarity to pubic hair. One sees the palm tree as a mammoth phallus. Can I ask what took place on the beach, Rusty? Did she stroke the tree's trunk?"

Alex said, "The two lovers lay entwined on the foreshore. A soft breeze whispered in the phallic palms. A dark sea reflected a waning moon. Eleanor spoke to him tenderly. Rusty answered – while gently stroking her lovely hair which curled deliciously at the nape of her slender neck – 'I love you so much, my darling-darling. When shall we wed? Soon, my love, for the ship sails Tuesday, on the flood tide'." Alex's voice hardened. "Suddenly the sand was cold and the dying moon gave no colour to her titian hair."

Rusty pushed a fist into his mouth and tears rolled down his cheeks. "Help me, Alex? You are my bestest mate."

"But you said earlier that Rusty rejected the proposal of marriage?" Trimmer then tried to get through to Rusty. "What did actually happen?"

Rusty sat bolt upright on his bar stool. "She said it."

"Said what?"

"I am going to marry you!" Rusty, in alcoholic shock, almost fell off his stool, but with rubber resilience came back up again. Wiping away tears, he pleaded: "Please help me." Then remembering the previous evening, his alcoholic mood altered. "Alex, you stirred it waffling on about the joys of motherhood."

"I hate children. They are uncivilised and noisy and smell and always lie."

"And then you..."

"I said marriage was a manufactured state. A set-up by the church. Eleanor is hardly saving herself for the nuptial bed."

"I'm not having that."

"Many have."

"Jesus God, Alex, what you said to Eleanor's mother."

"What?"

"Show me a virgin over eighteen and I'm straight."

"Surely not? I am always sensitive to any social occasion. I've been on passenger ships, you know."

"And you camped it up. And lisped. You lispingly lisped that even if you didn't have a longing for endless anal sex, you wouldn't get married."

"I do remember lighting up in the hall when we were leaving and Mother of Eleanor pulled a tendon sprinting for an ashtray and the Airwick."

"Eleanor said that you would never be my best man – not in a million years. It was then I started to shake. Best man? They were making the wedding arrangements." Rusty said, "You slag off Eleanor because she is a woman. You're not capable of liking any woman. You're an ageing homosexual in love with me."

"Until death us do part. Which will be quite soon, if you go on like this."

"You're the gaucho's fag. Walk!"

"What?"

"Walk! I want to see you mince under pressure."

Near to them a fraught young woman in a yellow dress gave her friend a look.

Rusty said, "I'm leaving now. Meeting the parents at eight."

All, including the girl in yellow and her friend, glanced at the clock above the bar which showed ten o'clock. All checked their watches before staring at Rusty questioningly.

"Where are you meeting them?" said Trimmer.

"Wasn't it *The Golden Futtock* restaurant?" prompted Alex.

"*The Golden Futtock.*" Rusty standing, had his feet cemented to the floor. He swayed so that his shoulder brushed the bar counter. He bounced back upright as if he were made of rubber. Then he bobbed in the other direction. Trimmer put out an arm to catch him but Rusty stayed at an alarming angle before slowly coming upright. His hands were clenched in red fists of frustration. They unclenched to embrace Alex.

"Sit!" said Alex.

Rusty's eyes were wide open but there seemed nothing behind them. "I've always loved you, Alex." He must have been reading one of Eleanor's magazines for he added, "Ours is a love that is made in heaven and because of convention we dared not tell others of it." Then abruptly he abandoned Alex to pick up his glass and drain it. When attempting to place the glass on the bar counter, he missed by six feet.

The barmaid came from behind the bar to join them with a dustpan and brush. As she swept up the pieces of glass, Rusty embraced a pillar and swung around it.

"Mind your feet," she snapped.

Rusty stopped swinging and focused on her, for here was possible sex.

"He'll drink himself sober," said Trimmer to the barmaid. "I'm a doctor."

"Alex, my darling, phone Eleanor for me. Tell her you and I are together."

"Not."

"I'm begging you!"

"Get off your fucking knees. Mind the goddamn glass," said the barmaid to Rusty. Then in a sympathetic way she addressed Alex, "You look a decent sort for a Pom. Be fair to Eleanor. Get on that phone to her right this minute and tell her you're one of them."

"He's not faithful to me. That's why I drink," groaned Rusty.

The woman in her role of barmaid-psychoanalyst, nodded at Rusty, giving him a chance to explain.

"He had sex with a man in Brazil. A gaucho. There were guns involved. He was thrown in jail with this South American lowlife and I was worried sick."

"When you were having it off with a fourteen-year-old nun in a convent," shouted Alex, escaping the glare of the barmaid for the safety of the telephone.

But the telephone was not easily reached. It was at the rear of the barroom. Alex squeezed passage towards it between a line of stools and the wall. Customers were sitting on the stools and they were not friendly. As he eased by the girl in yellow, she sharply drew herself in. A massive guy overhung his stool, and made no attempt to move, as Alex flattened himself against the wall.

He had trouble dialling. At a third attempt he heard someone answer. He slowed his speech, trying to sound sober and impressive. Then he put the phone down, silencing the babble in his ear.

The fat guy said, "Watch it!" as he squeezed by.

The girl in yellow hissed at her friend, "It's the Pom."

Rusty was overjoyed to see him. He kissed him on the forehead. At the same time he addressed the intrigued barmaid with a wail, "His problem has always been dick. Nine inches isn't enough for him." Rusty looked pleadingly at the woman. "I can't blame him. The poor bastard's had an operation down there."

"Oh, my God," she said.

Alex was wondering what the operation might have entailed. He certainly felt castrated at the moment.

"I've done everything to please him. He makes me drink his urine."

"He must be real sick," said the woman.

"As it comes with a twist of lemon. You should try it."

"Try drinking his piss?"

"Warm with a twist of lemon. Trust me. Are you going with anyone?" said Rusty.

"I'm married ten years."

"I feel so close to you. Your husband treat you all right?"

A customer on the far side of the bar banged his empty glass demanding service. The barmaid screamed at him, "You got no fucking manners!"

Through a fug of tobacco and insane companionship, Alex saw Cadet David Jones standing outside the bar on the pavement, peering through the glass door.

Alex waved him in.

Trimmer said, "I must get pissed. Therapeutic. My treat. Can you lend me a tenner, Alex? I know a club which is raided often."

"Alex, come back to the ship with me?" said Cadet Jones.

"What you doing ashore, Dave?"

"Looking for you."

"Why so?"

"Rodney saw me earlier on and told me where you'd be and I was to rescue you from the mad people."

"Come and have a drink? I need someone to talk to who is sane. On me." Alex opened his wallet.

Jones shook his head and put his arm in Alex's.

Rusty shrieked at the barmaid, "He's picking up rent boys now."

Walking outside, Alex said, "David Jones, take me home."

"We walk?"

"You'd come expensive."

"Sorry?"

"As rent." Alex hailed a taxi.

"CAN I SAY SOMETHING?"

"Am I in the shit?" Alex poured himself a large scotch.

"You don't have to get drunk to escape me."

"I'm escaping my upbringing."

Dave Jones pushed a protesting Alex onto his bunk and pulled off his trousers, which he neatly folded, then he unbuttoned his shirt. Alex, almost asleep, rocked on the bunk's edge.

"You only like me because I am a father figure," he said, throwing his folded clothes in the air.

A generator, below in the engine room, was running noisily and vibrated the empty peg glass against the whisky bottle which had dregs in it. Dave moved the bottle before climbing on the narrow bunk alongside Alex and held him tight.

"We can't be much closer, can we, Font Pisser?"

Without warning a squall hit the ship. The two men were startled at its suddenness.

Alex slid his hand down and held Dave's cock, saying, "I reckon, the shit between us has about run its course now." He eased back on the cuddling but Dave clung to him and rocked him like a child as he came in Alex's hand.

Before leaving, Dave grasped Alex's feet and held onto them, urging him to wake up and be with him, but Alex only snorted in a drunken sleep. Then the young man carefully covered him with a lightweight blanket which had the Bede

Line's blue crest, large and dead centre, on it.

THE ALLEYWAY was brightly lit. The vibration from the generator grew more intense when Dave reached the after end of the midships accommodation where a sound-proofed steel door led to the engine room. The door was ajar and he could hear the clanging of metal on metal as the engineers worked below.

On the afterdeck Larry was smoking; his white boiler suit limp with perspiration. The rain had almost stopped but the scuppers were still running water. Larry came into the alleyway, and indicating Alex's cabin, said, "You okay with him?"

Dave went on deck. "This air smells so good after the rain."

"I'm on a break." The second engineer's was about to open the steel door to return below but changed his mind. "Wait." He trotted forward along the alleyway and returned minutes later, holding two hard boiled eggs. Two cans of Cokes bulged in his boiler suit pocket. He gave Dave a Coke and a can opener. He handed him the two eggs. "My hands are shitty."

On deck they stood in the hard light from the suspended cargo lamps. Number four hatch was open but protected from the squall by a tarpaulin. Dave shelled the eggs and gave them to the second engineer, saying, "Make you constipated."

Larry stood with his right leg resting on an iron cleat, his boiler suit unbuttoned.

"Taken six salt tablets today. Two more hours and it's finished, thank fuck. Would've been done by now, if Rodney had turned to."

"Right."

"Come and talk to me – my cabin? Have a cold one?"

"You've got to work below."

"I'll take an hour off. You up for it?" Larry's left hand caressed his hairy chest.

"Why aren't you wearing underpants?" Dave put the unopened Coke into the second engineer's deep pocket in his boiler suit. He then moved purposely forward leaving Larry alone on the wet iron deck that shone like a mirror after the downpour.

ALEX was disturbed by an irritating tapping on his bunk-board. Awake he felt so ill, he swore he would never drink again.

"You'll kill yourself," said Francis, retrieving a sock caught in the metal fan that was fixed to the forward bulkhead; then, as the nagging wife, he gathered the strewn clothes. Picking up the white shoes to clean, he left the cabin and later returned with *chota hazri* which he dumped, together with a bottle of one thousand aspirins, on the ledge by the side of the bunk.

"Are these suicide pills?" said Alex.

"Take the lot and give me a break."

"Where's Rusty?"

"Shitting himself in the pilot's cabin."

Alex's shaking hand dropped the aspirin bottle. Tablets cascaded on the breakfast tray. Francis scooped them up and put them back in the bottle before crossing to the sink where he held down the cold water tap to soak a face flannel which he placed on Alex's forehead. "Think of me as the Red Cross," he said.

An hour later, seated at his office desk, Alex gingerly sipped his tea.

Eleanor banged open the door. "I've a lecture at nine."

He was trying to add up a column of figures for the third time.

"I'm staying here until you tell me where Rusty is hiding," she said.

"What?"

"Your ramblings."

"What?"

"My poor mother was inconsolable after hearing your filth on the phone."

He wondered what he had said, wondered how he could get rid of Eleanor, wondered when the fullness in his stomach would be relieved.

"Mother had to lie down."

"Wish I could."

"Where's that pathetic creature?"

"Rusty's heavily sedated – in shock."

"I want to see him."

"Eleanor?"

"What?"

"Drop the volume a bit."

"I'm not shouting!"

"God help me when you are," he said, as a sudden spurt of acidic bile hit his mouth. It tasted revoltingly green. Tentatively he sipped his cold beer. He felt he was in danger of going mad and shuddered recalling last night's drinks in *The Gitchie Goomie* and the killer whisky chasers he had knocked back in the company of a concerned cadet. Silence might help him now. To vomit certainly would.

"You turd," she shrieked.

The morning held the nightmare unreality of a five-star-hangover, and hearing Eleanor shouting was signalling him it was time to get out of town. The bile came again. He might well pass out. He smoker-coughed for several minutes. While coughing himself red in the face, Alex imagined a caring and distraught Francis silencing Eleanor with a right hook, as he jerked his last on the office floor next to the cockroach trap.

"Where's Rusty, you pouf?" she screamed with such force that Francis dropped his tin of lavender furniture polish.

Alex had had more than enough. And in a truly British way he called on his stiff upper lip. He operated at his best when under attack, even when severely unwell.

"Pouf with a double 'F' or without a double 'F'? Think very carefully before answering."

Eleanor would take none of his nonsense. She spun about, hitting his cheek hard with the flat of her hand.

Alex got to his feet and hit her, matching the force of her blow, then he grasped her wrists as she tried to attack him again.

He held her tight. "You any idea what you sound like?"

"You bastard!"

"You that desperate to get married?" He let her go.

"He promised." Eleanor quietened some.

"This is Rusty we're talking about. Bow out and salvage some dignity."

"I must talk to him."

"You think shouting at him will make him marry you?"

Privately, Alex thought it might.

"I don't underestimate the power you exert over him. He's weak and you're a domineering bully."

"You're marrying a weak guy you despise?"

"You hate all women." As though she had had enough she crumpled on the office desk, sobbing.

Eleanor's face, undeniably beautiful, had broadened in self-pity; the mouth quivered and seemed larger, the eyes were spoiled by tears. Alex was grateful that his own family were not given to such scenes.

He took charge. "Francis, ring for a taxi, please."

While waiting for the taxi, Eleanor rummaged in her bag for a mirror. When she checked out her reflection, she rushed through the doorway into the cabin where she busied herself with cold water and tissues, peering at her reflection in the mirror above the wash-hand basin.

Alex thought it amazing how women care, in times of crisis, what they look like. His imagination captured an all-female infantry platoon applying lip gloss and eyeliner before going over the top.

"Can that steward use a phone?" she shouted from his cabin.

"Third World Francis is, but stupid he ain't."

Ten minutes in makeup and she had undergone a transformation. With head held high and her shoulder bag adjusted, she gave herself an approving glance in the mirror.

"You look bloody sensational, Eleanor."

"Thank you, darling." Shrewd and hard-nosed, she was a siren out of a high-class detective novel, a siren with fabulous looks and expensive clothes.

A wry smile of farewell then she calmly walked down the awkward ship's gangway, which was almost level with the jetty. She had a certain sway that caught the eye. Feminine and aloof. She did not look back. Alex watched the taxi drive away between two warehouses.

"You know how to make an exit," he muttered.

The Indian *kalassi* at the top of the gangway said to Alex in Hindi, "You all right?"

"I'm never all right," he said, dashing into the officers' accommodation. He raced along the alleyway to the heads.

Slamming the cubicle door shut, he clung to the lavatory bowl. His right hand held down the flush so that the continuous force of saltwater rinsed away his vomit. In minutes he was feeling not quite so close to death.

But his troubles were not over.

THE MAN WHO BOARDED wore a black, creased suit, and had the high voice of a dry academic. He carried the authority of age.

"Alex, isn't it?"

"Right. You are?"

"Anthony." The brilliantine in his hair did not mask its grey.

"Thank you for taking Felicity."

"I love cats. Rodney told me that Alex could fix things."

"What needs fixing?"

"Rodney's in hospital for observation in case of delayed concussion."

"Tell me?"

"Extensive bruising and a cracked rib or two."

"How?"

"He was beaten up in a lavatory not far from the docks."

That was enough detail for Alex but not for Anthony. He had to listen as the man elaborated. He flinched at his graphic description. He did not care at all for the enthusiasm the man showed telling the tale.

He noted the name of the hospital and said he would deal with it. They shook hands. Anthony said he could find his own way off the ship.

But he did not hear the clatter of footsteps on the aluminium gangway. Instinct told him to go up top. He eavesdropped briefly outside the captain's door before barging into the dayroom.

"Get off this ship," he said.

Anthony started to protest but Alex grasped tight hold of his arm and marched him through the doorway to the head of the stairs where he pushed him with force. Anthony stumbled, grabbed hold of the banister to regain his balance.

Alex strode into the captain's dayroom, opened the outside door in order to watch Anthony rush down the gangway.

"I was about to telephone you, purser, when you arrived somewhat dramatically – if I might make such a timorous observation, without you hurling me off my ship."

"Went over the top, didn't I, sir?"

"I do hope that you are over it. You did indeed play the captain in my accommodation, but I'm well used to that. One is often humbled in the presence of your authority."

"He's a malicious bastard."

"The man has an axe to grind, one suspects."

"What're you going to do, sir?"

"I shall have you log the incident."

"Give Rodney a break?"

"I'm logging the incident."

"It's hearsay."

"One does not know the facts – other than gossip from that shabby man. But the authorities may be involved. The engineer may demand compensation. The reporting of the incident must be recorded in the Official Log Book."

"He's got a ticket, sir."

"I take your point. There could be an enquiry but I have by law to note in the Official Log Book that an officer has been discharged and I'm obliged to give the reason. You know all this, purser."

"It sounds as though Rodney will rejoin in Brisbane. I'll check with the hospital."

Frogmore stared unhappily at the pad of lined foolscap on his desktop. His right hand crawled towards the glass of bicarbonate of soda. Alex handed him a teaspoon. The captain stirred the liquid then drained the glass. He did not look up.

Alex said, "There are moments when anger surges up, when I want to lash out at the system, lash out at your unfair authority."

"I'm not unfair authority." He looked up, looked his purser in the eyes.

"I'm a coward. I should have stood up to you from day one."

"Cowardly? My God, I tremble to imagine you in aggressive mode."

"Don't you realise what you are like? You spread your

unhappiness throughout the ship."

Alex and Frogmore had finally grappled. Caps and inconsequential stuff were not considered.

A rap sounded at the dayroom door.

"Pilot on the bridge, sir," said Cadet Jones.

"Apologise to the pilot. Tell him I am detained. Tell the O.O.W. to report when we are singled up."

After Jones left Alex said, "What're you going to do about Rodney?"

"You write the log entry – something along the lines that the officer did not rejoin the ship because of an unsubstantiated report of his hospitalisation."

"Yes, sir. Thank you, sir."

Frogmore focused his rheumy eyes on his purser over the top of his half-glasses, the monocle hung; his silver beard needed a trim, small purple veins showed in his cheeks. "You can telephone Sydney agents once we're at sea. Have them contact the hospital in which he is confined and find out all details and if..." He studied the crew list and put a red line through Rodney's name. "...if the officer is going to be fit enough to rejoin in Brisbane." Showing a familiar spark, he added, "Quite frankly, purser, I've only that Man in Black's word for what happened. A man who sat down uninvited, and spoke with unnecessary relish. I did not care for the cut of his jib."

"I'm really sorry I lost it just now."

Frogmore lit his pipe. Leaning back in his desk seat he said, "On your way below, would you ask my steward to come up?"

"You don't look well."

"I asked you to summon my boy not comment on my appearance," the captain said. "You practised deceit, purser. That man told me that your cat is alive."

"There's no come back..."

"That is not the point and you bloody well know it. You implicated the cadet – that is what is unforgivable."

"You're not going to...?"

"Don't you know me by now?"

Alex stayed silent.

Frogmore hadn't finished. "The animal is old and would have been humanely put down. Human beings aren't so fortunate. It's your betrayal that shocks me far more than that Man in Black's sordid revelations."

"You're not shocked by sex between men in a public lavatory?"

"You must be aware, purser, that I am a captain of considerable experience. I have oft witnessed the shame of human misery and I am an intelligent man. Intelligent men do not hold illogical prejudices." He paused. "The time for insolence is over."

"Sir!" Alex was rooted to the spot, fascinated by his captain.

The phone from the bridge buzzed. Frogmore listened, said, "Yes" then replaced it.

"We're delayed, waiting for a tug. It will be some time. You recall the mendicant in Brazil?"

"Who became Maria Mendes' gardener?"

"He was more than that. Sit down. Sit down."

Alex took the armchair the captain indicated. "Was he begging for alms? A religious man?"

"A youth who was sent to the hacienda where..." Frogmore seemed to drift. It was as if he were recalling a pleasant incident, "...he helped with the horses."

"The hacienda?"

"A good deal south. It entailed a lengthy journey."

"The mendicant, sir?"

"Ignacio. Ignacio taught me to ride 'not as an Englishman'. I took to the saddle like a gaucho, he told me."

"You would teach him English?"

"Why do you smile? Are you imagining a gaucho using my rhetoric, ordering a ponderous beer perhaps in some isolated cantina? Would that be such a bad thing?" As Frogmore talked, both men understood that their conversation was exclusive. "He had a dashed fine seat. It was as if he and the horse were one. Praise from him was the praise I sought. Several of the guests had travelled with us to the southern boundary. The cold came up from the ground at night and was intense. It penetrated our bones, despite the sleeping bags and the covering of heavy blankets woven from alpaca and the heat from the fire that blazed all night. Maria could not sleep either and at three in the morning we drank coffee gone beyond its prime, but it was eased down by a shot of something to warm us. Ignacio had placed potatoes in the embers and we three ate them later: their tough skins we tore at with our teeth, the steaming innards dripped butter. That first night, rather that early morning, Maria talked of the land, of the route that Ignacio and I should take when we explored." Frogmore paused. "If there is a God, It is in such a place. It was there. One felt close to It."

Alex wanted to blurt out, *So you do believe in a supreme power, a force, an It?* but he kept his counsel, only saying, "I can see you on a horse. But I cannot understand how you discovered such peace so far from the sea?"

"Isn't that strange." Frogmore was suddenly on the telephone to the bridge. He said, "I see." and put the phone down. "Still delayed."

"Our phoney doctor?"

"I'll swot him like a fly."

Chilling, romantic, vulnerable; he was no martinet. The captain had dismissed the doctor and wanted to talk of more important matters. "Mornings we washed in a stream after breaking the ice."

"But the others?"

"There was Maria and myself and, of course, the two men to look after the horses. The other guests, caring for their comfort, returned to the ranch house at sun up. I was glad to see the back of them. After two days Maria had to return too. He left me with Ignacio and horses and provisions. To get on with it, he said, but instructing us to keep to the planned route – in case we got injured. And got on with it we did. The going was not hard, nor the land spectacular other than the distant mountains which one acknowledged each day with a period of quiet wonder."

Alex nodded. He would not interrupt. He allowed an old man to relive an important part of his life.

"That tract of land was silent at night other than the sounds we made: the rasp of a sulphurous match, a grunt as Ignacio shook himself in a deep sleep. Always on rising and looking at the horses at first light, I would think how beautiful they were. So loyal, so unaware of their power." Frogmore paused, deep in thought. "One careless slip, as I was walking my horse, and a rock cut my calf. It became infected. Ignacio covered the wound with sugar and the flesh from a cactus."

It seemed to Alex that the potion administered by Ignacio relieved Frogmore's inner torment.

"It was the lack of noise, Alex. No transport, no people only Ignacio and those splendid beasts." Frogmore jerked back to the present day and flicked the silver table-lighter and lit Alex's cigarette.

"Are you a mystic, Rupert?"

"You have moments of perception. The stillness of the night hinted at an inner silence we crave."

"You attained a union," Alex said softly. They did not need to talk to be comfortable in the other's company but he had to know for sure if Ignacio was the Man from the Pampa. "How old would Ignacio be now?"

"So many years ago..."

Cadet Jones was tapping at the door.

"Hatches closed up, sir. We're singled up. Tug's on its way. The pilot says ten minutes."

The cadet left but Frogmore did not head for the bridge straightaway. It seemed that he was held by something more important than the ship's departure from the sophisticated port. Nor did the luxury of his dayroom hold his attention, for his mind was on a gaucho and on horses. "You get to know your animals. You feel a pride being associated with such beauty; humbled by such devotion. Such dignity too. One has to make sure they are looked after. It was a privilege to be with the splendid creatures. The responsibility is to one's friends: human and equine."

He was repeating himself. He was talking about love, thought Alex who said, "You mentioned some time back that you stayed with Maria – but only for a weekend?"

The captain shook his head impatiently. "No, no. I went back to South America a number of times, during my leaves. In those days the Bede Line subsidised flights for all officers and Maria's plane sometimes picked me up."

"Golly, how splendid."

"That first time on the hacienda, Ignacio and I spent two weeks together. The nights grew even colder. We shared blankets and took turns to tend the fire. We drank a glass or two of fiery liquor to warm us. For such moments of great happiness and companionship one is grateful."

"You found contentment – not in a ship but with your fellow man."

"Few men have been privileged to experience the silence held on the plains before dawn, to glimpse but fleetingly the hidden truth."

Alex acknowledged the depth of the man, but said, "Did you take photographs?" For he longed for a much fingered snapshot, taken in black and white, kept in a wallet. A snapshot not so often looked at nowadays because Frogmore had moved on. But a photograph that could confirm and would link him and Frogmore in a surprising way.

"To take photographs would have been inappropriate at the time, but now, as one grows old, one wishes one had." An Indian seaman shouted on deck. "He is telling his fellows that a tug is coming." The captain crossed to the liquor cabinet and into a crested Bede line glass poured a good measure of whisky. He handed the glass of golden liquid to Alex. You will say nothing of this to the cadet?"

"The cadet is something else, sir."

"No exceptions."

"No exceptions." Frogmore had given a great deal of himself and Alex was not insensitive to that.

"You'll have to excuse me, purser, I'm due on my bridge."

Alex sat on for a while, realising that he would have had time to telephone the hospital ashore, but all thoughts of Rodney had gone out of his head.

TWENTY-FIVE

AT SEA

THE SHIP CAST OFF to sail under the Sydney Harbour Bridge. The marvellous daylight intensified the colour of the many yachts' sails, it highlighted the near completed Opera House.

The *John Bede,* when clear of the Heads, had the decks hosed down. The ship heeled, setting a course for Brisbane.

Alex caught hold of the inner slatted jalousie door before it banged shut. The outer weather door was already hooked back. The strong breeze blew papers off his desk onto the strip of Axminster. His tea-tray was untouched. He speared the dry rock cake with a ballpoint pen. The chief cook would bake frightful cakes now and then as a treat. And Alex could not bring himself to tell him not to. He hurled bits of the cake high in the air but could not reach the oar-winged albatross keeping station on the port beam.

HE dawdled gossiping to Sparks, then he detoured via the galley, and when he got back to his office Dave was sitting in the spare seat with two books open in front of him.

"Why aren't you working in the mate's office, cadet?"

"Kicked out. Doesn't want me to see how much he drinks."

"Work in your own cabin."

"I'm a bother?"

Alex got a kick out of working alongside Dave. He got a kick out of a sneaky glance at the mulatto boy too, only it was much better with Dave.

Not saying a word, Dave pushed the door shut and kissed Alex on the mouth.

The telephone buzzed and it kept on buzzing.

"He'll send the *seacunny* for you if you don't go up."

Alex stood and adjusted his underpants. "What's that book you're reading, cadet?"

"Ships construction."

"Hot stuff."

ALEX TREKKED UP TOP.

"You wanted to see me, sir?"

"A passenger ship might be best for you."

"Things which are best for you seldom are, if I may say so."

The captain turned in his desk chair to get a better look at his purser. "Not best for you?"

"I enjoy the fast-paced hard work in cruise ships, but the passengers…? And bingo…"

"Bingo, purser? You do not care to be appointed to passenger vessels because of bingo?"

"Not when bingo is known as tombola because tombola is posh. I don't want to clap adults who dress up for fun at the fancy dress parades. Deck quoits are games, and games I'd hoped to leave behind at school. The Race Meetings are particularly disgusting."

"As a senior purser you can sit back and become anaesthetised on free wine and then all becomes mellow and seen in a beneficent light."

"The *Clerk of the Coarse* and his banal 'humorous' commentary? Dear God, I want so much to run away and hide. It is just too embarrassing. And the sod awful cocktail parties where one has to be nice to people one does not know nor wants to know."

"You cannot dismiss all the passengers. There are those who smile benevolently and who have accents that are cut-glass. They are above it all. Look carefully and one recognises them. People who pull strings, put pressure on where they think pressure is needed. Words are dropped in high places by these people of power."

"Could you be one of that exclusive band, sir?"

"All the 'fun' in passenger ships, can be balanced when one considers the ports: Leningrad for the Hermitage, Malaga for the Alhambra, Alexandria for the Pyramids."

"Why bring this up?"

Frogmore sifted through papers on his desk, stopping at a letter headed *Private & Confidential.* "Between ourselves, it looks as though general cargo ships are finished."

"Then I'm fucked, sir."

"That's not quite the way I would've phrased it."

DAVE HAD GONE when he returned to his office.

A toy Koala bear sat on the typewriter's carriage.

Ernest, who had been watching from Alex's cabin door, made himself comfortable in the spare chair. Alex, standing behind him, cuddled him and pushed his face into the Scotsman's warm hair.

Seated, he was admiring Ernest's snaps from home. "She's gonna look after you, I can tell. But have you told her about you and I being together?"

"You can tell her when you're up for the wedding."

"Will there be bagpipes? I can never tell if they are being played well or badly," said Alex, side-stepping the wedding invitation.

The way the two got on annoyed Rodney. Rodney had tried it on with Ernest and had been ticked off. Alex never would try it on 'cos he valued their friendship. But he could flirt with impunity.

Francis doted on the junior engineer too because Ernest did not smoke nor drink and he tidied up the cabin. "*Ernest sahib,* please, I beg of you, let me be your steward? I will pay you much *baksheesh* for the privilege and honour of serving you, *sahib,*" Francis would say. Ernest was delighted with the attention he received in Alex's cabin.

He came to the point. "Why's Rod in hospital?"

"Accident, or something."

Ernest, usually diffident, shied away from unpleasant matters, but his concern for Rodney made him say, "Was it sex?"

"Don't ask. Sydney agents cabled he'll rejoin in Brisbane."

"He told me how he sucked strangers in public – to shock me." Which it plainly had, thought Alex.

Then Ernest turned to practical matters. "I'm on watch with Larry now. Larry'll have me running all over the shop and insisting I read the domestic freezer temperatures at night." He reached out and placed his hand on the back of Alex's neck. The warmth and affection of his grip trickled down to Alex's loins. "I won't know what to say to Rod when he comes back."

"Thanks for the Koala."

Ernest smoothed his hand round to the front of Alex's

neck. "I can feel a pulse. It's as strong as anything."

"You want I read the temperatures for you?"

"In the middle of the night?"

"Wake me," said Alex, thinking that David Jones and Ernest shared a tangible purity, but while Dave would certainly cut the mustard, Ernest would not. Or would he? He would never know because he was obligated not to try it on.

HE stormed into the mate's office where Cadet David Jones was working at the long desk. "Be like that!"

"The mate asked what I was doing in your office."

"You taking me ashore in Brisbane?"

"You're getting the message," said Dave.

That evening Alex turned in early to rest up so he would be fresh to go ashore and get pissed in Brisbane. In an uneasy sleep, he heard Eleanor shouting and ranting. He woke sweating, grateful to escape the nightmare. The only sounds were the thudding pistons and the hissing punkah louvres blowing air, and the sea racing along the side of the ship.

IN THE LOVELACE era the three days transit to Brisbane was a time to take it easy and recover from the excesses of Sydney.

Frogmore ordered rounds *after* lunch. Rounds *after* lunch was taboo because afternoons were siesta time for the *sahibs.* Morgan excused himself, saying he had to check the disposition of the cargo remaining on board.

Frogmore's heart was not in rounds. In the smoke room, heavy with lavender aerosol, he failed to interrogate Alex about the delinquent bar refrigerator, though his attention did linger on the fitment where the framed tie had once hung.

Frogmore and Alex, with Francis in tow, crossed the alleyway to inspect the spare cabin at the starboard side of the wide staircase.

Alex had not had a nightmare. Eleanor was on board and she hadn't masochistically stowed away in a lifeboat to drink rainwater and suck barley sugars, she had taken over the spare cabin. Perhaps she considered the spare cabin her territory and, not being a woman to shy away from conflict, had stowed away first class – as if wanting to be discovered. A teddy bear glared aggressively from the easy chair; the wide-mouthed vacuum flask on the dressing table spilled fresh ice – ice she must have filched from the engineers' mess room. Some leftover cans of soft drinks from the party were positioned neatly on a tray next to a full bottle of vodka. Alex noted an electric kettle, a twenty-four pack of tea bags, a tin of reduced-fat milk powder, and a bone china cup and saucer decorated with roses. There were screwed up floral tissues in the bin and a trail of talcum powder on the dark carpet.

A housecoat in a green and yellow daisy pattern hung on the outside of the bathroom door. Singing could be heard above a running shower. Frogmore rapped on the door. The singing stopped. The shower stopped. The door cracked open.

Without makeup Eleanor's face was transformed; her features less intense, her lips pale and her eyebrows had lost menace. Her glorious hair was shrouded in a green and yellow floral shower cap. She appeared almost naked, like a baby bird.

The captain stood centre carpet. "Up to Victorian times slatterns in Portsmouth boarded the fleet in droves to satisfy Jack Tar's needs."

She pushed into the cabin. A green and yellow floral towel was held by a knot above her bosom.

"I'm faithful to one man," she said.

"I would hazard a guess," said Frogmore, in shock but in control, "from the fact that you are not encamped in the third engineer's cabin, that you are a woman in pursuit." He shook his head. "You will lose him. An air of desperation clings to you. I might advise you – and I say this with considerable experience of life – that to pursue with such obvious intent terrifies a man."

If he had spun about on his hard-tipped heels and continued rounds, thought Alex, that would have left Eleanor up in the air and disadvantaged, but Frogmore, never one to avoid confrontation, hung on in.

Eleanor was off balance but this scrubbed and singing stowaway could still deliver the goods. "You tyrant."

"Tyrant, eh?"

"I lecture in economics."

Francis nudged Alex in his back and both had great difficulty not exploding into laughter. Alex turned and gazed through the open window at the deck crew painting near number three hatch, but the powerful drama in the small cabin drew him back.

"It would seem that the engineer did not smuggle you on board?"

"Him!" She snarled then stepped back onto Alex's white doeskin shoes. "This excrescence struck me – a defenceless woman."

Frogmore said nothing. All colour had left his face.

"Your officers are scum. A mate and chief engineer who are never sober..."

Frogmore turned but lost his balance. As he stumbled, Alex grasped his arm, steadied him, said, "Water, Eleanor, please."

Frogmore sat in the chair at the dressing table.

Eleanor picked up a tumbler and turned her back as she put in two ice cubes from one Thermos and water from another.

Frogmore, breathing through his mouth, was gazing out of the window at what was familiar: at the derricks, at the expanse of number three hatch-cover.

"Your nieces..."

"Stop this now, Eleanor," said Alex quietly.

"I expect you've told the captain how you shat on his desk?"

Francis tugged at the back of Alex's shirt, indicating that a speedy exit might be expedient. But Alex felt at ease. He was experiencing the cleansing of the confessional. "Sir, I...

"Enough is enough."

"You okay?"

The captain eyed Alex almost humorously. "Old age, I'm afraid. I shall be in the cuddy, as always."

Francis followed him out, leaving Alex alone with Eleanor.

"You don't play sport. You haven't got that natural desire to win." Then she made a self-condemnatory remark, "It's the feminine in you."

She went back into the bathroom but before slamming the door shut, said, "I spiked his drink. L.S.D. from the ship's quack."

ALEX sped up top.

"Make yourself vomit. I'll get salt water." As he rushed into the bathroom, the captain called him back. Unfolding a white handkerchief on his desk, he revealed a tablet. "Whatever it was didn't dissolve."

"L.S.D. She told me."

"You will say nothing of this to anyone?"

"Why did you get giddy, sir?"

"Events get even the toughest of old seadogs down. It has not been the easiest of voyages, Alex."

"You okay now?"

"Indeed. Might I suggest that you attend dinner this evening. It could well be a bit of a gas."

"SHE'S TOLD everyone," hissed Rusty from his seat at the engineers' table.

Sure as hell Eleanor wouldn't be nibbling cheese shamefacedly in the spare cabin. She arrived in the dining saloon with hair bouncing; evidently the hairdryer had been packed too. Most officers mouths were hanging open, seeing her in a diaphanous frock, which was too clinging for her robust figure. Alex wondered if she had chosen it because it was easy to pack or to drive the crew wild. Unsuitable for the all-male cargo ship certainly, but he was thankful that the dress did not follow the green and yellow floral theme.

Larry, who had not eaten in the saloon since Christmas, sat at the top table. His appearance indicated the unusual, as did Morgan who had been taking his evening meals in his cabin of late. Morgan arrived on a gin-humming high. The cloud of melancholy, which usually followed him around, had vanished.

Looking at his fellow officers, Alex thought they were voyeurs – voyeurs sipping their amber cigarette holders in the art deco saloon, waiting for the cabaret. He imagined a fanfare as Frogmore left his suite. And, as the hands on the oblong clock showed five minutes past seven, Frogmore was heard approaching. The businesslike heels, the smell of pipe tobacco: Captain Rupert de Vere Frogmore entranced.

Francis at the sideboard stopped reading the French label

on a brown sauce bottle. Cadet Jones' face lost all expression. Conversation stilled. Frogmore did not check his step upon seeing Larry and Morgan. He acknowledged no one other than Alex and the chief engineer who both received a curt nod.

The doctor arrived ten minutes later. He placed a folded Marconigram on the linen cloth.

Frogmore broke a cracker and sipped his minestrone soup. "You have a medical degree?"

"I've never said that."

"It is a fact that you are not medically qualified. You have masqueraded as a ship's surgeon. This deception I will bring to the attention of the police."

"Police?"

"You are a charlatan, sir."

"Check with London office," said the phoney doctor.

He's wallowing and he's undeniably pissed, thought Alex.

Ice clinked as Gomes topped up the captain's water glass.

"I am cabling head office." The doctor tapped the Marconigram. "I'll tell them my detailed report will be telexed from Brisbane."

Frogmore studied the menu. "Turbot, boy."

Trimmer was notably dishevelled. His black formal trousers hung loose, his bow tie was askew, his suffered cotton shirt showed damp at the armpits and it could have done with an iron. His vague interpretation of evening dress did not work at all. He wore his clothes as unconvincingly as an actor wears a military uniform. Irritated by the captain's lack of reaction, he said, "You're steeped in nostalgia and inefficiency."

Frogmore ate his steamed turbot with delicacy. He took a second cracker.

Alex's digestive tract balked at the *pommes frites*. He toyed with his side salad.

Trimmer was disadvantaged by an afternoon's heavy drinking and Frogmore's cool manner. "You're not a well man."

"Trimmer, I take no account of your medical observations. Indeed, your judgement on all matters, I discount. And, at the moment you are intoxicated. You'd do well to hold your tongue."

"My report will go in." Trimmer floundered.

"You have never talked of this report to me nor have you discussed your brief. You have refused to attend the morning meetings which you yourself instigated. You have not familiarised yourself with my ship. You know nothing of the deck or engine or saloon departments. You have, on many occasions, been grossly drunk. You have never asked my opinion on matters nautical, on cargo or personnel. And whenever you have opened your mouth – and, by God, that has been often – it is to make a puerile joke. Your aim appears to have been to create havoc and to undermine my authority."

Trimmer rubbed his forehead.

Frogmore fixed him with the eye of the executioner. "I have informed head office of these facts. At my suggestion, they telephoned the Medical Council's library who keep records of qualified medical practitioners. On discovering that your name was not recorded, they telephoned Australia where they also drew a blank." The authority of a man which had caused Alex to involuntarily salute him, triumphed, it silenced all talk in the saloon. "You are not only ill mannered, you are a master of camp and a doyen of the snide remark. You cover your malice with liberal claptrap. There is a destructiveness in you which fills me with contempt."

"You will be superseded," bleated Trimmer.

Frogmore contemplated his serrated steak knife and nodded to Gomes who drew back the captain's carver chair. The captain then purposefully strode to the other side of the large table to stand behind Trimmer. His left knee, he thrust with force against the back of the chair so that Trimmer was wedged against the table's edge. The captain jerked Trimmer's head up and held him in a vice grip. His left arm tightly encircled Trimmer's neck. His right hand was raised. His right hand held the steak knife.

"For Christ's sake!"

All the officers and stewards watched.

No sneak attacks here, thought Alex, as the knife slashed down to cut Trimmer's shirt sleeve. Its point sank into the cloth and penetrated the thick layer of protective felt, to lodge in the walnut tabletop. It pinned Trimmer's cuff. The officers watched in awe. The impostor doctor trembled.

"He's mad," said Eleanor.

But in control was the man who'd sailed before the mast, who'd hove-to under goose-winged fore tops'ls off Punta Areanas, who'd rounded the Horn, and there he had watched seas cascade green and deep over the main deck. He was a seaman who had commanded men of all races and beliefs, men whose home was a narrow berth and a fitted locker. This was a captain who had sailed out of Liverpool during the War and had sunk two submarines. His medal ribbons attested to that.

Trimmer was held tight in the vice created by chair and table and the captain's arm about his neck. Blood clung in droplets to the hairs on his wrist; blood stained the cloth to the size of a medium Jaffa. A nod from Alex and all four stewards withdrew and waited silently in the cross-alleyway behind the glass doors.

Frogmore had lanced the boil and his lance held the troublemaker.

No one spoke. The thudding pistons of the main engine sounded. It was evening so the shutters were up and the lights on. The ceiling fan, above the familiar oval table, rotated but slowly. It's shadow flicking, flicking, flicking on the stretch of Irish linen stained with blood.

Morgan broke the spell. "Is his wrist all right?"

"It will take years for him to bleed to death," said Frogmore in a rasping voice. His eyes were ablaze. "I should go for his neck, do you think? He has enough of that."

Trimmer was ashen, his uninjured left hand clenched the tablecloth.

Frogmore wrenched out the steak knife to study it with some care as though he was going to strike again.

"Jesus, it'll need stitches," said Trimmer, writhing feebly in the captain's grip. He showed stark terror when Frogmore spoke;

"You are the man who served me with The Black Spot."

"For Christ's sake."

"Or was it Blind Pew?"

Stillness. The pistons thudded. The punkah louvre blowers hissed air. The ceiling fans rotated.

"Admit your guilt, Trimmer. But it isn't Trimmer, is it?

You're Long John Silver." The steak knife was raised, poised ready to strike.

Alex studied all faces. They were agog, thinking Frogmore had lost all reason. This is truly The Last Supper, he thought.

"Someone help me!"

"Admit to me, Long John Silver, that the floozy is Blind Pew!"

"Oh, dear God!"

"The tap, tap, tap in a night blacker than black, as you nailed The Black Spot to the bulkhead in my smoke room. You are an evil man, Silver."

Trimmer stared at the condiments, at the flowers – lasting brilliantly – stared at the white cloth with its livid stain.

"The bilge rat has a poisonous bite, Silver. It has the filth of decay between its teeth. The rat gnaws at the wounds, leaps at the nether regions, acts vilely." Alex wondered whether some of the L.S.D. had taken hold when the captain said, "You squalid fucker." It shocked him greatly. It was as if his mother had blasphemed.

Frogmore let go. He stood erect.

The gaze of H.R.H., whose portrait was fixed to the forward bulkhead, gave no comment to the captain's actions.

Gomes held open the glass doors as Frogmore left the saloon to enter the spread of foyer. Standing to attention on the art deco linoleum waited Cadet Jones who held the captain's cap.

As the captain took it, he said, "The purser's idea?"

"The third mate, sir."

The captain put on his cap; its oak leaves on the peak would intimidate any timid soul. "Tell the third mate that he need not try so hard. My recommendation for his promotion has already gone in."

"Yes, sir."

"Perhaps you'd best keep mum. He'll only speed his way to my quarters."

Cadet Jones, encouraged by the captain's manner, said, "He's bound to ask what you said, sir?"

"Tell him I was very much out of sorts. Can you do that?"

"Yes, sir."

But Frogmore seemed reluctant to leave. "Speak only to

the purser of this conversation."

"Sir!"

"Goodnight, Jones."

Very much in awe of Frogmore, and acutely aware of the captain's confiding in him, Cadet David Jones nodded.

The captain's face expressionless as he made his way up the broad staircase.

The unconventional man is often misunderstood, thought Alex, as Frogmore went out of sight.

Cadet David Jones, deep in thought, returned to the saloon to finish his meal.

Morgan, in his cups, broke the silence: "You've got him, Doc. His cutting you will cost him his command." Morgan, the hoverfly, had landed, but in the wrong camp.

Alex examined the doctor's wrist, stanched the slow-flowing blood with lint and a bandage brought by Francis.

He said, "The captain was slipped L.S.D. supplied by Trimmer. Eleanor spiked his drink. I'll attest to that."

Eleanor's chair was noisily pushed back. She ran from the saloon.

Morgan tried to drain a peg glass already drained.

"Alex," said Trimmer, "you know I've always been on your side."

Alex pushed the pseudo-doctor's face hard into the remains of his meal. He turned to Francis. "Close his wine account. Clear his cabin of alcohol. You've got the dispensary keys?"

"Yes, sir."

"I'll be up top."

OLD JACK was on watch on the bridge.

"I hear the shit hit the fan?"

"He tell you?"

"He told me."

"He commanded the saloon. The spotlight was on him all the time."

"Always has been, hasn't it? He's in the radio room telephoning London head office and Brisbane agents."

"It's almost over," said Alex.

TWENTY-SIX

BRISBANE

DOWNSTREAM FROM THE ABATTOIR two tugs had pushed the *John Bede* alongside. The harbour water was muddied and it was said that in it sharks swam.

The Muslims in the crew had checked out the direction of Mecca with Jack, and were praying on the poop. From a locker, on the sundeck aft of the funnel, Captain Frogmore's trunks were being manhandled by four Indian seamen. Gomes had retrieved the Martini umbrella and was carrying it forward with noticeable enthusiasm; his handsome face smiling, his white hair recently trimmed, his film star moustache dyed black. Budhia, the *topass*, ate his breakfast alone on number five hatch scooping up herring and boiled rice with his fingers. Alex skirted number three hatch and climbed the companionway to the boat deck. He entered the captain's dayroom after a perfunctory knock.

Frogmore wrote *Immediate For Ship's Master* in red ballpoint on a slip of paper and pushed it in a bulldog clip holding the official mail which had arrived that morning.

"The secret documents I've handed to my first mate."

"Why are you leaving, sir? You won."

"Purser, it is not a question of winning or losing."

"But it is exactly that."

"Some men are not suited to the sea. For them it is an uneasy marriage. They carry on in a manner which is close to insane. I ran across it in tankers. In tankers, with their abysmal voyages from pipeline outlet to pipeline inlet, there might be some excuse, but in this ship? Australia? Brazil? New Zealand? What better countries could a seafarer want? The charlatan doctor seemed to represent the unwashed of the sixties who squatted on their heels, mimicking ash-coated fakirs, who chanted OM to achieve a stillness of mind while they shrieked to the hyena's wail of electric guitars."

"An ageing hippy."

"His was a transmogrification."

"Maybe he's someone who hates all authority not realising he's authority himself. I know the feeling. You reporting him to the police?"

"One must consider the publicity. I've informed head office that it is to be kept in the family, as it were." Frogmore carefully positioned his pen so that it lay parallel to the pad on his desk. "I thought my use of an expletive at dinner was a touch you'd appreciate."

The remark revealed much of the man, but Alex made no comment.

"But I had no stomach for what I did, but it seemed an expedient way of ridding the Bede Line of that flawed man."

Alex said teasingly, "You took a chance on me. I could've said that you had not been fed L.S.D."

"But I am a ship's master who knows his officers. Is the harpy still on board?"

"You mean the floozy known as Blind Pew?"

For several moments there was no reaction then the captain's mouth twitched, the lines deepened about his eyes. He bellowed with laughter so loud that Alex stood back. After the laughter ceased, the captain said, "Charge her passage money from Sydney to Brisbane. Log her in the Official Log Book as a stowaway. Report her to immigration. Report her to the police."

"The publicity?" said Alex.

"Trimmer admitted to the mate that she hid in the ship's hospital until the ship was at sea."

One of the band.

Alex said, "Do you believe that I shat on your desk?"

In slow motion the captain repositioned his pen and adjusted his monocle before examining Alex. "It has been said, purser, that I have little imagination. Despite that, I'm trying to visualise a person of your character performing that act." Alex felt relief when Frogmore said, "I knew from the start what Trimmer's game was. His misquotations of Freud were intended to irritate me. His literary illusions were supposed to go over the head of hoi polloi – but hoi polloi, I'm not."

"That you ain't."

"There is no tavern near the Royal Docks named *The*

Admiral Benbow, eh?"

Alex hesitated.

"A landlady with a metal hook for a hand?"

"Absurd."

Frogmore was smiling his familiar death-mask smile, showing old teeth worn down by his pipe stem. He waved Alex to sit down then pushed the cigarette box, with the mother of pearl inlay, towards him. Gomes held a hissing sliver table-lighter. Alex inhaled.

"Beer, *purser sahib?*" said Gomes, judging the moment.

"You played the child's game goaded by a man of prejudice. You were seduced by a glib tongue. But you are but a simple seafarer."

Alex blushed.

"From a personal standpoint, it was naïve of me to think that my return to sea could be an escape from people."

"You can't escape people."

"Few true seamen remain."

"And me?"

"Are you seeking my approval?"

"Yes."

"I've managed what is best for you."

"Oh dear God, we've been here before," said Alex, taking the glass of beer from Gomes and drinking deeply.

"The *Atlantic Bede* you will join. You will fly to UK to take leave prior to reappointment."

"Streamers thrown at the quayside. Rousing sailing music. Ten cocktail parties in as many days."

"With one of this company's finest captains... Did you mutter 'Oh, fuck.' purser?"

"Me, sir, no, sir, your recommendation is everything."

"Put the irony aside."

"Race Meetings."

"One sincerely hopes that you are not going on about Race Meetings again."

"Passengers who wind a length of string that pulls a wooden horse..."

"Desist! But I will agree that there are occasions when one does pray for a machine gun, and indeed, one can understand the mass murderer who finally snaps and can take no more. We are but simple seafarering folk stuck with the sophistication of passenger ships. Your urge to escape should be suppressed for to escape means leaving the sea for there is little else now. The *John Bede* is scheduled to load Brisbane for Japan where it will be scrapped."

"Aren't you saddened?"

"As I would be with a favourite dog. But the time has come to put it down."

"I love this ship. It's like being with family." Alex glanced up sharply when the captain said,

"Part of your family is being appointed to the *Atlantic Bede* with you – Cadet Jones." After making his point, he added, as if to steer the conversation away from the cadet, "Do you consider the third mate part of your family?"

"Brewer's like my brother – he takes the piss."

"Cargo ships are being replaced by container vessels. No pursers – very few crew, come to that. These new goliaths are to be controlled by a computer and manned by technicians in white coats, and a handful of low paid ratings from the East. Conrad would have had none of it, but I'm a modern man." He paused. "What I'm about to tell you is something so intimate that you will honour my confidence."

"Sir."

"A man very close to me – you may have seen his photograph besides my bunk?"

"Your…?" Alex was so shocked by this revelation, he was quite unable to say 'boyfriend'.

He was very glad that he didn't when Frogmore said, "My brother."

"And he was queer?" said Alex, suddenly seeing the light.

"If he was, he hid it well."

The captain called Gomes in. After his steward had poured the purser another beer and left, he continued,

"He was married."

"Two daughters in Australia."

Frogmore's gaze was on the shoreside sheds seen through the doorway on the port side of his cabin. It was as if he were talking to someone outside the dayroom. "He was at sea and gained command in a lesser shipping company – so no gossip of him haunts me now. His breakfast was two lager beers, his lunch God knows how many. And he gambled. The sums considerable."

"And you helped him?"

"I bailed him out on condition that he emigrate to *Aus*tralia."

Alex thought, condemned to the colonies, but said, "Why are you telling me this?"

"He died when drunk; fell down a hatch. However, I'm trying to convey to you that I can detect the bad egg, and while I felt a great deal for my brother, I could see and comprehend his weaknesses. Your own attitude, purser, was due, I believe, to you being part of a minority."

"How'd you mean?"

"Society condemned you for being not as the majority of men and consequently you rebelled against authority. Is that plain enough for you?"

"Refreshingly so but I'm not unique. And you can call me a nancy boy, if you like."

"You can be most irritating, purser."

"Isn't it bad form to discuss another's sexuality?"

"Not with you it isn't. You were discussing it with me when you took me to that Melbourne bar where the men wore frocks and earrings."

"You're poking fun at me."

"You have afforded me more than one light moment, purser."

"Can I say something that will upset you?"

"You have upset me on numerous occasions and have never asked my permission, so why you bother to ask it now, I do not know. After you have left my dayroom, I have taken deep breaths often, attempting to calm myself. Indeed, my steward will confirm that I have resorted to smelling salts. You have been fortunate, for my self-control is legendary."

"Can I say it?"

"I won't stick a knife in you – if that is your concern."

Alex said, "You should've trusted me."

"Obliquely, I have." Frogmore added, "As men, we cannot weep, we cannot confess nor can we confide as we might. We are clothed in guilt. We are stuck in this detestable existence. There is much unfairness in manmade rules and bigotry."

"The Melbourne bar?" said Alex.

"I admired your guts taking me to that homosexuals' trysting place."

"And you thought?"

"A touch of Sodom but not truly Gomorrah. One has been in worse, but if you quote me, I will deny it. Gay it was not. Men overtly postured. Men stared with intent. It was the sort of meeting place I had not before encountered, I will confess. I was not prepared for such frankness and to that degree I found it enlightening."

"Would you have gone into a queer's bar by yourself?"

"Nice eyes or not – I might well be too long in the tooth."

Alex felt distinctly light-headed. "Why the hell did you act like that at dinner? I mean, you could have nailed Trimmer – no problem."

"You've sussed me out. Meals with Trimmer were uncivilised. His presence created the zoo. Food was thrown about by a jabbering gibbon. I thought it time I called the shots. And I wanted to give the meal an extra dimension – an element of the unexpected, a little drama. Something for the gawping officers to chinwag about in the future while they take a refreshing glass ashore in some tropical port where the heat hangs like a cloak and where tired fans make scant impression on the humid air. A bearer to hand. Cicadas noisy in the darkness. And the officers reminisce, as seamen do, about the time Frogmore went berserk. Reputations are made by such gossip, purser. Such will be my legacy."

Frogmore, with the habit of command, said, "Come!" And in a manner alien to anything that he had displayed before, he grasped Alex's arm and led him out over the weather sill onto the deck. Together they walked to the ship's rail. Leaning over the side Frogmore nodded at the abattoir upstream then at the muddied water.

"The sharks had gathered. Who was it said that the sea cleanses all wounds?"

"Are you retiring?"

"You'll be delighted to hear that I've graduated to hands-on management. I confess a not altogether unpleasant appointment. Ms Oliver asked me to head personnel department in London during the transition period."

"Transition period?"

"The replacement of the general cargo fleet with container ships."

"You'll be a director?"

"Yes. And I shall at times be a relief captain. Keep my eye on things while the regular captain is on leave."

"Personnel means dealing with people."

"There is a certain irony, I agree. But as you said, one cannot escape people."

"As *el supremo* – you'll have all us reprobates quaking in our boots." Alex almost said, 'shitting ourselves' and wished he had for he knew he could have got away with it.

The captain strode back towards his accommodation. There was a tinge of colour in his cheeks, a spring in his step. He stopped at the doorway to his dayroom. He faced Alex who had stayed at the rail. "I can understand that being a member of your tribe could well weaken one. And, when vulnerability shows, the enemy attacks."

"And Eleanor? Keel-haul her?"

"It's best left." He gave a nod of dismissal but the purser hurried up to him.

"Sir, about The Last Supper?" said Alex, not wanting their conversation to finish. It was the realisation that The Last Supper had been an unnecessary event, a theatrical happening which had smacked of triumphalism. Constraint had given way to a show, something to entertain the troops. Frogmore had played a game, and he had gained glee from it: something to gossip about in some far flung land; a hissing paraffin lamp on a verandah, mosquitos in the long grass... Alex looked enquiringly at the captain, a man outwardly a disciplinarian but inwardly screwed up, a man who would never come clean.

Staring each other in the eye, Captain Frogmore shook his purser's hand, saying, "I suspect, Alex, that we have at last reached a mutual understanding."

"Yes, sir."

"I have to bathe and pack." Then with a finality, he turned away and was giving orders to his steward to run his bath. Without looking back, he strode towards his bedroom.

TWENTY-SEVEN

BRISBANE

RODNEY sat in the passenger seat, saying little.

Alex turned the hired car off the road onto a wide track. "Excellent, I sense a dump," he said as he braked, then took a left to bump on the dirt surface of a car park adjacent to a long wooden building with a corrugated iron roof. He steered clear of a bunch of down and outs drinking beneath a gum.

He saw through the open door that the drinkers inside were wearing sweat-stained bush hats. "Australia without the *Aust*."

"*You* wanted a beer. I'll wait in the car."

"You won't," said Alex.

"I prefer to."

"Don't play the fucking martyr. They took your cash?"

"The agent paid my airfare. I'm to refund it – he said. Can I get out of that?"

"Don't push it. The less said the better."

Rodney strode up to the barman. "Where's the sitdown, cunt-face?"

The barman, big enough to intimidate any man, said, as if clairvoyant, "You got beaten up chasing cock, Rod?"

"Alex, this peasant is Max."

"You should try packing your manners. Your aunt warned me you'd be sashaying into town. Keep it down. Get dirty and I'll throw the vegetables at you." He nodded at his grinning bush-hatted clientele.

"Aunt Margaret would be lost without your cutting wit, Max. She okay?"

"Always chipper." The barman eyed Alex. "Beer, is it? Rod has a cherry in his."

Alex nodded, thinking that Rodney wore his injuries badly. Swelling had almost closed both eyes, and the bruising showed purple and yellow and tender down the left cheek. Alex suspected his nose might need corrective surgery. All nails on both hands were black. It is when secrets are made public then comes shame, or maybe maturity to the sufferer, he thought.

Rodney said, "While I was strumming painful fingers, waiting for you at the airport, I caught up with Eleanor. She was withdrawn. Something happened?"

"She tried to destroy one of the few men I've ever respected."

"No one respects Rusty."

"Frogmore."

"Eleanor got bitter after her abortion – unstoppable bleeding at one stage."

"And Rusty was the father. Why didn't someone say?"

"You're too superficial."

"Cut the crap, Rod, and tell me how you are. Or am I too superficial to be told?"

"I ruined a very good pair of shoes. But one survives, dear, even after rape." Rodney's talent was to use camp to mask his feelings, to survive without crying.

"Who was that creep who slimed his way on board in Sydney?" said Alex.

"Distinguished? Dressed in black?"

"Tacky in black. Looking after Felicity."

"Wasn't Anthony all right?"

"I did detect a cutting edge to his tongue."

"That's him. He'd be upset because I'd been out on the town."

"You mean sucking dick."

"Don't get superior with me, Alex."

"Don't thank me for covering for you and making it okay with Frogmore who was for logging you."

"What?"

"Your friend was graphic. Your friend relished in the telling of the tale, spilling every sordid sperm to Frogmore. I grovelled and pleaded your cause, because that's what we superficial people do, Rodney."

"You talked Frogmore out of logging me?"

"You've got it."

Rodney's painful face showed unhappiness, then anger. "I should've guessed. Anthony told me he likes John Wayne."

"John Wayne? Am I missing something?"

"He likes John Wayne's politics. John Wayne is as right-winged as you are left." Rodney downed his beer and waved his glass at the barman. "I sort of knew something was up. He missed out visiting me in hospital, making some pathetic excuse, but you know these queens, they can be moody. When I asked him to buy me clothes, he got *this*." Rodney shuddered his horror at the concentration of khaki he wore: long stockings and baggy shorts, a crumpled shirt which had damp patches under the arms.

They looked army surplus, but Alex had thought that maybe it was Rodney's latest fashion leap; aping the military perhaps, the kind of military portrayed in *The Bridge on the River Kwai* or *Ice Cold in Alex* – who wore khaki uniforms which had suffered. The idea of *Ice Cold in Alex* had Alex musing on the appropriateness of the film's title, not only the *Alex*, but, he thought, that the *Ice Cold* could refer to his own sometimes frigidity. "I should take up psychoanalysis," he said.

Rod glared at him, as he often did, with a look that signalled puzzlement. "You can wear anything. Denim and you're it."

"I love John Mills. He's so splendidly British in a way that Frogmore is not."

"John Mills?"

"Ice Cold in Alex."

"You carry on a conversation with yourself in your head and expect me to join in."

The barman put two fresh glasses in front of them. "No swearing, Rodney, please. We're not used to it."

"Max, do something about your halitosis, though it's a plus in a place like this – keeps the flies away."

Max ignored him; joined his regular customers.

"Anthony is going to look after Felicity okay, isn't he?" said Alex.

"Thank God, you've got your priorities right."

"Will he?"

"His home makes Buckingham Palace look like a slum."

"If the under-footman at Buckingham Palace doesn't like cats then it's a sad billet for them."

Rodney angrily fed Alex's change into the jukebox at the end of the bar. He punched buttons. "I'll pay you back."

Max lowered the volume of the music with a control behind the bar.

Rodney said, "I'm getting at you. Take no notice. Don't tell me I've got to report to Frogmore? I mean, it's all so humiliating."

"The matter's closed."

Rodney reached across and helped himself to a Pall Mall, struck a match and inhaled. "It's got me smoking your fags again. It'll be on my mind forever. I wish I could say I'm surprised about Anthony but I discovered a long time ago that because a queer is a fellow-queer one cannot assume that he is on your side. Queer friends make dangerous enemies. It's the bitch revenge thing. Hell hath no wrath like a queer scorned. I'm so fuming, Alex."

"You still getting at me?"

"Oh, shut up. I love you, for fuck's sake."

"Let's go visit your aunt then get back on board and start the joke."

"Joke?"

"The ship's loading for Japan. Captain Lovelace has flown in. I missed picking him up at the airport – the agent drew the short straw."

"Japan? Ernest will be distraught."

"I phoned London office from the agents. They're going to fly a relief out for him."

"You're such a good person. And you fancy Ernest."

"Rodney, any more of your shit and I'll abandon you here so you can camp it up with the not-camp natives."

"You won't."

On their way out, the barman winked at Alex.

Opening the car door, Rodney said, "I've never understood why you're so popular. It's certainly not your personality," he hesitated, "nor your looks, come to that."

In the car Alex said, "Am I okay on this road?" He always leant heavily on others' directions, seldom bothering to understand maps, and often asking the way.

"Straight ahead for a mile – watch for a lone house – then turn right."

The town was small. Its only street deserted other than a stocky youth, maybe sixteen-years-old, kicking a tin sign, advertising Colas, that stood outside the store. An

Aboriginal man, with hair so thick that it was a mass of black curls, came out to see what was causing the din. Alex thought the man had an original beauty.

"Go away," the Aborigine said to the youth, who two-fingered him arrogantly then stood some ten feet off. Alex guessed that as soon as the man went back in the store, he would kick the sign again.

"The shopkeeper's an Abbo," said Rodney. "The boy's white. The Abbo don't integrate well 'cos some of the locals won't let him integrate. And the Abbo ain't a local, see? It's the human condition – they want someone to bully and the Abbo does them nicely in the someone-to-bully department – no queers around until I ride into town, but I'm built like a brick shithouse and I have a mouth, and my Aunt Margaret packs a hefty punch – so there you go."

The shopkeeper was now out of sight so the youth started running up to the sign, swinging his foot.

Rodney opened the car door. "I know you. Do that and your mamma is are gonna find you with your throat fucking slit wide open."

He bolted.

The shopkeeper stuck his head out the door to see what the commotion was about. His smile was a smile of recognition. Rodney waved at him, said to Alex, "You got twenty dollars on you?"

Alex chucked him his wallet. Rodney caught it and ran after the shopkeeper and put his arm in his as they disappeared into the shop. In minutes Rod came out with a large paper-bag.

"What do you think of that little shit?" He slammed the door shut, glaring at the young man at the far end of the street.

"Fantastic bone structure. An amazing face," said Alex dreamily, gazing at the shopkeeper who had come out to watch them drive off. "That face demands painting but he would be a restless subject, I fear."

Rodney, watching the young man, not notable for anything other than his bullying, said, "At times I swear you're on something." He angrily tugged off his khaki shirt but calmed as he sprayed his armpits with the antiperspirant he had bought in the store. Pulling on a new plain white T-shirt, he said, "Terrible quality but I feel cleaner."

"You look good – shows off your muscles. Keep it simple, that's the secret." Alex glanced at the map, then slung it on the back seat. "Is your aunt like you?"

"You okay with visiting her?"

"I'll wait in the car."

"You'll make me feel I have to rush."

"I'm not good at the social stuff."

"That is so much shit and you know it. Margaret'll think you're being funny."

Alex realised he was being churlish. "I said, Is she like you?"

"Nothing like."

"Then her and I can talk about what a prick you are."

"Lift up." Rodney pushed the wallet under Alex's bum and wiggled his fingers.

Alex started the engine. "I'm lost. Directions?"

"It's staring you in the face. Number eighty-four. I forgot, you've no common sense, no road sense and no sensitivity to my feelings, come to think of it." He pulled his hand away.

"Ease up on me, for fuck's sake."

"I'm scared, Alex. What's she gonna say, seeing me like this?"

"Tell her you slipped in the engine room."

"See the house that the sign-kicking-shit went into? Aunt Margaret is next door. When I spill the beans about him, she'll wring him out to dry."

AFTER RODNEY told his aunt about the youth, he said dramatically, "Can you do something with this?" and dropped the khaki shirt on an armchair.

"It'll make dusters," said Aunt Margaret who was smartly dressed in a bright print cotton frock; her jewellery was a wedding ring and a string of pearls.

Rodney mentioned they had popped into the bar on the way down and spoken to Max.

"His wife told me that he wears his hat in bed," she said.

"Auntie, I got my injuries picking up men in a lavatory." Rodney's face was expressionless as he talked. Alex smiled at him and sipped his tea, relaxing on a settee that was modern but nicely comfortable.

Aunt Margaret listened attentively to her nephew who spared few details. Alex was amazed at such frankness. Rodney went on at some length about Anthony, who Alex thought of as The Man in Black.

Aunt Margaret said, "Remember last year when Anthony invited me to stay?" Alex then marvelled how Rodney had introduced her to his boyfriend. "Was I glad I opted for a hotel. All he needed was a flag up his arse to see which way the wind blows."

Rodney laughed. He looked younger, almost boyish when talking with her.

She said to Alex, "Anthony couldn't buy the second Bentley until the third garage was built. Have you ever heard such bullshit?"

"Alex sussed him out. 'Course he would, wouldn't he."

Embarrassed, Alex looked out the window at a threadbare lawn at the front of the property.

"It's a blessing it's so dry. I don't have to mow it," she said. "We'll go out back in a minute. You've got good hair."

Alex thought she might've added 'for someone your age'.

She said, "Don't wait to be asked."

The sandwiches were nearer doorstops than filigree. The tea was so strong that it merited a proof rating. "This beef's tender and tasty," said Alex.

"I know the butcher."

"Your home is secluded yet near the sea. Your food is my kind of food. Can I stay?"

"That's his charm," said Rodney. "He's full of it."

"You save room for my speciality – it has pineapple in it." She turned to her nephew. "They take you for much?"

"I can always buy another watch. But pride, you know."

"You won't scar?" she said, then not waiting for a reply, turned her attention to the dog at her feet and said with authority, "Move it!" The old dog, with grey in her muzzle, thumped her tail on the wooden floor, but stayed firmly in the way so Aunt Margaret had to step over her to get to the teapot on the square dark wood dining table. "Always have a bitch. Stubborn, but you know where you are with them. Rod, you won't be telling Enid."

The easy and intimate way Aunt Margaret and Rodney talked, showed Alex that they were family in a way that his own mother and he could never be.

"Let's sit outside?" She opened double doors that led onto a patio.

As they traipsed after her, she said, "Enid lives her life in terror that something bad is going to happen and it does."

They sat on comfortable upholstered garden chairs. The breeze smelt of salt.

"He did all the gardening." Aunt Margaret nodded at the dying and dead plants in terracotta pots.

"Get succulents," said Rodney. "Mam never reads my letters. I could send her a page out the telephone directory for all the notice she takes."

The sea at this distance was a layer of light, so strong that Alex wished he had worn sunglasses.

"The medication holds her down, but is it doing her any good." The aunt turned to Alex, "Her nerves. I flew back to see her six months ago. I'd forgotten what the place was like. Noisy pubs and takeaways – dried up pies and disgusting chips. The litter!"

Rod leant across and stroked Alex's knees as he spoke to his aunt. "Two brilliant fish and chip shops, Margaret."

"I saw two children drop a rock on a hedgehog and it spilled its intestines. I cried at the ugliness in them."

"How about your shitty young neighbour who taunts 'The Abbo'?"

"But there the shops have shutters up at night to stop the vandals. The shutters are covered with obscenities. Broken glass everywhere. It rained and rained, as it can rain on the wrong side of the Pennines. But she won't leave her 'lovely friends'." Aunt Margaret added, as though to stop any suggestion that she should uproot from her Australian paradise and settle in the damp Northwest England, "I try to go to the old country every two years. It's a relief to get back here. Don't you go leaving the sea to look after her, Rod. You've your own life to lead." She added, "She drinks but swears she doesn't. She won't help herself."

She caught Alex looking over his shoulder at the framed photograph that stood on the polished sideboard. "We were both a good few years younger. She came out for the wedding. Enid never photographs well. Lovely complexion." She added, as if trying to drum up support from Alex,

"Rodney's face has a lot of character – takes after my side of the family."

"Rod's a good friend," said Alex, then laughing as if he had showed too much affection, "And he's an idiot."

"My Ted was a good few years older than me. I married him 'cos he had this wonderful sense of humour – he laughed at my jokes. I miss the way he said, after every meal, 'I only married you for your cooking'."

Alex nodded.

"He left me the house. And they're developing the area, if that's a plus. Property values are going through the roof." She concentrated on the view. "I wanted Enid to come out, live here, get out of that grim mill town. That was me talking to a brick wall."

"I love your use of colour. The terracotta urns and the different fabrics," said Rodney, dragging the conversation back to matters of importance.

Aunt Margaret was not deflected, "Family's family."

And, as they chatted about family, no mention was made of Rodney's father. The way the father was left out of the conversation gave Alex the impression that he was not worthy of mention – a brutal Northerner perhaps, much in the pub. And he would have bullied his wife and blamed her for his defiantly queer son.

WHEN THEY WERE DRIVING back to Brisbane, Rodney said, "Well?"

"I could never tell my mother I was caught having sex in a public lavatory."

"Go for it. You'd be surprised. Scratch these classy birds and underneath…"

"My mother is way beyond being a classy bird, Rod. She took her PhD in class. Even my mother's dogs do class. Dog walkers in the village treat them with deference. I was sent to an elitist school to get an A level in class, to get the right accent, to learn how to communicate with the lower orders, to know how to take my place as a leader; to know how to walk into a room filled with people and take charge with a lift of a superior hand."

"You've got a nice packet."

"There are times when you and I could almost be friends."

"Your shit doesn't work with me, Alex."

"It does."

"You know what Aunt Margaret said when you were in the bog – 'He's the one, isn't he? He can come and stay with us when you move in with me'."

"It's right for you – here." Alex nodded his approval. "I wonder if Australians really appreciate how beautiful their country is." He peered to his right at the stunning shoreline and the surf rolling in, white in the sun.

"It's a good town but some of the people are crap."

"Same like anyplace."

"You held back on the smart remarks."

Alex nodded, becoming aware, as if for the first time, of Rodney's pleasant Lancastrian accent.

"I begged Mum to come out. At home the mills are shutting. The gutters at Roddicks are blocked and overflowing. The ground floor windows are boarded. The upper windows are smashed to fuck. And there is buddleia growing out the roof. The stream – that onetime powered the mill – is now a dump for prams and anything plastic." Rodney rested his injured hand on Alex's bare knee. The intimacy of the hand was of friendship – but sex was on the cards, Alex suspected. And in the emotion and warmth of the afternoon, he let the hand be. And when it moved to rest gently between his thighs, he was grateful for it.

"Mam accepts her roots – I can't do that. I know what I don't want. I don't want that Lancashire town."

"Why?"

"It's a town of heterosexual men. The local lavatory is where the heterosexual queers hang out. They advertise at the urinal, peer through holes drilled in the cubicle walls to drool over each other's bits." With Rodney's hand on his hard cock, Alex glanced at him. Rodney's face was expressionless but his gaze was on Alex. "The queers were heterosexual men in cloth caps and working men's boots. The effeminate gestures kept under wraps."

"Did you ask your aunt about your mum's fall?"

"A neighbour pops in twice a day. You'd go home, if your mum fell, wouldn't you?"

"There's a place to park," said Alex.

As the car veered to the right, it ran onto sand that coated the tar macadam and dragged at the tyres. Alex switched off the engine. In front of them was deep golden sand and lines of powerful surf. There was no one about; not a soul on the beach. The car's side windows were open and Alex, now relaxed, watched the sea.

"No one to see us. No holes in cubicle walls," he said. "I reckon yours is the practised hand."

"There's no point hiding your confusion beneath wit; sometimes acting camp without doing anything about the sex. That leads to unhappiness."

"I'm just so soaking up the wisdom of a philosophising engineer. As my queer guru, what path do you advocate – cock sucking in public?" Alex pushed his legs forward.

"You're so bitchy."

He felt the breeze off the sea on his face. The surf was clean and surging and came in strong along the miles of foreshore. He could taste salt on his lips. His legs stiffened and widened. The roll of surf was fierce, crashing and curling back in an undertow, dragging sand with it, pulling at any swimmer foolish enough to venture in. Further out the wave tops were curling and cresting in white foam, breaking and disturbing the turquoise sea.

"That's so good. Thank you."

"I caught it in my hanky," said Rodney.

He held onto the refrigerating engineer's small ears. Rod's face, never one to grace a chocolate box, was disfigured and puffed, the nose was off to one side, and the bruising was in full colour. Alex stroked his undamaged ears as if he were a dog. "Your injured hand seems to be working okay," he said.

"You know how to make me feel like the only girl in the world."

"What the fuck are you doing?" he said, alarmed when Rodney's mouth was on his softening sex.

"Tidying up." Seconds later, Rodney sat up, lit a cigarette.

"You want we stay a bit?" Alex zipped up and opened his side door. He pulled off his shoes and socks; his feet were moving, his toes lifting and sifting warm sand. He looked with longing at the dunes, wanting to sleep off his lunch in the company of sun and sand and be near Rodney and later wake up and talk to him, sort things out. And in the background would be the sound of the waves surging and crashing on the shore, giving them seclusion as they confided in the other, and that way they'd be close.

And importantly he wanted to talk about Frogmore, about The Last Supper which was rapidly becoming a sour memory. An event that had revealed flaws in Frogmore: his desire to win and let everyone know that he was in charge and that he was right.

Rodney usually understood Alex. At special times his sensitivity would surface from beneath the layers of camp and snide. This wasn't one of those times.

"If sunbathing is what you want – sunbathe. You're in charge. You're driving."

"Stop being so petulant."

"Who the fuck would say petulant?"

"You would. What's up, Rod?"

"I'm dressed in the uniform of the urinal."

"Then take the uniform off and stretch out naked, you miserable sod. We can talk."

"You can't talk to Dave Jones?"

"Of course I can."

"My mum's okay. Aunt Margaret told me while you were having a piss," said Rodney, his guilt pushing through.

On the drive back the pair fell into an uneasy silence. To get Rodney talking, he said, "I'll be stuck in Brisbane for at least two days 'cos I've got to hand over to my relief."

"Right."

"There's a rainforest someplace. You up for it?"

"What?"

"If you don't fancy it…"

"A favour?"

Alex glanced at his passenger. "You've caught the sun. And you've been in the car all the time – that's crazy."

"It's the bruising."

"What favour?"

"I want to go to my aunt's tomorrow?"

"Sure."

"Is this the right road?" said Rodney, studying a road sign.

"I'm not that bad."

"Tomorrow you ask Dave Jones along?"

Alex said, "Is sixteen too young to drive out here?"

"Just so long as he can drive."

"One of his mother's boyfriends raced cars. Dave'll be Le Mans standard, bound to be. We could still do the rain-forest." When Rodney did not answer, he said, "Your aunt wants another stranger foisted on her?"

"Dave worships you."

The ship's iron hull loomed high and black. He parked the car and after they got out, he felt confused when Rodney kissed his cheek and said, "It was just a wank."

"Rod..."

"I know."

"You've left your antiperspirant on the back seat."

"The brand I use is made in Milan not Melbourne."

Alex locked the car, and as they walked towards the gangway, he said, pointing at the small carrier bag which Rodney carried, "So you do have luggage?"

"You're breaking the ice again."

"How can you dismiss our sexual adventure in such a way?"

"And now who's camp?"

"Rod!"

"You're getting over your hang-ups."

"What's in the parcel, you miserable shit?"

"More of that pineapple tart from Aunt Margaret – I'll bin it."

"No, you won't."

"I can give it to Dave Jones from you?"

"Okay. Tell him he's gonna have the day off tomorrow and he's driving. I'll clear it with *el capitano nuevo.*"

HE HEARD the hacking smoker's cough on the stairway leading up to the dayroom. Captain Lovelace looked more under the weather than usual. The flight, and the alcohol consumed during it, had taken its toll.

"The chief tells me you're leaving us, Alex?"

"I've been seconded to a passenger ship. At last I'm appreciated."

"The rats leave."

"Welcome aboard, Fred. Good flight? Sit next to a kangaroo? I'm taking notes for my next *Tatler* piece."

Lovelace took the sheaf of official mail secured with a

bulldog clip and shoved it into the lower desk drawer. Alex attempted to grab it.

"Watch your manners. I haven't flown twelve thousand miles to be attacked by a fucking clerk."

"If I could glance at it, Fred? Please?"

"How are you?"

"Nice seeing you again, to tell the truth."

"How's Francis?"

"Reading Proust or some writer no one ever reads unless they're studying for a degree – or unless they're quite unusual. But then you're quite unusual, but you don't even read the official mail."

"Take it easy. I've been with normal folk." He chucked the creased correspondence at him. "The Big File."

"Glad to see you haven't lost your administrative touch, Captain."

"My way works. The ship functions. We glide from port to port. The crew are happy."

"I've always considered your leadership was your genius."

"How'd you get on with Frogmore, you sarcastic bugger?"

"Last thing I said to him was that I thought he was nicer on drugs than off."

Lovelace was besides himself at the remark. His hacking cough mingled with his filthy laugh. His eyes watered. This was not the first time in their three year friendship that Alex wondered about Lovelace's health.

"Rupert sees little good in anything nowadays. Everything good must be in the past."

"That right? You heard that he's gonna supervise the manning of the container fleet?"

"You know the old bastard was asked to join the Foreign Office as an advisor to the minister on the Middle East?"

"I'm impressed."

"Turned it down. Hates fucking politicians. Got that right." Lovelace lit a cigarette, chucked Alex one. "The chief told me about the fracas at dinner with him and the mad doctor."

"Showdown at the *John Bede* corral."

"Rupert under the influence of L.S.D.?"

"Flying high."

"I would have given my back teeth to have been there."

"Everything happened – except for the monarch breaking wind."

"She did that in my bathroom. You smelt it?"

Alex strolled into the bedroom, helped himself to a wire coat hanger from the wardrobe. When in the bathroom he unscrewed a plate in the ventilation system's trunking. The bent wire coat hanger hooked onto the fetid wad, which he eased out and dropped into a waste bag. When he returned to the dayroom, Lovelace said, "Larry's over the moon about Japan."

Alex said, "How'd you know I was leaving?"

"A charming women in London. A Ms Oliver. The dear lady wears a wig."

"You mean the old dyke who sits on electrical appliances?"

"Your remark is unnecessary, purser, and in appalling taste. I can only assume that you have acquired the manners of the lower deck under Frogmore's captaincy."

"The vibrator bitch in a wig, you said."

"You are a misogynist. Ms Oliver owns thirty-seven percent of this shipping company and she reappointed me. The most delightful lady."

Alex was thinking that Ms Oliver had only appointed Lovelace for the short journey to Japan. In Japan he would be scrapped along with the *John Bede*. But that would be in the hands of personnel department controlled by Frogmore. Frogmore had won again. Lovelace had not much time left at sea. His appointment as ship's master was a sop before an enforced retirement.

ALEX was wakened by Francis' relentless tapping on his bunk-board.

"I dreamt of you."

"Not a word," said Francis.

"Not wet, but I woke up with a can of beer between my legs. Unyielding – hard and with no emotion."

Francis positioned the plastic tray, with its good Bede Line crockery, on the ledge alongside the bunk. "Is your tea all right or shall I shovel in bromide?"

"Keep going that way and I'll put you up for promotion."

"No provisos?"

"You insult me as usual." Alex rummaged underneath the blankets and found the can of Foster's. "Change it for a cold one."

"It's almost eight."

"Frogmore's gone. No caffeine session. I feel relaxed. Do you fancy anal sex?"

"I should hit you hard but you'd probably enjoy it." Francis took the can. "Now that Captain Lovelace is on board, it's comforting to be back to the abnormal." He undid a small flat oblong package which was wrapped in brown paper with Indian attention. "The Black Spot. Gomes retrieved it from Captain Frogmore's gash can. Chippy made a frame. You will observe it matches exactly..." and with the theatre of a conjurer, Francis took from the top of the desk the framed tie.

"Where'd you get that?"

"The doctor's bottom drawer. It's all he left."

"You're telling me that he gave you no *baksheesh*?"

"Not even the ten pounds he borrowed."

Alex swung out of bed. Opening his wallet he pushed twenty pounds into his steward's trouser pocket. "I'll have head office deduct it from his fee."

"Acha, burra sahib. You're so wise and caring."

"Stop playing me for all I'm worth. Why aren't you in tears at the news of my departure?"

"Is our superficial friendship worth a tear?"

"You are faithful to me in sarcasm."

Francis sat on his heels in a chair. "The doctor had a brilliant mind – so he told me. But, brilliant mind or not, without integrity he was not worth talking to."

"They both misused power."

"Who?"

"The doctor and Frogmore. Two actors, both playing the lead, but resentful of the other. I'll really miss you."

"Me too – read your mail." Francis nodded at the postcard on the office desk.

Alex recalled The Man from the Pampa's square hands. He remembered how he had cared for Alex in the police station, and told him who to see, a man who would get him out. Ignacio was now free, probably sprung by Maria Mendes. The writing on the postcard was old-fashioned, as if he had used a steel nib dipped in black ink, and written at night in the poor light from an oil lamp. The edges of the dog-eared card were tinged sepia, as if it had been on display for years – perhaps in a rack outside some remote cantina with a tiled roof. A cantina over the southern border, a cantina on the pampa where the gauchos drank.

"As the oracle, what do you think, Francis?"

"I seriously worry that you are thinking of joining The Man from the *Pampaz.*"

"Pampa."

"The plural is *pampaz* – try it with a 'z'."

The second engineer tapped the open door and came into the office followed by Rodney.

"What you brought him for, Larry?"

"Because we're heading for Surfer's Paradise, so move it." Rodney sat on the desk.

Larry said, "I need money."

"Tea, sir?" said Francis.

"You're acting like a normal steward today. Why?"

"The *purser sahib's* outrageous behaviour affected me in the past. I will now have to revert to being a conventional subservient steward, sir."

Rodney said, "The only time you're subservient is when you're taking the piss. You're the most un-Goanese Goan, I've met. Cut back on the yap. With me, you've met someone who can out-camp you – if only just."

After the jalousie door shut behind Francis, Alex said, "Rod, you and him have much in common: Your obsessive neatness and the lavender furniture polish."

"Not lavender!" said Rodney horrified. "No one can say that your problem is being neat."

Larry pushed between the two men and signed the advance sheet. He took the Australian dollars and put the notes unchecked in his back pocket.

Alex said, "My leaving do tonight. I'm thinking of joining The Man from the Pampa."

"Right."

"What's that mean, Larry?"

"Do what you want to do."

"You are just so commenting. Say it."

"These are your tickets to UK." Larry took hold of the two

flight tickets from under a glass paperweight and smoothed them flat on the desk. "What'd you really want?"

"I don't know."

"You've got money in the bank and your ma is hardly on skid row – in case it all goes to fuck. And you're looking at your tickets to the passenger ship. They're negotiable."

"You mean…?"

"He means grow up. You want to be gay but not part of the gay society. If you weren't queer you'd probably pretend to be, just to be different," said Rodney, whose bruises had matured. His face was a sallow yellow-brown as if he had jaundice.

"Shut up, Rod." Alex then spoke to Larry, "If I swop these flight tickets for South America that means I'm finished with the sea."

"Jesus Christ, you call him The Man from the Pampa," said Rodney.

"So?"

"Who the fuck calls their boyfriend The Man from the Pennines, you silly bitch."

"I'm into wild nomenclature, at the moment, cunt."

"It's so fucking butch in here, I'm starting to lisp," said Larry, blowing smoke. "I'll just slip into my new frock and fetch my magazine on hemlines this season."

Alex folded the tickets carefully and put them back under the paperweight. "It's all right for you, Larry – you're without hang-ups."

"Is it me in the bitch house now?"

"Should I be jealous of *el gaucho*?" said Rodney.

"He's sort of short. Very broad and powerful. Thick dark hair. Seldom smiles. Unusual face with a wide almost Asiatic nose. Smooth, dark skin."

Rodney said, "What's Dave Jones like?"

"Too good to be true."

"Did you know that Cadet Jones is getting a transfer to the same passenger ship as you?"

"Shut up."

"You're thirty-five and you haven't aged well. You want I spell it out? You're alone. He fancies you," said Rodney. "And he sleeps in your cabin."

"That's male bonding."

"Oh, such shit."

"Okay?" said Larry, from the adjoining cabin, taking the crown top off a large bottle of Foster's. "You two are driving me to it."

"You're supposed be ashore, not going on the piss. I'll have one. Give *him* one too," said Alex.

"Dave Jones had better be driving – you're scary enough behind the wheel sober," said Rodney. "You know what your attraction is?"

"Please don't bitch."

"You and Cadet Jones stink of integrity."

Larry dropped an opener into Alex's hand and placed two bottles of beer on the desk. "Tonight, how about us getting together like we used to? Drink in the radio shack to avoid Lovelace."

"Frogmore gone. Doc gone. I'm going. Dave's going..." Alex sighed. "After the ball is over..."

Rodney turned to Larry. "And you say he isn't camp?"

"I've an invite for a week or three in Sydney. I've gotta ring Debs," said Alex.

"And?" said Rodney.

"And what?"

"The cadet?"

"This is about me, not a sixteen-year-old boy who is straight."

"So am I straight, but you and I fucked and it must've been something real good 'cos I remember it – and that don't happen too often," said Larry, emptying his glass.

After Larry left to go ashore. Rodney went into the cabin and sat on the bunk with his chin in his hands. "Francis didn't bring us tea."

"He knows we'd be drinking."

Rodney leant forward but couldn't see the wall clock in the office.

Alex said, "It's nine-thirty."

"Dave will be ready before ten. You help me?"

"I'm here."

"Have a word with Ernest."

"What's up?"

"He doesn't say a fucking thing, commenting with his silences."

"You told him about it, didn't you?"

Rodney glared. "See him, okay?"

"I'll set Dave on him."

"Ernest said he'd rather be on watch with Larry. Jesus Christ!" Rodney's eyes were damp. "Dave said he might get off early. I'll go chase him up."

"Ask Dave to talk to Ernest. They're both young. Dave's been round the block and he's level-headed."

"And they both worship you."

ALEX woke. The luminous hands on his travelling clock showed two. The alcohol was wearing off.

Francis had requisitioned a Boots' pack of bicarbonate of soda which had been left in Captain Frogmore's bathroom cabinet. He mixed himself a draught. It settled his stomach, so much so that he half filled a tumbler with dry sherry which he nursed in bed. He looked for his paperback and found himself pouring another.

In the light that filtered in from the alleyway, he watched a cockroach speed its way up the bulkhead. It was said that once cockroaches were in a ship, they could never be got rid of – seal the ship and pump it full of cyanide gas, or whatever, and they would survive. He thought of his telephone conversation with Debs. It was so good to talk with her again.

TWENTY-EIGHT

ASHORE

ULANA was all for it, so they were both flying to Norfolk Island, Debs had explained on a bad line. The surfboards and all that 'essential' holiday stuff was in the basement. And Martin had the key to the flat. And if Alex didn't make proper use of it, she'd fly back and cook for him. Debs had come up trumps and he was grateful to her, and thought of her as he collected the key from Martin in the only other flat in the building.

"Hello, Martin. You're the wit."

"I am?"

"Debs tells me so."

"That puts me at a grave disadvantage. It's like you saying, You are funny, make me laugh. All I can do now is freeze. You're definitely Alex – witty and caustic and adept at the putdown, so I'm told."

"Why do I get the feeling you're gonna win?"

"Come in."

"I'm kinda waiting for two phone calls."

Martin rummaged in the small drawer in the telephone table and produced a bunch of keys which he handed over. "You can hear the phone from here – that's if you stay in the hall and leave the front door open." He lifted a pile of ironing off the only chair. "Sit. I'll get coffee. Two shakes." He opened the inner door leading to the living room, letting out a large black dog.

Debs' dog nuzzled Alex in affectionate recognition.

Martin reappeared with two mugs on a tin tray. Alex shook his head at sugar and cream.

"No wonder you're slim. Debs was right. You're distinguished."

"She okay?"

"She saw the priest after she visited you – Melbourne, was it?"

"That's bad."

"Why?"

"She sees me and rushes to the priest?"

"Debs is smitten, you know that."

"Right."

"She thought it would come to something... I was her confessional not the priest. Such feelings are not sins."

"These things pass."

"Many relationships stay the course and develop. There's milk in your fridge. A loaf too."

"I am grateful."

"That your only luggage?"

"Yeah."

"You're staying three weeks?"

"I planned on it." Alex had left his heavy baggage with the ship's agents to be air-freighted to the UK, but he did not want to involve Martin too closely in his personal arrangements.

"She wanted to hang on to talk with you but it was arranged in a rush. Evidently they were desperate in New York..."

"I thought she said Norfolk Island?"

Martin said, "Definitely New York. Debs' heart is in the right place. I wish mine was. My heart takes orders from my dick and it's disastrously instructed." He got on his knees and tugged at the black iron handle on a small low cupboard that was hidden by hung up coats. He surfaced, holding a bottle of whiskey. "It was either there or under the sink. Last month I found a half bottle in my wardrobe. The dog hides them." He poured a shot of whiskey into his coffee after Alex shook his head. "She cares desperately about people, you know."

"Debs is very religious?"

"She quit the hospital to do charity work full-time."

Alex moved uncomfortably on the hard chair in the miniscule hall. Martin lolled in the open doorway, poured another shot of whiskey in his coffee. "You sure?"

He put his hand over his mug; looked at the telephone numbers written on the magnolia wall. One was so passionately crossed out that the pencil had dug into the plaster. Above the numbers was a drawing in a gimcrack frame.

"People think it's a forgery," said Martin.

"Right." A daub is now a talking point, thought Alex.

"A present from an admirer – long ago."

"You're hot stuff." Alex realised what he had said was flirting, but he couldn't say, you must have been hot stuff – as though Martin was past it.

"Debs said you wanted to do a Greta Garbo."

"I'm Debs' charity case?"

"If charity is defined as love. Have a whiskey – make that chair, and my conversation, more comfortable." The liquor trickled into Alex's mug.

Martin was not as Debs had described. In a bathing costume maybe his chest was magnificent but now he was shapeless in a sloppy denim shirt and paint-splattered jeans. His hair had thinned on the crown and the thickish fringe needed a trim.

Alex said, "Your flat looks comfortable."

"Debs and Ulana and I have the same interior designer – Mister Fucking Disinterested. I've just had two days off and haven't talked to anyone but the dog. Don't worry, I'm a good listener to friends."

Alex was unsure if he wanted a friend, instant, like the coffee.

Martin had no such reservations. "You can't prefer the monastic life to the social?"

Alex smiled but made no reply.

"You bodysurf – Debs said?"

"Joke."

"One surfer came back here to give me pleasure. He left at two in the morning with my wallet. Never dared show his face again on the beach. So short-sighted of him."

Alex had the feeling of being there to listen, to help Martin with his loneliness.

He shook his head at the proffered whiskey, but Martin said, "Go on," and tilted the bottle so the golden liquor ran into his mug. He held up his hand. "You'll get me pissed."

"Would you have sex with me – nothing torrid?"

Alex said, "My friend. He'll be arriving today."

"Go on – get upstairs."

Standing, he embraced Martin who held onto him; pressing his erection into him.

"Anything you want, just bang on my door, anytime. Now piss off before I make another pass at you," he said, pushing Alex out the door into the bright entrance hall.

MARTIN'S overpowering neighbourliness should have had him bolting up the stairs and deadlocking the front door, then ramming the sideboard hard up against it, in case his new-found neighbour had a spare key. Instead, he debated whether he might go down later and chat with him.

The flat was much as he remembered. One wall was dotted with framed photographs: Debs' father, several weddings, Debs as a bridesmaid, a snapshot of himself laughing and two photos of an angular woman of around forty, her blonde hair too short – Ulana, he guessed. He smiled approval at the new silent-running refrigerator.

The telephone began ringing. It rang so urgently that he thought it was Martin checking that he had made it safely up the twelve steps to the flat.

Dave Jones' voice.

"How'd you get this number, cadet?"

"You gave it to me."

"Are you at the airport?"

"Sort of."

"You in Sydney?"

"I said."

"You did not. You said 'sort of' which sounds like insecurity to me."

"Shall I buy food?"

Alex reached over and tugged open the refrigerator door and read Debs' note propped in front of containers.

"We've been catered for."

"I AM DEFINITELY in demand. First him downstairs and now you reporting in. Why aren't you high-jinking it in the East End, me old china plate?"

"Because you asked me to stay."

Alex casually switched on the radio and caught the hit parade.

Dave Jones dropped his holdall; closed the front door, then took off his shirt and hung it on the back of a chair. He pushed the window wide open and gazed at the sea on the far side of the road. "I'll have a shower first."

"First?"

"Before sex."

"I haven't had sex since you and me in Sydney," said Alex, then hesitating, "unless..."

"You're blushing."

"I sort of remembered – someone did it for me."

"Did what, Alex?"

"I'm getting hot under the collar – and crotch."

"We could shower together and then you can tell me how Rod pulled you off."

Alex had wondered at the cadet's sudden found confidence. This was explained when he mentioned Rodney.

Still looking at the sea, Dave said, "Rod told me that you were imagining it was me doing it – I mean, when he jacked you off in the car."

"This is getting so romantic. Sex by a proxy hand." He took two cans of beer from the fridge but put them back when Dave shook his head. "Rod try it on with you?"

"He's a chancer, isn't he? You jealous?"

"I don't do jealousy only disappointment."

"Can I?" Dave turned the dial of the radio, then gave up and switched it off. "You mind?"

Alex watched him, said nothing.

"Nice place – sort of homey. Sort of studenty too." Dave kicked off his moccasins and peeled off his socks, then sprawled on the settee wearing only faded blue jeans. In the days since Frogmore's departure, he had grown sideburns which shone henna and they did not stop below his small ears, but drifted into soft stubble. David Jones 'going scruff' added to his physical appeal. His thick hair, which would have been trimmed under the Frogmore regime, was curling, and it flattered him dreadfully.

"That's you on display. I love your feet." Alex went to him. Dave pulled him up close, his broad chest hard against Alex's shirt. His mouth was damp and soft. Everything about the youth was wholesome. The kiss had Alex dizzy. He pulled away and sat opposite.

Dave said, "A woman in a shoe shop in Poplar said the same thing – about my feet."

"You were flattered?"

"I was fourteen and blushing. She took me back to her bedsit after the shop shut. Paid for my shoes. She was fifty."

"Go on."

"I felt evil about her buying me shoes. Mum said I was to give the money to the Battersea Dog's Home." He reached up and drew the curtains but light seeped into the room, catching his tanned forearms.

"You been with a man before, Dave?"

"Only you."

"Loneliness pushes some people together."

"Fate pushed us together – like you and me in the same ship. Frogmore fixed that passenger ship for us."

Alex said, "Frogmore as a matchmaker bringing together two queers. Love it."

"You know it."

"Frogmore was getting you off the *John Bede,* away from Evil Lovelace, and appointing you to a ship where you wear a cap a great deal – that's known as discipline and character forming." Dave didn't say anything, forcing Alex to speak. "There's a queer downstairs called Martin – gay and very gay, in fact gay-gay-gay and gay. And on the prowl. My guess is he is due up here any second and will be inviting us down for sipping-whiskey."

"I don't drink whiskey."

"Very wise. He pours it by the pint."

"Met him. He was tweaking his nets when the taxi dropped me. He yanked open the front door, grabbed my wrist and screamed, You're gorgeous. Are you Alex's friend? And would we both be charity-visiting him – the lonely fucker in the ground floor flat? He's terminally embarrassing. He's gonna lend me a surfboard tomorrow."

"He wants your body. The signs are not difficult to read."

"Never happen. I got jealous thinking that you and Rod were together."

"Why'd you think that?"

"You bickered like a married couple."

Alex gaze was on the young man's light blue jeans that were moulded to his muscular legs. He knelt on the carpet. Dave cradled his head, touched his hair.

"Alex, suck me. I can hold some back then that way I get to come again when I suck you."

Alex got frantic trying to pull off Dave's jeans. He yanked them down and flung them across the room; coins rang and rolled on the floor. He tugged off the tight underpants and pushed his nose into glistening pubic hair. Dave's hands were on his neck; hands that were rough and exciting.

"Suck me hard and suck me quick, 'cos what I want is to hold your spunk in my belly," Dave said.

And it seemed only minutes that Dave was above him, lifting him, putting a pillow under his head, pulling down his jeans. Dave's mouth was on his. His tongue slithered down his chest and stomach and his mouth was gently on his balls, damp on his cock. Dave's finger was inside him and his other hand held his balls. He was in a vice of ecstasy and it was almost that he wanted to push him away because the inevitable was happening too soon. As he spurted into Dave's mouth, he touched the head of Dave's cock that was above his face.

Dave sat up, bright and cheerful. "I needed that. Sorry about my small cock."

"God!"

"You don't do romantic." He pointed at the framed drawing on the mantelshelf, his other hand on Alex's inner thigh. "That Debs?"

"Yeah."

"You drew it?"

"Don't you go telling Picasso downstairs I went to art school."

"He cocked up the eyes."

"It should've been left in the pad."

"Don't you want to draw me?"

"I want to do Debs' dog, capture her innocence. You can watch – in the nude with a hat on." Alex got to his feet, checked the curtains were shut properly, then walked naked across the room.

"Where you off to?"

He opened the fridge and found the milk. As he was taking down a brown teapot and two mugs, there was a knock on the door.

Dave was at his side, whispering, "Make it three mugs. Give him booze and he'll be here all night." He raised his voice, shouted at the door: "Two minutes."

Martin replied from outside: "Okay, if I leave the dog?"
"Sure," said Alex.
"I'll get her."
Dave said to Alex, "We're surfing tomorrow."
"I am *not* going native."
"You can use my camera, make snide remarks."
"You gonna be long?" said Alex, raising his voice as Dave had disappeared into the bathroom. When he came out he was wearing a towel about his waist and carried another.
"Put it on. Show him he's interrupted something," said Dave.
"Anything else?"
"The lavatory flush – I'll fix it tomorrow."
"You do plumbing too?"
Alex heard the dog scampering up the stairs. He moved towards the door to unlock it. "Where exactly was your progressive finishing school?"
"You leave the door for a sec?"
"He'll be saying there's a cheese dish, he's dying to try out, and he'll be inviting us to dinner after we get settled in. And he'll be showing us the place to shop for *Chateau Melbourne* and I'll be saying, Isn't this nice."
"It's swimming tomorrow and hamburgers. He's an okay bloke and this is the world of compromise. And there's no you pissing off to Patagonia."
"Where's Patagonia?"
"Bottom of the map of dried spunk on your cheek." Dave held a teacloth under the tap then wiped Alex's face.
"You done?"
"I'm wiping Patagonia off the map."
"This is so symbolic and you're getting aggressive too. I like it very much." Alex pretended to panic: "Biscuits? We simply *must* have biscuits. I fancy a digestive. Check out the blue tins but wash your fingers first."

TWENTY-NINE

ASHORE

"DAVE'S just been telling me off 'cos I bellyache too much. Trouble is he's right," said Alex opening the door.

"He can tell me off anytime," said Martin. The Labrador jumped up at Alex. "She's been fed."

"Right."

"She breaks wind notably – always when people visit. The conversation stops, then starts again. I never explain."

"Sugar?" said Dave.

"Can't stay long. One, please."

"You look smart."

Martin was in a dark suit, white shirt and a plain navy tie. The thick fringe had been brushed and was held down with pomade.

"The ballet. *Romeo and Juliet* – I'd rather spend my time looking at you. Isn't he superb?"

"He palls on acquaintance. Trust me."

"I have a micro penis – tell him, Alex."

"Exaggeration but one needs a decent magnifying glass."

"You could get a job modelling anywhere."

"Alex's surfing tomorrow. I'm gonna photograph him. I'm into the aggressive look. I go for the mean man with the mean one-liner." Dave pulled back the curtains. Light coming from a lowering sun coloured the room pink. Looking down at the MG parked in the street, he said, "Yours?"

"I'm too old for it. And tonight I'll be driving it to the ballet to ogle buttocks and bulges. How sad can I be?"

"Why too old?" said Dave.

"You can drive it – anytime."

"Don't drive. I'm getting us lunch tomorrow."

"On me – at Mario's."

"Please..."

"My treat. The young..."

Dave came away from the window and sat facing the two older men. "I'm not The Young."

Martin went to say something but Alex checked him by frowning.

Dave's face had lost all expression. And beneath his calm and sensible manner, Alex could detect annoyance. He'd never seen it in him before. He watched and listened intently; for the controlled irritation had given power to the man who now dominated the room.

"Alex didn't find me. I've always made the running."

"When I first met you..." Martin then talked to Alex, "The immediate impression I got was he's straight. Outgoing and good at games, popular at school." Martin reached across and rested a well-shaped hand on Dave's towel-covered thigh. Dave crossed his legs. The hand slid off.

Alex said, "In the shower, we were having the most intense discussion about which waxed hats we will wear on the grouse moors. Stitched brims are so much in this year."

Martin said, "Superb physique. I must draw you."

"Leave it, Martin," said Alex.

Dave said, "I wanted him from day one. But he refused to pick up the signals. For someone so sophisticated he has a block. I did everything but take it out and wiggle it."

The room was quiet. Alex, hearing the traffic for the first time on the road below, got up and shut the window.

Dave said, "He pursued two members of the crew 'cos he prefers older men."

Alex was aware of Dave's diplomacy and drew comfort from it. He filled their mugs with tea, tentatively nibbled a biscuit, saying, "You did wash your hands?"

Dave smiled, but undeterred he went on talking to Martin, "Alex's steward – Alex thought the world of his steward – had a squint and he had this Neanderthal hair that cut a straight line across his forehead. He was skinny, and had this sharp tongue. Together they were a double act. Like all good double acts, they cemented on stage, feeding each other lines." Dave gripped his mug of tea in both hands. "They were so much in sync that I would be brushed aside now if Francis were to enter this room and lay it on the line for him."

What he did not say, but might think, thought Alex, was that stand-up comedians who gel, do not have sex. No more than long-standing great song-writing teams – from Gilbert and Sullivan onwards – had sex. However closely they collaborated or performed together, on or off stage. They went back to their partners in their mansions in some desirable part of town where the little woman, or man, slaved over the kitchen staff.

He studied his own unattractive feet, wondering what Dave saw in him. "My toenails need clipping. I hate that."

"You two have everything," said Martin.

Alex revised his opinion of Dave's mum for she had done a fine job. He was without hang-ups. He had skilfully put a middle-aged academic in his place, and he had seduced and entranced and converted, the bound-to-fuck-it-up Alex who now wouldn't give Francis a second glance.

Dave switched on the table lamp that was decorated with pink shells, then he moved to another lamp.

"I've got two complimentary tickets for tomorrow night's performance?" said Martin.

"I'd love it but I can't speak for Mister Micro Pecker."

Dave, drawing the curtains, said, "It's a suit and tie do?"

"I'm only dolled up 'cos I'm on the committee."

"Thanks, I'm definitely up for it. I've done ballet."

"You did ballet?" said Alex.

"Soccer."

"Ballet? Soccer?"

"Ballet teaches co-ordination and self-control. It's okay."

"Define okay. Blokes after your tackle?"

"It was movement not sex."

"I guess the butch boys from your neck of the woods, who do the ballet, get the girls." The dog rested her muzzle on Alex's knee. He said gently, "Piss off, you." The dog wagged her tail and slumped on his feet.

A cloud came over Martin. "Even the dog likes you best."

As he made his farewell, shaking hands in a formal way, his attention seemed to be on Alex. It was as though he was wondering what the attraction was. The two men were not far apart in age, but Alex had a desirable companion who leapt on a soap box to drool over him.

"Shopping tomorrow?"

"I thought it was boards at dawn?"

"Make it after ten. I feel sorry for myself when I turn in, so down a peg or two." His hand was firm, holding Alex's. "You will not believe what a sad man I am. The other day I was in urgent need of an electrician. I couldn't take my eyes off him. I dashed to the kitchen and made him tea and fed him chocolate bars and bright conversation."

"You make yourself sound old."

"My dear, such thighs. Thinking of them now, I rush for a Kit Kat and the K.Y."

The door closed. He was gone. The dog followed Alex when he filled her bowl with water and placed it under the sink.

Dave nodded at the dog. "Someone else for you to look after." He unzipped the side pocket of his holdall. "Nail clippers. You want I do your toenails before we shower?"

"Clip away." Alex ditched his towel and sat naked with his feet up on the settee. The dog followed, watching him.

Dave grasped one of his feet and positioned it on his lap, rubbing the heel against his sex which was hard beneath the bath towel.

The dog stirred, put her head on the settee.

"She smells like Billingsgate," said Dave.

"Doesn't your dog pen and ink?"

"Pen and ink?"

"Apples and pears speak. I'm preparing myself to meet the family."

"My mum does not sound like Eliza Doolittle."

"Sheba only wants attention and she doesn't pen and ink, do you, my darling?" Alex stroked the dog's head.

Dave was silent.

"What's up? I didn't mean to be rude about your mum."

"I know that."

"Tell me?"

"It's the way you give such love to the dog."

"I feel deeply about people but am unable to show it. You're 'people', by the way. Martin gets a kick out of treating you. Let him buy lunch tomorrow. He's not hard up. He's got some high flier's job."

"What's he do?"

"Wank excessively is my guess. You okay about me paying for you?"

"No."

"Say no to me again and you get to fuck Martin without

earplugs." Alex thought that Dave was a gem cutting his toenails. "Did you bring shoe polish?" he said.

"Under the sink. I'll give yours a rub over in the morning," said Cadet David Jones. "Martin's as gregarious as you are not."

Alex was certain that Rodney had been coaching Dave. Gregarious was a Rodney-word.

"We shower now?"

After Dave got the shower running at the right temperature, they both squeezed into the cubicle, relishing the warm water sluicing down their smooth bodies.

The doorbell rang.

Dave stepped out of the shower dripping onto the terrazzo floor. Wrapping a towel about his waist, he said, "Gotta let him in."

"I'll go. Seeing you damp and glistening, his hand will go out of control."

"Be subtle."

"He don't understand subtle."

"*Please* answer it."

Alex padded to the front door dripping water.

Martin held out a long white envelope. "This came by special messenger. I had to sign for it. Such drama."

"Bless you."

"Love to you both, my darlings. I'm running late. Late, late, late."

Alex dried his hands before slitting open the envelope with a knife out the cutlery drawer.

Dave was behind him. A drop of water fell on the sheet of paper, smudging the print. Alex held it higher, at the same time pushing his back into Dave's damp body.

"Important?" said Dave.

"It'll wait."

"I want to fuck you."

"Do not laugh but I am a virgin in that direction."

"But with Larry?"

"I screwed him."

"Monica in number twenty-seven – the house with the heavy nets that drove mum out of her skull – had a dildo. First off, she pushed it in me. Was that something. But oiled and slow – you know."

"Rod told you I'm frigid, didn't he?"

"I got used to Rod," said Dave.

"You're just so up for it. It must be all that free school milk."

"You say that, I want to explode, but when Martin says stuff about me, I want to explode in a different way. How about you fucking me?"

"DID I FALL ASLEEP?" said Alex

"I'll fix us soup."

"It's not late. Let's eat out?"

"We'll have soup here and save money on a first course. The bread's brilliant." Dave eased Alex gently off him. He sat up. "You all right about me asking Martin if we can shop tomorrow afternoon. Get stuff in."

"Whatever."

"You packed the painting of the mulatto boy, didn't you?"

"I knew you'd check," said Alex.

"Why did you say you'd leave it?"

"I told you. I sucked a man off and that was payment."

"Six hundred pounds for a suck?"

"Treble it, I reckon. Does that make me cheap?"

"That's not cheap. Hang it in your bedroom in Mincing-on-Sea."

The large Labrador stood up and wagged her tail, as if commenting.

"Sweet Jesus, it's the quiet ones. No wonder Martin ditched the bitch on us." Alex rolled off the settee and curled up on the square of rug. The dog thinking he was playing, barked at him. "I do hope the dog doesn't want sex. There's only so much one can take."

"Can we wear waxed hats next time we do it?"

"You and me arrested in matching waxed hats, dripping water and fully soaped, has an appeal. We could wear them in court. I can hear the judge: 'And the elder of the two Pommy brown-hatters is not only into sticking it up boys, with his British-fucking-hat on, but he's a dog-fucker into the bargain'. They're terribly coarse in *Aus*tralia, you know." Alex's fist was in his mouth, his eyes were running tears. "Sheba's dropped another one."

"We're supposed to be discussing penetrative sex not

dog farts," said Dave.

"Penetrative? That's so Rod. Charcoal biscuits for the dog..."

The telephone interrupted. Alex hurried to the kitchen area to answer it.

He again thanked Maria Mendes for the painting.

"Did you think him a slave?"

"I thought him very sexy," said Alex.

"It was me as a boy."

"Oh my God, I've been having underage sex with you."

"It was at the gallery for restoration and reframing after it self ignited."

"I wondered 'cos the gallery undervalued it. I thought that the receipt was a ploy to make Rodrigo jealous and humiliated."

"My dear Alexio, how could you think me so devious? Truth is, I've never dared hang it – it makes me look so available."

"But you are."

"Come and stay and reassure me that I'm the only man in the world?"

"I'm with my other only-man-in-the world at the moment."

"Sleep in my favourite room with the most fabulous of views. All facilities – Rodrigo comes with the en suite."

"Hot and cold, I don't think so."

"Then bring your friend, my dearest Alexio."

"Will The Man from the Pampa be there?"

"Who?"

"Ignacio. Did you spring him from jail?"

"Spring him? Goodness, this is not the Wild West. I had a coffee and cognac with the charming official you met. Ignacio's at the estancia. You and your friend can take the plane south. Ride the land where the en suite is a shovel and Ignacio is your guide. An exciting and loyal companion. He spoke of you with much respect and affection. You are so much like me, Alexio. You have superb taste. Did you have sex with Ignacio?"

"He didn't say?"

"Do you ride horses too?"

"How old is Ignacio?"

"Must be forty-five."

"He looks thirty."

"And he has integrity and discretion too. I adore him."

"Inquisition time, Maria. Are you ready?"

"Am I to be punished, my darling? How marvellous. I'm panting. You look at the painting while I open my fly."

"It's about Rupert."

"I've closed it."

"Rupert and Ignacio. You knew Ignacio wouldn't turn up at the party, didn't you?"

"When I saw him earlier in the day to invite him, he put his hands together, as if praying, and said that Rupert was an important man now. There was pain in his downcast eyes. To humble a man of Ignacio's stature – Rupert could not be allowed to get away with that."

"But why did Rupert Frogmore run scared?"

"Do you remember Ashier at the party?"

"The smooth operator who invited me back to his house for a nightcap – something long and hot. I told Captain Frogmore about it and how I was quite taken aback."

"Rupert certainly wasn't, but if he had been, it would have made his eyes water. I instructed Ashier to tell Rupert that he was sexy which he did, as he clung to his hand, stroking it."

"Captain Frogmore would not have experienced such passion in many a year," said Alex.

"Rupert tried to break free of Ashier's relentless grip – but to no avail. They were a tableau. Then Ashier went over the top, and said with a languid sigh, 'Rupert, my darling, I think I am falling in love with you'."

"How can I believe you?" said Alex.

"Rupert broke free and scurried away, terribly flustered. I followed him and when we were alone I told him that a car had been sent for Ignacio who would be arriving any minute. I then mentioned that Ignacio was these days often maudlin in drink. That did it. The thought of Ignacio arriving pissed and weeping at a shippers' party, which seemingly had turned into a gay fest with no holds barred, had Rupert down with a very sudden migraine. I sent him flowers."

"And you blabbed to Rupert Frogmore. Told him about you and I in the courtyard, didn't you?"

"Alexio, with you I am always discreet."

"Don't bullshit. You told him, and in graphic detail."

"We did chat on the phone and something may have slipped out – as these things do."

"I'm devastated that something so meaningful between us should not be kept private. How could you, you beast?"

"I am distraught, Alexio, and am on knees – as you were in the courtyard."

"I shall never forgive you."

"You will. You have. You too are a passionate man."

Alex smiled at such an absurd idea.

"You're refreshingly not British," said Maria.

"I bathe in your flattery."

"In British society the ruling classes keep their indiscretions hidden. Britain is controlled by the dull middle-classes and the *eminence gris.*"

They talked some more then Maria said, "Britain is a lessening power. Brazil will be huge one day. Be my personal assistant, Alexio – you are a fixer."

"I fuck up."

"Utter rubbish. Beneath the throwaway remarks you and I are serious men. That is why, at times, we seek out Ignacio in search of his clean mind and his simplicity and his love of nature, for that is in us too. Ignacio is like you – never are his fingers in the till. Trust is all, my dear friend – and when trust is combined with affection..."

"I am half in love with Brazil but with you...?"

"Alexio, I shall tonight pray that you change your mind. And shall immediately have a secretary transfer funds for two flight tickets to be issued to you at your Sydney agents."

"Maria, behave!"

"You are putting me in my place, but I deserve it. I will make amends. You will have to accept a small token of my affection. I know just the painting..."

"Oh no, Maria, no!"

"You sound like *West Side Story.*"

When he finally put down the phone, Dave said, "Wasn't it Anita – not Maria – in *West Side Story*?"

Alex realised that Dave must have heard both sides of the conversation.

"You going?" said Dave.

"Where?"

"To sleep under the stars. Beans and coffee on an open fire."

"Brazil! I'd sooner die! You up for it?"

"It's not about me."

"You heard – all we do is pick up the tickets."

Dave said, "He gave you a portrait of himself which he treasures."

"He's sixty and wears corsets – whalebone and embroidered."

"You can't pass up on an opportunity like that. I mean, the way you two gel, it'd be the job of a lifetime."

Alex sighed. "I have so much to contend with. I'm fatigued after being courted so relentlessly. Martin downstairs is hot for me, and the dog is gagging for it. There is Ashier in South America and the official who gave me his card. Maria will simply have to join the queue."

"I am trying to crack the irony. I think that means you're not going to fuck off to Brazil."

"You don't swear, Dave?"

"I'm upset."

"I'd be a mug to leave you. You do all the chores and don't complain. After Moaning Francis you're it."

"Balls. The reason you won't leave me is 'cos you're your mother's son."

"Oh God, that sounds deep."

"Loyalty makes you stay with me; makes you do the right thing. You always choose loyalty over self-enjoyment."

"Has Rodney been making me out to be a martyr?"

"I don't come with no dowry, Alex."

"You do – the dowry is you. Is this about the oil painting?"

"What'd you reckon it'll be?"

"A large courgette."

"Explain?"

"A courgette is gaucho rhyming slang for an erect penis. Didn't they teach you anything at Eton?"

"East End, mate, the East End."

"Eton missed out stinking."

LATER that evening, they sat outside a brightly-lit restaurant not far from the flat. The remains of their meal having been cleared away; only two cups of tea were on the table. Cars on the road masked the rush of the sea only a hundred yards off. And looking at that ocean, Alex thought how, when at sea of an evening, he'd put down his book and listen to the thump of the massive pistons driving the propeller, as the ship steamed on course for Australia.

He took the folded long envelope from his back trouser pocket and extracted the single sheet of paper.

"What is it?" said Dave.

"It's a telex from personnel department in London saying I'm to join the *Atlantic Bede* as senior purser in four weeks at Genoa. Frogmore signed it. He will be relieving as ship's master for two cruises – and he's sure that will be something for me to look forward to."

"Is it?"

"He holds summit meetings like he's planning the Normandy landings."

"You fancy a beer?"

"Listen to this! *Cadet Jones will be joining at the same time. I expect that you will be splicing the main brace at the news of your prestigious appointment and in eager anticipation of salting it with an old shipmate.*"

"He knows about us."

"Not."

"Alex, you stop shitting me. I heard you on the phone."

"So?"

"Question for you. What's a cuddy?"

"You're the seaman."

"It can be a closet. You told Rod that Frogmore said to you 'I'll be in the cuddy'."

Alex yawned.

"Think about it. He lets the mate get away with murder. I mean, what's worse than being pissed on watch? Okay, you're a bit mad but you function good enough for him to have you appointed to the *Atlantic Bede*. Me, I'm dead keen and okay at my job. Who does he bully? Me and you. Why?"

"I thought I'd escaped all this analysis crap after the stabbing of Trimmer. Do you have a knife?"

"You've known all along – or guessed anyway."

"Go on."

"He bullied us both 'cos what he saw in us he hated in himself. You wouldn't have sex with me 'cos you didn't know which way he would jump. You couldn't take that chance."

"Keep this to yourself, Dave."

"In the end he confided in his own kind and you know that and I know that. Maybe you didn't strike any deal but he's appointed you and me to the same ship. At last he gave us respect."

"Amongst his generation there are a legion of queers who had to pretend to be straight all their lives. So best leave them alone, let them be."

Dave stood up. "I'm off for a leak. Beer?"

"Not for me thanks, I've eaten too much. You have one."

Alex watched Dave as he chatted with the waiter who was about thirty and had a red face, his ears were red too, painfully mauve in places.

When Dave returned, Alex said, "You coming to live with me when we get back to the UK?"

"I want that, but I must talk to Mum first; put her in the picture. You can come visit and sleep overnight – same bed, no bother."

"I'm quaking. I'm no spring chicken."

"Mum won't think about age. It's how you treat me."

"Right."

"We're great together. I love you. And I love you hard and inside me."

"I'm having a hot flush."

"You look after people. You looked after me, Ernest, Rusty, Rod. And you looked after Brewer, for God's sake."

"I don't want to visit your mum – that's me being honest, and running scared."

"Mum didn't take to Monica – that's Monica at number twenty-seven – 'cos of her mum's nets."

"Because of the net curtains? I can see problems."

"The clincher was that Monica's mum wore her rollers to shop. So my mum said, like mother like daughter. That put the kibosh on it. On the other hand Mum was okay about me doing the ballet. Kept me away from the roughs, she said. Until a couple of the blokes gave me the glad eye."

Alex thought that 'the glad eye' sounded old-fashioned from this modern young man. "She put the kibosh on that too?"

"Mum said best not do it with them 'cos homosexuals are

promiscuous so I dated one of the ballerinas. She was so elegant." As Dave talked, his hands stretched across the table towards Alex, not touching him in public, but reaching out.

"So your ma's only prejudiced against queers 'cos they play the field. I won't do that."

The dog moved her bulk and was heavy on his feet. He pushed her away but she moved back again. Fact was his own mother would like Dave who was quietly British. Few women could resist him.

Beyond the road, the low moon was reflected in the dark ocean and he thought how some nights, when the ship was at sea and he was alone on deck, he'd watch the deep folds cut by the ship's bow, watch the folds broaden to a wide wash; a wash that glowed white with phosphorescence, a wash that caught the light from the same moon. And he would think how fortunate he was to have such a job.

Listening to Dave, and feeling the weight of the dog on his shoes, he marvelled at how lucky he'd got.

"You sure about not going to South America?" said Dave.

"How can you *think* about South America when I'm hanging five tomorrow?"

"Truth?"

"It's a once in a lifetime opportunity for us."

"Truth is, I'd give my back teeth to go. Except I wouldn't want him paying."

"I'd fund you."

"Forget South America. Instead we can have the maters down to stay at your place in Mincing-on-sea."

"Oh, God."

"It's gonna have to happen sometime."

"David, please, please, could you ask the waiter – the one who can't take his eyes off you – to get me a very weak China tea, with a twist of lemon and a teaspoonful of Australian honey?"

"You want a brandy?"

"How about I get the bill and we piss off back to the flat?"

"I've paid it."

They crossed the road and strolled along the beach.

Dave glanced at the dog walking to heel and happily wagging her tail. "You see the waiter's face when she dropped one?"

"He sniffed the scampi."

Dave jammed his arm into Alex's, and pushed his body into him as they walked. The dog followed.

Dave said, "Did you know that you smiled at the dog when you filled her water bowl. You talk about dogs like Frogmore talks about ships. With passion."

"Decision time."

"South America or get our mothers down to stay at your place," said Dave.

It was dark away from the harsh light of the restaurant; pale stars showed in the sky. The sea surged and crashed against nearby rocks. A sudden flash of spray caught the light from the headlamps of a passing car.

"My wonderful David, there are riches in South America that we must grasp. We will fly south and when there, explore the land on horseback. The mountains that we see in the distance are where the condor flies. In the morning, before we wash in a cold stream, or have a shit, or brew tea in a billy, we must look after the horses."

"You ride?"

"Yes."

"And what about Ignacio?"

"Our friend, our guide who will teach you to ride a horse and evenings we will sit around the fire and we will talk and be with him."

"And if he comes close to you and wants to be with you?"

"I wrote to him about my passion for you," said Alex.

"Phone Maria."

"If Ignacio confides, as I think he will, after a glass or two, he will have an interesting tale to tell."